ROAD TRIP
EVANGELISTS

SOUTHWIND

ED WACASTER

WESTBOW
PRESS®
A DIVISION OF THOMAS NELSON
& ZONDERVAN

WestBow Press books may be ordered through booksellers or by contacting:

WestBow Press
A Division of Thomas Nelson & Zondervan
1663 Liberty Drive
Bloomington, IN 47403
www.westbowpress.com
844-714-3454

ISBN: 979-8-3850-3953-1 (sc)
ISBN: 979-8-3850-3955-5 (hc)
ISBN: 979-8-3850-3954-8 (e)

Library of Congress Control Number: 2024925730

Print information available on the last page.

WestBow Press rev. date: 01/14/2025

Dedication

This book is dedicated to my family

Debbie Tipton

Jennifer Lambson

Brandon Wacaster

And

Brian Wacaster

Preface

This project has taken quite a long time to come to completion. It started around 30 years ago. It took a few years to write it originally, then have it edited and put on a CD to go to the future published that was unknown at the time.

Unfortunately, that CD was lost during a move and the project stalled for what seemed to be an eternity. Then, during yet another move, I found what I called my "bookbag." In it was a hard copy of the manuscript, or most of it anyway. The ending was missing. But since I wrote it, I was quite sure I could find it again, that that little brain of mine.

As I read that I had become a much better writer in the preceding years as I had written multiple newspaper and magazine articles during that time. So, I began to rewrite the book and change a few things here and there to my liking. Although it took a hew more years to complete, and some huge life struggles, here it is.

I hope you enjoy reading this book as much as I enjoyed writing it twice.

Acknowledgment

There is no way that I can remember all of the people that helped and encouraged me during the writing of this book. I am so terribly sorry for not remembering some of their names and I know that I have forgotten some others. A project this long takes a toll on a finite brain, and mine might be more finite than others.

First, I would like to say an incredibly special thank you to Debbie Tipton. She woke me up one night by grabbing me by my neck because I had stopped writing at a certain spot when she wanted to know what came next. Well, I had no idea what came next and said as much. She gave me bruises. Since she so rudely awakened like that, I thought it appropriate to tell on her like this. And even though she was so mean to me, her encouragement meant more than I can tell you. As time went by and this story progressed, she was able to steer me in directions that changed the story slightly and it made more sense. I can never thank her enough.

My Sister Denise Toupin also read this as I was writing it. I would print out my latest pages and let her read them as I went along with the story. And, just like Debbie, she would encourage me as it progressed and make suggestions here and there. Again, I think I made one change due to her encouragement, and it made the story better. Thank you, sis.

To my children Jenniefer, Brandon, and Brian. Not only do I love you more than you will never know, but I thank our Good Lord for allowing me to be your daddy. I know I spent time working on this story when you would have liked to be playing outside or watching a movie together. Thus, I will never claim to be the world's best daddy. But I thank you for your love and friendship and for allowing me to become one of the proudest fathers alive and I am so proud of the adults you have become.

Chapter 1

Southwind

BOOM! Larry woke up with a scream! Bob started laughing and pointing at him. "I finally got you back you mean, mean person you!!" Which got a smile onto Larry's face as well.

Larry said, "This road sure has its surprises for us without any warning. Makes a guy wonder how long he's going to live with surprises like that and getting scared half to death out of a dead sleep." He started praying: "Lord, please let this road become smoother as we travel toward the next adventure You have for us. Please keep us alive long enough to where we can get married and have kids. Then let the kids kill us or something, but I am *begging* You to not let us be killed by a loud tire noise from hitting another huge pothole. And please teach Bob how to start missing every hole in the road, this guy can't drive for thirty seconds without hitting a hole the size of Delaware. Amen."

Bob echoed the Amen and started laughing. "Did you ever think that maybe I look for those holes the size of Delaware just for fun?"

Larry looked at him for a moment and said, "Nope, you love me too much to do such a thing."

"You are so right, I do love you enough not to look for them, but not enough to avoid them." Bob began to laugh almost hard enough to wreck the car.

After they both composed themselves and got the car settled back into the proper lane, they began to talk about the town they had just left and what had happened there. Exciting and worrisome at the same time was the case in that town. God had done some serious miracles in those people's lives and the town for that matter.

Bob and Larry had just finished a month-long meeting at a church in Southwind Nevada and were heading towards Boise Idaho but didn't know where they would be stopping next. This car Sally Walker had given them before they left Southwind was an absolute blessing. The air conditioning was going full speed on this sweltering day in the desert. The poor car they had arrived with in Southwind had died a slow painful death and barely limped into town the day they arrived there. That car was a gift from Brother Rector, and it was such a blessing when he gave it to them. But that was so many millions of miles ago and the Lord had kept it running well past it worn out date.

Bob, being six foot three could barely fit in that little Japanese import car and was finding the leg room in this new car really nice. Enough so that he could get comfortable enough to sleep while he trusted Larry not to kill them with his awful driving. And this air conditioner was blowing his hair around, which bothered him a little bit as he was hoping to hang onto what hair he had left.

Larry was a bit shorter at six feet even with jet black hair and a full head of it. He was always rather muscular, but after Southwind he was looking a bit bigger to Bob. Bob just wished he would shave those sideburns and Fu Man Chu mustache; the seventies had been gone for a while now.

The two were now eating the egg salad sandwiches Sister Wilson had made for the trip today. She was such a sweet older lady and had taken them into her home like they were her very own as soon as they arrived in town. Sister Wilson had arrived at the church when the two Evangelists pulled into the parking lot. They already had the familiar feeling that God had something for them to do in this town before they ever got out of the car.

Pastor Brown met them outside as he heard their loud car pull up and he was curious to see who it was in this ugly thing that so profoundly announced their presence. Pastor Brown was a tall man in his sixties, slim and quite handsome. Bob was instantly envious of his full head of silver hair. The pastor had a huge smile as he watched the two weary travelers climb out of this thing they just parked in front of his office. He was glad they had parked there so he didn't have to explain the huge oil spot from his own vehicle which was in the shop that day. Bob and Larry made their way to the shade where Pastor Brown waited for them, and they noticed that he seemed preoccupied with something as they approached him. They met and exchanged handshakes as Pastor Brown invited them in for a nice glass of ice water. There was no way these two guys were going to turn down a nice glass of ice water after the ten-hour trip they just finished.

About the same time the two boys arrived, another car pulled into the parking lot. A woman with a huge smile met them on the porch as they made their way inside for that much coveted glass of ice water. Her name was Sister Wilson, and she had been going to this church for decades.

The group went inside, and Sister Wilson graciously told the men that she would bring them ice water in a couple minutes, so they could talk business like the men folk like to do. Sister Wilson was slender with silver-blue hair and had been a widow since 1966 when her husband was killed early in the Police Action in Vietnam. She never really could figure out what a "Police Action" was, but it killed her husband. That's all she knew about it. She never remarried or had any children prior to her husband's death, but she was one of the sweetest, kindest, loveliest people on the planet to most of this town. Everyone who knew her adored her and that beautiful smile. In her seventies now, she knew she would see her sweet husband soon, but for now, this church needed her and all she could give it. So, she planned on being here, in this church, every time the doors were open.

Bob and Larry were surprised to feel such a chill in Pastor Brown's office when they sat down. Pastor Brown stated proudly that he had installed that wall air conditioner himself without any help from sister Brown thank you very much. There was that great big smile again. Bob and Larry were beginning to like this man already.

Pastor Brown began the conversation by asking the obvious question: What brought these boys to town.

Bob and Larry looked at each other with a smile of their own. Larry spoke up: "Pastor we travel all over the country and stop when God tells us to stop. We love meeting the Pastor and his staff, if they have one, and find out what's going on in the church, as well as look for needed repairs that have been waiting to be done. Most of the time we end up helping out with a service or two, then move on. Other times, we end up in a town for a couple of weeks, sometimes longer, then head off to the next town." As Larry was speaking, he could see small tears welling up in the Pastor's eyes but didn't need to ask why.

Pastor Brown spoke with a hoarse raspy voice after taking a moment to compose himself. "Boys, I have been praying for about two years now for someone to come here to help me with my congregation. This congregation is full of really good, genuinely nice people and I love every one of them dearly. But for the life of me, I cannot get them to respond to my preaching at all. I feel Gods' anointing every time I preach on Sunday's, but they don't respond anymore. We ended up canceling the evening service on Sunday because the congregation had quit coming. It was usually Sister Brown, me, and Sister Wilson. But she had a health setback last year leaving just the two of us here. Sister Wilson is one of the special people that everyone just loves, including Sister Brown and me. She has been such a huge help around here. If it weren't for her, things would have been so much more discouraging. That smile and sweet spirit of hers has kept us going through some pretty rough times.

Bob interrupted: "Pastor, what did you mean by 'anymore?' Had the congregation been responding to the Word previously and then quit or something?"

"Yes, they did, and it was an awesome congregation. A teenage girl was raped and murdered outside of town some time back and after that the entire town just seemed to go into a fog or something. People don't smile as much and seem to be a bit weary of everyone after that. The person who did that hasn't been arrested yet, so no one knows who to trust. It's sad to see this once great town have the air taken right out of it like that. So, yes Bob, prior to that incident this church was a lovely place to be each week. Now it's a shadow of itself. It was at that point that I began to pray a little harder for help, because these people are no longer responding to me, so I figured they might listen to someone else.

"They still show up every week with their smiles and are friendly with my wife and I, but it seems to stop there. If we run into one of them at the store, they to avoid us, or just exchange pleasantries and move on. Of course, not all of them are like that, but some of them are. If I knew what happened I would probably know how to fix it, but I haven't even a hint of a clue about it. These are really good people and for them to act like that now, it just kills our hearts for them, and I'm a little scared for them not being as happy as they used to be.

Pastor Brown looked at his two new friends. "I think I may have just confirmed why you guys are here didn't I?"

Bob spoke without looking at Larry. "Pastor, we would like to stay for a while and see how we can help. Let us just sit back and take in the service tomorrow. That will give us a good idea of what you are dealing with, and we can take it from there?"

Right then Sister Wilson walked in the big pitcher of ice water and three glassed filled to the brim. She announced with that huge smile of hers: "I would just love for you two to stay at my house while you're here in town. It'll give the town something new to talk about. I've got this huge house with everything you need, even your own bathroom, as long as you don't mind sharing it. I'll go make your beds and make sure there are clean towels and such in the bathroom for you." Without waiting for an answer, Sister Wilson walked out, got in her car, and drove away, leaving Bob and Larry with a quizzical look on their faces.

Pastor Brown laughed as he got up out of his chair, "You two are the newest townsfolk. Welcome to Southwind boys!" They all chuckled. "Let me show you what we've got going on around here before you go have one of the greatest meals you have ever eaten. That lady can cook man. It's such a shame she never remarried after her husband died. She would make someone a great wife and companion." He smiled as he walked them around the building. It was pretty hot as they got the tour of the outside of the church.

Larry looked at Bob and Said: "Dude! That woman could smell you from the doorway! Of course, I noticed it myself about five hours ago."

Bob responded, "You still smell like that rabbit we ran over yesterday man. I tell you what, I'll wait for you to go first in the shower. If Sister Wilson has any brains at all, she will vacate the premises until we both are all cleaned up and ready for dinner. I thank God for that air conditioner in that beautiful car, but it can't keep *you* from stinking up the joint."

Larry laughed. "I love you brother; you can hand out the greatest sarcasm I've ever heard and still make me laugh."

The two newest townsfolk got the entire tour of the church, and it was in a decent phase of disrepair. It needed new doors and door jams, some of the pews were in such bad shape they couldn't be sat on anymore. Every faucet in the building leaked. The sound system was so old that it could barely get the volume above the kids in the next room. The cabinets in what appeared to be the fellowship hall were barely hanging on or leaned up against the wall next to the refrigerator that had quit working last week.

Bob knew they had enough to keep them busy for a long time. He and Larry were their own kind of handymen. They loved to sing and pray as they worked on churches, and they always had a fun time as they worked. Most of the churches they had been to since this "road trip" started had always needed repairs, some more than others and this church was one of the worst they had seen so far.

Bob put his hand on the Pastors shoulder, "Pastor, why don't we pray before Larry, and I head on over to Sister Wilson's?"

"I was just thinking the same thing, Bob. But let's go into the sanctuary because it has carpet and it's easy on the knees. At this age you need every comfort you can find. My office has faux carpet without any padding under it and it kills my knees." They chuckled and headed in there.

As Larry kneeled, he told Pastor Brown to pray for specific things that he had on his heart and then He and Bob would pray after him.

Pastor Brown began his prayer: "Father, only You know why these young men are here and I thank You in advance of what glorious things are going to happen to this church and thus this town. Thank you so much for hearing my prayer when I thought it was falling on deaf ears. Lesson learned Father, forgive my doubt. There was a time I thought this prayer was going to be answered after I was already up there with You. Now Lord, I ask that You keep Your hand on Brother and Sister Young and their two precious daughters. Poor little Nancy has had so much trouble with whatever is going on with her abdomen and little Chelsea is worried she's going to lose her best friend. Those two parents appear to be on the verge of collapse and need a true miracle from You. Father they could use a miracle touch from You today, please heal that little girl today. Also, Father, Brother Warren has been missing a lot of church recently, bless his health and please draw him back toward You. He seems to have cooled towards You and this church, and we miss that awesome booming laughter around here and we miss him. His kids seem to have gotten cold in their relationship as well. As for the rest of this congregation that has quit coming Father, please bring them back, or help them find a church that fits them better than we have. The Wagner's come to mind as do the Maguire's and the Hopkins' the Torensens' and the Caldwell's Father. I love them all and miss them dearly. Please bring them back and restore our friendships, as well as drawing them closer to you. Please bless our City Council and our Mayor. Please let them all to know Your love, mercy, and grace oh Lord. Save them all. I would love to have all of them as part of this congregation. I thank you again for these two guys. Let them stay forever. Amen."

Larry prayed: "Thank You Lord for all of the hospitality You have shown to us at each place You have sent us. Thank You also for all the wonderful people that come into our lives. We know they have burdens and some of those burdens are bigger than themselves. Thank You Father for Pastor Brown. I can sense he loves You more than most Pastors that have been here in the past. Not many Ministers would have stuck with such a cold congregation. Please help all of them to be sensitive to Your leading. Help us to keep our focus on why we are here and get this church back to being successful once again and being that evangelical tool, you need it to be. Amen."

Bob prayed: "Father here we go again. Once again, we are going to be involved in something big. I look forward to this new challenge with a thirst for Your presence in this situation. Larry and I know it's going to get ugly pretty quickly, but You *always* come through with a victory for Your Kingdom, and we expect nothing less this time. Who does the devil think he is even bothering Your people? It just goes to show us all that he just ain't smart once more. Here he is again standing in Your way of showing this town just who You are. No wonder You threw him out of Heaven, he's still just as senseless as he was then. Well, here we go again. Please keep all of us safe. Every member of this church, the three of us and all those who are going to be helping us here. Let the miracles begin!"

Pastor Brown opened his eyes and looked back and forth between Larry and Bob a few times shaking his head. He finally spoke with a broken voice: "What have you two been through in your short lives? Those prayers kind of scared me boys, I'm not even kidding, I'm a little scared here. But at the same time, I have a peace within me. You two are so calm and it's comforting to me even though I know we're getting ready for a spiritual battle like I may have never seen before. I'm going to be leaning on you guys for strength, while until I get my feet under me like you guys do."

"We have definitely been through this before Pastor." Bob said. "But in *every* place, we have been God has shown just how *huge He is!!* We have had the hair on the back of our necks stand at attention more than once because of the devil. *But!* We've had just as many goose bumps because God showed up. So, Pastor Brown, we are in good hands. In fact, the best hands that ever existed. God's hands are bigger than everything! Even better. I think you will see they are so much bigger than you have ever seen."

"I sure hope so, but I've seen some pretty great things in my sixty plus years." Pastor Brown told them as he looked at his watch. "Hey! We better get going before my wife thinks I ran off with the circus again."

"Ya and Larry here is stinking this place up really bad anyways. So how do we get to Sister Wilson's home?" Bob asked.

"Good grief Bob, my nose was hurting so bad before we even got here, it's turned itself off at this point. Now I'm hungry, but I won't be able to smell that good food we're having for dinner!" Larry retorted.

They all laughed and soon headed in different directions. These two guys were looking forward to a home cooked meal. It had been quite a few days since their last one and the food at most of the eateries on the road was forgettable.

As Larry drove away from the church he began shaking his head. Bob saw it and asked what he was thinking. "I'm just glad we're wearing shirts and pants today instead of our normal shorts and tank tops. Had Pastor Brown seen all of these scars we have; he may have *really* gotten scared once we got down to business in that conversation."

"I agree." Bob said. "He's afraid enough as it is, that would have definitely raised his fear level. We'll pray for him like we always do, and he'll be fine. God hasn't let us down yet, even though we've been knocked around pretty good a few times. Pastor Brown has such a huge heart and burden for these people, maybe more than I've seen before. Most ministers would have packed up and run out of this town, but not this guy. I like this guy a lot. His maturity and wisdom are above all others. Plus, that huge loving heart of his. His integrity stares you right on the face. This is one Pastor that we can count on in the fight this time brother. I don't know about you, but I'm quite sure this Pastor is going to be good for us in the long run. I already love the guy more than I deserve."

"No doubt about it Bob, *that* is one impressive Christian man right there buddy. And like you, I love him as well. He's more up for this than he thinks he is. He just might surprise himself when this is all over and this whole town is on fire for God." Larry was beginning to feel rather good about this town already.

Chapter 2

One Year Earlier

Summer vacation had already started for the high school this past Friday, but boredom had already set in for Jimmy and Zane and it was only Wednesday! Jimmy was five feet, ten inches tall and weighed about 155 pounds and looked like he just walked off the front of a magazine. He never thought a thing about his looks and always wondered why the girls at school smiled so big at him in the school halls. Did he have something in his teeth? Was his zipper down? He never knew why and quit trying to figure it out. To say he was shy is an understatement.

Zane was just as pretty but a bit taller at six foot even and weighed about 170 pounds. Jimmy told him he could hide behind a broom handle because he was so skinny. He was just as skinny as Jimmy and just as shy.

They had been best friends since kindergarten and in a couple of months they were going to be seniors in high school. As Jimmy was thinking about it one day, this senior year had really snuck up on him rather quickly. Zane was talking about joining the military and Jimmy didn't really want him to go. Who was he going to hang out with when he left? Zane was like Jimmy's brother, maybe even closer than that. Jimmy decided to think about something else. Friday was coming, and they hadn't discussed what they were going to do.

Zane was sitting on the fender of a classic car that he was given for his sixteenth birthday. It was bright red with chrome baby moons and chrome bumpers. It had a three twenty seven in it with dual carbs and a really nice tuck and roll interior. His dad had his friends at the upholstery shop put it in for him. When he punched the throttle, it would scream! When it was freshly waxed it shined like the noonday sun.

His dad had put this car together over a lot of years just for Zane. His dad wanted him to have a car he would like to keep for a long time, as well as remember where he came from when he left home, when the time came.

Zane and his dad had a special relationship that made his friends envious as they would have loved to have that same relationship with their dads. Billy Warren, Zane's dad had been the mechanic in town for Zane's entire life. This car had been Billy's dream car, but he ended up making it for Zane as the years went by. Zane had always admired this car over in the corner as he was growing up. He knew his family was going to climb in it and go for a drive in it when daddy got it finished, but never in his life did Zane think he would be the one driving it. Zane really appreciated this car and took great care of it, hopefully just like his dad would have if it were his car. Zane had never seen his dad smile so big as he was the day Zane saw the car in the driveway on his birthday. He could tell his dad was really proud of this car.

Billy Warren was a good man and was loved throughout the town. He was always fixing cars that people couldn't afford to get fixed. He just told them to pay him when they could. For the most part, those people always paid his dad over time.

Zane began to think of how much he had appreciated Jimmy's company over all these years. After being friends for so many years, almost since they could talk it seemed to Zane. They had never gotten into any trouble growing up and had never been arrested. These two weren't mean at all, like some of the other kids in town. They did have their times when they would have gotten "whooped" big-time if their parents had ever caught them doing some of the things they did when they were feeling ornery. They weren't perfect, but they were pretty solid in their character.

Neither one of them had much to do with girls thus far in their lives. Not that they didn't pay attention to the girls in town, they were just too shy to ask any of them out. There were plenty of pretty girls here in town, but Zane and Jimmy just didn't think about them too much. But Friday was coming and both of them were thinking it would be nice to take a couple of girls out on a date.

"Hey!" They both said it at the same time. Jimmy said: "You first. What were you going to say?"

Zane replied with a sigh: "Well, it's our first Friday out since summer started, so what do you want to do?"

Jimmy thought for a moment and answered: "I was just thinking about that. What do you think about asking a couple of girls to go to a movie or something like that Friday night?"

"I was just thinking the same thing! Wow! That's interesting," Zane said. "I think it's a great idea, but I don't have anyone in mind and I'm not so sure I have the guts to ask anyone either. Do you think anyone wants to go anywhere with either of us?"

Jimmy shook his head sideways "I don't have anyone in mind but listen here Zane. We're not exactly the ugliest boys in town, but we're not ready to put on those brown robes and move to a really quiet place either. We're pretty nice to everyone and people seem to like us. Besides, who wouldn't want a piece of us anyways?" They both laughed and gave each other a high five. "So, let's think about it for a minute and decide who to call today, okay?" They both grabbed their chins and looked down. They had been friends for so long they had a lot of the same mannerisms.

After a couple of minutes Jimmy spoke first. "How about that girl you took to the Valentine's dance a few months ago? She was really pretty, and you two seemed to enjoy each other's company. Was her name Rebecca, or something like that?"

Zane's eyes brightened. "Ya, that's her name. I'll definitely be giving her a call! What a really nice girl, not to mention pretty." Rebecca was tall at five foot nine and slender, with big blue eyes and reddish hair. They both enjoyed each other's company that night, but Zane had heard she was sweet on John Sweet. Zane had kind of thought maybe she wasn't his type, like he would know what his type was. But he was so shy he never pursued anything, plus he was too shy to do so anyway.

Zane looked at Jimmy. "What about you buddy? Suzy left in a huff from the dance that night. What was her problem anyway? Did you ever find out?"

"No, I never did. She wasn't mad at me. That's all I know." Jimmy Said. "She and Sally Bigelow had some words in the powder room I heard, and Suzy just came out, got her stuff, and told me she would see me at school. Then she left without telling me what happened. Besides, she was stuck on herself anyways and I don't really want to call her. She was already telling people how well she had things planned out and that she was going to be pursuing a career in management at Burger Box. For some dumb reason I would like more than that for my future mate. I wish Suzy all the luck in the world, but I have bigger plans than that. She was a pretty nice girl though."

They were leaning on the car again with their hands on their chins, looking like mannequins in the store. Jimmy spoke first. "Ha! What do you think of Connie Mickler? She's pretty, she's smart." And on her way to college." Zane interrupted Jimmy's thought. "She graduated this past Friday remember?"

"Oh yeah. Shoot!" Jimmy squealed. "I always had a crush on her, but I could never get the nerve to even say hi to her in the hallways at school. What a smart girl. She's probably going to an Ivy League college or something like that. Well, that shot that one down like a dead pheasant. You got any more girls in mind?"

Zane's eyes narrowed. "What about that girl that took you to the Sady Hawkins dance? What was her name anyway?"

Jimmie's face scowled. "No way dude! Her name was Laura Kilderon. She asked me and I went because I didn't want to go alone, but she paraded me around and introduced me to everyone she knew like I was a piece of meat or something. She's smart and pretty, but not enough for a second date. You know what though? I think I'll call Betty Jo Miller. She's such a nice person with the sweetest smile in the world. She's got those pretty freckles on her nose and such a cute round face. Not to mention as smart as a set of encyclopedias. I don't remember her having too many close friends either now that I'm thinking about it. Meaning, I think she should be available for a movie Friday night. What do you think?

"Now that you mention it Jimmy, I don't remember her hanging out with anyone on a regular basis. Good call Jimmy. You're going to marry a hermit and live a nice quiet reclusive life." Now Zane and Jimmy were both laughing.

Jimmy said, "Come one Zane, you know she not a hermit, but she is so smart and just as cute as a bug. I think I really will call her. She's so sweet that even if she tells me no, it would just be nice to talk to her." Now the two of them were standing there looking pleased with themselves and smiling. So, it was settled; Zane was going to call Rebecca Turnbull and Jimmy was going to call Betty Jo Miller.

Zane looked at his watch and it was five forty-five, time to be heading home for dinner. They hopped into his hot rod and headed towards home.

As Zane walked in his dad was washing up for dinner. He looked at Zane and gave him a big smile. "How are you doing son? Did you have another boring day with that poor slob Jimmy again?" Now his dad was giggling. Billy Warren, Zane's father, was a hard looking man. The desert seemed to have weathered him a bit for his 45 years, and he was starting to show some gray around his temples. His belly was getting bigger as the years went by as well, but at 6 feet even he carried it well.

Zane's mother was stirring the vegetables at the stove. She was the prettiest mom in town. According to Zane. She was the same 45 years old as his dad but looked much younger. Zane was asked a few times about his beautiful sister, when in fact, they were asking about his mother. At five foot four, Zane wondered how she was able to get up high enough to kiss his dad.

Zane's sister, Laura, was only thirteen years old and getting pretty with a nice figure. Zane always watched out for her at school as she was a bit naive when it came to the boys flirting with her. He found himself hoping she would wise up soon before he left for the military.

His dad asked if he and Jimmy had gone out kissing girls and pulling their ponytails today. Zane looked at him and answered: "It may surprise you that Jimmy and I decided to call a couple of girls and ask them out to the movies on Friday, you ol' coot.!" And he let out a big laugh.

"Did you hear that, Helen? This little skinny, wet-behind-the-ears kid just called me an ol' coot!" Billy had an amused look on his face.

Helen replied: "And it looks good on you too dear. You should wear the ol' coot thing more often." She flashed a huge smile at Zane. "It sounds like our son is trying to feel his way to manhood, finally. Actually, Zane, I though it sounded very masculine for a boy your age."

"Is that a compliment, or a put down mom?" Zane had no idea what just happened.

His mother simply answered: "Yes."

"Mom!" Zane protested. His dad and sister laughed at him. His mother just smiled that "gotcha" smile she always wore at times like this. She was the one in the family with the real sense of humor, which he really loved about her, except when it was at his expense, like it was now.

"Well, now that we're finished teasing you at this point, who are you going to call for that date. I already know she's not as pretty as your mother." Billy winked at Helen who blushed.

"To that we agree old man." Zane said with a smile.

"Did you hear that, Helen! There he goes with that "old" stuff again!" His dad protested.

His mom was on her son's side after that statement. "Actually Billy, I am beginning to like this young man that's visiting with us for dinner. He is very charming to say the least. Wherever did you find him, and could you find another one just like him?"

"I don't know where I got him Helen, but I'm more inclined to put back after all these "old" jokes he has got flying' out of his mouth from the other side of the table." His dad winked at him and stuck his tongue out at Zane. "That was surprisingly good Zane. A guy could do a lot worse than picking up his mother's sense of humor like you have. Just be sure to treat your date like a Princess and you'll have a lot of fun. So be on your best behavior and don't be in a hurry to be so grown up. So, what's her name?"

"Her name is Rebecca Turnbull, for your information, and we went to the Valentine's dance together a few months ago." Zane had always listened to his dad when he was dishing out good advice like this, but he wondered what "being so grown up" meant."

Meanwhile, Jimmy was having dinner at his home too, only the conversation was not so pleasant. His stepfather was looking at Jimmy like he had just stolen the family silver or something. "What are you going to do with yourself this summer boy? Waste the entire summer away like you have all the others? You know, when I was a teenager, I had my own paper route and mowed lawns. I fixed things around people's houses for them too. I was so busy working that I didn't have time to spend all the money I was making, because I was too busy making it! I can't believe the way you kids are now days. You just expect things for nothing don't you?! You don't work for anything, yet you expect people to just give you everything. That's why we have Welfare because kids like you grow into lazy adults! You think the world owes you everything when in fact, it owes you nothing but a swift kick in the pants for being lazy!"

Jimmy had never liked this guy from the first time they ever met. He was a jerk then and now he was just a bigger jerk. In fact, he gave jerks a bad name. His mother told Jimmy that she was going to marry this piece of whatever when he was about nine years old and he begged her not to, but she did it anyway. He treated both of them like garbage and Jimmy could not put his finger on it, but something was more amiss than him being such a hard person to get along with. There was something mysterious about this guy that made Jimmy wonder about him, but Jimmy didn't like him enough or care enough to find out what it was. At this point he was just hoping to get this next year or so under his belt and get out of town on the first bus to college, far from here. Jimmy had once told Zane that He wished this guy would just die, but then his mom would be a basket case all over again.

Ken Walker was Jimmy's stepfather's name. Jimmy called him Matilda under his breathe because if he was a woman he would be a witch. He was short and chubby with dark black hair. Sometimes when the sun hit his hair exactly right, it had blue streaks in it.

Jimmy's dad had been killed in a car accident while he was headed to San Francisco to say his final good-byes to his mother who was dying of cancer, but he never made it. Jimmy and his dad were as close as Zane was with his dad, and Jimmy found himself really missing him today. He thought his mother was going to cry herself to death when it happened. He was really worried about her because he didn't know if he could get over losing both of his parents all at once. But one day this preacher came over the house to see her. That Pastor was a really nice man and very gentle in how he spoke to his mom. That Pastor even got tears in his eyes as his mom was telling him the story of how his dad died. He still sees that preacher around town and makes it a point to wave at him and smile. That guy really helped his mother get back on her feet again. Soon she had a job at the elementary school working as the Principal's Executive Assistant. It always helped having her there, as he could threaten the other kids with telling his mom to tell the principal on them.

Now his mother was thirty-nine years old and looked much older than that. Jimmy figured she looked about fifty right now, but what really bothered him was that she rarely smiled anymore. Jimmy loved his mom more than he did himself and it killed him inside to have watched her personality fade since she married this monster. Her name was Sally Drummond before she married, and he wished it still was. She was always nice to Jimmy but had quit sticking up for him when Ken was having one of his fits, like he was now. What in the world could she have seen in this guy anyway? Other than the fact he had a lot of money, and they moved into a huge four-bedroom four-bathroom house, luxury cars and nice clothes, what did he have? Jimmy knew money didn't bring happiness with it. Shoot, they didn't even have anyone in that fourth bedroom and bathroom. Who was this guy kidding?

"Do you hear me!? Are you listening to me!? You better listen to me when I'm talking to you son!" Jimmy found himself back in this conversation he was hoping to not hear, but not this time.

"Ken! Ken!" Jimmy had to yell to get his attention. "I don't mean to be disrespectful, but I don't deserve this. You keep screaming at me about how ungrateful I am, but that's not true. I am incredibly grateful for all that you have done for mom and me since my dad passed away. But I don't know what you want from me. You're always accusing me of being lazy, but you hire out all the work I could do around here Like the yard, I can mow that myself and help out around here. But you pay that simple little guy, who is so kind and friendly to do it. What's his name? Oh, Delbert. Then you gripe about how much you have to pay him, which is nothing compared to what you would pay a professional to do it. Poor Delbert is even afraid to come to the door for his money when he's finished, so he has mom get it for him. I'm going for a walk. I don't want to be here right now. I even know as soon as I'm out that door that you'll start in on my mom. What have we done to you that makes us deserve this, Ken!? Nothing! Absolutely nothing! But I'll tell you this while I'm on a roll here, if you ever lay a finger on my mom I'll beat you within an inch of your life, I swear I will. She's all I have left in this world, and I love her more than my own life. I will fight you to the death before I ever let you hit her. So, go ahead and drink another glass of that expensive wine and shut up!" With that he stormed out the door with a thundering slam!

Jimmy had put up with all that he could at this point. He wanted to punch Ken so bad right now but knew he wouldn't be able to. He never was a fighter, so he would take a walk and calm down.

Across town Zane and his sister had finished the dishes and put them away while that "ol' coot" and his beautiful wife watched the news.

Zane got online and found Rebecca's number. "Hi Rebecca, this is Zane Warren, how are you tonight?"

"Zane Warren! What in the world are you doing? I'm fine by-the-way and this a welcome surprise." Zane could tell she was genuinely surprised.

"Well, Laura and I just finished getting the dishes all put away. I was just curious as to what you have been doing this week. Jimmy and I are already getting bored, how about you? Are you bored too?" He was hoping her answer would be yes.

"Actually, I've been talking on the phone all week with Tammy, Sue, and Terry all week. In fact, I thought you were one of them when my phone rang. But yes, I am a little bored. I wish I could have gotten a job again this summer, but this is going to be my last summer at home, so I didn't. What are your plans for the summer?" Rebecca sounded as excited as a five-year-old on Christmas morning.

That question caught Zane off guard, even though he had some plans to talk to her about. "Well, I haven't really thought about it much. I usually go help my dad at his shop after a week or two. He pays me for the help, but I think it's one of those things to keep me from asking for money, so he makes me think I'm earning it. It spends good though and it keeps me in soda and burgers and gas for my car. I've even managed to save some of it. Do you have any plans for this Friday night? Are you and your friends doing anything?"

Now she was really excited. "No! No, nothing at all planned. Why? Did you have something in mind?" Rebecca couldn't wait for the answer.

Now Zane was getting nervous. He had no idea what he was doing because he had never asked a girl out before. But she sounded like she was ready to go anywhere right now. "Well, Jimmy and I were talking today about who we might ask to go to the movies on Friday and... well, we thought of you...I'd like to know if...you would like...Well shoot! Would you like to go to the movies with Jimmy and his date this Friday night?" Zane got frustrated with himself. "I would really like to take you out. I will pay for everything, popcorn, soda. And if you're hungry afterwards, we can get some burgers or pizza. Whichever you prefer." Now Zane was talking fast, and his adrenaline was moving good.

"Oh, Zane that sounds wonderful! I would love to go, but my cousin Linda, from California is coming for a visit tomorrow. I wouldn't want to leave her here alone." Rebecca was so disappointed.

Without even thinking, Zane said, "Oh bring her along, that would be fun to have her too."

"Oh Zane, that' nice and all, but that would be imposing on your kindness. I couldn't expect you to pay for everything for both of us. But I really do want to go. I tell you what, let me pay for Linda's stuff okay?"

"I don't know how to do that Rebecca. It's a good idea, but that would be awkward, I think. Just let me pay for everything. If I get short of money, I'll have no choice but to say so. How does that sound? I don't want her to feel out of place." Zane was grasping at straws now that he knew she really wanted to go.

Rebecca was really excited now. "Yeah, I guess that would work. But I really would like to pay for something that night. I'll definitely bring some money. You know, I've always paid my own part when I've gone out on dates before. It's nice to know that there are still gentlemen in this world. Oh, I'm so excited! Why did you wait so long to call me? I haven't heard from you since the Valentine dance. I'm really curious."

Zane blushed every shade of red ever invented. "I don't honestly know Rebecca. I had a wonderful time at the dance just like you did, but we seemed to be two different types of people, so I didn't think you would want to go out with me again. Earlier today Jimmy and I were talking about taking a date to the movies on Friday and we started throwing names out. When Jimmy mentioned your name, I got really excited. But I heard you and John Small were dating, so I wasn't really sure you would want to go. Whatever happened with him?"

"Oh, John was a really nice guy, but we didn't have anything in common. Every time we got together it was just silence. We didn't have anything to talk about or anything. Both of us even recognized it. So, we wished each other the best and now we're friends." Rebecca was nice as she talked about him.

Zane said, "Yeah, he really is a nice guy, which is why I thought you two would be together for a while at least. But when Jimmy mentioned your name today, I suddenly remembered not seeing you two together for a while prior to school letting out last week. But listen, I will have you and your cousin home at a decent hour, so your parents don't have to worry about you guys, okay?" Zane let out a big breath.

"Okay Zane. I'll see you about 5 o'clock on Friday then." Rebecca was going to seal the deal right now and not let Zane Warren off the hook. She really liked this guy, and he was on the top of her list of people she could see herself with for a long time. There were others of course, but Zane was on top of that list with no close second.

"Five o'clock it is my dear. I will see you then if we don't bump into each other sooner." Zane was a happy boy right now. He wasn't going to be able to sleep the next two nights before this date. He felt like he had just had the best conversation of his entire life!

Jimmy had walked a while and had calmed down from his fall out with Ken. He finally took out his phone as he was walking down the main street and decided to call Betty Jo. He had gotten Betty Jo's number and had written it down before he left the house, now he was glad he had put it in his pocket. He called the number, "Hi Betty Jo? Oh, I'm sorry, you sound just like her. Is she there by any chance? This is Jimmy Drummond. Yes, I'll wait. Hi Betty Jo, how are you tonight? Did I catch you at a bad time?"

Betty Jo was definitely surprised to be getting a phone call from a boy she barely knew but was excited at the same time. "No Jimmy, you caught me at the perfect time because I was just thinking I wish Jimmy Drummond would call me, and here you are calling me.

She caught Jimmy off guard with her humor, which completely embarrassed and dumbfounded him so bad he didn't know how to answer her. "Uh...well... Hi Betty Jo...um...uh."

Betty Jo giggled a little. "I'm just teasing you Jimmy, what are you up to tonight?"

"Man, you got me good Betty Jo. I forgot you had such a good sense of humor, and I definitely wasn't ready for it. Are you getting bored yet since school is out? Zane and I are bored to tears already."

Betty Jo noticed Jimmy didn't sound like his typically happy self. "Well, I've been home all week helping with the housework and watching a lot of TV. It gets kind of boring watching people win prizes and I'm not one of them. I've had a few conversations with some of the girls from school but haven't left the house yet. Say Jimmy, is everything okay? You don't sound like yourself tonight? You sound sad and I've never known you be even slightly unhappy."

"Oh, my stepfather and I got into an argument earlier and I had to go for a walk. That's why you hear this background noise because I'm calling from in front of the pharmacy." He stopped and took a deep breath. "I'm Sorry Betty Jo, I should have waited to call you when I wasn't so upset. I thought I could call you, ask you to go to the movies and be a happy boy again, but I'll just call tomorrow when things are better. I'll talk to you tomorrow, Betty Jo, bye-bye."

As he was hanging up the phone, he could hear Betty Jo talking. "Jimmy! Jimmy! Do not hang up. I would love to go to the movies with you anytime. It would get me out of the house." She didn't mean that like it sounded. "Oops, I'm sorry Jimmy. I would love to go to the movies any time, not just to get out of the house. You are one of those guys that's fun to be around and I would totally love to do that. So, when are we going to that movie? But I require that all my dates pamper me like a Princess or it's just not going to work out." She started laughing as did Jimmy. Jimmy had forgotten how much fun she was, or they may have already been dating.

"Now that you mention it Betty Jo, why do you stay at home all the time? Zane and I were talking about that today when we decided to go the to the movies." It was just a curiosity the two boys shared aloud.

Betty Jo was a little embarrassed at needing to defend her mother like this and her mom's strictness. "Actually, Jimmy, my mother is trying to protect me from something that happened to her right out of high school. You see, my dad left when he found out my mother was pregnant with me, and she's never seen him since then. She has a lot of trust issues with every guy she sees and isn't even interested in dating again or a relationship at all. That guy flat out crushed her spirit and it ticks me off sometimes seeing her so unhappy at times. She doesn't smile quite often, except when I tease and make her laugh."

Just then Betty Jo's mother took the phone away from her.

"Jimmy?'

"Yes Mrs. Miller?'

"Are you asking Betty Jo out on a date?"

"Yes ma'am, I am, but only if it's okay with you."

"That's fine Jimmy, but I want to meet you in person first. Come over to our house at six o'clock tomorrow so we can talk. Can you do that for me?" Mrs. Miller wasn't rude, but very matter of fact in her tone.

"I will be there at six for sure Mrs. Miller. Please don't worry, I think I understand from what Betty Jo had told me so far." Jimmy thought he was helping.

"Well Betty Jo talks too much sometimes." And she handed the phone back to Betty Jo.

"I didn't mean to get you in trouble Betty Jo, I'm really sorry." Jimmy really felt bad.

"It's okay Jimmy, I'll see you at six tomorrow and I'm looking forward to it." She hung up sounding as depressed as Jimmy was.

Friday finally got here, and Zane and Jimmy were finally taking their dates to the movies. Jimmy had just finished the interrogation of his life yesterday and was looking forward to being Betty Jo's date for the night. When he met her at the door earlier, it was all worth it. Betty Jo was even prettier than he remembered.

Zane was having difficulty keeping his eyes on the road as he drove, because he kept looking at Rebecca and trying to carry on a conversation with her and her cousin, Linda, at the same time.

They made it to the theater twenty minutes before the movie started. Jimmy would have been happier just sitting in the car and talking with Betty

Jo. He was a little embarrassed as he felt underdressed for the date. He had just put on a new pair of jeans and a western shirt, just like it was any other day. He shaved for the first time in three weeks, which wasn't saying much. He usually only needed to shave every three weeks.

Betty Jo must have really taken her time in front of the mirror tonight. She looked great and Jimmy was smitten to the bone. She was wearing a light-colored linen dress with small white and yellow checkerboard pattern on it with lace around the collar. The white stockings made it even prettier. The yellow in the dress seemed to really make her blonde hair shine like gold. Yap, Jimmy was definitely smitten in every way imaginable.

Zane had actually dressed up a little bit. He was wearing his white shirt with that thin black tie he usually wore to the school dances and his cowboy hat. He was looking really good tonight. Rebecca had just worn a pair of jeans and a white knit shirt. It didn't matter though; she was a pretty girl. Zane was really glad he had asked her out. She seemed to come alive when she met him at the front door. Her cousin Linda was just as pretty. She was a tall girl at five feet eleven inches and slim. Zane was looking her right in the eye, or even looking up at her a little bit. She was wearing all black, but Jimmy and Zane just figured that's how they all dress in California.

They went inside and got their popcorn and drinks, then went and found their seats. The theater was pretty full tonight. Maybe because it was the first Friday of summer vacation. They all saw some of their friends on the way to their seats and had small conversations as they walked by. A few of the boys took jabs at Zane and Jimmy for finally taking girls out on a date. Some of the boys were even teasing Zane and Jimmy about being in love with each other. Jimmy had no idea what that even meant.

The movie finally started, and everything got quiet for the first time. The movie was surprisingly good and held their interest, for the most part. Jimmy, for most of the movie, stared at Betty Jo. Jimmy was wondering if he was in love or was it just the fact that she was so pretty tonight. He was beginning to wonder if he was staring at the girl he was going to marry. If her mother would let her marry, of course.

Zane was holding hands with Rebecca. They would look at each other throughout the movie, exchange smiles from time to time, then resume watching the movie.

Linda was enjoying herself watching the movie from several seats away. She told Rebecca and Zane she didn't want to bother them tonight and sitting away from them seemed like a good idea. Linda had also told them she felt as if she were intruding on her favorite cousins first date. But both Zane and Rebecca assured her she was most welcome to be there, and Rebecca told Linda she wasn't going without her. Thus, Linda was trying not to be noticed by either of them tonight. But from the looks of things, Linda would not have bothered them if she were sitting in their laps.

Linda was a really nice girl and had graduated from high school two weeks ago. She had been accepted into one of the prestigious Southern California colleges and majoring in Marine Biology. She was hoping to get a job at one of the theme parks working with either whales, or dolphins. She had photos of them both on her phone and little else. Her family was just visiting for a couple of weeks this summer, just as they did every year, and Rebecca was really looking forward to spending a lot of time with her this year.

Zane thought that it was really cool for Linda to be testing for her black belt in martial arts when she got back home. She was so tall, why would anyone pick on her to begin with? But in Southern California, why does anyone do anything? Life sounded like a jungle there, at least to Zane.

When the movie finally ended, Jimmy was jumping out of his skin to get in the car and out to the park, so he could show off his beautiful date. Jimmy caught a look at Zane and Rebecca. They were really enjoying each other's company. Linda looked like she had an enjoyable time too. Soon, they were all in the car on their way out to the park but stopped by the frosty to grab a few burgers and drinks to take out there with them.

Once they arrived at the park, Zane and Jimmy realized this was not going to be an average night at the park. It was wall to wall cars and people, and it looked like everyone was having a fun time. That pretty red classic car caught some eyes as it rolled in and parked. At this point, everyone knew Zane and Jimmy had brought dates to the movies, but not everyone knew who they brought. Some of the girls were already jealous as those two boys had been the most eligible and sought after boys in the entire school. They just seemed oblivious to all the advances girls had made towards them in all those years. Whoever those girls were, the jealous girls just hoped they knew who they had, because if not, the line for those two guys had already started.

They ended up parking clear in one of the back corners because this place was full and jumping with excitement. The two couples started making the rounds and talking to their friends. The two boys had their chests stuck out a bit because they both knew they had two of the most beautiful girls in school with them tonight.

Rebecca and Betty Jo kept getting sideways glances from some of the other girls. They both knew why, but neither of them said anything to each other. Linda tagged along with them for a while, then decided to go her own way and mingle amongst the crowd. She thought it was like the county fair back home, as you ran into a lot of friends there.

No one noticed the black limousine in the back corner of the park, close to where Zane had parked his car. The occupants of that car were watching the crowd looking for something that might pique their interest. They all noticed the tall girl wearing black clothes; she might be someone of interest, but later. If things kept going the way were, they might get a chance to approach her, and with no moon tonight, they wouldn't have to worry about being seen.

Zane and Rebecca had caught up with Sandi and Marvin, while Jimmy and Betty Jo had caught up with Ed and Diane. Everyone was chatting and having a good time tonight, especially the two boys and their dates. Jimmy was able to make his way through the crowd and show off his date. At one point he caught a girl giving Betty Jo a dirty look, so he asked Betty Jo about it. She just shrugged it off and told Jimmy that the girl was just a snob.

Zane and Rebecca were mostly talking with Sandi and Marvin. Zane and Marvin had played baseball together for years and they were talking about all thing's baseball. Meanwhile, Sandi and Rebecca were talking about their dates tonight and how proud both of them were to be out with such great guys.

Finally, Sandy asked Rebecca how she was able to snag Zane for a date tonight. Rebecca told Sandy that she had Zane wrapped around her little finger. They both laughed liked little girls, as they both knew it wasn't true. It was funny though. Rebecca told Sandi the truth after a few minutes, about how Zane had called her out of the blue.

Jimmy and Betty Jo were holding hands now while they were visiting with Ed and Diane. They were both enjoying their evening together. The four of them were talking about the fact they were starting their last year in school in a few short weeks. Now that their senior year was here, it seemed to have snuck up on them. Ed wasn't sure what he was going to do yet but had thought about staying in town and working in the mine like everyone else. The pay was okay and if things got serious with Diane, he would have a steady income to start their lives together. "If not, I'll just marry someone who really cares about me, whoever that is." Diane punched him in the arm pretty hard. Ed Said: "Well, we know it ain't her" as he was looking at Jimmy and started laughing. Diane had no intention of letting Ed get away.

Jimmy echoed Ed's uncertainty. He mentioned that Zane was thinking pretty seriously about going into the military, but Jimmy hadn't made his mind up yet. Jimmy even mentioned how much he was going to miss Zane after he left town. Jimmy mentioned that he just might follow Zane into the military, but he really hadn't put much thought into it, at which Betty Jo squeezed his hand hard enough to get his attention. Jimmy gave Betty Jo a look as if to say, "what was that about?"

At that point Zane came and mentioned to Jimmy that it was getting close to eleven o'clock and they should probably get their dates home, so he didn't have to go through another third-degree interrogation from Betty Jo's mom. Zane definitely didn't want to jeopardize any future dates with these two girls. He knew how he felt about Rebecca already and he was quite sure Jimmy felt the same about Betty Jo. Zane had a smile on his face that Jimmy had never seen before. It was so big it was like the sun shining on his entire face.

The four of them got in the car and Zane started to leave when Rebecca remembered her cousin. "Wait Zane! We forgot Linda, have you guys seen her? We can drive by and pick her up."

Jimmy said that he hadn't seen her in about an hour and asked Betty Jo if she had seen her. Betty Jo said: "I bet she met a cute guy and just lost track of time. But we do need to find her pretty quick, we don't need me getting in trouble because I was late getting home.

Rebecca had a panicked look on her face and told them she had to find Linda. She could never forgive herself if something happened to her tonight. Zane put his arm around her. "Rebecca, remember where you are. This is Southwind, nothing bad ever happens here because this town is full of really great people, and we watch out for each other. Please don't be upset, we're going to find her." Rebecca squeezed his hand and gave him a weak smile.

Zane turned off the car and everyone got out. Jimmy said, "why don't we split up and just meet back hear after we've found her?" Zane and Rebecca liked that idea and headed off in a different direction.

Jimmy ran across his friend Joe, neither he nor Kim remembered seeing her. They asked Roger and Linda and got the same response. But Jimmy and Betty Jo hadn't lost hope at all. They both knew they were going to find her.

Zane and Rebecca were a little more deliberate and impatient with their questions as Rebecca began to break down each time someone told them "No." Zane had to continually stop walking and console her and he was beginning to worry a little more. They got back to Sandi and Marvin, but they hadn't seen her either.

Jimmy and Betty Jo had made it back to the car and were just waiting for Zane and Rebecca to bring Linda so they could go home and not get into trouble for missing the curfew he had promised Betty Jo's mother. Jimmy was getting a little concerned the closer it got to eleven o'clock.

As soon as Rebecca saw Jimmy and Betty leaning on the car without Linda, she absolutely lost it. She took off at a dead run towards Jimmy screaming, "you didn't find her either? Oh no! Where is she? She has to be here! We have to find her! Please! God! Let us find her!" Then she screamed towards the entire park in an awful, hysterical voice: "Has anyone seen my cousin Linda tonight?" Then she fell on her knees and openly sobbed.

Rebecca's screaming got the attention of most of the crowd in the park and some of them came running trying to see what was going on. Marvin and Sandi pushed their way through the crowd as did Ed and Diane. Fortunately, Zane was as calm as ever, but Rebecca was still on her knees sobbing. A group of girls had gathered around hugging and trying to console her. Not one person in the crowd thought anything sinister had happened to Linda. They all figured she had just lost track of time and was still talking to someone in the park, and she would be here in a few minutes.

Zane knew that Marvin and Ed had bright lights on top of their trucks, so he asked them to drive around with them on looking for Linda outside of the park boundary. Unfortunately, they didn't find her the first time around.

Zane was absolutely dumbfounded. How could Linda do this? She was sweet and seemed to be pretty intelligent as well. Losing track of time like this just didn't make sense to him; not the Linda he thought he met earlier tonight.

Zane wouldn't accept this. He asked everyone to turn their lights on and point them towards the desert. Since most of the kids had pulled straight in, this was pretty easy. Ed and Marvin came around and shined their lights above the cars which seemed to work as far as vision was concerned, but still no Linda. The only car that didn't participate in this was Zane's car, which he figured out after taking an exhaustive look around the outskirts of the park. Even if they were to leave now, they might still get the girls home on time, but without Linda, that wasn't possible.

Since Zane's car was the furthest from the street, no one had thought anything about it until the second look around the park came up empty.

"Hey Marvin! Bring your truck over to my car and shine your lights out there." Zane prompted. Ed's truck was already pointing onto the desert. Marvin brought his truck over and shined his lights out there also. Zane told the two boys he had a sick feeling in his stomach at this point. Both their faces sank, as neither of them had any bad thoughts; until now.

Marvin and Ed stood next to Zane's car without saying anything to anyone, so the rest of the crowd stayed gathered around Tammy Mayo's car as the girls were still trying to get Rebecca to calm down. But they weren't having any success.

When Marvin's truck arrived at Zane's car, they turned on their lights. They all looked around Zane's car first, then out into the desert. Still nothing. Marvin thought he may have seen something with his little spotlight he had plugged into the power socket. He shined it on the object again and pointed it out to Zane. No one could make out what it was, so Zane said he'd be right back thinking it was an animal or a bush. Marvin and Ed waited by their trucks.

As they watched Zane walk out there, he was suddenly on one knee, then he vomited. The two took off running as fast as they could towards him. When they got there, they both got sick too. Linda was lying on her back with her eyes open and in an awkward position. She was obviously dead.

Zane was finally able to whisper: "One of you please call nine one one. One of you take your truck to the entrance of the park and block it so no one can leave and wait for the police. Don't say anything to anybody, including your girls." Ed told Zane he would go block the back gate and they both left.

Marvin made the call as he was driving towards the front gate. "Miss Mabel, there's been a murder in the park out on highway one forty. Can you send someone over?"

Miss Mabel came out of her chair. "There's been a what?!" Miss Mabel was one of Marvin's aunts and thought for just a second that Marvin was playing a joke on her, but Marvin wasn't like that.

"Miss Mabel, listen to me. You know Rebecca Turnbull, don't you?"

"Yes, of course I do. Everyone knows that lovely girl. It wasn't her that got killed was it, Marvin?! Don't joke with me like that!"

"No Miss Mabel, it was her cousin who is visiting from California. Zane found her out on the southeast corner, just outside the park boundary. He said he would wait there until you got someone out there. Miss Mabel, we are really scared, please get them out here really fast." Marvin was openly crying now. He had never seen anything like this before, and he already knew he never wanted to see it again. He would definitely remember tonight as long as he lived.

It took a moment, but Miss Mable finally got herself together enough to get a sheriff's unit on the way out there. "Marvin, do you know what happened?"

"No, I don't Miss Mabel." Marvin was losing control at this point and having difficulty talking in between sobs. "No. We just...Rebecca... was really upset... when she found...that her cousin was missing...then about...forty-five minutes later...we found her...just outside...the park. Rebecca still...doesn't know...Linda is all broken up...Miss."

"Marvin, it's okay. I've already got someone on their way out there. I'm so sorry you had to see that sweety. You're a strong young man, so try to get yourself together and be a good witness when the officers get there, okay? Do you want me to call your mom and have her come out there?" Now Miss Mabel was crying as she listened to her nephew.

"Yeah, why don't you do that. I'm not sure I can drive home tonight. I'm really sick to my" ...Marvin threw up.

The sirens were getting closer now which sent Rebecca out of her mind. She pushed everyone out of Tammy's car door and was screaming: "What's going on? What's going on? Where's Zane? ZAAANNE! Please somebody! Tell me what's going on! Pleeeeeeeeeeeeeease!"

Betty Jo was no help now as when she heard the sirens, she started sobbing herself. Could this night get any worse? She would soon find out.

The first police car finally arrived, and Marvin moved his truck. The officer asked what was going on and Marvin could only point in Zane's direction. The officer was hoping this was a teenage prank, but when he saw Marvin's face he knew better. He shined his spotlight in the direction Marvin pointed at and started driving towards Zane. In the Meantime, Rebecca had climbed to the top to Tammy's car and saw Zane when the spotlight hit him. Now she was outrunning the police car. Zane spotted her about the time the police car parked beside his car. Zane started running towards Rebecca to keep her from making it all the way to Linda's body. He caught her in front of the police car and held her as tight as he could to keep her from getting passed him. She was screaming as loud as he had ever heard anyone scream and still trying to get passed him. He ended up tackling her and holding her on the ground. Zane had a fleeting thought that he would never get a date with this poor girl ever again and just hugged her. He was crying too, but nothing like she was.

About that time, Marvin pulled up behind the officer and offered to help. Officer Mark asked Marvin what he knew about the situation. Marvin pointed out towards the desert in the general direction of where they found Linda. Officer Mark asked if he could shine his lights on that area for him, and Marvin didn't hesitate. The officer called Miss Mabel on his hand-held radio and asked her to send two ambulances, one for the body and one for Rebecca. He also asked for the Chief and detectives be sent out there. Officer Mark looked at Rebecca and saw Zane holding her as best he could to keep her from getting to the crime scene. He then noticed Betty Jo standing there crying and holding Jimmy's arm. They both had wet clothing, but he asked them if they could make sure the entrances were still blocked. They both nodded and took off walking.

When they got out to the front entrance, they found Marvin standing there. Marvin was still weeping, but nothing like he was earlier. Jimmy asked Marvin if he could use his phone to call Betty Jo's mother and let her know what was going on. Marvin handed him his phone without speaking.

Betty Jo held onto his arm while he talked to her mom. "Mrs. Miller?'

"Yes, is this Jimmy?"

"Yes," Jimmy didn't know what to say next. He had no clue what to tell Mrs. Miller as his mind was completely blank.

"Jimmy, is everything all right? Where are you? Is Betty Jo hurt? What is it, Jimmy?" She was really nervous at Jimmy's short answer.

"Betty Jo's fine Mrs. Miller. She's fine, but..."

"But what Jimmy?" She interrupted him. "You're starting to scare me now son, tell me what's going on?"

"There's been some trouble out here at the park and I was wondering if you might want to come pick Betty Jo up and take her home. Would you do that Mrs. Miller? I'm so sorry to call like this, but..." He started to cry.

Now Mrs. Miller was really scared. "What kind of trouble Jimmy?! Talk to me son! Please tell me what's going on! You have me scared Jimmy! What's going on?!"

"Do you remember me telling you yesterday that Rebecca's cousin was coming with us tonight?'

"Yes, I remember."

"She was killed tonight Mrs. Miller, we just found her about an hour ago, but I told you I would have Betty Jo home by midnight and it's pretty close to that now. I didn't want to disappoint you, Mrs. Miller. Betty Jo and I had such a wonderful time together, until this happened. I don't want to jeopardize us getting to date in the future. Please forgive me for scaring you Mrs. Miller, I just didn't know what to say." Jimmy was still weeping a bit, but able to talk.

Mrs. Miller felt her heart sink. "Jimmy, it okay. I'm so sorry this happened. Are you sure it's Rebecca's cousin? This kind of thing doesn't happen in Southwind, which is why we live here. Don't even worry about dating my daughter. After what I put you through yesterday, you proved you're a true gentleman, and now this call. You stand tall among men Jimmy Drummond, really tall. I'm really not mean Jimmy; I was just protecting my daughter. I don't mind coming to get her. You're at the park out on one-forty, aren't you?"

Jimmy answered: "Yes. Out on one-forty, and Betty Jo is fine Mrs. Miller. She's upset and crying, but physically she's not harmed at all. Here, I'll let you talk to her." He handed Betty Jo the phone.

"Mom." Betty Jo began crying all over again. "Yes, I'll be fine, but how can this happen with all of us here? I can't believe this is happening. Oh mom!" She started crying again. Her mom told her she would be there in a few minutes to pick her up and hung up the phone.

Jimmy gave Marvin back his phone and handed him some money, but Marvin wouldn't take it. Jimmy thought that cell phones had a fee for every minute, but Marvin assured him those days were over. Marvin said, "That was really nice what you did for Mrs. Miller Jimmy. In fact, I'm going to call Sandy's mom and ask her to come get Sandy as well." With that, Jimmy and Betty Jo walked over to the fence and sat down to wait on Mrs. Miller.

Back at the scene Rebecca was still hysterical. Officer Mark had done a preliminary investigation but didn't say anything to anyone. When the detectives arrived, Officer Mark showed them two teeth in a small puddle of blood.

They looked around and found that one of the killers had been dragged to a car. They could see where he fell but didn't know why just yet. The teeth were close to where another person had fallen. Maybe the teeth belonged to that person. They found Linda's undergarments. They had been cut, but she was fully clothed. Her shoes were still tied, and she was wearing her socks. With all of the footprints, they could find six different shoe soles, besides Linda's. The detectives were able to see Zane's shoe prints, as well as those of Marvin and Ed. There had been one terrific fight here tonight before Linda died. The tire tracks were different than anyone had seen before. It appeared that the vehicle had been a limousine as the tread pattern was pretty long.

The ambulances finally arrived, and the Chief told one of the ambulances to go help Rebecca, as she was the one needing help right now. She couldn't stop crying and shaking. The EMT's were calm in speaking with Rebecca and asked her to roll up her sleeve. She resisted at first, but Zane talked her into it. The EMT's got the ok from the hospital to give Rebecca a shot and she began to calm down.

Shortly afterwards, Rebecca's parents and Linda's parents arrived with the other cousins. The Chief caught them all before they rushed out to the body.

Linda's mother passed out when she noticed the lights shining on something black in the distance. Linda's father looked horrified; he couldn't believe it. That was his little girl lying over there dead! This cannot be reality right now, it can't! She was only eighteen years old. She knew martial arts and how to defend herself. How could this even happen to Linda, of all people? Linda's mom woke up and started letting out some blood curdling screams, that made the hair on the back of Zane's neck stand up straight.

Rebecca's parents were with her but couldn't get her to calm down much, even with the shot the EMT's had given her. One of the EMT's suggested they take her over to the ER before she went into shock. Her mom rode in the ambulance while her dad drove the car.

Meanwhile, the other Ambulance crew was trying to help Linda's mom without success. She was in the same condition Rebecca was in at this point.

The Chief told Miss Mabel to send two more ambulances out to the park just in case they need them. They needed one for sure, but things were unraveling pretty fast right now.

Zane went over to the where the detectives were talking while leaning up against one their cars to offer whatever help he could. He was hoping they could catch the guys that did this tonight.

Betty Jo's mom arrived at the front gate and found Betty Jo and Jimmy still sitting on the fence. Mrs. Miller got out of the car and ran to her daughter as fast as she could and hugged her tighter than she had in years. They both cried aloud. Mrs. Miller was so thankful her Betty Jo was alive. She had no idea how she could have lived if Betty Jo had been the one killed tonight. Jimmy was standing close by, and Mrs. Miller grabbed him and pulled him into the hug. It was a total cry fest at this point. Mrs. Miller told Jimmy he could call or come over to their home any time he wanted. She was completely impressed with the way he managed what she had put him through the day before.

"Mrs. Miller." Jimmy said. She interrupted him.

"Sweetheart, you can call me Louise from now on. Mrs. Miller is much too formal for the boy who has proven himself to be a big man at this point. Okay, Jimmy?"

"Thank you, Louise. I was just going to say I really wish we hadn't brought Linda tonight. She would be back at the house safe. I am so sorry Mrs... Louise" Jimmy's face was still wet with tears.

"If it hadn't been Linda tonight, Jimmy, it would have been someone else, maybe even Betty Jo. Besides, what happened here tonight is not your fault. It's the fault of the person who killed her, no one else. I hope they find them soon." With that, she grabbed Jimmy and hugged him tight again. She really liked this kid. He had a strong enough personality to take what she threw at him yesterday and he didn't flinch.

The three of them walked over to the car and Jimmy opened the door for Betty Jo. "Jimmy, you better be calling me. I will hunt your fanny down if you don't. Do you hear me?" Betty Jo had the first smile since they found Linda. It warmed his heart a little bit.

"Well, I know I'm not going to be sleeping tonight. It may even take a few days before that happens. So, give me a day or two to regroup and get some rest, okay? I promise to call and visit. Louise, take this beautiful girl home and tuck her in tight tonight, okay?" Now Jimmy had a little smile.

"I'll do more than that Jimmy. She's sleeping with me tonight in that King size bed. I just might hug her all night if she doesn't wiggle too much." They all laughed. Louise held her daughters' hand as she drove away. Jimmy went over and stood next to Zane.

The detectives were trying to figure out what kind of tire had this unusual tread none of them had ever seen before. Zane was close enough to hear that part of the conversation, so he suggested they call his dad, who had been around cars since his childhood. He might know. They told him to call him and get him out there.

They took a closer look at Linda's body and got as much information as they could before the ambulance took her to the morgue. Her parents wanted to give her a hug, but the detectives couldn't let them because she might have evidence on her. They assured them there would be a time soon enough where they could hug her all they wanted, but just not right now.

Zane's dad arrived and found out what had happened. He was so, extremely relieved his son was okay that he hugged him for a long time. Zane began crying again while he was in his dads' arms. It felt good to be there again. He couldn't remember getting a hug like this since he was about ten years old. His dad wiped tears from his own eyes as he walked over to the detectives.

Billy took one look at the tire tracks and immediately told the officers that it was an old style of tire. They were still made, but not by very many companies. They were wide white walled tires like the ones used in limousines in years gone by. The detectives hadn't said anything about the limousine to Billy.

They asked Billy if it were possible to find a such a tire on a newer limousine, or even a different type of car. Billy doubted it as the tread was one he hadn't seen in decades, with no steel belts, so the ride was just terrible and rough. Officer Mark radioed Miss Mabel and told her to put out a statewide bulletin for an older limousine with wide white walled tires. Now maybe they could catch these guys.

The detectives finished about six thirty in the morning. Zane and Jimmy were still there, as was Billy. The detectives decided they were finished for now and they would call if they had any further questions.

Zane gave Jimmy a ride home. They didn't talk much as both of them were pretty tired and both still felt guilty about what had happened to Linda. Zane was hoping Rebecca was going to be all right. He figured he would call her tomorrow after he got some rest. After a few minutes Zane asked Jimmy if he had seen a limousine tonight. The tire tracks in question lead right to the front of the park.

Jimmy thought for a minute but couldn't remember seeing such a car. The only cars he saw were all parked, until they started shining headlights everywhere. "Boy that's some kind of nervy person you know it. They killed her right there while we were all over the place. Then they drove right past us after they did it and no one noticed. That's nervy right there boy." Jimmy had some anger in his voice.

'Yeah, I was thinking the same thing. We were having such a wonderful time with those two girls. Wow, I had forgotten how beautiful they are when they get really dressed up. Dude, we hit a grand slam with those dates tonight. I sure hope Rebecca is able to calm down. I've never seen anyone that worked up before. I was really scared for her." He started to cry. "I thought she was actually going to die too. I was holding onto her as best I could, trying to keep her from dying. I don't know about what happened to you tonight, Jimmy, but when I saw her for the first time tonight, I knew that's my wife. I just hope what happened at the park doesn't mess that up."

Jimmy thought for a minute before he answered. "Not really. I certainly had the thought about how neat it would be to marry someone like Betty Jo, but no, I didn't think she was the one. I kind of hope she is though. Goodness, she's an awesome person. We got to talk about a few things tonight and she has the biggest heart I have ever seen. And that smile of hers melted my heart boy. Wow! We did good bro. But it's going to take me a while before I get rid of the guilt for taking Linda with us tonight. I'll never get that vision of seeing her out of my head." He started to cry again.

Zane pulled over and they both sat there and cried for a while.

Chapter 3

(Present Day)
A Bad Day at the Office

Bob and Larry were at the church at eight o'clock still licking their lips from that huge breakfast Sister Wilson had made for them. Steak and eggs, hash browns and biscuits so fluffy you would swear they were made by the clouds. And gravy! Oh, that gravy was wonderful. If Sister Wilson were thirty-five years younger, she would have two guys fighting over her no doubt.

They were getting out of their car when the Pastor pulled up in the exact same car, only his ran much better. It had been a while since the boy's car was that quiet. "Good morning fellas! I'm sure you slept well at Sister Wilson's, and I will bet you ate even better."

"You know Sister Wilson, man can she cook! And those beds were fantastic." Larry offered.

Bob said, "If I had a grandma like that, I'd live with her until she dies, I ain't kidding! That is one fantastic woman!"

Pastor Brown was rather proud of his friend, Sister Wilson. "She is one great lady, Bob. It's a shame she never took a liking to anyone after her husband died. She's really a woman any man would be happy to call her his wife. To be honest with you, she's a much better cook than Sister Brown, but you didn't hear that from me. Sister Brown is a great cook, and I have no reason to complain about what she fixes for any meal. But Sister Wilson is in a league of her own. Let's go inside and get started."

They walked straight into the sanctuary where Pastor Brown started every day with prayer. Today he had some friends that he was proud to pray with. Larry spoke up: "Good idea Parson, we still don't know what we're up against in this town yet. But you can bet your bottom dollar the devil ain't gonna like us butting into his business of destroying this church."

Bob added: "He likes to fight good Christian people every chance he gets. But let's not forget that he ain't nothing to tangle with compared to our God. He cannot even stand when God enters the fight. So, let's roll up our sleeves and be done with him."

Pastor Brown took note. "Bob, I've noticed that you're a bottom-line kind of guy. You just state the facts and get on with business. We would sure save a bunch more time if everyone were more like you. So, let's roll up our sleeves and be done with him!"

Bob smiled: "That's a great idea Pastor, I cannot tell you how happy I am that you came up with it. Let's just kick his hide out of town and all of his ugly friends too. Kick them all out of town in their little red wagon." He chuckled.

Larry wrinkled his nose at that one. "What's with the little red wagon thing?"

Bob smiled: "Everything that devil has is red, don't you remember? Red pitchfork, red horns, little red wagon. It all fits."

"If that don't beat all." Larry mumbled.

Pastor Brown got a kick out of watching these two interact like this. Even if the situation got really bad, he would laugh all the way through it with these two involved.

After they finished their morning comedy session, Bob asked Pastor Brown if he had thought of anything else they might need to know from the previous night. Pastor Brown started by saying, "You guys sure gave me and Sister Brown something to think about last night. She's so glad you two are here, even as glad as I am. We talked a bit about what has happened this past year and what may or may not be happening to this town. One thing she told me that I had forgotten, was the fact that Billy Warren's son, Zane and his and his best friend, Jimmy, were out there that night with the girl that was killed. They didn't have anything to do with her death, but it shook both of those families to their very core.

"Both of those boys have been friends since they were knee high to a gopher and they still are. It's really taken a real tole on both of them, however. If you remember, I prayed for both of those families last night during our prayer. If you remember, I prayed for Billy and Helen to get back with us and bring their two kids with them. They have a thirteen-year-old daughter named Laura too. She's just a pretty little girl and looks a lot like her mother. Billy keeps my car running when I need to have something done to it. He usually tells me it's on the house if it's something that doesn't cost much to fix. When he rebuilt the motor on that car out there, he just charged me for the parts. He's a really good man, and his son Zane, he must be about sixteen or seventeen about now, he seems to be taking up right behind him. It's such a shame what happened to that girl though."

Larry wanted to know more about his shadow Jimmy. Jimmy's a really great kid as well, said the Pastor. "I remember when his father died on a trip to Sn Francisco. He was one his way to see Jimmy's grandmother for the last time before she died, and he would end up dying before he got there in a car wreck. Sally, Jimmy's mother, was absolutely devastated. I guess her husband, Tony, had been dead for about two weeks, when Billy Warren asked me to visit her.

She was barely sleeping and eating even less. When I got there, she had terrible bags under her eyes, and you could tell she had been crying for a long time. As soon as I laid eyes on her my heart just sank to my knees. It was all I could do to keep my composure, but I didn't do a very job of it. I cried right along with her. Jimmy kept peeking out from behind the door of his bedroom with big ol' tears in his eyes. He finally came out and I hugged them both and cried with them.

"Sally married a wealthy man about two years later. He was really good to her at the beginning. He was good about bringing large bouquets of flowers when he came to see her. They he bought Jimmy a new bike and some other big toys. Now he just mistreats everyone in town. The guy bullies his way through the grocery store at a breakneck pace. He yells at the cashier for being too slow and overall seems to be a miserable man. Sally is just a skinny little thing now; she almost looks as bad as she did when her husband died. Jimmy is just as nice as Zane, who is a bigger influence on him than Ken is. Jimmy and Sally could really use our prayers today. And Ken needs really big prayers. You know those people that we think may too far from God to ever get saved? Of course, we know that's wrong, but Ken has that flavor to him. He would be a great Christian too. He pours his heart into everything he does and does it all well." Pastor Brown was just shaking his head back and forth at this point.

Larry knelt at the altar and started praying without saying anything to the other two. "God, we love You today. We love You because are a God of the people. You made us in Your image, and You love us even though we tend to mess up on a regular basis. But You are so swift in forgiving us for being so ignorant. I praise You Father for Your Son Jesus who came down here and walked among us, and set us free from the bondage of sin, that once had a death grip on our souls. You are so much bigger than anything we can even imagine or dream of. You see all things before they even take place, and even know the outcome before we do. Awesome is an understatement to say the least. Lord, please take these two families who were so devastated by this murder and wrap Your loving arms around them both. Let them feel Your Spirit run through their being. God, touch Ken in a special way. Let him realize the situation he is in right now and let him realize how hurtful he is towards those he cares about. Bring him to know You Lord and save his soul from eternal destruction." Larry sat quietly waiting on the next one to begin praying.

Pastor Brown didn't hesitate. "Lord, You are unbelievable when it comes to miracles like You've done here. These two brothers are such a blessing and I've only known them for less than 24 hours. Keep us safe throughout this ordeal Father. Help us use the wisdom You have given us. We pray for a special hedge of protection around us and our families, as well as the church family Father. Keep us all safe during this ordeal oh God. Let us not lose sight of You and what is actually going on right now. Help us to keep in the forefront of our mind that this is a Spiritual war and the fact that You are always victorious. Continue to bless my new friends here Father and let them continue to grow in the wisdom You need them to have. And please help me not get too scared if this situation seems to get out of hand."

Bob was right on his heels. "Father, we need You again. But we already know that You are already here and have been for a while, or You would not have sent us here. We also know that You have everything under control. Help us all, once again, to be sensitive to what's going on around us. We've missed some things in the past and it's impeded our progress. Help us to not let that happen this time. But for now, let us get this church back in shape. Let the money come in as it's needed and let some of the congregation come out and help us as well. For now, Father, just supply the paint for us. Thank you, Lord, for being there for us, and for letting Larry and I be part of such an awesome ministry. I actually enjoy this. Forgive me if that's wrong, but it's the truth. But for Larry Father, he needs a special touch. He always holds me back. Could You find a way to increase his IQ? Amen."

Larry had a wry smile on his face. "Your prayers are a work of art man. Did you hear that, Pastor Brown? This guy over here is a real piece of work. I just don't know about you Bob." Larry was smiling and shaking his head.

Pastor Brown laughed out loud. "How long have you two been friends?"

"We've known each other since our senior year in high school. We were both surprised to run into each at Bible school. We knew each other to be Christians, but we didn't know we were going to same college. We started hanging around each other after school, and we got jobs at the same pizza joint for a while. We even roomed together for a year. The two of us weren't necessarily the best of friends, but friends that liked each other quite a bit, would be accurate. Then, we were making plans for what ministry we wanted to get involved in after we graduated one night, and Bob suggested a road trip for a month or so. You, know, just drive around, and see the country for a while. The first weekend, we were looking for a church to attend on Sunday."

Bob butted in. "We arrived at a church in Arizona on Saturday evening and found some teenagers drinking whiskey and smoking pot in the parking lot of a church. So, we pulled up, got out of the car, and shared Jesus with them. A few of them gave their hearts to Christ right there in the parking lot. The next morning, we were in Sunday school, and the teacher was talking about all the drinking that went on in the parking lot on Saturdays and stated he wished someone would do something about it. Me and my big mouth asked him why he didn't do it. You could have heard a pin drop on the carpet just then. The looks we got from that entire crowd that morning still give me chills. I still have daggers in my chest and my back from that morning."

Larry jumped back in at this point. "I thought they were going to throw us out. Then this guy asked us what we would do to take care of the situation. I told them what had happened the night before in the parking lot, and you should have seen their eyes light up. The kids had only been there for a few months, but no one had done anything. Suddenly, the Pastor comes in and asks if we can meet with him in his office. It was like being called to the principal's office, but he was very pleasant.

"He asked us what happened in the parking lot the night before. After we told him, he just sat back in his chair completely shocked. He had gone out there and talked to that same crowd of kids a hand full of times and knew that someone else would have to talk to them before they would actually hear the message of Christ. He had prayed off and on for them from time to time but had given up talking to them himself. Then here comes the Dynamic Duo and saved the day.

"The Pastor asked us if we would share a message in that morning's service, and the Spirit of God filled the building. God was already moving in the church before we ever got to the platform. The song service was absolutely impressive and must have lasted a good hour. Then we got up and Bob started off. He talked about what had happened in the parking lot the night before but didn't dwell on it. Then went on to talk about John three sixteen. You know, a basic message. But it was so anointed."

Bob butted in, "I cannot take all the credit here, Larry and I did a tag team kind of thing. When he got up behind me the entire church began to weep. It seemed like every person in the church had tears in their eyes. It was like a release this poor church needed for years. When the alter call was given, the entire church came forward. People were asking forgiveness from others for things that had happened years before and they would cry and embrace each other and heal. A few of the teenagers from the church came down to the altar for the first time and got saved. But the biggest blessing of all were those kids from the night before. They brought everyone they knew to that alter call; there must have been about fifty of them. I have never seen a response to an alter call like that, even at a district meeting. All the kids had tears all over them and each other. And saved! Those kids got saved! We found all kinds of thing on the alter after church was over."

Larry spoke with tears in his eyes this time. "A big bag of cocaine, a ton of cigarette packs, earrings, nose rings, switch blades and even a satanic bible."

Bob was wiping his eyes and nose after remembering that morning. With a raspy voice he said: "I'll never forget that as long as I live. Pastor Walker had some things inside of him that he was able to let go of that morning as well. That entire church was blessed in that one service. We stayed and held services for a week. Each night the Lord brought more people into His Kingdom. We still stay connected with Pastor Walker, and his church is bulging at the seams. They had to draw up plans for a bigger sanctuary. One of those kids saved in the parking lot that night, got his ministerial degree and is the Youth Pastor there now. He's running about seventy-five kids and has his hands full already. His kids are reaching other kids at the high school, and they bring 'em in every week. The Student Body President is a Christian too. Man, God is so much more than we will ever know."

Pastor Brown had a tear in his eye now. "That's quite a movement of God, I must admit. I guess we could use a dose of that around here too."

"Don't be surprised if it happens here Pastor." Bob offered. "It happens a lot, so expect big things from God in the coming days. Larry and I will know when it's time to move on. In the meantime, why don't we go scrape some paint?"

With that Pastor Brown showed them where he had gotten to thus far. He had actually done a little more than half of the building. He had been at it since spring started, but he was only able to get to it a few times each week. Then of course, the heat had kept him from doing anything serious the past few weeks.

"There's a wire brush and a scraper over there in that bucket boys. If you don't mind me taking about half an hour to make some calls I need to make, I'll give you a hand." Pastor Brown was wearing that big smile of his, as he so glad to have some help with this. Finally.

"Oh no you don't!" Bob said. "You keep yourself inside that chilly office you have in there and work on a bunch of other stuff. We have this brother, without any help from you. And don't worry; it will be done correctly."

"Yeah, besides, you would just slow us down." Larry said as both of them began to laugh.

Pastor Brown looked at both of them with those smiles they made a habit of wearing and decided not to argue with them. "Okay, but I'm going to call sister Brown and see if she can bring us lunch. She makes a mean tuna fish sandwich. Tuna salad sound good to you."

They both started licking their lips and rubbing their stomachs simultaneously. Pastor Brown took that as a yes, waved at them with a smile, and went into his office to call Sister Brown. He already had deep feelings for these two and he already began to think how much he was going to miss them when they left town.

Bob and Larry began scraping away on the church and singing worship songs as they went along with their work. After a song got old, one of them would start in on another song and the other would join right in.

An hour had gone by before they knew it and they were getting a little thirsty. ZAP! Bob was stung on the ear again! All of a sudden, he was holding his ear and jumping around like a chicken with his head cut off. Larry was laughing so hard he thought he was going to pass out. Pastor Brown heard the commotion and came running outside to see what had happened.

It took a few minutes for Bob to quit dancing around and Larry was able to calm down to a chuckle.

"What happened out here? Are you okay Bob?" Pastor Brown was genuinely concerned.

Bob was finally able to take his hand away from his ear and grimace as he said: "Yeah, I'm okay. Man, I hate it when that happens."

"How can you explain how that happens so often, and only to you? It's unreal man." Larry said with a chuckle.

Bob said: "I have no idea why that happens to me so often, but every time it happens, it hurts worse. God must be trying to tell me something. Man, I don't even have a clue why this happens to me and not you Larry. Just one time, I wish the tables would turn on you, so I could laugh at you like that." Bob was able to smile now, but it still hurt.

"It's not the pain I'm laughing at Bob, it's just the fact that this happens everywhere we go." Larry said. "It just weird and honestly, I really feel for you brother." Larry was trying to keep his friend from being too upset with him.

"Oh, I guess I can't blame you for laughing. But you're right, it's flat out weird." Bob said to his best friend.

Pastor Brown was smiling, but he didn't know why, as he invited them in for a cold glass of water he had put into the refrigerator earlier. "You boys didn't waste any time out there, did you?" As he noticed all that they had done in just an hour's time.

Once inside, Larry took a look at Bob's ear to make sure the stinger wasn't still there. "It's not in there buddy. I didn't even see that thing, but once you started dancing around, I knew what had happened."

"This is ridiculous! I'm going to wage a war on bees that will make World War two look like child's play. I'm going to kill every last one of them! I'm gonna sic God on them, is what I'm going to do. He's gonna make bee soup out of them all, that's what He's gonna do." Bob was smiling as he talked.

Larry was sitting next to Bob when Pastor Brown brought a nice big glass of ice water to them. "That really is strange Bob. Has this happened since you were a kid? You're not allergic to them, are you?" Pastor Brown was really concerned for his new friend.

"Not at all Pastor. Bob said. Only since I started hanging around this guy. I think I'm going to trade him in for a newer updated model once we get back to headquarters, wherever that is. I think I'll have him reprogrammed into a garbage truck or something like that."

"Garbage truck, or something? Is that the best you can come with?" Larry and the Pastor were chuckling.

"Yes." Bob said with a grin on his face. "At the moment anyway. But garbage truck seemed appropriate. If you don't like being a garbage truck, maybe you'll annoy some garbage, and they will have you reprogrammed into something else. Besides, it's my delusion, leave me alone."

"My goodness, you need help brother!" Larry was shaking his head sideways and smiling. "But the help you need costs about a hundred and eighty-five dollars an hour." They all laughed at that one.

Pastor Brown was beginning to wonder about these two. "Hey, why don't you two take a break. Sister Brown is going to be here in about 20 minutes with our lunch about then. Besides, it's getting hot out there, and I'm starting to think it's effecting both your brains the way you talk to each other. My goodness, I've never seen friends talk to each other like this. It must be that new type of Christianity I keep hearing about, or something like that."

"Did you hear that, Bob? Do you see what you've done here? You've got this poor man thinking we're a couple of nitwits. Garbage truck? If that don't beat all." Larry was still jabbing his friend.

"Ah Parson don't pay any attention to us. This is how Larry and I tease each other. It's one of the reasons we're such good friends; because we both can give it and take it too. We definitely get our share of teasing here and there. We won't get cheated on that teasing, that's a fact." Bob was letting the Pastor know everything was just normal with the two of them.

Larry added, "He's right Pastor. We've never had a quarrel in the two and a half years we've been on this road trip. I have a huge amount of respect for Bob, as he does for me. With all that we have been through together, it's hard to imagine anything but God breaking this up. I can guarantee you that even a woman couldn't break this up."

Bob chuckled, "I don't know about that one there buddy. I almost walked away from you last year with that Kelly girl. Wow! She was so pretty, Unfortunately, her mustache was better than yours and we can't have that kind of competition."

"You know that wasn't it man! It was the fact her muscles were bigger than yours. That's what you couldn't handle." The two friends were really laughing now."

He's kidding Pastor, there was no Kelly. But good grief Bob; she really did have a mustache though. That's funny!"

"Oh, you liked that one did you bud?" Bob was still in a giddy mood." Pastor, Larry's right. It would have to be God Himself that breaks this up. I really love Larry and he's a great man of God. There will come a day when do say good-bye to each other, but it doesn't look like it will be any time soon. There seems to be so many churches out there that need outside help. We literally stumble on them. As we drive around the country the Lord sends us right to them. But as for us, we have no idea where they are. We pass through more towns than we stop in, but we always find a church, just in time it seems."

Pastor Brown was shaking his head. "You have such a unique ministry, and it seems to fit you both. With the personalities you two have, I can see why you never argue. You're both just so easy going that I'll bet you don't bother each other much. I've never heard of a ministry like this, but I'm glad you guys are involved in it."

Bob spoke up. "I'm fairly sure there isn't another ministry like this one. I would never say it's absolutely true, but we haven't met anyone else doing this. It's very humbling to be involved in this. We go into these churches and see the hurt that the devil has caused, sometimes a very deep hurt. And then we watch God heal everything. We've been able to see kids reconciled to their parents after being ridiculously rebellious, and even runaways come home. We've seen broken marriages mended. But even bigger than that Pastor, we've seen churches mended. Pastors who have been so discouraged that they were ready to quit the ministry all together, have their spirit renewed. Then the church goes off on a tirade and changes the entire town.

"In fact, one story comes to mind. We were up in Montana and there was this kid that just didn't fit in anywhere. He didn't fit into the town; he didn't even fit in with his own family. He had taken on this persona of a goth. He had spiked his hair, wore white make-up and black lipstick. He wore black leather studded clothes and had a nose ring with a chain that went to his earring. His mother came to us the first Sunday we were there asking if we could help her son. Keep in mind, we're from California and we don't exactly fit in up there either. Talk about your ultra-conservative redneck town, this was the epitome of it.

"Anyway, we invited this kid out for a burger the next day. Much to our surprise he actually came. He looked so depressed we wanted to cut *our* wrists. So, we buy this kid, Norman, a burger and strike up a conversation with him. This kid was intelligent, almost too intelligent for his own good. He had everything figured out. He even told us why he dressed like he did, the makeup, the chain, all of it. Norman had decided since he was different from the rest of the town, he would completely separate himself by dressing that way. Then he looked Larry right in eye and asked him what his God could do for him. Tell him what you said Larry."

Larry started off: "Actually the Lord was up to the challenge before I was. When Norman challenged me like that, my first response was to swallow hard and gasp for air. But instantaneously, the Lord stirred me and told me what to say. I just followed instructions. Anyway, I told him that God didn't need to do anything more for him than He hadn't done already. He had already sent Jesus down here to die and pay the price for his sins. The only thing left to do was to accept the gift of salvation and let the Lord take it from there. Norman had this idea that God was something man conceived in his own image. Apparently, he watched too much TV. So, I asked him if he had ever accepted Christ as his savior before, and he said that he had. So, I asked him how he felt about God when was living the "Christian Life." He said something about being deceived into believing that the Bible was the absolute Word of God, and everything in it is absolute fact. He just couldn't buy into that myth. When I pushed him to find out why he had walked away from God, he said that there was a Utopian kind of lifestyle. A place where there was no right or wrong. When I asked him again why he walked away from God, he got a little angry at me. But then he told me was ridiculed at school and bullied. When he changed his lifestyle, the kids at school were nicer to him and accepted him.

"I then pointed out that Bible told us ahead of time that this type of behavior would happen to us, yet Paul told us to count it as a blessing. Plus, the fact that he must have been living the right kind of life in front of them, or they would not have bullied him so hard. Then the Lord brought that Scripture to my mind that we are a chosen generation, a royal priesthood, a holy nation, a peculiar people, that you should show forth the praises of Him who has called you out of darkness and into his marvelous light. That's first Peter two, nine. Then I pointed out that he must have really been living the Christian lifestyle in front of those kids and the devil wasn't going to let that happen without a fight, thus the harsh bullying that took place.

He told me it just wasn't worth the hassle to endure that day in and day out, it was just too hard for him. I asked him if he would enjoy being in hell with those same kids that bullied him, or would he rather take them to heaven with him, if he had the choice. His answered that his choice would be to take those kids to heaven. He even added that he always felt hell was for losers, but he was powerless to do anything about it, and he ended up becoming the weirdest kid in school. In fact, from one extreme to the other. When I asked him if he wanted to begin living for Jesus again, he started to cry, and his makeup began to run down on his shirt. After he cried big sobs, and slobbered on his clothes, he said that he had a feeling God wasn't finished with him yet. He had actually been thinking about it when we called and asked him to meet us at the burger joint.

"Anyway, we prayed with him, and he accepted Christ all over again. He was a messy mess when it was over. We had makeup on our shoulders from hugging him and laughing with him. All of a sudden, the door burst open and in walked his friends from school. They were dressed like he was, but none to that extreme. You should have seen their faces. It was funny because Norman was only wearing half of his smeared make up and looked like as total wreck. He motioned them over and introduced us to them though. We got to share Christ with them and all seven of them accepted Christ as their Savior that day. So, we bought them all burgers too and had a great visit.

"One of the kids said he was the one who teased Norman the most, because he knew Norman had what it took to go to Heaven and deep down, he wished he could be just like him. But for whatever reason, he bullied him instead of asking Norman to pray with him so he could go to Heaven too."

Bob cut in. "We gave Norman a ride home and went inside with him when we got there. He took one look at his mother and took off in a dead run towards her. He scooped her up in his arms and they both cried like babies. We even got a tear in our eye just watching them. They both apologized over and over. About then, his dad walked in from work. As soon as he walked in the door, he looked at Norman and broke out sobbing openly. They apologized to each other as well. Make up was everywhere I'm tellin' ya.

"I'll tell ya Pastor, you can't pay money for memories like that. It so exciting to watch God do those things right in front of our eyes." Bob wiped a tear away.

Pastor Brown was smiling. "I was telling you yesterday that I thought you two had some stories to tell, and I like that one a lot. I'm looking forward to stories like that one happening here before you leave town.

Larry was wiping tears from his eyes as he spoke: "Oh, I'm sure you'll have your fair share of stories too brother. Incidentally, Norman was able to start a Bible study at school and was able to lead ten other kids to the Lord the last time we heard from that church. Of course, he got rid of the makeup and studded clothing and is a senior now. He's going to go a certain our old Bible college when he graduates."

Just then they heard the back door to the fellowship hall open. An extremely attractive woman in her forties walked in. She was carrying a picnic basket in one hand and a pitcher of lemonade in the other. Bob and Larry were on their feet instantly and went to take the items from her in a flash. She then walked straight over to Pastor Brown and kissed him on the lips. She said: "Hi honey, these must be your two newest friends you were telling me about last night."

Bob and Larry had their mouths open. Pastor Brown started laughing at them both. "I suppose you were expecting someone much older than Rachel here. Yes, she is Sister Brown. Let's get this out of the way first. Sister Brown is forty-four years old. We were both widowed on the same night twenty years ago when our spouses were involved in a huge pile up out on the interstate. We went to the same church and were already friends. The tragedy brought us together as we both missed our spouses. We mourned, cried, and ended up on the phone for hours talking about them as though they were both in the next room. As time went on, we grew pretty close to one another and ended up getting married two and half years later. And before you say it Bob and Larry; she's the prettiest wife I have ever seen."

Bob was really embarrassed, "I am so sorry Sister Brown at being so surprised. Please don't be offended at the look on my face."

"I'm not Bob, it happens a lot when we get new people in the church. We're used to it at this point. Sister Brown walked over to Larry. "You must be Larry." And she put her hand out to shake Larry's hand.

"Larry too was embarrassed, "Yes ma'am, I too must apologize. I sure hope I can find a miss's half as pretty as you are Sister Brown."

"Oh Dennis, I do like this one very much. Can we keep him?" She said with a huge smile on her face.

"I'm not sure either one of them are potty trained my dear." Pastor Brown said laughing.

"But look honey, they're so cute. Can we take 'em home and feed 'em on the back porch?" Sister Brown was too good at this game.

Bob said: "I think we better sit down and eat, before we get hit with the paper Larry."

"Good idea buddy. This must be the famous tuna salad we heard about, Sister Brown." Larry said with a delightful, playful voice.

They all sat down in the fellowship hall and began to eat. They ate without talking for a few minutes, when Sister Brown asked Larry how long he had been a Christian and where he had accepted Christ as his Savior.

"Well," Larry started, "I've been a Christian sine I was about twelve years old, so I guess that would be about 13 years now. I accepted the Lord as my savior while I was on vacation with my family in Idaho. We had gone up there from California, where I was living with my mother and two sisters. The Pastor at this small church, had been our Pastor in the small town we lived in. It had been about three years after he moved up there, I think. But there was a huge camp meeting in Boise we went to that had this choir for the main service. One of the lead singers would speak for a moment or two, then the choir would sing. Then he would preach for a moment and the choir would sing again. The Lord was moving all over that building so strongly they pushed the devil clear out of the state. I began praying at some point during the service right in my chair. I was slobbering all over myself. Boy I was a mess. I had this really nice blue shirt one that day and flat messed it up. The front was completely wet with my tears and the sleeves were soaked as well. I was an ugly mess, but I got saved baby, and I mean saved."

"When we got back home, for some reason my mom decided to change churches. This new church had a really dynamic youth group that I got involved with and even started singing in the choir there. I felt the call to preach at an early age and preached my first sermon there at the age of thirteen. I've been preaching ever since then."

"What about you Bob, when did you get saved?" Pastor Brown asked.

"I accepted Christ into my heart when I was in high school." Bob looked off in the distance as he spoke. "I was going to church with my aunt at the time. My cousin Phil and I are about the same age, so we were in the youth group together. The youth Pastor, Roy, was a really great guy. He really had a heart for the kids there in that town and he made sure we had plenty to do. Larry was head of the Bible Study group we had at school and did as good a job as could be done with all the constraints they had on us. But when I got saved, I immediately started going to the Bible Study group, so I could learn more about the Bible and Jesus. I never really heard about Jesus at my house growing up. My parents drank a lot and were gone most weekend nights to the bars. My brother Steve and I were basically on our own. It's a wonder neither of us got into any serious trouble during that time or became some sort of deviant. I guess I've been saved for about nine years now. And from what I've seen so far in my walk with God, I will always be involved in sort of ministry. I love leading people to Christ and watching them grow as Christians.

"When he sends Larry and I into a town, things begin to happen that no one knows about. Like families being reunited, that no one knew were in complete chaos. People get healed from all sorts of things, including cancer. A woman who had a compound fracture in her leg that shortened it about two inches, had her leg completely restored to its original length. No more huge platforms anymore. More things than I can list here; unless you have a couple of years for a long lunch."

"My husband was telling me that you two had some great stories to tell about all that you've seen. Have you told him any yet?" Sister Brown seemed too anxious to hear one of these stories.

Bob said: "Yeah, we had just finished telling him one as you walked in the door with lunch." Sister Brown looked at her husband and said: "You'll have to tell me that story when you get home tonight, Glen. In the meantime, I've got go visit with Sister Wilson for a while and get some groceries. It was a pleasure meeting you two. When you get your rabies shots, let me know." She had a huge smile as she spoke.

Larry said: "Alright, alright. If rabies shots are required to be friends with you two, I'll pass. Did you know that you and Pastor here have the biggest smiles I have ever seen?"

Pastor Brown said: "Yeah, we get that a lot. That smile of hers will melt your heart, won't it?"

"There you go Parson, trying to get us into trouble again. But yes, she has a very pretty smile." Bob said with a huge smile of his own.

Sister Brown blushed as she waved and moved toward the back door.

Chapter 4

The First Sign

It was Thursday now, and the two preachers had preached during the previous evening service. They got a good look at what Pastor Brown had told them was happening, when he mentioned how the congregation responded to his sermons at this point. The two guys had done a tag team sermon the night before. As Pastor Brown had told them, they felt the anointing of the Holy Spirit during the sermon, yet the people just sat there, looking bored. The three of them were discussing this very issue before they started their day in prayer.

Pastor Brown was shaking his head back and forth totally bewildered with what to do. "What do we do guys? I'm wide open to suggestions and I'm hoping that you two can come up with something just because there are now three heads thinking about this instead of just mine. I've done everything that the Lord has led me to do and probably some of my own, which is not such a good thing. But how can we fix this? Well, that's a silly question. We know God's the answer here, but how can we get these really good people to respond to the Lord?"

Bob said: "Pastor don't worry. This will be answered before we leave town, but I have the same questions that you do. Larry, you spoke a bit longer than I did last night, did you get a sense of what might be going here?"

Larry pondered that question for a moment before answering. "Guys, these people are spiritually bound right now. I think that's pretty clear for the three of us to see, and it reaches the entire church. Am I correct Pastor?" Pastor Brown nodded yes. "Well then, the devil has done his job here, as far as he's concerned. We just need more information before we can figure this out though. Which ones in the congregation are helping the devil out, but don't know that's what they're doing, and making it hard for this church to progress? Sometimes people get cold spiritually and then become puppets for the devil without knowing they're doing it, until it's too late.

"So, get ready Pastor. This is going to be an all-out dog fight for this congregation brother and fight we will. But so will the devil, so lace 'em up tight boys, this going to be quite a ride. We can expect some kind of action from the adversary soon, but I'm ready for it, how 'bout you guys?"

Bob's head was already bobbing up and down, but Pastor Brown was looking off into space. He wasn't quite ready for an all-out spiritual war with the devil, but here he was knee deep in the middle of it. So, all he needed to do was the lace 'em up like Larry said and get busy.

Pastor Brown looked Larry and Bob right in the eyes and spoke softly, "Larry, Bob, I'm not as young as I was when I first got into the ministry, but I already know this is going to get rough, we know this to be a fact. Yet even though I feel a peace spiritually, my first thought is to run to the hills and get as far away from this place as possible. But! I'm going to trust my God just like I have always have. But there seems to be a bit of a mystery to me about this congregation. When I sit and ponder what's going on with them right now, I keep going back to what happened last year to that girl. So, for a while now, I've been wondering if that could have something to do with how cold they've grown. Could that incident have shaken everyone's faith in God? It certainly could have, but is that really the issue here? I guess we'll know when this is over."

Larry saw the weight of the congregation on his friends' shoulders while he spoke. "Parson, you can't carry the weight of this on your own shoulders. It's much bigger than you. In fact, it's bigger than the three of us. But it doesn't compare to our God. Our God is bigger than this. Remember in the Old Testament when God only wanted a few guys who could drink water like a dog going forward towards the enemy? When they got there, the enemy was so confused that they ran in all directions and started killing each other. In that fight there were only three hundred people who could drink water like a dog. In this case, it's just the three of us. But now that I'm thinking about numbers, we also have sister Brown and sister Wilson and our God against who? The guy who got himself and all of his friends thrown out of Heaven? I kinda like our chances at this point you guys." Larry had a huge smile that made the other two smile as well. He was beginning to feel the presence of God in the room. "The victory is ours brother! You're going to get your church back Pastor, just accept it and go forward."

Pastor Browns face no longer had that dreadful look on it. He was suddenly looking completely refreshed and ready to go.

Bob was just sitting there watching his friend go. He had seen Larry go on like this before and he liked it. Larry could get carried away at times and he was usually correct in what he was saying when it happened, like he was now. The three of them looked at each other and the camaraderie was in full force. This was a team that would be as skilled and effective as any team could be and it would prove to be just as formidable.

They finished praying in the sanctuary and were standing in the kitchen enjoying a drink of ice water before they began their day. The three were all silent and deep in thought. God was going to show His mighty hand in this situation and none of them doubted it. After a few minutes all of them said simultaneously: "Here we go" and laughed. Bob said to Larry: "Let's go scrape some paint bro." And with that, they put down their glasses and went outside.

As they got outside, they picked up their tools and got to work without saying a word. But after a few minutes, they were singing praise songs and having an enjoyable time.

Pastor Brown went into his office and called Billy Warren. "Billy! How are things going over at your shop my friend? Busy huh, well that's good for business. Hey, listen, I would like to personally invite you and your family to our Sunday morning services this week."

Billy was wondering why the Pastor was calling him with a special invitation like this. He and Helen were there every week, with few exceptions. "I don't understand Pastor Brown, Helen and I are there every week. What so different about this Sunday than any other Sunday?" Billy was taken aback at this phone call.

"Well, you weren't there last night Billy. We have some special guests with us right now. I'm not sure how long they will be here, but I invited your entire family. Bring Zane and Laura with you this week. They only come once in a while, and I have a feeling that something wonderful is going to happen this week. My spirit tells me so. What do you say? Will you make a point to bring your kids this week?" Pastor Brown was really feeling something about Sunday.

"We will all be there this week Pastor; you can count on it. I appreciate you calling and letting me know about our visitors. How is that car running right now?" Billy was just being Billy. He really was a good man and great friend.

"Oh, it's okay, I guess. It's kind of old you know, like Sister Brown." Pastor Brown was in a fairly good mood this morning. "It's got some rust in its joints sometimes though, especially on those cold mornings. But it actually runs good right now Billy. Thank you for asking. I'll see you Sunday. Give my best to Helen."

"See you then Pastor. Don't ever hesitate to bring that car over here. I always enjoy the visit when you come by here." Billy really liked Pastor Brown and considered him one of the best people he had ever met.

"I know you do Billy, and I appreciate everything you've done to that car for us over the years. You've been great about it." Pastor Brown was beginning to sense some warmth in Billy's voice that he hadn't heard for a while now. Maybe this spiritual battle wasn't going to take as much participation as he thought.

Larry and Bob were outside working away. They had that church about scraped in no time at all. When they got around to the sunny side of the church, they decided to take a break and get some ice water. They were standing and facing the building, when all of a sudden, they heard deafening thunder as the wall right next to them exploded close to Larry's face. He was on the ground in a flash with his hands covering his face. Bob dropped to his knees next to him not knowing what had just happened. At the same time, Pastor Browns chair exploded about chest high. Fortunately, he was in the kitchen making some ice water for his friends when the thunder happened. He heard something whizz past his head, but he didn't pay any attention to it. Then tires squealed down the street and around the corner.

Pastor Brown put the water down and took off at a dead run down the hallway until he was outside looking down at Larry. "Oh Lord, don't let him be dead" was Pastor's first thought. "What has that devil done now? Please God, heal him now in the name of Jesus!" Pastor was so scared he couldn't move once he saw Larry on the ground holding his face.

Larry was telling Bob, "Get these splinters out of my face! But whatever you do, don't mess up my face. It's the only face I've ever had. If you mess it up my mom won't let me in the door anymore because she won't recognize me the next time I go home. I'll never get married because I ain't got no face."

Bob told him: "Would you quit with that nagging already. No wonder you're not married yet. Besides, I'm not sure these splinters are going to help or hurt your looks. You ain't that pretty, so there neener neener.

Pastor Brown was so relieved when he heard Larry talking that he almost cried. Instead, he chimed in with Bob: "Son, your face was messed up long before you ever got to this here town." Then he chuckled at his joke.

Bob was pulling the splinters away from Larry's eyes when Larry told him something was poking him in his right hip. When Larry rolled over to let them see what it was, there was a big spot of blood there. Pastor Brown's heart sank. "Oh, dear Jesus, don't let Larry be hurt very bad. Keep him safe until we get him to the hospital. Oh, Jesus help us now." The poor Pastor was scared all over again. "Come on Bob, let's get him in the car. It'll be quicker than waiting on an ambulance."

They got him in the car and sped off in an instant. They had Larry in the Emergency Room in no time flat. Pastor Brown was feeling nauseous and pacing the floor praying over and over again. Bob tried to console him, but it didn't help.

There were two nurses working on getting Larry ready for the doctor. They noticed a hole in his pants pocket that went through his underwear. They cut his pants and underwear off and laid them next to the gurney Larry was on. When the nurse laid his clothes on the floor a metal ball rolled out onto the floor. The doctor was standing in the doorway as the ball rolled out and he picked it up.

As he looked at it, his eyes widened. He rolled Larry over on his left side so he could see the wound. He kept looking back and forth between the bullet and Larry's backside and shaking his head back and forth in disbelief.

About that time Bob stuck his head around the curtain to check on his friend. "What is that, Doc?" Bob asked.

The doctor, still shaking his head said: "It's a piece of buck shot from a double ot shotgun shell, and it should have shattered this guy's hip to pieces. I've never seen anything like this before in my life. This is absolutely amazing and impossible. There is no way this can happen. It defies physics and logic at the same time." He sat down on the stool and continued to shake his head while looking at the buckshot. "Absolutely unbelievable."

Pastor Brown came over and asked the doctor to see the ball. He wasn't going to let this opportunity get away without sharing how big his God is. "Doctor, what you're looking at right here is an absolute miracle from heaven. You are correct when you said that should have shattered his hip, but God was watching out for my friend today. Do you believe in God doctor?"

At this point, the two nurses were standing there listening to the Pastor. The doctor answered: "Pastor, right now I believe in whatever it was that made this possible. I've been an Emergency Room Doctor for twelve years and I have seen more than my share of gunshot wounds, but I have never seen anything like this. This defies everything I know to be true, physics, logic, and even basic science. It defies it all. I am completely dumbfounded at this. With all of my education and in all of my forty-two years of life, this defies everything I have learned. But to answer your questions Pastor, I guess I would qualify as an agnostic. I would love to believe in a God that is bigger than us and watches over us. But yet when I look at all the wars and how mean and heartless people can be, it makes that 'good thing' hard to believe in."

"Well doc, that's a miracle that you're holding in your hand. Do you need any more evidence than that?" Pastor Brown didn't skip a beat. "You can see all of the good things this life has to offer, but then we weigh it all against the terrible things that happen at the same time. A battle of good and evil. God has a plan for each of us and this world we live in, yet sin, or the devil, if you will, has his plan also. The Bible tells us that every good thing comes from God, and I'm telling you right now that what you hold in your hands is a good thing.

"You know, God sent His son Jesus down here so that we could have a friendship with God and live in heaven for eternity. Jesus sacrificed His own life to make it happen, by accepting all of our sins upon himself as He died. That being the case, the only thing we need to do in order to have that friendship and promise of eternal life in heaven, is to simply ask for forgiveness of our sins and allow Jesus to live in our hearts and guide our lives from that point. I would hate to walk away from this hospital today and not let you three wonderful people have the opportunity to accept Christ as your Savior today. I would love to pray with you all if you're ready to do that. What do you say?"

All three were ready to accept as their Savior right there on the spot. After what they had just witnessed, it was the next logical thing to do. Besides that, the three of them were also experiencing the Holy Spirit tug on their hearts and had a tear in their eyes as well. They all simply nodded their heads yes and wiped tears away when Pastor asked them if they wanted to pray.

"Okay guys, just repeat after me, okay?" Again, they nodded. "Father I ask right now...that you forgive me of my sins...and make me a Christian today....I know that You are God now...and I accept...Christ as my Savior...please help me live...my life according to Your ways...and not my own...fill me with Your Spirit...and help me...show others the joy...that You have put in my heart...thank you Father...Amen.

"You are now new Christians guys." And with that, the doctor and the nurses let the tears flow down their faces. The nurses began to sob quietly, and before long the doctor was smiling from ear to ear.

Bob went over and hugged one of the nurses as Larry hugged the other one while sitting on the gurney. Bob said: "You guys just made the biggest decision of your lives just now; you have every right to cry. I bet you feel lighter than air right now, don't you?"

The nurse he was hugging said, "I do feel like a heavy weight has been lifted off of me. I feel joy, that's why I'm crying. It's like a huge release of some sort. Wow! Doctor, that talk we had yesterday started me thinking about where I would spend eternity and hell just sounded so unpleasant to me. I was going to find a church this Sunday and go. I am so glad you came here today, although the circumstances aren't ideal. Hey Bob, what caused that bleeding anyway since it didn't penetrate the skin?"

The Doctor looked at Larry and said: "You had a blood blister, and it popped. When that ball hit you, it did nothing more than make the blood come to the surface because of the sudden impact on your skin. Somewhere during the deal, it popped and made a mess of your clothes. You'll be fine and it may not even leave a scar."

"It would be one more for the collection at this point." Larry said, then he realized they didn't even know the names of the people with whom they had just prayed. "By-the-way, what are your names?"

The Doctor spoke up: "My name is Doctor Bob Franklin. This is Cindy and this is Roxanne. Please call me Bob, the nurses do."

Bob said: "We can't call you Bob, that's my name. How about we call you Doctor Bob?"

"That sounds perfect, that's what my mom calls me. It's got a good ring to it too." The Doctor still had a smile on his face that would outshine the noonday sun right now.

The two nurses introduced themselves and shook hands with the three preachers. Cindy was still wiping tears from her eyes. She asked: "Pastor, where is your church? I want to come Sunday." Then she turned to Doctor Bob and Roxanne and asked if they wanted to go with her.

Roxanne said: "I'm supposed to work that day, but maybe Trish can switch days with me. I'll be there Pastor, one way or another, I'll be there. Thank you so much for being such a good Pastor. When I was a little girl, our church never grew. It was the same people every Sunday. As I got older, I realized that the Pastor and the congregation liked their little family and when anyone new would come around, they just weren't that friendly to them. Man! I feel so light right now! I can never go back to that life I just prayed away. Just WOW!

"I've been staying with my alcoholic boyfriend, but I'm going to move to my mom's house when I get home today. I'm not going to take that abuse that anymore."

Pastor Brown said: "Roxanne, that's a great idea on your part. Moving out of an abusive relationship is a good start, but God loves your boyfriend too. Why don't you see if he will come with you on Sunday? Then he will have a chance to pray like you did just now. Does that sound doable for you?"

"Yeah, it does Pastor. I really love Steve when he's not drinking. He's a great guy when he's sober. He's smart, friendly, genuinely nice, and handsome. He would be my choice of a husband if it weren't for the drinking. I'll do my best to get him there. I mentioned God to him the other day when he got home from work, but he didn't say much. I could tell he was thinking about it though. I'm glad you suggested that Pastor, that really gives me hope for him, and us going forward. I had already made up my mind that I was going to leave tonight and not look back. Thank you, Pastor." She gave him a big hug. Now Roxanne was wearing the same smile as the Doctor.

Doctor Bob said: "I'll be there too Pastor. It's obvious now that this blood blister thing was meant to be. This was no accident."

Larry spoke up: "You're right Doc but let me shed a different light on this. The devil had that guy let go of that blast to kill the three of us, but that didn't happen. Instead, we end up here because a minor injury that made a decent amount of blood. Then, you three accept Christ into your hearts and are the newest members of a great family. What the devil meant to be a really terrible thing, ended up being a really good thing. That just verified a verse in the Bible that talks about what the devil meant for bad, God turned to good. That's paraphrased but you get the jest of it. I just wish it had been Bob's rear end that got the blister though." Everyone laughed.

"That's what you get for laughing when that bee stung my ear yesterday. You mean mean person you." Bob was laughing while he spoke.

The Doctor noticed Bob's ear was a little red. "Let me see that ear, Bob." As he reached for his ear. "I'll be. Man, it's good thing you guys came in here today. Bob, you have the very end of that stinger still stuck in your ear. If you hadn't stumbled in here today, you would have definitely been stumbling in for real tomorrow or the next day. Let me get that out of there." With that, he grabbed some tweezers and pulled a tiny piece of stinger from the top of his ear. "I'm going to give you an antihistamine shot and some cream to put on there for the next week. Make sure you get it on there twice a day, okay?"

Bob said, "My goodness. I noticed it hurt more than usual, but it never dawned on me to have Larry look at it for me. Thank you, Doctor Bob. Larry gets to wear a hospital robe the rest of the day while we go back and scrape some more paint off the church, right doc?"

Larry laughed and said: "What robe, I'm under a sheet right now! There's no robe! A robe would be an upgrade at this point."

Bob laughed. "Well get yourself rapped up dude, we gotta go." Pastor Brown echoed Bob. "C'mon Larry, we have work to do, let's get going already!"

Cindy walked over with two robes and handed them to Larry. "Here you go Larry. You can wear these robes. I'll see you all on Sunday morning as well. I really admire you guys, all three of you." Pastor Brown asked why?

"What you all do lasts an eternity. What we do is try to help people live a better life than what they walked in here with. But it's finite. Everyone is going to die someday, and some even die right here unfortunately. But you guys get people into heaven and that lasts forever. I don't know what you make in the way of a salary, but it could never be enough."

"You're right Cindy." Larry had put on the robes while Cindy was talking. "But you can't measure what we do in the way of money. The feeling we got when you three just prayed that sinner's prayer was awesome. We get the satisfaction of watching people not only change their earthly lives, but their eternal lives as well. And knowing that we're doing what God has called us to do, then seeing the fruits of that labor, are just flat out awesome."

Bob Chimed in: "He's right Cindy. We get the best feeling in the world watching people pray to accept Christ as their Savior. In fact, there's a party going on in heaven right now because of you three. According to the Bible the Angels rejoice when someone comes to the Lord, it's true. Then of course what we have just witnessed with Larry's hip, you can't deny that God wasn't watching over his child can you?"

Dr Bob said: "There is no doubt that there is a God in my mind anymore. That is an absolute miracle if there ever was one. I still can't wrap my head around that wound. There is no scientific reason for his hip not to be shattered. It even defies physics. WOW! Just WOW!"

Pastor Brown gave the doctor a hug. "Guys I know you're busy and that you have people waiting for you. Why don't we get out of here and let you get back to work with those big fat smiles you're all wearing?" With that, everyone got hugs from everyone that the three preachers went their way.

They stopped at Sister Wilson's house so Larry could put on some clothes before heading back to the church. Fortunately, Sister Wilson was in the backyard weeding her garden. She didn't see Larry in hid hospital gowns, so they didn't have to explain what happened. Now that could wait until dinner.

Once they got to the church, they noticed the outside wall looked like it was in a war zone. They counted six bullet holes in the wall, one through the door and one through the Pastor's window. The one that hit Larry would be nine shots from that shotgun shell. They walked down the hallway of the fellowship hall to find the one that went through the door and found it in the wall at the far end of the fellowship hall. They went into the Pastor's office and sat down to talk about it all when Bob told Pastor to stop! "What?'

"Oh my." Bob said and pointed at the pastor's chair. It was an executive style chair with a high back on it and dead in the middle of it at chest high was a bullet hole.

Larry shot to his feet as the pastor gasped. "Good grief!" Said the pastor. "That devil tried to kill to kill all three of us today. And now that I'm thinking about it, that bullet in the fellowship hall whizzed right by my ear. I heard it but didn't even pay attention to it because I couldn't get outside fast enough to make sure you were okay. He missed me twice with one shotgun blast. Oh, my goodness, I'm going to be sick now." And he grabbed his stomach. The seriousness of what had happened a few hours earlier just became real to the three men in the room.

Larry began shaking his head sideways as he started to pray. "Father, we now know the full extent of what the devil tried to do to us earlier. This is the first time he has tried to kill me and Bob. He's beat the snot out of us a few times, but never anything like this. Thank You so much for Your protection today. Please don't let this incident distract us from what You have coming to this town. Speaking for myself alone, I'm a little angry at the devil right now and I want to get as many souls saved and safely into Your Kingdom as possible before you move us on to the next city. Father, please, give us a huge harvest while we are here and show Satan, he can't mess with Your children like that. And I pray this in all the power in the name of Jesus Christ Your Son. Amen." Bob and Pastor echoed an emphatic "Amen."

"What is my sweet bride going to do when she hears and sees this? This is going to scare her more than anything ever has. How am I going to tell her about this. As scared as I am right now about this whole thing, this just might kill her. Oh Father, how do I do this?"

Bob seemed to be the only one not totally shaken about this. He was certainly a little scared as well, but still had his wits about him. "Guys, look at the big picture here. The devil truly meant to have us dead today, but we ain't. He tried to stop whatever God has planned for this town, but he didn't. And we are sitting here scared out of our wits for still being alive. Does that make any sense to you guys? Larry, I'm with you. I'm so mad at the devil right now I want to save the entire state just to get back at him. Pastor Brown, your lovely wife is going to be simply fine and even a bit more emboldened like we are right now. But first, let's call the police to let them know what happened, then invite sister Brown and sister Wilson over here to see what happened and tell them all about it. Does that sound like a plan?"

Pastor Brown took a deep breath: "Yeah it does Bob." He picked up the phone.

Pastor Brown called the police and had them on the way over to the church. Then he told Bob and Larry that he was making some ice water for them when the blast occurred, so they all went into the kitchen. The ice had melted while they were gone, but the water was still cold. They all stood in silence looking at the hole in the wall still in disbelief. Larry was so thirsty he ended up drinking three glasses of ice water while they waited on the police.

The police were there pretty quickly since it was a shooting and that just didn't happen in Southwind. It was a small and quiet town, just the way the townsfolk like it. Even Chief Lee was with them today. The three preachers went outside with the police officers and showed them the wall. Chief Lee asked where everyone was standing when it occurred. They dug two balls out of the wall then went inside to follow the path of the balls. In a storage closet and they found one of the balls in a box of quilting scraps and two more in the wall. They collected the one from the fellowship hall and the pastor's chair. None of the police officers had any idea who would have done anything like this. They knew all of the "bad guys" in town, but none of them was this violent.

The pastor asked Chief Lee if he was going to be at church this Sunday. He had been AWOL for about a year and a half at this point. The chief made a poor attempt at explaining his absence but relented to come. The two officers with him agreed to come as well. Now Pastor Brown was getting excited about the crowd this weekend. Just the fact that the crowd was going to be bigger than normal warmed his heart and encouraged him.

After the police left sister Brown and sister Wilson arrived. They were hoping that the ladies would show up while the police were still there, but that didn't happen.

Sister Wilson was never one to waste time. "What happened to the wall Pastor? It looks like a war zone out there."

Sister Brown was just as curious. "Howard, what happened?" She could tell something wasn't right by looking at the men's faces.

Pastor Brown instantly had her in his arms trying to keep her from getting too upset. He nodded to Bob to tell them what happened. Pastor Brown sat her down next to him as Bob told the story.

Both Sister Brown and Sister Wilson were completely horrified by what had happened. But as Bob began to tell how God had protected them all, they calmed, but only a little bit. Sister Brown was clinging to the pastor as tight as she could and was crying. Sister Wilson had her head in her hands sobbing as well.

Sister Wilson spoke through her tears: "I have never seen the devil be this bold before. He literally tried to kill you all today and yet you're so calm. What's the matter with you?"

Larry laughed as he stood up. "Let me show you two a couple of the most amazing things that happened here. You see that hole there in the wall?" The ladies both nodded yes. "That whizzed right by the pastor's ear close enough for him to hear it. Let's go back to his office." They all walked down the hallway to the office. "That hole in the back of that chair is where they took out another ball. That would have hit Pastor Brown right in the heart, but it didn't because God is still on the throne, and He is the King of Kings and the Lord of Lords and He has a hedge of protection around all of us. The devil knows that we are getting ready to start something here in town and it must be going to be a humdinger, or this wouldn't have happened. So, instead of being so scared, this is a time to rejoice that God is here in a big way and we are getting ready to reap a huge harvest of souls for God's Kingdom. In other words, we're getting ready to make a lot of new friends!"

Pastor Brown looked at Rachel. "Sweety, that ol' booger tried to get me twice today and missed both times. It scared me too but look at it in a spiritual sense; God didn't allow either one to happen. How much more encouraging can it be? I'm alive because of the very hand of God, nothing less than that. God's here and working for us right now Rachel. And because of that, we still get to be together for a long time yet to come. So instead of letting this rattle your faith, it should strengthen it in a huge way." He kissed her forehead with a gentle sweet kiss.

"Oh Howard, why can't God just come down here and give us a back rub to make us feel better. All this drama is just not necessary." Sister Brown smiled through her tears, as the rest of the crowd laughed.

Sister Wilson was in full agreement with that. "I'm telling you right now. I could sure use a big back rub right now." Everyone laughed again.

Bob spoke up. "I know this has been an interesting day to say the least, but that shot the doctor gave me is making me really sleepy. So, if you don't mind sister Wilson, I'm going to turn in early tonight so I can get to it first thing in the morning."

Larry agreed. "Yeah, we need to go get supplies tomorrow, so we can get to work on this place. And this little thing on my fanny needs to get some weight off it. Time to be laying down for sure."

Sister Wilson was curious about something. "You two say that you mostly end up at small churches. That being the case, how do you support yourselves? There's no way small churches can keep you on the road like this.

Bob said: "We get that question from time to time, and it's an easy answer. I have a trust fund that my grandfather left me when he died. I was about ten when he died, and we were really close. He used to take me fishing and to all kinds of sporting events. He was a sports fan from the word go. If it involved a ball, he knew all about it. Anyway, I call my mother from time to time to move some of that money over into my checking account for expenses and church supplies when the time comes. But the churches do help. Some of them give us money and others simply give us food and groceries while we're in town, because that's all they can do. But whatever it is, we really do appreciate it. Neither one of us wants to be a burden on the church's finances while we're at their church. So, whatever they give us is plenty and good enough."

Larry told them, "I have something similar to Bob, but it's not as formal.

My uncle Jack sends me money whenever I ask for it. He told me when I went to Bible college that he would give me every dime I ever needed as long as it was ministry related. Uncle Jack is rather comfortable in his finances, and he uses his money to bless as many people as he can. He told me it doesn't do anyone any good just sitting in the bank. Although he lives off of the interest of the money he has, he still has enough to give to those who need it. He's always helping people, but no one ever knows it's him. He told his Pastor to call him personally if the church ever needs anything or anyone that attends there. He got really upset at the Pastor when he took a benevolence offering one week. He told the Pastor to put that money into something else, because as long as he was alive, *HE* was the benevolence fund.

"I end up calling him seven or eight times a year to chat with him. He's one of those guys that's so easy to love. Every time he asks me how things are going and wants to hear some good stories. I told him about Norman once and he wanted to know if Norman or his family needed anything. They didn't need anything in the way of money, so he sent five hundred dollars to the church's youth department. He's that kind of guy. Bob gets money from his trust fund about as often as I get it from Uncle Jack. We alternate each time we need to ask.

"We would end up calling more often if the churches didn't pitch in as often as they do. But hey, it's all God's money anyway. We have yet to go hungry even once since we've been out here. So, Sister Wilson, you need to let us help you with all the groceries. We can afford to help out. And you two pastors over there, you can let us pitch in too. We know you are helping her out with that food bill."

Pastor Brown looked at the two young men sitting across the table from him. "You can just forget that ever happening. We're going to help out as often as is necessary while you're here, so just get used to the idea. As far as what's needed to get this church back into shape, we will definitely need help with that. So please let us do what we can. Don't deny us that blessing. And you're right; it is all God's money so just accept it and be quiet about it you young whipper snappers." He laughed as he said it.

Larry looked at Bob. "Whipper snappers, well now we've been labeled Bob, and I don't care. As long as we can eat Sister Wilson's cooking, I don't care what they call us."

Bob echoed Larry: "Exactly Larry. If I can't find me a woman that can cook like that in a few years, I'm going to be back in this town and ask sister Wilson if she'll either marry me or let me be her newest son." Everyone laughed at that one.

"I would marry you in a minute Bob. If you were forty years older." She laughed as she spoke as did the rest of them.

Chapter 5

Sunday Morning Service

This Sunday morning was an exceptionally beautiful day. No clouds in the sky and it was a beautiful shade of blue. The breeze was perfect as it blew through town. It was most welcome after this super sizzling summer in the area thus far.

Pastor and Sister Brown woke up this morning with a peculiar interest in the day. Excitement was in the air and both of them knew something was going to happen today at church. Pastor Brown had invited everyone he ran into during the week to today's service, but he did that most weeks. However, today was special and he knew it. He was really hoping that Billy and Helen would bring Zane and Laura today. He just knew that today could change all of their lives if they would just give God a chance.

Pastor Brown knew that Jimmy was thinking of coming, but he wasn't sure if he would be there, so he Called Sally and invited her, Ken, and Jimmy to come today. It would be so great if all three of them came today. Pastor Brown knew that Ken had gotten pretty ornery about this time last year, but as of yet, the Pastor wasn't sure if Ken had committed his life to Christ. Today would be a great day to do that if he would come.

Larry was in his room praying and getting prepared for his sermon today. Bob was in the kitchen visiting with Sister Wilson. She was sweet, sincere, and just seemed to love everything and everybody. Bob was thinking that she was one of the sweetest people he had ever met. There was no more question as to why she insisted that he and Larry stay at her house. And oh man! Could this lady cook! Bob and Larry had more than one fun argument as to who was going to marry her first.

Larry came out of his room with a great big smile. That was Bob's favorite smile, and he knew what it meant. Larry announced: "It's going to be a good day boys and girls."

"You've got that smile going on brother, and you know how much I like that smile. Are you feeling what I think you're feeling?" Bob was getting excited just looking at Larry's smile.

"I'm telling you brother; I have never felt the Holy Spirit on me as much as I do right now. I can tell you this already, there will be a good number of souls saved today as well as a lot of rededications. That church might even be packed wall to wall. We are going to see a mighty move from the hand from God again buddy. Man, I love this job!" Larry was a happy preacher right about now.

Sister Wilson was intrigued by the banter of these two. "What? Holy Spirit on you Larry? It sounds like you have been through this before. It sounds like old hat for you though."

Larry answered her questions: "Sister Wilson, we have been through all of this a few times now. The only difference is the people and the location. We go from church to church and hold a few services and help out the local Pastor. So, we basically know what's going to happen, but not down to the nitty gritty details. The Pastor is going to get a good blessing today as well.

"People don't realize what a Pastor has to endure from the church he's called to shepherd. Someone is always complaining, while others have legitimate needs, which the pastors freely respond to. We were at a local minister's breakfast one morning when the head of that section told us two Pastors had just quit. It's one of the most difficult jobs out there. Yet most of the Pastor's will endure the junk because on the other end God is moving all over the place. People are being saved and healed. They get to watch God work His work and it's flat out amazing. The devil tried to kill all three of us the other day, yet here we stand just as strong and healthy as we ever were. It scared the daylights out of us, no doubt. But God was already standing there protecting us. You have to admit Sister Wilson, that day was a scary and amazing day all in one."

"It got my attention. When I heard you had been shot Larry, I hit my knees and started crying, then I prayed. That scared me good. But look at you, you're laughing about it now and for good reason. As for Pastor Brown, you never think he was having a bad day. He's always smiling that smile of his and he's just such a warm person. Even my husband wasn't that easy to like. I've never even seen a hint of a bad day from him." Sister Wilson was shaking her head in disbelief.

Bob said: "We agree with you Sister Wilson. Brother Brown is an exceptional man. He stayed here when a lot of Pastor's would have been long gone. He really loves everyone who has ever attended the church, not just the ones that continue on every week."

Sister Wilson said, "Well we better get going. It's not a good idea for you two to be late. Unless you two just need to make an entrance."

Across town Billy and Helen Warren were getting breakfast ready and getting dressed for church. Billy went into Zane's room. "Hey you! Let's get you up and ready for church after some breakfast."

Zane stirred a bit and asked why he needed to go to church today all of a sudden. "It's not just another Sunday today, Zane. Apparently, we have two guys from out of town that are preaching today. Besides, Pastor Brown asked us to bring you two today. These guys have been involved with some pretty amazing works of God. I personally wouldn't want to miss today, especially if God has something amazing planned for our family. These guys work a lot with kids while they're in every town they visit. So, I want you and Laura both to tag along today. Come on bud, it won't hurt that much."

"Okay dad. I could use some direction from God today. I still haven't made up my mind about the military yet. Maybe I can get an answer today. I'll be out in a few minutes for that steak and lobster breakfast I can smell." Billy laughed sarcastically.

Jimmy was up and already ready for church when Sally came downstairs. "What are you doing up already Jimmy?"

Jimmy looked at her with a question in his eyes. "I'm going to church mom, aren't you coming with me? Don't you remember Pastor Brown asked us to come this week and I'm looking forward to it. I don't really know why, but I'm going anyway. Aren't you coming with me?"

Sally was caught off guard. "Oh Jimmy, I forgot. What time is it?"

"It's only nine o'clock mom, you've got plenty of time to get ready." Jimmy smiled at her. "Please come with me mom. We've never to been to his church yet. He was such a big help when dad died, and I really want to go today. Please mom? Bring Ken too." He was trying to pry her out of the house. She hardly ever left it anymore.

"Well, I guess I should go over there at least a couple times each year. Ken won't go and I'm not even going to ask him to. But I'll be down in a little bit." Sally had no idea why she was going to church today, but she really had appreciated that Pastor for all he had done when she really needed someone. She remembered his warm tears running down her cheek when he gave her a hug that night. Yeah, it would be good to see him again.

Chief Lee and his wife were getting ready for church today, but Mrs. Lee would rather have slept in today after a night on the town. However, her husband had made her promise to the preacher that they both would be there today.

Dr. Bob was eating breakfast at the town diner with Roxanne and Cindy. He was really anxious to get there and hear some of God's word today. The nurses were getting nervous just watching him eat. Cindy mentioned that he might want to switch to decaf.

Both of the nurses had tried to invite some friends along this week but had no takers. Even Roxanne's boyfriend wouldn't come. He was really mad when she moved out the other day. But she would ask him again and maybe he would come with her next week. Dr. Bob was so busy this past week he didn't even think about inviting anyone to come today, but he would do better next week.

Betty Jo woke up feeling a little different than normal and didn't know why. But she knew she wanted to go to church today. Maybe that had something to do with it. She was more excited this morning as well. "Hey mom, are you up yet?"

Louise had just awakened and was walking into her bathroom. "Ya sweety, I'm in the bathroom, what's up?"

"Nothing really, I was just wondering if you would go to church with me today?" Louise hadn't gone to church with her for a while now.

"Church? Where did that come from? You haven't been to church in a couple of weeks, why the change?" Betty Jo was standing at the bathroom door now and Louise could see a big smile on her face. "What's different about today pumpkin?"

"I don't know, I just want to go to church today that's all. And I would love it if you came with me this time. We haven't been there together in a long-time mom, and I miss our time together there. Please go with me. Purdy please. With sugar and big fat cherry and whipped cream with nuts. It is Sunday you know." They both laughed.

"Not today, Blondie, but maybe next week. Okay?" Louise really didn't want to go today, but Betty Jo had a point about missing those days together at church. Louise missed them too. Just not enough to go to church today.

"Okay lady, I'm going to let you off with a warning this week, but next week I'm throwing the book at you, so you better duck!" Betty Jo walked over and gave her mom a big hug.

"Okay you wicked little monster you." Louise was kind of proud of this young woman standing in her bathroom. She was already beginning to dread the day she left home. That little woman had become Louise's best friend these past few years.

"Tell ya what. I'll drive you to church so you can get there on time and we'll talk more about it this week. How's that sound?" Louise kissed Betty Jo's forehead. "Do we have a deal?"

"Deal" Betty Jo had no problem with that deal. She always loved visiting with her mom.

Pastor Brown was beginning to pace in his office in anticipation of the morning's festivities. In just a few minutes Sunday School would let out and everyone was going to get to see God do some mighty things for this little desert town. He was almost feeling like he did just before his dad took him to his first professional baseball game. Larry was in an empty room praying and getting Spiritually ready for his sermon. Bob was in the adult class sharing some of the things the two of them had experienced during their short time in this unique ministry. Some of the people that morning had never heard such things that had happened in present times. People were being healed and all sorts of nasty people getting saved. Bikers, homeless people, and people from all walks of life, the mercies of God were transforming lives.

Finally, Pastor Brown found himself by the front door to the sanctuary and greeting everyone coming in with that great big smile of his. He saw Betty Jo getting out of her mother's car walking towards the door. "Hi, I'm Pastor Brown and you are?"

"It's me, Betty Jo Miller. Don't be silly." She was easily embarrassed. "I woke up this morning really excited to be alive and wanting to come to church. I love coming here, but I can get a little lazy some Sunday's."

As she was talking, she felt a tap on her shoulder. She turned around and saw Jimmy standing there and gave him a big hug. "What a surprise Jimmy! What are you doing here? I never even thought to call you to see if you might want to come today. Oh, this day is getting better by the minute."

"I had a special invite by the preacher and thought it might be a good idea. You're right, this is a really nice surprise." Jimmy was really glad they had come this morning now.

Betty Jo said: "I was just telling the Pastor here that I woke up this morning feeling a little different, but I still don't know why. Man, I'm glad you're here Jimmy. I was telling him I was wondering what else would happen today and you tapped me on the shoulder. This is really a strange but fun day. I haven't met your mother yet. Hi, I'm Betty Jo Miller." She was so glad to see Jimmy that she was all giddy now.

Sally shook Betty Jo's hand. "Hi, I'm Sally Walker. It's a pleasure to meet you, Betty Jo. Have you and Jimmy known each other very long?" Sally had a curious look on her face.

Betty Jo slapped Jimmy's arm and had a puzzled look of her own. She thought that Jimmy would have told Sally by now that they were a couple.

Jimmy looked at Sally and Said: "I'll tell you all about it after church mom. I haven't had much time to chat with you. I apologize to both of you."

Sally shrugged her shoulders. "Okay, whatever it is can wait an hour or so." Apparently, Jimmy finally looked at a girl and liked what he saw. It could happen, she thought.

Just then the Warrens walked up with Rebecca and Zane. Betty Jo looked at Rebecca and went right in for a big hug. Zane was standing right beside Rebecca with a huge smile. Rebecca asked Jimmy what he was doing there today.

Jimmy shook Rebecca's hand and said: "Hi Rebecca, the Pastor invited us recently. Man, this is turning out to be a really weird day, isn't it? It's most excellent to see you guys this morning. Let's see if we can all sit together. They walked in and found an empty pew and completely filled it.

Pastor Brown was so excited to see a lot of people at today's service. Some of them hadn't been there in quite a while. Brother and sister Young were able to come together today as God had healed young Chelsey. Usually only one parent could come because of her illness.

Also in attendance today were the Maguire's, Hopkins,' the Torensens, the Caldwell's and everyone else that Pastor Brown had prayed for the first day Bob and Larry arrived in town. It warmed the Pastor's heart to see everyone there today. He knew God had heard that prayer just because they were all there. Yap, God was already at work in this little desert town. And He was just getting started.

From all appearances, it looked as if the entire congregation was at this little church today. This is most unusual for any church, and it was packed. The place could only hold one hundred and fifty people and there were only a few sporadic seats open as the service got under way. Pastor Brown asked Brother Lewellen if he could grab some chairs from the back and lean them up in the foyer, just in case they needed them today.

Sister Brown was playing the piano as she did every week and sister Wilson was at the organ. Billy Warren brought his guitar as always and young Brandon English played the drums. The worship service was awesome! God was moving all over the place and people were crying like they had just received Christ as their Savior for the first time. Visitors and regular attendees had tears on their faces, everyone was getting blessed this morning.

Chief Lee had his hands in the air, as did his wife, who usually hated coming to church. Church was only for weak people, she used to think, but God was definitely blessing her this morning too.

Zane and Rebecca had their eyes closed as they worshiped God. Rebecca's make-up was running down her face and Zane's eyes were wet. Betty Jo had both hands in the air, and she was praying out loud. God was blessing her big time. Jimmy was more solemn but did have one of his hands halfway up and tears running onto his shirt. Sally was sitting with both of her hands reaching skyward. She was getting touched by her Master today and loving it. It moved Pastor Brown to tears just watching God move on His people this morning. How he longed for a day like this for so long.

The Maguire's were holding their two young daughters in their laps and exchanging looks at each other once in a while with huge smiles as they sang loudly. This was truly a Sunday to celebrate for this family.

Dr Bob was a mess. He had tears dripping on his shirt all the way down to his belt. Roxanne and Cindy were almost as bad and crying and praying at the same time. These three were getting a blessing they had never experienced before. But they knew who God was and appeared to be enjoying His presence. That Emergency room better be ready this week, because if these three have anything to do with it, there's going to be revival in that place.

Everyone in the church felt the presence of Almighty God this morning. From young to old. God had visited with all of them today. When the worship service was over Pastor Brown told the congregation to come down to the front of the church if they had specific needs they would like to pray for.

Sally was the first one there without hesitation asking prayer for Ken. As they prayed for Ken, Sally felt a calmness come over her she hadn't felt in years. She and Jimmy had been living with a moderate level of fear lately, but that feeling was totally gone right now. For the first time in a long time Sally felt her shoulders relax and the tension just eased away.

Sister Wilson had been complaining about her hip this morning at breakfast, so the three preachers prayed for that hip to start working like it did when she was a little girl. Suddenly the organ music quit, and Sister Wilson stood up and looked at the guys with a great big smile. She pointed at them as she knew what they had just done. She put her hands together in a prayer symbol and gave them a slight bow, then went back to work on that organ while prayer time continued.

Zane was watching everything that was going on with wide eyes. He saw Sally Walker's face when the guys were done praying for her and watched her visibly relax and smile. He saw Sister Wilson get up from the organ and do that little prayer symbol at the preachers in front. He watched people just flat-out cry like little kids, and he knew it was because God was blessing them. Zane nudged his mom's arm and asked: "Does this kind of stuff only happen in this church mom?"

Helen leaned and told him: "No Zane it doesn't. There are a lot of other churches all over the world that allow God to come into their church and do whatever He wants to do for the people that day. This is only one of those churches. That's why I love coming here. Pastor Brown gets things started, then God is invited in to visit with us, then Pastor Brown steps aside and lets God do His work. A lot of good things happen in here Zane. It's something you really need to think about making a big part of your life. Visiting with God like this is just awesome sauce bro!" She kissed his cheek and made him blush. Billy and Helen got a good chuckle out of it too.

Chief Lee felt a conviction in his spirit that he could take another minute, so he went down and had the boys pray for him. His reaction gave his wife a huge smile. He stood there with the biggest smile on his face, and he just started laughing. Whatever it was that was on his mind was now making him laugh. His wife just waved at him every time he looked her way and was really curious what load just left his shoulders.

Betty Jo went down and asked for prayer for her mom. She knew her mom was a really good person, but she wasn't very happy these days and Betty Jo had no idea why. She asked God to put the smile back on her mother's face, because God had a habit of doing such things.

The Young's took both little girls down for prayer this morning. Chelsey, who was three years old now looked really scared. Pastor Brown took her in his arms and talked softly to her and told her Jesus was going to heal her little sister. Chelsey asked if they could pray for her dolly because her arm fell off last night. Pastor Brown prayed for Chelsey's doll and then began praying for her little sister. As soon as he had placed his hand on her arm, her color improved. Although Nancy was feeling much better today, she was still a little pale when they arrived earlier. Now little Nancy was awake and smiling and giving her parents big kisses. Her parents were a wreck crying and hugging each other and kissing their little girl. Nancy was able to lean over from Pastor Brown's arms and give her sister a big hug too.

After the prayer service everyone continued to pray in their seats and settled in when they were finished. Today was a day for healing and putting families back together. Pastor Brown let things stay quiet for a few minutes and as people began to talk quietly in their seats, he made a few announcements and took the offering. As the ushers were collecting the offering he noticed how many teenagers there were today. He then stood and asked the people to be praying for someone to work with the crowd of kids they had in the church. He was suddenly aware he needed a Youth Pastor. But where did all of these kids come from?

Zane and Jimmy looked around to see all the kids and if they knew any of them. They saw a ton of kids from school that they didn't know came to church there. Kim and Joe were there, as well as Marvin, Sandi, Ed and Diane, Denise and Mark and a whole bunch of other kids they didn't know. This church definitely needed someone to work with this crowd of kids, because there were at least a couple of dozen teenagers and some college kids too.

Some guy named Ed something or other got up and sang a song that gave the entire church goose bumps. Man, that guy could belt out a tune!

After the offering Pastor Brown introduced Bob and Larry and told the story again how they came to town. He didn't talk about the shooting because he didn't want to scare these poor people who had just experienced a mighty moving of God. That story would come about in a suitable time.

Larry went ahead and took the lead from there. "Turn your Bibles to John the third chapter, but let's start with prayer, shall we? Father, we need You today like we've never needed You more in our lives. Some of us came with burdens today that we've carried around for years. Others here today Lord need to have hurt feelings mended that they've let stay hurt for too long. Some of us today Lord just flat out need to get saved. In other words, Father, we all need a special touch from You and a lot of us have already had it. Thank You for healing little Nancy today, Father, that's a pretty little girl who is definitely loved by her sister and her parents. Father let me be a spectator today and You can take it from here. Let everything spoken at this point be exactly what You want to be said. Let it fall on open hearts and ears. Thank You so much for sending Jesus down here to make a way for us to make it to heaven. We give You all the praise and glory, Amen.

"John three sixteen, For Go so loved the world that He gave His only begotten Son that whosoever believes in Him, should not perish but have everlasting life. I have a question for you. Can you tell me what's so difficult to understand about that verse?" Larry waited a moment. "I'll tell you what's so hard to understand about that one verse in that big thick Bible of yours. People don't know who that only begotten Son is. They know His name, but it pretty much stops there. They use His name in vain. Uh oh. They usually know at least one person that follows His teaching, which is now a bad thing apparently. Ooooooohhhh! Like we're the boogie man or something. But what name do they call on when they get into a bad situation? Could that be Jesus? That name they used in vain just a few minutes ago. The name that makes them cringe when they hear it. Some cringe because they hate Him. Others cringe because their heart is convicted of their lifestyle every time they hear it. They need to get saved. Yet when it comes right down to it, they don't know who He is. That doesn't make sense, does it?

"Jesus IS the only begotten Son of Almighty God! No big deal, right? Wrong. So wrong. It's big fat hairy deal with fuzz on top! Why? Because Jesus is the only one in the entire universe who could have done what He has done and that's give His life in your place. He died with every one of your sins all over His back. So yes, that's a big deal. Did anyone of us in this room today deserve that? NO! Not a single one of us, yet there He was, dying our death and carrying our sins. Somehow that just doesn't seem fair, does it? Cuz it ain't. That my friends is a measure of grace and love none of us can understand with our human mind. He died for us even though we can never live up to such a high standard. Jesus was watching us when we hit our pinky toe on the edge of the couch. He saw us when that wrench slipped, and He heard what you yelled too. Ladies, He's seen you without your make up. Oh! I just saw a couple of husbands cringe at that one." Everyone laughed.

"Here's the bottom-line guys; Jesus has seen every one of us at our absolute worst and He still loves us, and He would die all over again if it were necessary. Thankfully, that's not necessary." At this point Larry sat down on the edge of the platform and relaxed while he spoke.

"I can remember a preacher that came to my church when I was just a kid talking about why God even made man. I agree with what that preacher said. And what he said was this, God created us to have fellowship with us. To spend His time with us and love on us. Have a fun conversation with us and laugh. God's amount of love that He carries for us as a human race and as an individual is greater than we can ever know this side of heaven. The amount of grace and mercy that He shows us every day is more than we can comprehend down here. We don't deserve any of it. Yet there it is, available to us by simply asking for it.

"Do we deserve it? Absolutely *not*! But there it is right in front of us. All we have to do is ask for it and He gives it so readily and willingly. He even has it set up similar to a starving person in need of food. And as that person, which is you, sees Jesus with a platter of the most delicious food on a platter that He's holding in His hands. And as you approach with a stomach that thinks your throat has been cut, Jesus hands to a Rib eye steak with all the trimmings. The only thing you have to do is reach out and take it and eat it. But we're not talking about food here. We're talking about every one of us deserving to be sent to hell because of our lifestyle and bad life decisions. Here's some something interesting to ponder, God doesn't send people to hell. People decide to go there all by themselves. God has given us a map to follow that leads right to heaven's door. If you will follow that map exactly the way it was written, you're in baby! Walk right up and accept your reward. Unfortunately, as we walk along that road that leads ot heaven, Satan has put a great many distractions in our way. We end up taking a side trip and have a tough time finding our way back to the only road that leads to heaven. It's totally our decision to follow the map, or not. Jesus isn't going to jump in front of us as we go down the wrong road trying to stop us. We chose to go down that wrong road all by ourselves without asking Jesus for directions before we started that journey.

"But that wasn't what God wanted for us. God Himself desires that everyone of us choose to spend eternity in heaven with Him. I mean come on. Walking on streets paved with gold. Walking through a pearl as we enter heaven itself. Can you imagine how big that clam is?! No shadows. That's going to take some getting used to. I don't know about you, but I have followed myself around my entire life with that shadow always tagging along. Think about the size of the smiles on those faces up there. Doesn't that just make you smile down here? No more tears or pain or bad days. And in the middle of it all is Jesus loving on us. How can you not want that?

"Over in second Peter, three, nine, we're told that God isn't willing for any of us perish but all of us to repent. I paraphrased that one a bit, but that's pretty much a quote. And over in First John one, nine we're told that all we have to do is to confess our sins, and Jesus will forgive us and cleanse us from all unrighteousness.

"Folks, listen to this if you haven't heard a word I have said thus far. This is so simple. Jesus and His Father made it so simple for us to make it to heaven. And I mean no disrespect to anyone, but God made it as dummy proof as He could. Jesus paid the price for your sins and then went and made heaven for us like He said He would. The hardest thing we have to do is to make the decision to accept that most awesome and precious gift of salvation. Make no mistake about it, it's the biggest and most rewarding decision you will ever make in your entire life, because the results last for eternity. This is bigger than picking a college or deciding to ask that girl to marry you, or even accepting that proposal. It's bigger than buying that beautiful home of your dreams. We're talking about spending forever in heaven! So, will you go to Heaven with me? Let's all go together. It only takes one simple prayer to make it happen.

"I know that I've laid it on thick enough at this point, so let's pray. Father, we know who You are and thanking You at times like this seems so insufficient. But Father, we do thank you for sending Jesus down here to take our place on that cross and dying for our sins. Thank You so much for Your grace and mercy and that abundance of love that we've already felt here today.

"Okay guys, I'm going to say a prayer and I just want you to repeat what I pray. I'll make it short and to the point, so it won't take long. But if you want to say that prayer with me, would you just stand up and stay right where you're at?" The entire crowd stood on their feet. Larry began to cry out loud and couldn't hold it in. He looked at Bob and he was doing the same thing. Even the Pastor had tears streaming down his face.

Once Larry got to the point where he could talk and said: "You have no idea what you've just done for the Pastor and Bob and me. We pray every day for days like this and they never happen. We root for everyone we speak with to accept Christ as their Savior. Tons of them do so, but not all. So, when an entire crowd like this stands like you just did, it touches our heart to the very core. Thus, the tears. And congratulations to you all for making this decision.

"Let's pray, Father, here we are with open hearts and accept Your gift of eternal life. Help us all Father to live for You and live according to Your ways and follow Your directions. Strengthen us so we can withstand the battles and fights we're going to experience against the devil and his crew. Thank You again Father for this magnificent gift.

"Okay everyone, repeat after me. Father forgive me of my sins...please come into my heart and life...please change my heart and mind...to think and be more like You...thank you Jesus for taking my sins away for me...help me live for You... the rest of my life. Amen" With that Larry began to clap his hands and Bob joined in. Now the entire crowd was clapping their hands and worship God and hugging each other.

While some people were still standing praising God and as others began to sit down, God gave Larry an idea. "Now that we're all Christians and while God's Spirit is still here, let's do some house cleaning. Don't let God leave out of here with unsettled business. Don't let this pass you by without getting things set right. Some of you have hurt some people and need to ask forgiveness. Some of you have had some arguments with others here in the church and still have a little anger over it. Let's get those apologies made today guys. This church needs every last one of you to be at your best as we go through this brief period of growth."

Before Larry stopped talking Pastor Brown was at the alter on his knees crying. In the back of his mind, he had always wondered if he did the right thing when he married Rachel. He was so lonely when they met, and he felt like he rushed her into a relationship that she may not have wanted. He always wondered if she married him out of convenience. He felt maybe she wasn't ready for everything and was just going along with everything because she didn't have anywhere else to go. God had just told Howard that Rachel was there because He had sent her, and she was exactly where He wanted Rachel. God told him to relax already just enjoy his bride like God had intended for him to. Now Howard really could relax and keep his focus on the job at hand.

When he finished thanking God for what he had been told he stood up and Rachel was standing there with the most beautiful smile. Howard grabbed her face and planted a huge kiss right on her lips in front of everyone. He didn't care right now because he was free to love his girl as much as he wanted to now. Of course, Rachel kissed him right back without hesitation. This was one relationship that was now sealed forever.

Billy and Helen Warren could feel Laura's hands on their shoulders as they stood next to Zane, who was praising God with his hands raised. Next to him was his girlfriend Rebecca quietly praying with tears on her cheeks.

Sister Wilson was at the altar asking forgiveness for something she had done years ago and wasn't sure she had asked forgiveness for it yet.

Billy Warren needed forgiveness for something he had done about a year ago and he just didn't think God could forgive him for it. He was certain God forgave him today. Now the Warrens were hugging the Torensens. They had a falling out several months ago over a pair of pliers and it just wouldn't go away. Today, all was forgiven, and their friendship totally restored.

All of the teenagers were now huddled around Brother Lewellen praying for different things and growing closer as a group of friends. There were a lot of new kids today, so Brother Lewellen made sure they had prayed the sinner's prayer with everyone earlier. If they hadn't, he led them through it right there in the circle. The youth group today at least doubled in size.

Roxanne was sitting with her head buried in her hands openly sobbing and praising God. Cindy was standing and holding onto the pew in front of her talking out loud to her newest friend, Jesus, whom she met this past week. She started crying before Larry spoke a word today, now all of her makeup was gone, and she didn't care.

Dr Bob was a little more animated than his two friends. He was waving his arms and smiling from ear to ear.

Sally was openly weeping and crying on Jimmy's shoulder. Both of them had let everything go this morning in their feelings toward Ken. Now they just had to see how he was going to act at this point. Betty Jo had her hand on Jimmy's shoulder and her other hand in the air worshiping God.

At this point Bob and Larry had made their way to the back of the church and were watching everyone. They were both excited and enjoying what God was doing in this little country church. It was one of their favorite parts of what they did in this unique ministry of theirs. Watching God work never got boring, and just standing there watching Him work was the best part of the entire thing.

After a while things began to settle down and people began to leave their seats. The smiles were huge at this point, and everyone seemed to have one. Some people were saying their cheeks tingled. Ladies were noticing their makeup was gone but didn't much care. Some were visiting, laughing, and having an enjoyable time. God had truly done His work here today. Pastor Brown was thinking this was probably the best church service he had ever been in, and he had been going to church his entire sixty plus years.

The people began to make their way out of the church a little at a time. It was a little after three o'clock, but Pastor Brown made it a point to shake every hand and invite them back next week. Larry and Bob were able to get to a good number of them and exchange pleasantries and say a few prayers with those that asked. The folks really had no idea how to talk to these two new guys, but they were all very pleasant and gracious.

After everyone was gone Pastor Brown invited the boys over to his home for gourmet tube steaks. Also known as hot dogs. He bragged about the way that Sister Brown could cook the meanest hot dog in several blocks. They accepted the offer but offered to get some antacids on the way over to the house.

On the way over to the Pastor's house Bob had a question for Larry. "Did you forget your Bible today buddy?"

"I sure did, and it isn't the first time for either one of us. It's a good thing that we study that thing and read it a lot, or I would have been dead in the water. I was able to remember the Scriptures I wanted to use, and things really flowed well today, I think. What about you Bob, how do you think it went?" Larry knew the answer to that question.

Bob opened his eyes wide. "Man! That was an awesome service! I absolutely lost it when the entire congregation stood for prayer. That says a lot about the character of those people. They needed prayer, they heard what the Lord said, and they let it hit home in their hearts. We serve a big God Larry, but you already know that. How awesome is it that we get to be where we are in this ministry? I still have to pinch myself sometimes because it is so unreal. We saw it all today brother. We had a huge healing, tons of people saved, and you could see which lives were really impacted today. Dude, it doesn't get any better than being able to watch God work like that. The best thing about what we get to do is that we go up there, say what God tells us to say, then we step back and watch Him take over. There ain't nothin' in this world more impressive than that. And if I'm wrong, I want to see that too. Bob was shaking his head sideways the entire time he spoke.

Sally and Jimmy made it home with huge smiles on their faces and walked into the house chuckling at each other. Ken was curious why they were so giddy and asked what had happened. He had been so unhappy for so long that he had no concept of joy right now. He thought Sally and Jimmy had skipped church and went somewhere to get high and said as much.

"Don't be silly Ken, we just came from church. It was such a good service today. I wish you had gone with us, because it was the best service I've ever been to. I've never seen anything like I saw today, Ken, I'm not kidding. The Lord healed sister Wilson's hip right there on the spot. She isn't walking with that limp anymore. And then God healed this little girl. When she got there today, she was pale but appeared to be okay. But after God touched her, she had rosy, red cheeks and big ol' smile. Her parents had been so worried about her they burst out crying and none of us could keep from doing the same thing. I don't know how else to describe it other than "amazing." What did you think about it Jimmy?"

Jimmy was just standing there smiling. He hadn't smiled like this in years, and he missed it. "I'm so happy right now mom, I really don't know how to explain it. Betty Jo and I went over to pray with that guy she told me about. Zane and Rebecca had come over with us and a bunch of other kids from school. After we said that prayer with that one preacher guy, I felt totally different. I guess God really does miracles, even today. When I walked in that place today mom, I was all sad or angry or something. But to walk out of there with a smile like this, a smile that I haven't had in years is so cool. I can't explain how happy I am right now mom. I don't know how." He turned and faced Ken.

"Ken, while I'm thinking of it right now, I want to tell you how much I appreciate all that you've done for mom and me since my dad died. I know you don't think I appreciate anything, but that simply isn't true. I truly do appreciate everything, I'm just not good at telling you that. I mean really. You give mom money sometimes and she lets me have some once in a while so I can go to a frosty or something with Zane. I have my own bedroom now with a bathroom in it and a shower. I don't know where we would be right now if you hadn't come along when you did. I do appreciate you Ken, I really do." At that point he walked over and gave Ken and big tight hug.

Ken had no idea what to do, so he hugged Jimmy back. Suddenly Ken felt himself just let go and he began to cry a little. After he let go of Jimmy, he took a moment to compose himself. He was finally able to speak and said, "I owe you two the biggest apology known to humankind. Sally, I could not have married a better woman than you are. You are so great! I know you're still here because you have no other place to go, and I've used that against you and Jim. I know you don't love me any more Sally and I understand fully why. If I were you, I would run as fast as I could somewhere else, anywhere but here. In fact, I don't even love me and that's the problem. I have a bunch of money. Money you don't even know about. Shoot Sally, we are rich! Very rich, but I am so miserable. And

Jim, I know you appreciate it all. I don't know why I accuse you of the opposite. You are a great kid son, I'm not kidding. The way you love your mother is off the charts awesome and I actually respect you a lot for it. I don't deserve you two, not one tiny bit. Is there any way you two can ever forgive me?" He began to shed tears down his face in a most sincere apology.

Sally and Jimmy looked at each other totally amazed. Ken was totally giving them a sincere apology. Neither of them could really believe it, but it was obviously a sincere gesture. They both walked over and hugged him.

Ken asked: "Did you pray for me today? If so, I could actually feel it. That used to make me so mad at you when you did that. But today was different, I felt calm this time, maybe because I'm sober this time, who knows. I want to thank for it today though. I do not enjoy being that miserable and angry at everything. I take it out on you folks because you're right here. If there were other people were around, I would get them too. Please keep praying for me, I'm serious. I don't want to be that guy anymore. But I have no idea how to change. I can't quit drinking, and I hate that too. So please, I already know that God is my only hope, and I know that to be a fact. So please, keep it up. He still had tears in eyes as he spoke.

Sally asked Ken, "Will you go to church with us next week Ken? If it's anything like it was today, you'll be glad you went, honestly you will."

"I'm not ready to agree to that yet, but I won't say absolutely not. I really did feel your prayers today and I feel so calm right now. It's been a long time since I've been this calm and I actually like it. So, let's just see what happens next Sunday. Is that fair?" Ken was feeling like Ken of old and he actually liked that guy. Not this moron of late that hated everyone and everything and enjoyed scaring people with his obnoxious behavior.

Over at Pastor Brown's house they were having a great lunch together. Of course, if it's gourmet, how can it be bad; right? Even if it is tube steak, it's gourmet for crying out loud. Pastor Brown was still wearing his smile from the service this morning but did have one question. "Larry, I noticed you didn't use your Bible today, why?"

Larry blushed a little bit. "Well Parson, I knew the verses I was going to use by heart, so I didn't really need it. But the honest answer is that I plane forgot it at sister Wilson's. This being a new town and all, I'm a little out of my routine. Bob has done it too. It's just one of those things that happens to us once in a while, but not once have we missed the message God wanted to deliver at that service. God's able to do what He wants to do regardless of how much we try to mess it up sometimes." He chuckled and the rest joined him.

Pastor Brown wasn't finished. "I have never heard John three sixteen put like you put it today. But what really surprised me was when you asked everyone to go to Heaven with you. I have never heard that invitation before." Then he looked at both Larry and Bob. "Guys, you are obviously in a unique ministry, and you are definitely right where God wanted you to be. Larry, you blessed my heart more than it's been blessed in years. Don't change one thing in your approach or delivery. Well, maybe one change. Don't tease the women about their make up too much. You may end up with a bullet hole somewhere in that body of yours." And He laughed that big burly laugh of his.

"I'll definitely take that under advisement. I'm allergic to bullet holes in my body. I'm not allergic to bullet holes in Bob's body though. Those are okay; I guess." Larry had that ornery smile that Bob had seen so many times. Bob just shook his head with a smile on his face.

Pastor Brown asked the boys if they had seen that couple at the front of the church in a tight embrace. "That was the Frazier's. They've been separated for about a year now, but I'm quite sure they're having lunch at the same table today. In fact, did you see all those kids huddled around Brother Lewellen? It looks like I'm going to need someone to take over that group if they all hang in there and keep coming. I'm already excited about next week to see what happens then. I don't think we can hold any more than we had in the church today. Oh well, we'll figure something out."

Zane was at Rebecca's house having lunch with her and her parents. Her parents had really grown fond of Zane this past year. Not only had he shown everyone that he was a take charge kind of guy last year when that girl was killed, but he had also shown Eric and Peggy what a gentleman he was with their daughter. For them, they couldn't have hand picked a better man for their one and only daughter. And since she had just graduated from high school, they had no idea what Rebecca's plans were yet as she hadn't told them anything at all. They just hoped it involved staying close to home and keeping Zane in the family somehow.

"Mom, dad, you missed a great service this morning. There must have been fifteen or twenty of us teenagers gathered around that one teacher and praying for forgiveness today. I know that I've been a good person, but God was really tugging on me to pray that prayer the preacher had us all repeat. I don't smoke or drink, or cuss or anything, but I can't remember asking Jesus into my heart like I did this morning. That preacher this morning was saying the same thing that God was whispering in my ear. It was weird and kind of funny. Will you guys go with me next week please?" Rebecca was as excited today as Zane had ever seen her. She had that smile again that went away the night Linda died.

Eric and Peggy looked at each other for a moment. Eric finally spoke through choked backed tears. "Sweety, we quit going to church when Linda was killed. That shook us to our very core. We still can't figure out why God killed her like that. How could such horrible things happen to such nice people, and she was only eighteen years old. I don't know 'Becca. Maybe some other time, but not right now. Ok?"

Zane spoke up before Rebecca could respond. "Jimmy and I stopped at this church the other day and talked to the Pastor. The Pastor of the church we went to today said something to Jimmy when his dad was killed in that car wreck, and Jimmy told me about it the other day. That Pastor told him that God didn't kill his dad, but for some reason he let him die that day. The only hope that Jimmy had to see him again was to make sure he went to heaven. That pastor had prayed the same prayer we all prayed today, with Jimmy's dad a few days before he died. The Pastor also told him that even though his dad was gone now, all of what God said was still true; all the promises, all the rules, all the blessings and other stuff like that. So as Jimmy and I talked about it, we basically concluded that bad things do happen to really good people. You knew his dad; he was one of the nicest people I have ever met. He always made sure Jimmy, and I had everything we needed to enjoy ourselves. School supplies, balls, bats, and things. He even bought me a ball cap one summer, so I had something to cover my head in the blistering heat on the ball field one day.

"We also decided that the one responsible for Linda's death was the guy who killed her, not God. Jimmy has been blaming God for everything, even Ken being so mean. Jimmy thought about it that day and realized that Ken was the way he was because he was just that way, not because God made him that way. Jimmy made some pretty big decisions the other day, but we didn't even think about praying for forgiveness.

"I guess what I'm trying to say is that God is the exact same God that He was before what happened to Linda and Tony. I don't know if that helps you feel any better about Linda or not. But it came to my mind while you were talking about it. I hope I didn't upset you with all that."

Eric looked at Zane and asked him: "How old *are you*?" Peggy stepped over and hugged Zane. "Rebecca, if you don't marry this man, I'm going to." She winked at Eric, then started to cry on Zane's shoulder. Zane could only hold her while she cried.

Now everyone had years in their eyes. Eric came over and kissed Peggy's head. He tried to talk but couldn't just yet. It took a while before Peggy let go of Zane and went over and put her arm around Eric.

Eric finally spoke: "Wow Zane, you are definitely wise beyond your years. But you are so right; God does have everything in control just like He did when those things happened. I definitely lost track of that for a while. He tells us He is the same yesterday, today, and forever. How easily we get sidetracked when things like this happen. It didn't just rock my faith, it obliterated it. I can see now I wasn't as spiritually mature as I thought I was. Shoot, I might marry you myself if Rebecca doesn't step up soon enough." They all got a good laugh at that one.

Peggy suddenly began to pray. "Jesus, can You forgive us for being so childlike in our faith? Forgive us for those bad thoughts we thought about You and even said out loud. We know now how ignorant that was, and we repent of our sins. Please heal our pain, Lord. We lost sight of how important You are in our lives, please give us a bigger measure of faith so that we don't do this again. We love You Father. Amen."

By the time she finished her prayer, all four of them were in a huddle in the middle of the kitchen.

Zane said: "Wow! I've never done that before. I've gone to church, but I never took God home with me like this."

Rebecca was quick to speak up. "Did you ever think that you might be the answer the Pastor Brown's prayer for someone to work with Brother Lewellen? Maybe God wants you to stay here and not go in the military. I know I don't."

"You're just saying that to get me to stay home." Zane knew this would come around eventually, but he smiled at her anyway. He only said what he did because it was the friendly thing to do. Nothing else.

Rebecca defended herself. "Yes, I am! Of course, I am. But the way you just spoke to my parents, Zane; that was impressive. Maybe God has a calling on you that you aren't considering right now. That's all I'm saying. Plus, the fact that you going into the military scares me to death. Just consider it though. That's all I'm asking. Okay? Is that fair?"

"Fair enough." Zane said.

With that, Rebecca grabbed his face and kissed him while she was looking at her dad. Eric looked at her with an ornery look he was known for. Peggy just laughed while Zane turned every shade of red.

Across town Betty Jo was telling her mom about the service today. "Mom, it was like nothing I've ever seen before. It was like God was everywhere at the same time. At times it even felt like He was inside of my chest. The songs that they sang were so awesome and God showed up right then and never left. Then this guy gets up and starts talking to us like we're all best friends. He didn't have a Bible, but he quoted it like he wrote it or something. Then he just sits down on the platform and invites us all to go heaven with him. He spoke like there was a bus outside and it was leaving in a few minutes.

"He asked all of us to stand up that wanted to pray a sinner's prayer, so Jimmy and I stood up. Even the Pastor stood up with us. Mom, I don't know much about God, but I want to know a whole lot more than I do right now. Mom, there wasn't anyone sitting down at that point. God got everyone of us today. That guy preaching today talked about God like God was his best friend. And I can't tell you a whole lot, but there was no mistake, God was there today. I can't wait for next Sunday already!"

"Mom, please go with me next week, or even this Wednesday. I feel so clean right now, inside, and out. It's like I got myself scrubbed down or something this morning. I know you believe in God because you told me you do. Please go with me mom, please?" Betty Jo had the biggest smile on her face that Louise had ever seen. Even bigger than the first night Jimmy came over last year.

Louise was having a tough time believing what Betty Jo was telling her. "I don't know Betty Jo. This sounds like one of those cult-like things to me. The preacher says a bunch of really pleasant things and promises everyone a utopia of some sort. Then he ends up being some kind of weirdo. I don't think you know what happened today sweety."

"Mom, I told you that I have no idea what happened, but there was no mistake that it was all God. Nothing else could ever do something like that. And I've heard of those people too mom. The guy ends up driving a million luxury cars while telling his flock to give him all their money while they don't have enough to eat. Or they end up drinking something in a far-off land and killing themselves. But mom, this wasn't that at all.

"I tell you what. Why don't you come check it out this Wednesday and see if you can tell me if what is happening is good or bad. If it's one of those cult things, I will willingly walk away. I don't want anything to do with something like that. But! If it's the real deal mom, let's get involved together. If it really is God, it can only be good for our lives and our futures. I know I just challenged your beliefs, but that's not what I was trying to do. Mom, if this was the best piece of cake I ever had in my life, I would want to share it with you. I think that's an accurate comparison for what I think happened today. And I'm pretty sure I got this one right." But I don't know much about him. Only what I watch on TV once in a while. Those guys don't do much for me personally, but I know they have a lot of followers, and they seem to be sincere in what they say. Maybe I should go figure it out for myself and really see what it's all about. I don't know. Tell you what daughter, I'll go with you on Wednesday just to see what I can find out about God. I'll do my best to keep an open mind and not be so negative about it. I don't want to squash something that you are so excited about. And I really want to meet this guy that preached today. I don't think I've ever met a person like that before. How's that sound?" Now Louise had a smile.

When the Young's got home, the first thing they did was get both sets of their parents on a video conference and let them see little Nancy for themselves. They told them what had happened that morning and that they knew God had healed their little girl without a doubt. There was a lot of crying, but the parents were reluctant to believe God had done anything to their granddaughter. Jack Young got a little upset with both sets of parents and said as much. He told them they would have plane tickets waiting for them this week and he expected to see all of them on Friday. Then they could all go to church together and the skeptics could find out for themselves. Then he hung up on them before they could say "no."

He was mad enough to blow their hair back with his righteous indignation at that point. Ending the call was a pretty good idea. It saved their relationships, at least for now.

Billy and Helen Warren were eating lunch and enjoying it much better than most Sunday lunches. Everything was fantastic today and they knew they had been in the presence of Almighty God at church this morning. But today, they both got that "special touch" from God. The very thing they had been praying for and today it was answered. Billy still had a twinge of guilt about what had happened last year, but it was waning and knew that feeling would be gone soon. Helen was the happiest person on the planet at the moment, but the look on Laura's face stated that she would come in a remarkably close second,

Laura was the first to speak while they ate. "Hey, you all don't need to worry about me when it comes to boys. I hear you two talking about me at night and some of the fears you have. You're afraid I may like the attention I get from boys a little too much. Well, to be honest with you, I do like it. But I don't like to break your rules enough. You have your rules and God has His. And actually, those two sets of rules are pretty close. Just for your information though, the boys actually like hanging out with me because it makes them look good to their friends. I hear them talk about me in the halls at school and most of it isn't very nice. One of my girlfriends told me the other day that one of the boys had bragged to his friends about having sex with me one weekend. We weren't even together that weekend. I was with you guys and Zane at the lake that weekend. So, when I saw him with his friends the other day, I went over to him and acted all coy and like. Then I told him what I thought of him as well as his friends. I told him if I ever heard about another comment like from anyone, I was going to tell Zane and let him handle it. And we know what Zane would do. Somehow getting suspended from school wouldn't be a deterrent when comes to little sister's honor. I kinda like that about my brother.

"Oh, and by the way. I sneak around and spy on him and Rebecca when she's here. You don't have to worry about him either. He doesn't even kiss that girl, and she is gorgeous! So seriously mom and dad, you can relax with us. Zane and I know who God is and I think I can speak for Zane as well, when I say we will be a Christian before we'll be in a physical relationship based on feelings. You two have done a fantastic job raising both of us. I am so glad you're my parents too. I hear other kids say pretty often that their parents don't care what they do. I love it when I tell you guys where I'm going and when I'll be home. That accountability keeps me focused and on point. I can use it as an excuse when I get uncomfortable if that ever happens. I'm even thankful for that. So, relax y'all, you got some good kids." Laura was wearing a huge smile as she spoke. She had no idea why she had said all of that, but she was glad she did. Her parents were the bestest parents in the entire world. Of course, she knew other kids had the same opinion about theirs too.

Billy slapped her knee. "Liar!" And he laughed.

Helen spoke up. "Sweety, we have always trusted you. Zane somehow has his ways of keeping an eye on you and lets us know what's going on. Not once has he told us something you should be ashamed of. In fact, your brother's pretty proud of you. He's said something about a couple of the boys you've hung out with, but every time we hear about a boy like that, that boy seems to go away in short order. And Zane tells us he has nothing to do with it. He says you get rid of them all by yourself without his help. However, as parents we know that there will be a guy coming around that's pretty smooth and will get you to think about compromising who you are. You have our permission to punch that kid right in his snot box. You know better than to compromise anything and we're quite sure you won't."

Billy cut in, "We're not really pleased with the way some of these boys look that you bring home, but they seem to be pleasant so far. Of course, I have some tools around here that could be a deterrent for them. You know, crow bars, hammers, pistols. You know, things like that." Then he laughed and Laura hit him on his knee and laughed as well.

Helen spoke up, "So did you get saved all over again with the rest of us today Sweety?" Laura said that she had. "Then the Lord will help you to know when you're in an unpleasant situation, or one that can go that way. Make sure you're paying attention, but still keep your guard up.

"Billy, what did you think of that service today? Was that awesome and powerful and everything we've been praying for?" Helen was still giddy about that service too.

"I tell you what Helen. I'm still feeling it. And with what our pretty daughter just told us. I think I might have to get up and dance a little." Billy started doing something that looked like clogging, but he was just stomping his feet with a big ol' grin on his face.

Helen and Laura started clapping their hands. "Go Billy, go Billy, go Billy!"

Chapter 6

It was Wednesday already, and Pastor Brown was wondering where the week had gone. This week was flying by at a breakneck speed, and he was having difficulty keeping up with it. He wasn't sure how many people were going to be there tonight. He had talked to Mike Lewellen about working with the kids, but he wasn't sure how the kids would respond to him. Mike was forty years old now and not the ideal age to be working with teenagers. But, somehow, he seemed to have the energy and was really comfortable around them. And since he had worked as a Youth Pastor in years past, the Pastor asked him if he would consider working with the kids. Mike was such a great guy and the type of role model the kids could really learn from. But he hadn't gotten a definite answer from Mike yet. He felt like he was really pushing Mike into doing something he didn't want to do, and he was feeling bad about it.

Meanwhile, Larry and Bob were outside the church building scraping paint again early this morning. It was going to be a hot one today and they wanted to get as much finished as they could. Pastor Brown told the boys that the offering had been so big on Sunday that they had enough money to buy all the paint for the church, inside and out. So, they were working as hard and as fast as they could to get the building ready to go. That kind of information really put energy into their work this morning.

At about nine o'clock Pastor Brown couldn't bear the remorse he felt about Mike, so he called him at work to apologize and tell Mike he didn't need to follow through on working with the youth. "Mike how are you doing today, Brother?"

"Oh, hi Pastor, I was just wishing I had a riding floor buffer." Mike sounded a bit tired.

"You don't have one there I take it." Pastor sounded a bit surprised at this.

"No, we don't. They save that money for their bonuses at the end of the year. I just can't get them to put it in my budget year after year. The upside to it is that the one I do have keeps me in shape and on my feet. Maybe I won't get so old as the years go by and I can keep my baseball body a few more years." He started laughing. "So, what do I owe this pleasure to sir?"

"Well, I wanted to apologize for cornering you about working with the youth group. And I'm just trying to get my head around all the people and kids we're going to have here tonight and how many volunteers we're going to need." Pastor Brown was concerned about this one. The kids in this town really needed a place to land. A Godly place would be perfect, but this town didn't even have an ungodly place for them to hang out at that he was aware of. Having a place for them here at the church would be a remarkable place for them and give this town a great outreach for every family in town.

Mike told the Pastor, "What I'd like to do is get the group started and organized. I'm sure that would only take a few weeks. Then, hopefully after a little while someone will feel called to take it over and I'll gladly step aside and help them all I can. How does that sound my friend?" Mike had a big smile on his face. He was actually looking forward to seeing how many kids would be there and what kind of effort it was going to take to get the group to accept Christ as their Savior, and then get settled into a club type of atmosphere. This was either going to be a colossal failure or a story for the ages.

"Mike, I know you're the guy for the job. I was actually thinking the same thing about you getting it started and passing it off at the right time to someone who has the calling to step in. Only time will tell. Thank you do so much Mike! I thank you and God thanks you and the kids thank you. I think." They laughed for a minute then ended the call.

As soon as Pastor Brown hung up the phone, Billy Warren walked into his office. The Pastor was on his feet and hugging on Billy in a flash. It had been quite a while since Billy had popped in a for a visit like this, but once the Pastor got a look at Billy's face, he was sure it wasn't a social visit anymore. "What do I owe the most unexpected pleasure to today? Billy, it's so good to see you today. What's up?"

Billy held his ball cap in his hand while he looked at the floor. "Pastor, I have something that has been bugging me for a good year now. Maybe even longer. I know you've noticed a change in my attitude and my demeanor isn't what it was before either. I did something that I had never done before, and my conscience has been killing me ever since. I don't even know how to tell you about it."

Pastor Brown tried to alleviate the tension in the room a little bit. "Billy, everyone tells those fish stories, it's ok though, just tell me how small it really was."

Billy chuckled a bit, but his facial expressions didn't change at all. "Pastor, did you hear about those guys that went into Ken Walker's house last year and scared the living daylights out of all of them?"

Pastor Brown hadn't heard anything about it and said as much.

"Bluntly Pastor, I was one of the three guys that went over that night last year and scared him good. I kept hearing from Zane that Ken was getting more mean by the minute and making some pretty violent threats towards Sally and Jimmy. Apparently, Sally had been locking herself in one of the rooms at night so

Ken couldn't get to her so easily. Man, that was making angrier every time Zane would say something like that. So, I talked to a couple of my friends that are big as a bus and asked them if they would help me with what I had in mind. Neither one of them would have hurt Ken, but they both look like they just ate your dog. Anyway, one night I told Zane to have Jimmy get his mom out into the back part of the house and leave the front door unlocked. We went over there and gagged Ken, pulled his arms behind his back and pushed him around a little bit. But I told him that if he did as much as mess up Sally's hair, we would turn him into pig dooky. We left him gagged and tied up in his blankets, but we scared him good. We could see it in his eyes, and we had done what we came to do. Pastor, I'm dying over here. I had never done anything like that in my life. I didn't like the man I was that night. That man scared me too. I mean, if something ever happened again that made that guy reappear, I don't have a clue what I'm capable of anymore.

"God got a hold of me Sunday Parson. I was so full of Jesus and so happy I ended up dancing all over the kitchen floor while Helen and Laura cheered me on. I have to admit, that was fun. But here I am today feeling as bad as I have ever felt in my life. I know it's the devil trying to rob me of my happiness, but I don't know much about this. How do I get this gorilla off my back?"

Pastor Brown was sitting back in his chair and was silent for a few minutes while he thought this one out. "Pig dooky huh. I've never heard that one before. That's good one." They both got a brief laugh out of it. "Billy, I know the answer to this question, but have you asked the Lord to forgive you about this?"

"I swear I do it nine hundred times a day Pastor. I need this to be done with. I can feel it taking the life out of me man?" Billy had tears in his eyes again.

"Billy." Pastor said rather sternly. "You're forgiven brother, and it happened the first time you asked for it. All those other millions of times God doesn't even know what you're talking about. Listen to this again, I know you know this, but I'm telling it to you again God tells us in Psalms one hundred and three that he puts our sin as far as the east is from the west. That's a straight-line Billy. He also tells us in Jeremiah thirty-one, thirty-four that He will remember our sins no more, which is a repeat of Isaiah forty-three. Billy, I can go on all day with Scripture that tells us when we ask for forgiveness, *we receive forgiveness*. It's that simple. If it weren't for the amount of love and compassion God has for every individual, we would have no hope at all. But God loves us and wants to have a really close relationship with all of us. Buddy, you are forgiven a million times over and you only had to ask once. Now, go kick the devil in the teeth and get that lunch back that he's been stealing from you for about a year now." He stuck his hand to shake Billy's hand, but Billy grabbed him and hugged him tightly.

Now Billy was remembering why he liked this guy so much. Pastor Brown was, without a doubt, the wisest man Billy had ever met.

Pastor Brown was so glad to have one his best friends back. "Billy I can't even put into words what it means to me to have you back here. I really missed you folks."

"Yeah, same here Pastor. I missed on you the entire time we were gone, but I couldn't face anyone. I knew that as soon as I walked in here, that you were going to know exactly what I had done and call me on it. But until today, I just wasn't ready for that. Man, I feel so much better. I think I'm going to go grab Helen and take her to lunch." Billy was wearing that signature smile of his again. It was so good to see that. "Oh ya, I told Zane I was coming over here today and he wanted to know if there was going to be a class for the teenagers tonight. I told him I would ask about it."

"As a matter of fact, I was hanging up the phone with Mike Lewellen when you walked in. He's agreed to take on those duties for now. So yes, we have that handled for Zane and Jimmy and the entire town for that matter. He's taking all the kids over to the frosty for a sort of kickoff party tonight." Pastor was so glad to have that dealt with. That little issue had him really concerned.

Billy pulled some currency out his wallet and handed it to the Pastor. "You make sure Mike gets that and doesn't give it back. He always foots the bill himself out of that great big heart of his. He robs us other poor slimeballs of our blessing when he does that. So, tell him I know things about pig dooky that he doesn't want to know. Okay?" There was that ornery smile of Billy's. Billy had the biggest case of the "Orneries" than any three men Pastor had ever met. With that, Billy headed home to get his beautiful bride as Pastor Brown was rubbing his chin and thinking about pig dooky. It had never been on his list of things to ponder and now he knew why.

At that very moment, the two newest townsfolk had just completed scraping the paint and walked inside to tell the Pastor they were going to take him and his lovely wife out to lunch. Pastor Brown was reticent at first, but relented when he realized these two weren't taking no for an answer. He called Sister Brown to tell them of the lunch plans, but Sister Brown insisted on paying for the lunch. After what those two had done for the town after only being here just a few days, she felt the entire town owed them lunch.

Bob and Larry went by Sister Wilson's to clean up and took her with them. She had given so much to them; she deserved to take a break from all the cooking she had done already.

The boys took them to a steak house they had heard was really good. It turned to be much better than "good." Pastor tried to pay the bill, but Bob got wind of that silly idea and slipped the waiter his bank card before he ever brought it to the table.

After everyone had finished their meal Larry asked the Pastor, "How do you feel about things now brother?"

Pastor Brown got that huge smile of his all over his face. "Guys, I'm gonna tell you something. This is the single greatest thing that has happened to this church. It's not just this church though, this is going to radiate throughout the other churches in town. There is absolutely no way to contain what God is doing in just one church in town. I bet the devil is spitting all over himself right now. Just wait until this Sunday gets here, he thought he got thrashed before; this week will be even more powerful, and more souls brought into the Kingdom of God. It's going to be so much better. Our church is just too small to contain it guys. I'm telling you the truth about that one.

Larry told him: "You're absolutely right of course Pastor Brown. Not only will it continue to grow, but it will also probably grow beyond your tiny town even. Other churches are going to hear about what's going on here and they're going to want it for their church too, and they are going to want to get involved. It's going to be fun watching God do His thing these next few weeks. God has Himself a huge mission field here and He aims to harvest as may souls as possible during this time, no matter how much or how little time it takes. And brother, He's just getting started.

Pastor Brown jumped up out of his chair and shouted "HALLELUJAH!" and raised his hands and started praising God. "*I THANK YOU LORD FOR WHO YOU ARE! WHAT YOU'RE GOING TO DO AND FOR SENDING THESE TWO KIDS TO OUR TOWN. DON'T LET US MESS THIS UP! FATHER DO WHAT YOU PLAN TO DO AND KEEP US OUT OF THE WAY. HALLELUJAH! HALLELUJAH! HALLELUJAH!*

He suddenly sat down realizing where he was, totally embarrassed. But the couple sitting next to the group burst into tears. Sister Brown was the first to notice them and nudged Bob as she pointed in their direction.

Bob gave them a moment before going over to their table. "I guess my friend just scared the crud out of you, but I'll bet God is doing something here. What's up?"

Cathy Chandler spoke up first. "Well, your buddy over there brought Jesus into this conversation. Oh, this is my husband, Ben Chandler. I'm Cathy. We were just sitting here trying to decide how to divide all of our assets and who was going to get what and where. You see, we used to go to church when we were first married. We worked with the kid's part time, but we always had a Sunday School class we taught together. We eventually got away from that and went into business. We've been really successful and made a lot of money, but we have a ruined marriage and it's just over. Ben had just mentioned that he had wished we never quit going to church when that guy jumped up and started screaming." With tears in her eyes Cathy kept talking. "As soon as he jumped up, I think we both could feel the presence of the Holy Spirit right here. Ben looked at me after a minute and said, 'let's just stop what we're doing and pray.' When he ended the prayer, you were here already."

Now Bob had tears in his eyes, as he could feel the Holy Spirit there too. "Looks like Jesus just healed another marriage to me. Is that what's going on here?"

Cathy reached across the table and grabbed Ben's hand. Ben in turn, put his other hand on top of hers. They were both looking into each other's eyes, so Bob just walked away.

Ben looked at Cathy and said: "I think we just got our second wind, how 'bout you?"

Cathy began to cry again and talked through her tears. "We're going to be just fine Ben. I'm sorry for everything I have done. I can't speak for you, but I feel like I just got saved all over again."

"I was just thinking the same things Sweety." Ben said. "I am so sorry. Maybe 'second wind' is an understatement. We've talked over the years that we felt that God had something for us to do. Well, let's get ready for whatever it is. What do you say?"

"I'm all in." And she just started praying without taking a breath. "Lord, we're back. Tell us what to do and where to go. When you open the door for us, we'll be ready. Just let us know. Thank you for healing our marriage, Father. I was not looking forward to a divorce or anything that comes with it. Now we can brag to everyone that you did a complete and full miracle in both our lives. Thank you for your Saving Grace and saving us both while we were sitting here. And definitely bless that man that knows how to yell hallelujah."

Ben looked at Cathy with tears still in his eyes. "Can you even believe what just happened here? I'm going to shake my head every time I think about this for a long time. Praise Your Holy name Father. Praise Your holy name!!!" Now Ben was yelling a little bit and got the attention of others in the restaurant.

Pastor Brown turned his head toward Ben and said: "Looks like I have some competition over there. Well Praise God!" While he was looking at Ben and Cathy.

Pastor turned back to Larry and Bob. "You two started this big mess, it's only right you keep it going. I'm going to sick you two boys on the church tonight in a preview of a Revival we're going to start Sunday night. Let's go the entire week, including Saturday night. Then next week we'll see if God's done with His work, or we need to keep going. How's that sound guys? Do you have the time for that?"

Larry spoke right up. "Brother, we knew when we got here that we would be here for a while. But that always means something different in every town. In this case, we have all of the time we need. We're not scheduled to be anywhere in the future, so our time is your time. Or God's time for that matter. We'll be here working away until it's time to move on. Sound good to you?"

"Perfect. It sounds as appropriate as hot dogs on Sunday afternoon. Everyone sitting at this table knows that we're all in for the biggest treat God can give a church. This is going to be fun!" The pastor began pumping his fists in the air.

Bob let him finish his little celebration and spoke a word of caution. "Okay guys. We just planned an all-out spiritual war on the devil and he ain't going to like it one bit. So, let's not forget to read our Bible and pray at the beginning of every day just like we all do now. Pray for stamina and wisdom because we all know how smart the devil is. He can be right in the middle of something, and we won't even know it if we haven't spent time in prayer. Don't let your guard down even a little bit. But now that I've said all that, I kind of feel I wasted my breath because I'm not so sure you needed to hear that."

Sister Wilson said: "I needed to hear it for sure. I don't have morning devotions every day like I used to. I get in five days a week most of the time, but it's not very steady. I needed to hear that Bob, thanks for speaking up. I'll definitely be a lot more diligent about it now. I hate fighting the devil. That jerk is good at fighting, and I can't fight him on my own."

Sister Brown grabbed Sister Wilson's hand. "Sis, ain't none of us any good at fighting the devil without God in our corner. We are no match for that jerk at all. If you need a reminder, I'll call you every morning to make sure you got into the Word that morning. How's that sound?"

"That's a great idea. I simply forget to do it some days. Then other days I get my mind on the stuff I need to get done that day and I simply forget about it. So yes, I'd welcome that phone call. Hopefully, we won't talk so long that it's lunch time before we hang up." The two ladies got a laugh out of that.

"Okay guys let's do this. Pastor Brown had a plan. I'm going to let you two do tonight's service, mainly because I want to watch the crowd tonight from the back of the room. Basic curiosity is all it really is. But I'll preach Sunday morning and you two can take it from there. So as long as this lasts, I'll do the Sunday morning service, and you have the rest. You have absolutely no restrictions on you whatsoever. So, just do what you know to do and have fun doing it. Are we in agreement on that stuff?"

Larry and Bob answered at the same time: "Yes sir!" Larry offered: "You get those churches invited Brother and we will start studying for all those sermons. You're going to find out what an awesome opportunity it is to watch God do his work while we just stand there with our mouths open. We're ready Parson, this is going to be an all-out blast. Scary at times too, but it's going to fill our hearts and minds with great memories."

Bob had a thought. "WE" will be here for it Reverend. But you might want to call all of the people in your church to start gearing up for an influx of new believers in your church. You're going to need more teachers and group leaders. Your women's and men's groups will need to gear more towards discipleship to teach the new converts about Christ and the Christian lifestyle. Your congregation is going to grow, and their problems will need to be dealt with on a Pastoral level. That means you may need to get some of those people in the church to lend a hand once that happens. You may not be able to manage all of it. But if you can get up to speed before the growth gets upon you, you'll be fine. Otherwise, you're going to be behind and playing "catch up." That's something Larry and I have seen happen over the time we've been out here. The growth will happen, without a doubt."

Larry said, "It is going to be exciting to be able to watch this all take place. We're usually heading for the next town before all this stuff happens. But this time we get to watch. And we'll help out as much as we can Pastor. You can count on us." They both had big grins on their faces.

Pastor Brown was sitting on the edge of his seat. He knew without a doubt this was going to be big. He also knew that his little church was going to have to step it up a lot to be able to manage the new people. He had a few people in mind, but he also knew it was going to stretch their comfort zone. "I'll need to set up some training for some of my folks. I'm going to have to use people that have never done anything like this before, but they can do it. They've been good Christians all these years but with no teaching or discipleship experience that I know of. We're going to have to clean out some of the classrooms we have junk piled high in, but this is going to be that fun type of work.

Bob chimed in, "Feel free to ask us any questions Pastor. We know what a lot of the churches have done after their churches grew and they were able to keep up with it. We should be able to answer most of your questions. If not, we'll just get some of those Pastors on the phone for you and you can take it from there.

Sister Wilson butted in when Bob took a breath. "I'll take a class. I haven't taught Sunday School in a lot of years, and I miss it. So that's one less that you need."

Pastor Brown said, "I was just going to tell you to study up because you were getting drafted right now. So, you're in Sister Wilson. Welcome to the team." Everyone nodded in agreement with that little bit of news.

Sister Wilson had another thought. "Perhaps we should make plans to have a choir. I can help with it, but I've never led one before. Maybe we can get someone with more experience than I have. But if my thinker is correct, that person isn't in the church yet, so we'll have to keep our eyeballs open for that person."

Pastor Brown raised his eyebrows a little bit. "I hadn't thought that far ahead Sister Wilson, but I like that idea a whole bunch. Why don't you pick out a few songs that you know really well and could help get things started, and we can be looking for that new person as we go along. Does that sound like a good start?"

Sister Wilson nodded with enthusiasm. "I'm all in Pastor. Just let me know when the time is right, and I'll be ready to go."

Sister Brown said: Hey! I want to teach Sunday School too. I've been on the sideline's way too long. Just let me know what age you want me to teach, and we will have that classroom cleaned up already and waiting for them when they get here."

Pastor Brown looked at her with a lot of love in his eyes. "Sweety, you keep doing that and I'm going to marry you all over again and adopt your children."

Sister brown responded: "I don't know. We've been married for so long I don't know if I want to do that again. Talk to me later." Everyone got a good laugh at that. "Funny that you should mention children today sweetheart." And she gave him a worried look.

Pastor Brown got a quizzical look on his face. "What are you trying to tell me Rachel?'

"Nothing, but I gotcha didn't I?" And burst out laughing.

Pastor Brown took a big breath. "You sure did. I suddenly thought we had an oops baby on the way. Whoa... you got me good with that one darling. No dinner for a week because of that one, plus, you get to sleep in the garage now. If we had a dog, I'd sell it so it couldn't even keep you warm. You're really bad to me Rachel."

Everyone was laughing now. This was definitely a group of people that were about to have an awesome experience with a God that loved them more than they deserved, and they all knew it.

Sister Wilson broke the laughter. "You boys are going to need some space to study. Why don't you use my quiet room for that this next week? I've got an entire library right off the kitchen with concordances and such. I call it my quiet room. It's all yours now. I like to dissect the Bible from time to time when a Scripture hits my heart. I think you'll find everything you need in there and then some."

The boys looked at her with wide eyes. Larry said, "I have always wanted a library like that, but we can't haul it around in a car. That thing barely hauls us around at this point."

Bob looked at her in the eye. "Will you marry me? Please, I'll pay you."

"Oh, golly gee, what's a woman to do? But no, is the answer. I ain't training another one. But I don't mind you asking sonny?"

"You've been hanging around that Brown woman way too much sister Wilson and it just ain't right!" Bob was laughing as he spoke. The rest of the group got a good belly laugh at that one.

"I will take that as a compliment Bob. Glad you noticed." Sister Brown said laughing.

Pastor Brown looked at his watch and decided it was time to get back to the church to get things ready for tonight.

Sister Brown took the ticket and started to look at it when Bob grabbed it out of her hand. "I got this Sis, we were the ones that invited you out here, I already paid it."

Sister Brown squeezed both of his cheeks. "I ain't used to people paying for things like this. Thank you, Bob. But, please let us buy the next bis meal like this. We both love doing that for people. Seriously."

"Okay darlin', but this is the last time." Bob laughed and everyone joined him.

As they headed back to the church Pastor Brown thought that if Sunday were any indication, tonight was going to be a full house.

Once back at the church Bob and Larry began putting the extra chairs into all the classrooms that were going to be used tonight. As they were putting some in the sanctuary, Bob told Larry that he was going to sit in with Mike Lewellen tonight just to see if he might need a hand.

"I was going to ask to do just that Bob, but I never got a chance with all that fun were having. That's a great idea. I'm going to hang with the Pastor just for kicks as well. I gotta good feelin' about this place brother and I like what I feel."

Bob shook his head in agreement. "I love these feelings we get at most of the churches we've been in. It really saddens me when we show up at a church and they're not open to allowing God to do His wonderful work in their place. That "Us four, no more, close the door" stuff is dangerous to the soul, and every one of them in that church. But this Pastor has a burden and really fantastic vision for this church and town. It's going to be fun watch buddy, no doubt about it."

They all finished the preparations they needed to do and went home to get cleaned up for the service tonight.

As expected, the church was pretty full, but not as full as Sunday was. Mike put as many kids as he could into his van for the trip over to the frosty. Bob did the same thing in his little car. A couple of the teenagers had cars and took some as well.

Once there, Mike went over and ordered three dozen hamburgers. The cook told him it would take a while, but he would have them out as soon as he could. There was a total of eighteen kids there at the moment, but Mike knew there would be more showing up before they headed back to the church. Zane, Rebecca, Jimmy, Betty Jo, Marvin, Ed, Sandi, and Diane had all brought friends with them. Ed and Donna showed up a few minutes later with some friends as well. Billy had sent some money with Zane and told him to use it tonight, But Mike told him to keep for later, just in case the crowd got too big for his own wallet.

Zane looked in the window and saw the poor cook going as fast he could, but he was getting a little rattled. Zane grabbed Jimmy and went back to the window. Zane yelled at the cook to get his attention. "Sir, if you will allow us to, we would be more than happy to come inside and help out."

The cook's face said it all. "Oh, thanks man, I could really use some help right now, come on around the back and I'll let you in."

Once inside, the cook, John, told them to put some tomatoes and onions through the slicer and pull some lettuce apart into hamburger sized pieces. Then he gave them each a pair of gloves and a hair net. Once the boys got the hair nets on, John took a look at them and announced: "Now you two look like a couple of grannies and are fit for the job." Then gave them both a high five while the three of them giggled.

Soon, three junior high school kids walked up to the crowd on the patio. Rebecca handed them each a hamburger and asked if they would like a soda as well. "Save your money for the offering later, we've got this."

One of three named Brian asked, "Offering, what do you mean offering later?" Rebecca told them what was going on tonight and the new youth group starting at the church. She told them about some of the plans for the summer and the next year that she had heard Zane and Jimmy talking about earlier in the day. They were all invited to go over to the church after they finished their food and be part of the new youth group starting in town tonight. But they weren't obligated to go. They could just enjoy the food and the company and go home if they wanted to. The little group knew there wasn't much going on in this small town, so they decided to check it out.

A few minutes later, four freshmen with skateboards arrived. Jimmy had known one of them named Brandon when they were younger and had spent time at his house. He yelled out the window: "Hey surfer dudes, you wanna hamburger?"

It took Brandon a minute to figure out where that voice came from. He looked over and saw Jimmy with that big smile of his. "Hey Jimmy, what's going on here tonight? This place is packed. Do you have some free hamburgers in there or something?"

Jimmy smiled. "Not in here, but Rebecca and Betty Jo have a pile over there with them. Go get yourselves one. We've got a new youth group in town paying for everything, so go get it." Betty Jo was standing there with four hamburgers.

Now Brandon was a little suspicious. "Okay, what's the catch?" Betty Jo smiled and told them what was happening with the new youth group. They were invited to be part of it after they ate, or they could just leave when the group went back to the church. There was no catch at all.

The four of them sat down with the burgers as Rebecca came over with some drinks for them. "It's going to be an all-out blast you all. You really don't want to miss this."

Brandon wasn't that interested in church right now. "I don't know guys. I don't know that much about that stuff. When I hear about it, it gives me the heebie-jeebies. That stuff spooks me man, I ain't even kidding."

Bob was walking over when he heard what Brandon said. "Brandon, do you believe in God?"

"I've heard of lots of gods, which one are you talking about?" Brandon was being sincere in his answer.

"Well then, let me ask you a different question. Do you believe in Heaven and hell? Maybe this question will be easier to answer."

"Oh, okay. I don't know if I do or not. My parents do though. They tell me every once in a while, that if I don't make better decisions I'm going to end up in hell. But they don't go to church. So, I kind of think they're just messing with me. That's really all I know about it." Brandon was polite and not put off by Bob's question.

"Just one more question then. If Heaven and hell are real, which would you want to live in after you pass away?"

Brandon's eyebrows raised a bit, and he was wondering if Bob was trying to insult him. "I'm not sure I want to answer that one."

"It's not a trick question and I'm not trying to embarrass you at all. I'm really trying to find out if you know more than you think you do. That's all, really." Bob smiled and Brandon seemed to relax.

"Heaven of course. That's the nice place, right?" Brandon wasn't sure he answered the question correctly.

Bob smiled and said: "Yes, that the nice place. I tell you what, if you will skate over to the church in a few minutes, I'll show you that this stuff is very real, but not scary at all. It'll only take about a half hour for me to do that. Then you guys can be on your way, and you'll make some new friends in the process. Is that a deal?"

Brandon was up for it. "You guys want to go? I do." The other three agreed but they were looking at all the girls. "Okay sir, we'll see you over there."

Everyone seemed to be having a nice time tonight. Tons of laughter and good natured kidding. Then it was time to get back to the church.

Once they finally got back to the church all the kids were smiling and excited. Mike told Bob to do whatever he wanted to tonight. He knew Bob was in town for a brief time and he wanted to get every minute out him that he could.

Some good-natured kidding went on for a few minutes. Mostly teasing Zane and Jimmy about how bad the burgers tasted tonight. Everyone eventually found their seats and settled down. Mike had taken down all the tables earlier in the day so they could have a circle on their first night. Only a few of the kids had brought a Bible tonight.

Bob had everyone introduce themselves, which took a few minutes. Bob counted twenty-five kids in the room. "Okay. We're going to have a short Sunday School lesson tonight. If you can pay attention to what I'm telling you, you're going to learn something tonight, I promise. So please pay attention."

Bob held up his Bible. "What I have here in my hand is one of the biggest miracles in the world. I'm not kidding. It took thousands of years to write, and it contains sixty-six books in it. Many different Authors wrote it a few thousand years apart and yet I can hold in my hand right now. Even Jesus didn't have access to this book. In Jesus time they only had access to the Old Testament, because Jesus and His disciples, and everything that happened was the New Testament. We just needed those guys to write about all that stuff later.

"This Bible has been thoroughly challenged throughout the ages and has withstood every one of those challenges. It is historically correct. Of course, history isn't the source of the challenge. The source of the challenge has to do with the existence of God. Does He, or doesn't He exist? This Bible tells me He does. What I feel in my heart confirms that He does. History records the life of Jesus Christ and His death on the cross.

"Let me ask you a question Marvin. I know that you accepted Christ as your Savior just this past Sunday but let me use you anyway. Do you believe in Satan, the devil or Lucifer?"

Marvin was caught off guard. He wasn't expecting such a heavy question, but he answered "yes."

"Why Marvin?" Bob asked.

Marvin had to think about it for a moment. "Well, look at all the bad stuff happening in the world right now. Bombings, shootings. murder, rape, wars everywhere. A bunch of really terrible stuff and it's everywhere."

Brandon, would you agree with what Marvin just said?" Bob wanted Brandon involved so he could learn.

"Yeah. I agree with all of it. Satan, murders, all of it." Brandon was listening to everything being said tonight.

"Then why is it so hard to believe there would be a source of goodness going on at the same time as this messy crud, Zane?" Bob thought Zane might just nail this answer.

Zane had to think for a moment before answering. "I'm not sure I'm going to answer this question the way you would Bob, but I've read that in the Bible about a spiritual war. To put on the complete armor of God. Something like Principalities and demons and stuff like that. I'm sorry, it's been a while since I read that."

Bob was surprised at Zane's answer. "Wow, that's really close Zane. Excellent job. Zane's right everybody. It is an absolute spiritual war and every one of you are involved in it whether you know Christ as your Savior or not. Because the devil right now is trying to wipe every bit of knowledge we have of God completely out of this country and our minds. Zane nailed the scripture reference, it's in Ephesians chapter six. It tells us this war is being fought by angels and demons in high places. Those that we met at the frosty tonight are involved in this war too. It's a war for your very souls. The devil wants to drag all of us to the very pits of hell, but Jesus wants to spend eternity with you in Heaven. And yes, that's the nice place.

"Now here's the greatest news of all. Pay attention to this because it will change your life. Jesus came down from Heaven and lived with us for a while. He talked about God; He healed every person that He could. Thousands believed in Him and were sure that He was the Messiah that was foretold in the Old Testament. Then he allowed Himself to be sacrificed for every person ever born on this planet. It doesn't matter how good or bad they were or are currently. He died and shed His blood for them. And with that shed blood He paid the price for all of our sins. And now, all we have to do to go to the good place is to simply say a quick prayer with a sincere heart. A prayer asking for forgiveness of our sins does the trick. Once we've done that we get to go to Heaven when our life is over here on earth. We all know that we ain't getting out of here alive.

"The devil has nothing he can do that will stop us from going to Heaven. Nothing! So, what he does is try to get us so discouraged that we give up. So, it takes a little effort to keep our hearts and minds in the right place. But as long as are serving Christ and have Jesus in our hearts, Heaven is our reward for that. And ain't nothing the devil can do about it. So, it's important to have Chrisitan friends at school and around town. They will help you hang in there, and pray with you, and encourage you when the devil gets to you.

"So, who in here tonight wants to say that short prayer and accept Christ as your Savior?" Bob was a little surprised when every single hand went up, including the kids he was fairly sure had already accepted Christ.

Bob asked Zane. "Zane, haven't you done this before?"

"Yes, I have, but the way you presented it tonight, I want to do it again to make sure I'm right with God. That's okay, isn't it?"

"It absolutely is buddy. And for the others in the room who feel the same way, join right in here." Bob was taking a liking to this kid Zane.

"Okay here we go. Just lower your heads in reverence to God and close your eyes. Repeat what I say and when I'm finished, all of you are going to be Christians. Okay, repeat this: Father forgive me… take all of my sins away…fill me with Your Spirit…let me feel Your presence…every time I breathe…change my life…and help me live according to Your ways, not mine…Thank you for sending Jesus to the cross…to die for my sins…and don't ever let me forget that… Amen" Bob looked around the room and there were a lot of tears.

Kids had their arms around each other in support of each other. One of the kids that looked like the biggest jock in school was absolutely sobbing. In any other setting people would be laughing at him. But in here tonight, this was someone who just asked Jesus to change his life, and sometimes it makes people cry. Sometimes they cry a lot like this guy.

"Okay guys, let me get your attention for a minute. I know a lot of you are really emotional right now and that means Jesus really touched you heart tonight. Others of you are not emotional at all and may be wondering why. The reason is that all of us are different, and it's nothing more than that. Some completely lose it, like our guy over here. Others don't get emotional at all, like those of you over here. But as long as you prayed that prayer, you are now a Christian. An emotional response to that prayer isn't required. So don't let the devil tell you that you're not saved because you didn't cry. The only requirement was saying the prayer with a sincere heart, nothing more. Does that make sense to you all?" Bob wanted to make sure every one of the kids knew they had done the correct thing by saying the prayer.

All of the kids shook their heads yes.

Bob Asked Mike to finish things up tonight. Mike stood up. "Well, I certainly have nothing I could add to what Bob said tonight. I'll only clarify that since you all said that prayer with him, you are all new Christians and Jesus lives inside of every one of you right now.

"Just so you know, we'll be doing this every Wednesday night at seven. But I want to do something this week. I want you to go home and write down every question you can think of. Then bring those questions with you next week. We will go through all of the questions we can get to that night. But we will get every question answered for you during the following weeks, until all of them have been answered. If you don't have a Bible, don't leave until I give you one tonight. I'm pretty sure we have enough for everyone. I'll be your leader for this group so stop me if need anything. Okay?" Mike said a quick dismissal prayer, and everyone began to file out of the room.

"STOP!" Mike yelled. "I forgot. I need all of your addresses and phone numbers and email addresses so I can mail you, call you, email you and bother you as much as I want to. I put some paper and pens by the door for you to write it all down. This is going to be of those clubs that's going to be a lot of fun. So, invite your friends and family to come and enjoy it too. Goodnight you all, see you on Sunday."

As the kids were going out the door Bob grabbed Brian and Brandon. "Did you guys understand what went on here tonight?"

Brandon spoke first. "I understood everything. Even what Jesus did for me when He died on the cross. I know now that I'm involved in a spiritual war. So, when I'm tempted to do something wrong, I'll probably think about it in a different way now."

Bob looked at Brian for a response. "I know what I did tonight. I accepted Christ as my savior." A tear began to fall down his cheek. "I asked Jesus into my heart and now I'm a Christian. I feel lighter though. It's like a ton of bricks just left my shoulders or something. I'll be in this group as long as I'm young enough, maybe even longer. I'll be bringing my sister next week. She needs to this as much as I did. Thank you for everything you guys. I've never been so glad to eat a free hamburger in my life. Just keep 'em comin' boys." They all laughed.

Brandon said that he had asked Christ into his heart also. "I'll never forget this day as long as I live. Like Brian said, I feel so much lighter, and I feel different than I ever have. There's something to this Jesus thing and I like it. I like it a lot. I never knew it was like this. Everything I heard about God and Jesus was bad. I thought God sat up there in heaven and blasted people with all kinds of crud. I'm pretty sure that the devil does it to us now. All I can say right is WOW!" They all chuckled a little.

Mike put his hand on both the boy's shoulders. "You are now totally different people. You have a different life, totally. Your heart has been changed by saying that simple prayer tonight. Your heart is different and now you'll feel different about a lot of things that happen in your life. You're going to love your parents like you never have before. Ain't that a hoot?" More chuckles.

Bob patted them both on the shoulders. "You guys are going to be all right. You two also have some leadership qualities that'll come in handy as you grow up. So don't walk away when an opportunity comes up to tell someone what happened to you here tonight. Bring every friend you can and your sister too of course Brian."

Brian smiled." She'll be here. She a good girl, she just needs to say that prayer."

Mike said, "Well, we love you all, so go home and talk to your parents and see if they might come to church with you on Sunday. It'll be neat." Chuckles all around again.

As the boys walked away Mike turned to Bob. "I wanted to thank you so much for your help tonight. What a night huh? Twenty-five kids getting saved in one service. I've got goose bumps just talking about it. And I want to point something out to you. You are a natural at this Bob. You talk and make it so understandable to the kids. My word, no wonder you and Larry have had such success wherever you go. I'm flabbergasted. I have never met anyone like you two guys. I wish I could put you in my pocket and take you out whenever I needed you. Thank you thank you thank you.' Then Mike gave him a huge hug.

"Oh my. Those are really kind words Mike. But I have to give God all the credit for my manner of speech. When Larry and I got into that car to take a nice little road trip, I wasn't like that. I was shy and didn't really have that much self-confidence. But the first church we stopped at; there I was in front a fairly small crowd letting God use my mouth. Since then, it's become habit for me.

Larry will tell you a similar story as well. He was nothing like he is now. We were just going for a drive before we ended up taking a job at a church somewhere and that was the entire plan. But thank you for the compliment, it's good to hear Larry on I are making an impact."

Bob found himself wishing this was one of those times when he and Larry could just stop and settle down in this small town. But God had more places He needed them to visit.

Larry was standing in the foyer talking to some people when Bob and Mike walked into the sanctuary. From the way Larry was talking to them, they must have just given their heart to the Lord tonight. This Sunday was definitely going to be a hum dinger. When Larry finished chatting, he turned to Mike and Bob and said: "Guys, I'm telling you right now, this is only the beginning of an area wide revival. Southwind isn't the only church that God's going to work in while we're here Bob. Some of the other churches in the neighboring towns are going to feel the effects of what's starting right here in this little church. This is just the beginning boys and girls. Sunday is going to be a day to behold for sure. It's exactly what we were talking about at lunch today."

Just then the Pastor Brown and his wife walked over. Pastor Brown said, "Boys, I've got a feeling that Sunday is going to be a great day in heaven, this is just the beginning of something huge for this entire area. I've read about things like this before, but this time it's my turn to tell the stories. Satan better get packed cuz we're going to kick his hide out of town. That would definitely be something to see."

Mike had tears in eyes. "Yeah, Sunday should be a great day in this church no doubt." He was fighting back tears as he spoke. As he wiped his face he said: "I hope we have enough chairs to seat everyone this week. And by-the-way, we haven't heard from the devil in few days. I'll bet he shows up on Sunday trying to pull some crud out of his arsenal."

Now everyone was looking at each other with a big question in their heads. Pastor Brown said: "Well, I guess it depends on how many people show up. We better find every chair we can and get 'em set up before Sunday so we can get a count and see if we're going to need some more. Now that's a good problem right there buddy."

"I like that problem, Parson." Larry said.

Sister Brown bumped Bob's arm. "Don't forget your Bible this week Bob." She had that ornery smile on her face.

Bob shook his head as he chuckled. "I'll do my best ma'am. I guess we'll find out Sunday how good my brain works."

Chapter 7

Zane and Jimmy had decided to get a burger and visit, just the two of them. Since they had begun dating last year, they rarely took the chance to visit by themselves. Zane had mentioned the other day that he missed it, so Jimmy suggested a date with just themselves. So, here they were on their "date."

They finally arrived at the "Burger Joint" after a quiet ride over there. They were both in deep thought during the entire ride. Wilson was only half an hour away from Southwind, but today it seemed to take hours. "Come on Jimmy, lunch is on me today." Zane wanted to treat his best buddy to lunch for once.

The two boys ordered their meals and sat down to wait. Jimmy spoke first. "I've got something on my mind, other than Ken, and I can't shake it. But it's not the right time to make a decision about it. How do you feel about our girlfriends?"

"I don't understand your question, Jimmy. I think about Rebecca all the time. But what are you getting at?"

Jimmy was shaking his head from side to side as he spoke. "I keep wondering if Betty Jo is the girl for me or not. If not, I don't want to waste a lot of time. But if she is the is the one, how long do I wait until I propose? I mean, it's way too early to be making that decision. That's what I'm talking about. Am I off my rocker thinking like that at this age? How do you feel right now about Rebecca?"

"Oh, okay, I get it now. If I had to decide right now, I'm marrying that girl and I'd be over the moon about it. But you are correct oh wise one, it's way too early in the ball game to go there. But I don't mind wasting my time with her, even if she isn't the one. Is that what you were getting at?"

"Yeah! That's exactly it. And I feel the same way about Betty Jo, I'd marry her right now and love her until the day I die, I think. But I can't do anything because of Ken right now.

"He's got my mom so scared of him that she moved into one of the guest rooms last night and locked the door. I mean, this guy is totally off the rails right now. It's flat out scary just to look at him. His face has a constant scowl, and he growls sometimes when he's quiet. It's the most scared I've ever been and I'm not kidding Zane." Jimmy's bottom lip was beginning to quiver.

"You want me to have those guys come back over there again." Zane didn't like what he was hearing and now he was afraid for his friend and his mother.

"NO!" Jimmy shouted a little too loud for this little frosty type building. A lot of people looked over at them. "That was really scary that night. I know they didn't hurt him, but man they scared the crud out me and my mom. Forget Ken, mom and I can't take that again. But thank you for the offer. Anyways, I can't really decide about Betty Jo until something makes this Ken issue go away."

Zane was feeling bad for his friend all of a sudden and getting mad about it at the same time. "You know what we could do, and I'm not sure it would help very much; but we could start praying for him. I don't remember praying for anyone before, but I hear my parents talk about praying for people all of the time. Maybe we should give it a shot. Afterall what we've been seeing at church lately it's worth a shot."

Jimmy showed Zane an angry look, but it suddenly softened as he considered what Zane had said. "You know Zane, with all that's happened this past week at church, maybe it's not a bad idea. But my goodness man, that guy may be so far gone even God Himself can't reach him. I don't even know if I have enough faith to ask God for anything about Ken. Don't get me wrong, I would love for Ken to get saved, but that's asking for a lot more faith than I have right now. But! I like the idea now I've pondered it out loud. Clever idea Zane."

Their burgers arrived and the two best friends ate in silence for a few minutes. Both of them were just trying to focus on anything but Ken.

Jimmy had another thought. "Hey, I just thought of something. First, we have *got* to take our girls on a big fat date. The second thought is this though, we've been double dating since we started dating these girls. Do you want to start going out by ourselves at some point? I just don't want to interfere with anything you and Rebecca have going on. Maybe you two want some privacy or something, I don't know."

Zane already had an answer. "No, I don't want to stop double dating. I've already given this some thought. Rebecca and I, just like you and Betty Jo, spend a lot of time together at each other's' homes. So, us couples get our private moments. But I have no desire to get into a situation where Rebecca and I lose our focus and do something we know isn't right. I love that girl enough not to have sex with her before we get married. Some of the dates we've been on together have been so much fun and so deep at times, I can see where it would be easy to go there. So, no Jimmy, I want you and Betty Jo on every date until we walk down the aisle, if it goes that far. I'm sure there might be an exception or two down the line. We both know how sick the devil is, and I don't want to give him that tool to use against us, because what we both have is really special. So, let's just keep it this way for now, okay? Unless you guys want to go out alone."

"Absolutely not and for the exact same reason. I've never talked about this with Betty Jo, but I know she feels the same way. We love hanging out with you two anyways. You two are just fun to be around. Face it man, we're all simply good people and fun to be around." They both laughed but it was true, and they knew it.

They had finished their meal and the best visit ever and were now in front of Jimmy's house. Zane stuck out his hand to Jimmy. Jimmy took it and gave it a good shake. "I think this may have been the best visit we have ever had. It's like we're becoming adults or something." He said with a smile.

Zane was smiling back. "You're right bud. That *is* the best visit we've ever had. And I hope to have many, many more. I love you brother."

"I love you too partner; see you tomorrow probably." Jimmy shut the door and headed for the house.

As Jimmy walked into the house, he joined Sally on the couch. They were talking when Ken he walked in from work looking really tired. All the drinking was catching up to him. Sally told him to have a seat at the table, she had his dinner ready for him. He sat down and took a drink of water as he closed his eyes for a moment.

Jimmy came over to the table and took a long look at his stepfather. He had lost weight, and his eyes were sunk back into his head. He looked terrible. Jimmy wondered why anyone would want to live this way. "Ken, are you okay?"

He looked at Jimmy and answered with a hushed voice: "Yeah, I'm alright, why?"

"You look so tired. Is there anything I can do for you to help out tonight? I don't know much about your work, but I'll do whatever you need me to do. That way you can get some rest tonight" Jimmy just wanted to give him a few minutes to relax.

"I appreciate that Jim, but I didn't bring any work home tonight. But that's very thoughtful of you. Thank you." Ken was genuinely grateful.

"You're welcome, Ken. I have a couple of things I need to talk to you about if you're up to it. It can wait though if you'd rather rest up first." Jimmy didn't want to push it.

"Sure Jim. What's up?" Ken was looking at Jimmy and actually paying attention.

"Well, I've decided to go to college this fall. I know I haven't mentioned it before, but I just decided to start this semester, instead of taking a break. I know that in order to become successful in life, a college degree really helps in most cases."

Ken said: "You're right Jim in most cases it does. I'm not sure it will make you a better truck driver though." And he chuckled a bit. Jimmy had never heard

Ken chuckle before, and he joined in the chuckle. "But let me know how much money you need, and I'll pay for everything. Make sure you ask for enough money for your meals and clothes too. And don't worry about getting a job. Just worry about school. We've got enough money so that you can go to college and not have to work. Okay?"

Jimmy was totally surprised. He expected a little bit of a fight with Ken, but this was so much better than he thought this conversation would go. "Thank you so much Ken. That's so much more than I expected here, but there's one more thing and I really don't want to push my luck here. I'm going to need a car to get there and back." At that Jimmy cringed in his chair.

Ken looked puzzled. "What's wrong with the car in the garage?" He was very polite with that question. Not the usual outrage that Jimmy expected.

With a crinkled face Jimmy said, "It on its last legs.

Ken was genuinely surprised. "Oh, I had no idea that was the case. I guess I wasn't paying attention. But yes, we can get you a car. What kind of car you have your heart set on?"

Jimmy's eyes were wide with surprise. "Oh, Ken, I have no car in mind. I'm asking for a huge favor here and I know that. So whatever car you get for me is fine. You pick it out with no input from me. Well, it does need to go forward and backward though." They both chuckled again.

Ken looked Jimmy straight in the eye. "I'll buy you a car Jim. No problem whatsoever." Ken stuck out his hand for Jimmy to shake.

Jimmy almost shook his arm off at the shoulder. "Jim! Jim! It's okay I promise, but I really do want to keep my arm in working order so I can enjoy this meal your momma cooked for us." Ken had a big smile on his face as did Sally and Jimmy.

Sally leaned over and gave Ken a big hug around his shoulders. This was the Ken she married. It was good to see him again. "There's the man I fell in love with. I really love this guy sitting in the dining room right now. You look tired can I make you some coffee?"

"No honey. I'm going to go to bed early tonight. I'm really tired. But have a seat for a minute, I need to chat with you two for a minute." Sally sat down in the chair closest to Ken and grabbed his hand. Ken in turn reached over and kissed her hand.

Ken looked at their clasped hands as he began. "I want to sincerely ask for forgiveness from both of you for my behavior. And listen to this or you'll miss a huge round of thunder. I'm going to church with you two this coming Sunday. I'm tired of the man I've been recently. He's a really unhappy man. He yells too much; he hates too much, and he's one of the biggest jerks I've ever known. You know you're a bad guy when you think you're one of the worst people that you have ever known. I don't want to be like that anymore. I can't even remember how long it's been since I was happy. I'm not suicidal or anything, but that guy needs to go away.

"Jim, you deserve so much more than what you asked for tonight. I know what I've said to you about being unthankful and lazy. When I said that I knew it was so far from the truth and I was out of line. You have been such a good kid since I've been part of this family, and you amaze me and put me to shame. You are a better person than I'll ever be, and I am so sorry son. I can't apologize enough to you for all that I've put you and your mother through." He squeezed Sally's hand and kissed it again. "I know most kids that have stepparents usually get into some sort of trouble, but you haven't done a single thing that I know of. I'm totally impressed with you Jim and I appreciate you every time I think of you. Which is a lot since we live together." He smiled a huge smile. Jimmy hadn't seen that smile before and he liked it.

Ken turned his attention toward Sally. "Sally, I know that I've scared you to tears so many times that I can't count them all. I want you to know that I am terribly and deeply sorry. The amount of remorse and shame that I'm feeling right now is overwhelming. I can't apologize enough to you. I wish there were a different word in English that could communicate to you how awful that I truly feel. And while I'm thinking of it, have you been praying for me lately?"

Sally kissed him and smiled. "Yes sir, I have, and I make no apology for it whatsoever." She gave him one for her "cutsie" looks like she used to when they were dating.

Ken nodded his head up and down as he flashed that big smile again. "I knew it. I could feel it this week and please don't apologize for that, ever.

"Throughout my life I have noticed how happy and close some families are and I was envious of them. I've always wanted to be part of a family like that. That's one of the things that attracted me to you and Jim. You are so close, and I could see the love and closeness you two shared. But I've come to realize in these past few days that I'm the missing link to that family. So, I decided I'm not running from God anymore. I quit; I surrender. I know who God and Jesus are. I know Jesus died for my sins and all that stuff. But I also know that the devil is trying to drag my fanny to hell after a miserable existence here on earth. I don't care what I have to do in order to become a Christian I'm going to do it, because I'm done with that level of misery in my life and subsequently yours too. So, on my way to work this morning I prayed and told God if He would change the way I felt and behaved, I'd quit yelling at Him and saying vulgar words in His direction. I told him I was done being the guy that acted out towards the one who made everything beautiful on this earth and in our lives. That I wanted to be a happy man again. Like I was when I was a young man and smiled and laughed all the time. I ended up pulling over to the side of the road and I just cried like a little girl for a while. It actually felt really good to have a cry like that. But when I finally got myself gathered and back together and back on the road, I felt completely different. I felt so much lighter. When I got close to the office there was a mom walking across the street with her little kid and they were laughing, giggling, and having a good time. It brought a smile to my face for the first time in I can't remember how long. So, if this is what it feels like to be a Christian, I don't ever want to stop."

Sally went around the corner of the table and hugged her new husband and cried on his shoulder. He hugged her back and cried into her hair.

Jimmy decided this would be a suitable time to visit Betty Jo. He got on his bike and rode over to tell her the good news about Ken. Thus far in their relationship he had never said anything good about the man. Now he felt he could brag about him. He was smiling as he walked towards the front door.

The next day the two couples decided it was time for burgers and ice cream. Zane and Rebecca were all smiles while heading over to Betty Jo's house.

As they turned the corner towards Betty Jo's house, they saw her and Jimmy walking up the driveway. Zane honked to get their attention and met them at the edge of the sidewalk. Jimmy reached over and gave Zane some knuckles.

Betty Jo was laughing when she got to the car. "My mom is just silly sometimes! And funny too! She just asked me if the four of us were going to live together after we all get married." She and Rebecca started to laugh hysterically, Zane and Jimmy just looked at each other with a straight face.

Suddenly the girls noticed the boys' faces. "What?" Rebecca asked.

Zane said, "Of course we're going to live together. We already picked out a little two-bedroom one bath house for us to live in. I guess we forgot to mention that."

Jimmy continued. "We thought it would just be the thing to do since Zane and I have been friends since kindergarten. Why not still be best friends after we get married? You two seem to get along good enough, so living together just makes sense. I don't see why that would make you two laugh like that."

As they pulled into the parking lot at the frosty, the girls were looking at each other with worried faces. Rebecca looked like she was going to start crying. She got out of the car and leaned up against the fender with her face in her hands. Zane and Jimmy exchanged a look of complete bewilderment. Then Zane got out of the car and put his arm around Rebecca's shoulders.

"Rebecca, you have to know that we are teasing you two. There's no way that I want to be living with anyone after we get married. That's our time to grow closer together as a couple and make memories. Going places for the first time as a couple. Hanging out with our friends as a couple. Going out to eat as a couple. Playing jokes on people as a couple. All that fun stuff couples do when they first get married. Besides, this is all Louise's fault. Jimmy just ran with it, and I followed his lead. It's nothing more than a joke. I'm really sorry and a bit confused at the same time. How come you're so serious about something that we haven't even discussed yet? Marriage and places to live are still a long way to go for us. We get to talk about all that crud when the time gets here and this ain't it."

How did this teasing go so far sideways so fast? Jimmy had something he wanted to say before this went too much further. "Hey, you two, don't you think for a second that we would do something like that to you. As much as I love you, Zane, and Rebecca, I don't ever want to live with you. We were only teasing you two girls, but I guess it went too far. I'm so sorry."

Betty Jo went over and hugged on Rebecca.

Zane spoke up. "I got to be honest with all of you right here. I'm really uncomfortable talking about marriage and where we're going to live and anything that has anything to do with getting hitched right now. That's so far off in the future right now that I can't see it from here. Can we all just to decide to talk about this when the time is right? Don't get me wrong here. I'm looking forward to those conversations, but not just yet. Let's just let that time come to us, then we can decide who gets the bigger room and stuff like that." Then he laughed and gave Jimmy some knuckles.

Rebecca punched him in his arm again in the same spot that already had a nice sized bruise on it. "C'mon Betty Jo. Let's go." She grabbed Betty Jo's hand and walked away.

As the girls were walking around the corner, a local kid from school and a few of his friends came over and started to tease the girls a little bit. Rebecca was in no mood for anymore teasing and said so. But he wouldn't listen to her. As they walked a little further, Rebecca turned around and pushed him away from her. But when the kid started to fall backward, he accidentally reached out and grabbed Rebecca's blouse and ripped it before he fell down. She let out a scream.

Rebecca and Betty Jo were both totally shocked at what had just occurred. Betty Jo looked on while Rebecca took inventory of the condition of her blouse. It wasn't that bad, just a button missing was all.

The poor kid on the ground immediately started apologizing, saying it was an accident over and over.

Jimmy looked at Zane with a puzzled face. "Do you hear the girls yelling or something?" Zane heard it too and they took off running towards the girls.

As they turned the corner, they could see the kid on the ground and Rebecca holding her blouse. Now Zane was ready to fight. But the kid was standing there with his arms out in front of him apologizing over and over.

"It was an accident! I promise! It was an accident! I didn't mean to grab her blouse, I swear! Please believe me!" The poor kid had a look of fear of on his face and it caught Zane's attention as he began to back down from his anger.

Rebecca had run in between Zane and the other kid and wrapped her arms around Zane to keep from hitting the poor guy. Still a little angry Zane demanded to know what happened.

Rebecca and the kid that tore her blouse started talking at the same time and no one could understand what either of them were saying. Jimmy yelled: "Stop! We can't understand you both talking over each other. Just calm down and tell us what happened. That's all we want to know. Rebecca, why don't you go first."

"Okay. First Zane, it was only an accident I promise you. In fact, it's partially my fault. He was walking behind us teasing us a little and I turned around and pushed him away. But I was still kind of perturbed at you and pushed him too hard. He started to fall and reached out to stop himself when he grabbed my blouse. Total reflex thing, nothing more. Zane, I'm telling you the truth. Please don't be angry with him."

Zane looked over at Betty Jo and asked if that's what happened, and she said it was. Zane then looked over at the poor frightened kid and asked if he was okay. He still had his hands out in front of him, but nodded and said, "Yeah, still scared, but I'm okay."

Zane kissed Rebecca on the forehead. He stuck his hand out to shake the poor, frightened kids' hand. "My name is Zane Warren, what's yours?"

The kid grabbed Zane's and shook it. "I know who you are. You and Jimmy seemed to be the most popular kids in school. My name is Dustin Hensley and I'm really sorry about your girlfriend's shirt. I'll buy her another one, I promise."

That "popular" comment caught both Zane and Jimmy by surprise. "Jimmy, did you know we were that popular in school all these years?"

Jimmy had wide eyes at the moment, "No. I had no idea about that at all. Betty Jo, did you know about that?"

Betty Jo was smiling. "Of course I did. So did Rebecca. We were both totally astonished when you two called us last year and asked us to go to the movies with you. The two most popular boys in school. How did we even get on your radar was what I asked Rebecca. And now that I know you both so much better, I can't believe she and I got so lucky that you called us." She looked at Rebecca who was shaking her head up and down. Now the two boys were looking at each other and shrugged their shoulders.

"Well, thank you for that Dustin it's nice to meet you, even under these circumstances. Why don't you and your friends come over and eat with us, my treat. We were just getting ready to go over there and order something greasy and really bad for us. What do you say?"

Now Dustin Looked surprised. "Are you really serious? I just messed up her blouse and you're inviting us over to be your new friends or something? I don't get it, but yes, we'd love to hang out with you guys."

They all went over to where the tables and chairs were and put enough of them close enough, so they didn't have to yell at each other.

After everyone had ordered and found their places Zane tapped Dustin on his shoulder. "Hey Dustin, why don't you and your friends come to church with us this Sunday morning at about ten o'clock? We have a little youth group that seems to be growing pretty quickly. The guy who teaches this class is a really nice guy. Plus, he seems to know everything. If we ask him a question about the Bible or Jesus or something, he's got the answer for us almost without even thinking about it. This guy's amazing. We'd all love for you all to join us; if you want to that is."

Dustin looked at his friend sitting next to him with wide eyes and a quizzical look on his face, then back at Zane. "I don't know Zane. Church just isn't for me. I went to it when I was little, and what I heard was that I'm a rotten kid and going to hell. That might be true, but I don't need to hear that anymore. I think I'm going to pass."

His friend elbowed him and gave him a frown. "I would love to come. I've been thinking about God and Jesus this summer, but I just don't know how to find out more about it. I would love to come and maybe I can talk Dustin into coming with me by then."

Zane stuck his hand out to shake the friend's hand. "What your name?"

"Oh, I'm Steve, nice to meet you guys."

"What's your last name Steve?"

"Patton. Steve Patton, sorry. Call me Steve."

Zane chuckled at him. "I remember you from school. I think we had a few classes together over the years."

"Yeah, we used to tackle each other when we were playing touch football in P.E." Steve had a big smile because he was the one that started that part of the game.

Zane chuckled and pointed at him. "That was you? Now I remember you really well. That made the entire game fun. Everyone got a kick out of us tackling each other, even when we didn't have the ball. I'm surprised we didn't get hurt, the way we creamed each other sometimes." They gave each other explosive knuckles over that fun thought.

"So where are you at in school now? I know you didn't graduate with us this year, are you a senior this year?" Zane really liked Steve; he was feeling embarrassed that he didn't recognize him right away.

"Yap, starting my senior year, so it's time to decide what I'm going to do with my life. I'm leaning towards living in my parents' basement and playing video games until I'm 40, or they die first and leave me the house. But I haven't told them yet." Steve was smiling again. He was always a joker.

Their names were called to get their orders at that point and the group fell silent while they ate.

After a little while the conversations began again. Jimmy wanted to know if Dustin was actually going to make it to church on Sunday. "So, Dustin; are you going to be with us on Sunday morning?"

Dustin was getting annoyed at this point. "What's the big deal about going to church on Sunday with you? I just really don't want to go. It's not that I have bitterness or hatred for you guys, I simply don't want to go to church. Seriously. It's nothing more than that, I promise."

Betty Jo was listening in and had a question. "Dustin, can I ask you a couple of questions? No tricks, I promise, but pretty serious questions."

"Ya, I'm game, go ahead." He said without looking at her.

Betty Jo put her hand on his hand for just a moment. "Okay; first question: Do you believe in heaven and hell?"

Dustin was a little taken aback at her question, but he answered it. "Yeah, I believe in both heaven and hell. But I can't remember how I came to think that way. But the short answer is yes. I believe in both of those places." Everyone around began shaking their heads in agreement with his answer.

Betty Jo kept going. "Okay; question number two: How do you get to heaven or hell? And please know, there's no wrong answer. I'm asking what you believe, that's all. I'm not looking for a right or wrong answer here, just what your thoughts are. That's all." She had that sweet smile of hers that really kept Dustin relaxed and made it easy for him to answer the question.

Dustin thought for a minute before he began his answer. "Well, let me start with hell since that seems to be an easy answer. To go to hell, I guess, you need to be a mean kind of person who steals and robs and hurts people. You know, kind of like an all-around scummy snot ball." Everyone laughed. "But to get to heaven is a little trickier I think and takes a little more effort, I think. Obey the ten commandments, honor your parents, be nice to everyone. Don't use foul language or tell lies. I guess that's my answer Betty Jo. I've never thought about it like this before. I feel like you put me on the spot here."

She patted his hand. "I'm sorry Dustin. I was trying not to do that. I guess I could have asked the question differently, but I really don't know how to do that. I'm just a girl, not a preacher. But I do apologize for putting you on the spot.

"I have good news for you though. Getting to heaven is easier than what you just told me. It's hard to walk around following a bunch of rules. Not doing this, but definitely doing that. Jesus went to the cross and was crucified for all of us, including every one of us around this table here. He did it in order to forgive our sins. So that all we have to do now is just to simply ask Jesus to forgive us, and He does. And that's all it takes. A simple prayer and you can go to heaven. The other night one of the guys that's in town said something about using three words in that prayer. God forgive me, Jesus forgive me or something like that. I've been going to church most of my life, but I've really only been paying attention for about the last two years, so I'm not the person who can help you pray that prayer, I wish I could because I'd help you right now if you wanted to say it. I'm sorry. But if you don't want to come to church with us on Sunday, why don't you come hang out with all of us after church, because after church we're probably all coming over here to just hang out. It would be neat to have our new friends spend time together with us."

Dustin sat there for a moment shaking his head up and down. "Okay why not. Steve, you want to come with me too?"

"I'm in." Steve said.

Dustin was still into the conversation. "I kind of wish you could have helped me through that prayer Betty Jo. You made a good case for it, but I can wait until Sunday I guess, when we can get a preacher to help us out."

Rebecca butted in. "I can help you with that prayer Dustin if you're serious." Dustin looked at her like he was about to cry. "Yeah, I'd really like to say that prayer if I can."

Rebecca looked at Steve. "Steve, you want to get in on this too. Do you want to pray with Dustin?"

Steve had the beginning of tears in his eyes as well. "Yeah, I do." Rebecca looked around the small crowd and noticed there were a couple of others that looked like they were about to cry too. She raised her voice a little. "Okay you guys, does anyone else want to say this prayer to ask Jesus into your heart with Dustin and Steve here?" Another five or six kids raised their hands showing they wanted to pray too. Rebecca looked at Betty Jo with wide eyes. Now Rebecca looked like she wanted to cry. She cleared her throat really quickly and spoke up again. "Okay guys, repeat after me. Father... please forgive me of my sins..." All the kids repeated her words. Rebecca continued: "Please come and live in my heart..." Again, everyone repeated it. "Thanking you for dying for me... Amen" Again, everyone echoed her words. "And now everyone who just said that prayer is a brand new Christian. Let's give those guys a hand. Come on, let's clap for them." The little group broke out in applause right there in the parking lot at the frosty.

Zane and Jimmy were smiling at each other, pointing at their ladies and being really proud. "Can you believe these girls?" Jimmy asked. "They're already acting like preachers' wives. They're far ahead of us is all I can say."

Zane shook his head in agreement. "You said it right Jimmy, We're the ones standing in their shadow right now, no doubt about it."

Handshakes, hugs, and lots of high fives were given around the crowd. Some were wiping tears from their eyes, but everyone was smiling.

"WOW! You two are unbelievable. Just WOW! I don't know what else to say right now. I am so proud of you two ladies right now. WOW!

Jimmy was still looking down and shaking head as he spoke. "I told Zane earlier today that you two were acting like preachers' wives already. But neither he nor I have the calling into the ministry, yet. But I have to agree with him. The amount of proudness and respect I have for you ladies is off the chart right now. And yes, WOW! Zane is correct with that word. Goodness you two! WOW!" Jimmy started to choke up a little as he spoke. "Zane, there is no way that you or I picked these two ladies at random last year when we were looking for a simple date to the movies. I think our Father in heaven was planning ahead for us. We ain't that smart and we know it."

"Whoa, dude! I never thought of that." He looked both Rebecca and Betty Jo in the eyes. "He's right you guys, there's no way either of us saw this coming. Not for a second. WOW!" He shouted. "Jimmy, you are so right brother. I guess we better start listening for that calling or follow these two ladies around as preacher hubbies. It could happen you know." Zane was shaking his head sideways at the mere thought of being ministers. That thought both excited and scared him at the same time.

Betty Jo was finally able to interrupt the two boys. "Hey! I didn't talk to those boys so that you two could fall in love with us all over again, but I like it. I did it because it was the answer to the situation. I haven't been going to church my entire life, but long enough to get the conversation on the right track, or something like that. That's all. I asked questions that I've heard preachers ask at the end of their sermons. So, I don't know what the big deal is. What about you Rebecca?"

"They were ready to pray, and I remembered a prayer I heard someone pray once and that's what I did. Nothing more than that. So yeah, I'm with Betty Jo. The only thing we did was pay attention at some time in our history and remembered a few things. Nothing more than that, so I don't get what the big deal is here either." Rebecca had a sweet smile while she spoke.

Zane grabbed both of them by the hands. "Okay, maybe we laid it on a little thick, but listen for a moment here. Here's what you did in a nutshell; you took every last one of those souls right out of the devil's grasp and placed them in Jesus loving arms. Perhaps you'll figure out what a big deal that is some time down the road. But we are both still without question so proud of you. Does that make more sense to you? Maybe?"

Jimmy couldn't let that statement stand. Zane, the girls didn't do that, they only facilitated an introduction to Jesus. That's all they did. They don't have the power to do what you said. It's like Bob and Larry keep saying. They only talk a lot, then stand back and watch God do His thing."

Betty Jo and Rebecca looked at each other and just shrugged their shoulders and smiled. Betty Jo said, "Well, I know it's kind of a big deal. But at the time it really didn't seem to be such a big deal. I just did what I thought was right and answered a couple questions for them. It did turn out the way I hoped it would though. I had no idea how to pray for them. Rebecca, when you did that, I knew we both did the right thing. I was really happy to be able to help someone get saved. I've never done that before. It was even fun."

Rebecca knew what happened today was a little bigger than she had let on. "Well, I know helping someone get saved is a really good thing. I've never done that either Betty Jo. And it was fun too, I agree. So, let's just acknowledge the fact that we had a chance to do something we have never done before and enjoyed it. I just hope those people that prayed with us enjoy it more than we did. That's all."

Zane looked at Jimmy and asked., "Should we tell them about the date we were talking about at lunch?"

"Yes sir, we better or they're going to show up underdressed. Ladies, we are taking you two to that really nice steak house in Wilson tomorrow night. So, wear your best dress and we will wear our favorite pair of jeans." Then he laughed.

Rebecca squealed and hurt everyone's ears. "Are you serious Zane? We didn't do anything just now to deserve a date night like that."

Zane was still trying to hear again, but he caught most of what she said. "No, Rebecca, we decided to do this because we love you ladies and you're everything that you two say about us, even more. So really, this is a real date, and I know you both will be as beautiful as ever. And it had nothing to do with what just happened at the frosty."

Betty Jo looked at Jimmy, "This is really happening tomorrow night? You could have given us a little more notice. It takes time for me to be as beautiful as I want to be dear boy." She slapped Jimmy on his leg and giggled.

Friday morning Jimmy was so excited about the big date he didn't sleep much that night. He could hear his mom making breakfast downstairs, so he decided to go help out. He knew he had to go to town to buy a suit today and was fairly sure Zane needed to do the same thing, so he would give him a call later this morning to make sure.

As he walked into the kitchen his mom met with a great big smile. "Good morning, Jimmy. To what do I owe this pleasant surprise?"

He walked over and gave her a kiss on top of her head. "I couldn't sleep because I have a big date tonight. Zane and I are taking our girls out to a nice restaurant tonight and I need to go buy myself a suit that fits. The one I have now is the one I wore to dad's funeral. I don't think it fits anymore." He said with a chuckle.

"Good grief, why didn't you say something a long time ago about that? We could have gotten you one anytime you wanted." She gave him a big hug. "Sweetheart, we're not exactly broke around here. Of course, we ain't exactly wealthy but we have money for clothes and stuff you know."

Ken was walking in the kitchen as Sally was talking. "I beg your pardon, Missy? We certainly are most definitely wealthy, and I have a bank account to prove it. In fact, more than one bank account to prove it. Does someone need some money or something."

Sally was shocked. "You what? What do you mean that we're wealthy?" Ken was standing next to her now and gave her a big hug.

"Well, when we started dating, I didn't want to tell you because I was afraid you might just be after my money. You know like a lot of women I dated before you. But you were so much different than they were. You were so warm and genuine as well as just flat out one of the sweetest people I have ever met. Anyways, I didn't tell you after were married for pretty much the same reason. I didn't want to get divorced. Forget the money part. I loved you so much, and the thought of losing you because of something so shallow was *my* hang-up, not yours. Then of course I started drinking and everything just got lost at that point. And that's the entire truth without any sugar coating. It was all on me, you did nothing wrong. But since I'm a Christian now and I know that we will be together forever, you should know all about it. But until this moment I hadn't even thought about it. So, before you go asking where did I to get all that money, it's all legal money and I earned it all in my businesses. I've done nothing wrong or illegal, so rest easy about it." He squeezed her a little tighter with a big smile. "So, what's the deal about money this morning anyway and pass that bacon before I bite someone's arm off. I'm hungry." He gave Jimmy an ornery look.

Jimmy pushed that bacon over to the other side of counter. "I was just telling mom that me and Zane are going to be taking Rebecca and Betty Jo to a fancy restaurant tonight and I needed to go buy a new suit. The one I have in the closet right now was from my dad's funeral and it won't fit at this point; I think." Jimmy had a smile on his face.

Ken reached into his pocket and handed Jimmy a huge money clip. "This will take care of the cost of any suit you want Jim. Spare no expense, just get the one you want, okay? I wish I had thought about this sooner. Everyone needs at least one suit for whenever the occasion arises."

Jimmy looked at the clip as it was pretty fat. "Good grief Ken! How much money is in here?"

Ken just smiled. "I'm not exactly sure, several thousand dollars, I think, maybe more. But whatever is in there will buy that suit as well as everyone's dinner tonight. Dinners on me okay." Jimmy tried to give the wad back to Ken but Ken wouldn't take it.

"Listen here Jim Bob! I gave you that money and now it's all yours. It's not mine anymore because it's all yours. No giving it back. So there, neener neener."

Sally grabbed Ken's arm. "Ken!"

Ken gently put his hand over her mouth. "Sally, Jim, I insist. That money is yours now. Get that suit and order anything you want on that menu. Oh yeah, leave one those hundred dollar bills for the waiter or waitress. It'll make their evening, and they'll remember you the next time you go there. Seriously, make them smile with a big fat tip."

"I don't know what to say Ken but thank you. There's going to be money left over after tonight. I'll bring that back to you, okay?"

"No Jim! It's yours, keep it. Put it in the bank if you don't want to carry it around. But it's yours now. Oh! By the way. I was going to take you out tonight to get a car. But since you have that date planned, why don't we go do that in the morning? In fact, bring your friend Zane and the two girls. Why don't you have them meet you here about ten in the morning and we'll get it for you. Then you can go another date and get a speeding ticket or something fun like that." Ken was chuckling now.

Jimmy nodded his head. "Speeding it is! Coming right up!" Breakfast at this house was joyous today. Something that hadn't happened since just after Ken married Sally. Smiles and laughs filled the room. Ken looked at his watch and found it was past time for him to be on his way to the office, but Jimmy stopped him.

"Not before we pray for you Sir. Sit back down and mind your manners."

"Yes sir." Ken said and sat down.

"Father, we want to thank you for this most awesome breakfast that my gorgeous mother made for us this morning. And we want to thank you for allowing us the privilege of having that food in our home. Now with sincerity I pray for your hand of protection over Ken today as he drives to and from his office. Let it be a fun day, filled with lots of laughter for him and his peers and staff. Please draw all three of us closer to You and closer to each other as we enjoy our family time together. Amen."

Sally smiled at Jimmy for saying that prayer, it had never happened before. Ken was looking at Jimmy shaking his head. "Jim, I don't know what you did, but I could feel that prayer. I'm so new to this Christianity but I sure am looking forward to meeting all my new friends at church. Of course, I have a lot of apologizing to do around town, but I'm up for it. Who knows, maybe those apologies can lead to someone else getting saved and having this much joy in their hearts. I had no idea people could be this happy, I'm not even kidding right now. I am the happiest I have ever been in my life at this point. And something tells me there's more to come because I'm just getting started. Anyways, I've got to get going. I love you guys." He reached over and kissed Sally on her head, then reached over and grabbed Jimmy by his head and kissed his ear, then laughed all the way out the door.

Sally was laughing as Ken left. As she looked over at Jimmy holding his ear with a big smile on his face she said: "I think he actually like you son."

"I think you're right mom. I like this new guy a lot too. I was really questioning the fact that he really got saved like he told us the other day, but I think that's been answered. He seems totally genuine right now. I'll take every one of those kisses anytime he wants to tease me like that."

Then Jimmy lifted up the money clip. "I really don't know what to do with this wad of money mom."

"Well Jim Bob." Sally started laughing and Jimmy joined her. "I'm sorry Jimmy, but that kiss on the ear was just funny."

"You're right. He caught me totally by surprise with it. It happened so fast I didn't even get a chance to laugh at it myself. But really, what do I do with this money?" Jimmy was reluctant to accept the cash because of the amount. They sat and came up with a plan for it all.

Later that morning, Jimmy was getting dressed after his shower when his phone rang. It was Zane wondering when Jimmy would be ready to go shopping. "I'll be ready by the time you get here buddy."

"Good, cuz I'm sitting in front of your house right now." Zane chuckled.

Jimmy looked out his window and sure enough, Zane was sitting in front of the house. "Let me get my shoes on and I'll be right there, you silly boy you."

On the other side of town, the girls were already on their way to the mall for new dresses and other stuff that goes with a new dress. They both were so excited about tonight they were talking over each other. Smiles and squeals were abundant today.

The girls walked all over the mall going from store to store but weren't able to find that perfect dress for tonight. They finally decided to revisit the stores to find one of the dresses that would be only ok for the date. The time was going so fast they were wondering if they were going to have enough time to get ready for the date on time.

The boys on the other had walked into a suit store, shopped for a while, and picked out a suit. They had to wait a few minutes for the pants to be hemmed but were on their way home in just over an hour. They had time to stop for coffee on the way home and had a great visit. They talked about the loves of their lives but got more excited about what was going on at the church. Bob, Larry, and Pastor Brown seemed to have it all together and leading this thing right along without a hitch. Or so they thought. They had no idea about the battle going on daily at the church.

With all the new teenagers and college aged kids coming into the church, they both knew there was a need for a youth Pastor and knew that Mike would do an excellent job at it. Both Jimmy and Zane were excited to help as much he needed, but a crowd like that needed much more than either of these two could offer. Nonetheless, this new group was going to be a lot of fun as well as uplifting and helping their walk with God. They both continued to voice something pulling them toward working with Mike, but really didn't know much or in what in part they could help. Perhaps Mike Lewellen was the man with the answer to that.

The girls got home just in time to get themselves all dolled up for their menfolk and not much time to spare. After all the makeup and hair curling and a lot of attention to the details on the dresses, they were ready for their guys.

Both Zane and Jimmy gave each other knuckles as they pulled up in front of the houses awaiting to see their dates. Of course, both of them looked absolutely radiant and definitely would be turning heads tonight.

The date was going so well. At the restaurant, the guy on the piano, the staff and especially the food, were over the top nice. The conversation went from each other to the church and the girls stepping up last night with Dustin and Steve. They chatted about Zane's military decision, which he brushed aside. They also talked about having a double wedding. If there were ever two couples that a double wedding would make total sense, it was them. Jimmy was so excited about getting his car tomorrow that he kept bringing it up. Every time he brought it up, the car he wanted got bigger and more expensive.

As Jimmy was talking about his new car, Ken and Sally were out shopping for it without telling him.

They had been to several lots when Ken got a glimpse of a car that caught his eye. He pulled into the lot and walked over to a mid-sixties' sports car. It was a two door coupe with chrome wheels. He opened the hood and noticed some chrome on the motor. When he looked at the interior, it had a couple of rough spots on it, but nothing that needed immediate attention. The paint had faded a little bit but was still a pretty metallic green.

Ken walked around the car with his hand on his chin, then stopped at stared at it. He was allowed to take it for a test ride and put it through the paces of a sports car. "So, would fifteen hundred over your cost be a decent profit for you? I'm really just asking because I don't know."

"Oh, I wish you hadn't asked that question like that Ken. This might be where you lose your trust in me." Bill the salesman, literally let his shoulders deflate. "I knew the lady who sold me this car, and the story of her husband's accident, but I didn't know her. When she asked me how much I would give her for the car, I had the same question you have right now. I made a few phone calls and looked online to figure it out. It was worth about fifty five hundred dollars, but I gave her eight thousand because I knew she needed the money. She was crying the entire time she was here. She didn't want to sell her husband's car. I'll make that money back with sales on other cars a little a time, so your offer is way too much for that car." Bill was looking at the floor shaking his head back and forth.

Sally spoke up as she put her hand on Bill's shoulder. "Bill, you look familiar. Do you go to church here in town?"

"Ya. I go over to the Christian church every week. Why?" Bill looked a little confused at the question.

"That's why you look familiar. I go there too. I think trusting your story on this car is a little easier now." Sally gave him a big smile then stepped back.

"It is a small town. I'm wondering why I didn't recognize you until you said that? Ken, just make me an offer, I'm sure whatever you have in your head will be fine." Bill was a little more comfortable at this point.

Ken was a little surprised at this added information. "Okay, two things. I want that ladies mailing address. Second, I'm writing you a check for twelve thousand dollars for that car. Basically, one and a half times what you paid for it. Please don't object because I insist. You're a good man Bill. I could see it in your face as you were telling the story about the lady who sold it to you. So let someone do something nice for you. It's well deserved."

"That's just too much. I really appreciate the thought though, I do. But seriously?" Bill was almost in tears.

"Bill, I've been there, right where you are financially with my business and it kept me awake at night, caused stress in my family and all that crud. Please let me do this. My business turned around and I can afford to do this. So, seriously, please allow me to bless you just like you blessed the lady who sold you this car. It would be my honor." Ken stuck out his hand to shake for Bill.

Bill slowly accepted his hand while shaking his head back and forth. "Thank you, Ken, I sincerely appreciate it. That's more than nice of you."

"Again, it's my honor Bill. Our son is going to enjoy this car. I'm sure he will learn how to drive it fast and all that, but he's such a good guy that I doubt seriously he's going to hurt himself in it. So, if you don't mind, let's get the paperwork done so we get home before he does and surprise him with it." Ken had a huge smile on his face as he knew Jimmy was going to have and fit when he laid his eyes on this car.

Back at the restaurant the group was having playful fun and great conversation. They had already chatted about the events yesterday and were looking forward to church on Sunday. Dinner was winding down and the waitress dropped the check off at the table.

Jimmy touched her hand as she began to walk away to get her attention. "What's your name ma'am?"

"Jill, is everything okay?" She had a pleasant face and had served them well. She kept their drinks filled and always had a nice smile while she was at their table.

"Absolutely yes, everything has been wonderful tonight. But my question is if you share your tips, or does this tip go in your pocket?" Jimmy needed to know.

"Well, we have staff in the back that actually put your salads and other things together for us, so we can get your food to you sooner. So, they actually to share with us. They make us look good out here. They deserve everything they get, maybe even more." Jill smiled as she spoke about the staff.

"In that case, can I talk to the manager? I just need to ask him a question. I assure you everything was great tonight. I have no complaints. I'm just curious about something. That's all I assure you." The other three people at the table were wondering what was up.

"I'll bring him right over for you. Just give me a moment, okay?" Jill was really curious at this point. She wanted to hear this.

She was back with the manager in no time flat. "Here is my manager for you sir. His name is Joe."

Joe shook hands with Jimmy. "What can do for you tonight? I trust everything was within your expectations tonight."

All four of them were shaking their heads yes. "Joe everything was fantastic. And it exceeded my expectations by leaps and bounds which is why I asked for you. Jill did an amazing job for us tonight and I would like to give her a tip for herself. One that she can keep for herself, as well as one that would go to the group in the back. Would that be okay?"

Joe looked confused. "So, you want to give a tip on the check that goes to the group, but you want to give a tip to Jill all by herself in addition to that? Is that what you want to do sir?"

"Exactly. That's what I would like to do if it's okay. I don't want to get her in trouble. She's been fantastic tonight." Now everyone had wide eyes, including Jill and Joe.

Joe stuck his hand out for Jimmy to shake. "If there's one of my staff that deserves to be treated like that at this place, it's Jill. By all means sir. That would be really nice of you to recognize her like that. I can't do that in my position. I can only recognize her as employee of the month. All that does is give her a parking spot." Joe was noticeably happy for Jill.

"Okay, stand here for a minute with us if you don't mind." The wad of cash that Ken had given to Jimmy this morning was all one hundred dollar bills. He paid the bill and gave more than a one hundred dollar tip to the group. Then he handed two one hundred dollar bills to Jill. "This is for you Jill. Thanks for everything did for us tonight."

Jill put her hands up to her mouth. Joe's mouth fell open. Jill began to her head no as this was just too much. She was expecting a ten or twenty dollar bill, not one this large. "That's just too much sir. I can't let you do that." Jill was astonished. No one had ever been this generous before.

"First of all, my name is Jimmy, not sir. And Jill, you deserve every bit of this. I insist. Take it." Zane and the girls were just as astonished as Jill and Joe were. "My dad gave me this wad of cash today and told me to leave a big tip for the person who waited on us tonight. However, I would be doing this even if he hadn't told me that because the service you gave us here tonight has been off the chart great. You deserve this Jill, I promise. Please let me do for you exactly what you have done for us. Please."

Joe put his arm around Jill's shoulders. "Jimmy, I didn't see a thing. Jill put that in your pocket and say thank you."

Jill took the bills and stuck it in her pocket. "Thank you, Jimmy, that's more than generous of you. I sincerely appreciate this."

Rebecca spoke first, "You deserve it, Jill. Maybe even more. If I had any cash on me right now, I would add to it."

"Thank you, guys. You were so easy to deal with tonight. I hope that you all came back soon." She had the biggest smile on her face.

Zane looked at Joe. "Does Jill have Sunday off Joe? If so, we would like to invite her to church with us on Sunday in Southwind. We have a couple of Evangelists visiting our church right now and they are just fantastic. They're funny and they're preaching style is one I've never heard before. It's fun to listen to them. So, all of us here would be honored if you would come and be our guests and sit with us."

Joe's eyes got big. "Yes, she has the day off. In fact, if you don't mind, I would like to invite myself along if that's okay. What do you say Jill? Do you want to go?"

"Joe I'm scheduled to work Sunday." Jill looked confused.

"Jill, I work you like a rented mule around here and you deserve a day off. So now your schedule has been changed." Joe had a big smile on his face now.

Jill grabbed Jimmy's arm. "I would love to come to church with you all. I've been thinking of raising my little girl in church, but I haven't put too much thought to it. She's only six months old and there's no better time to train her, right? So yes, I would love to come. What time does it start?"

Betty Jo stood up and gave Jill and Joe a hug. "It starts at ten. It's the big Christian church on the main road in town, you can't miss it. Oh, and we have a nursery for your baby. That way you can sit and enjoy the service."

Jill looked at Joe, "Can I ride with you Joe? I don't have a car anymore since my boyfriend took it with him when he ran off."

"It'll be my pleasure, Jill. I'll be prompt, I promise." Joe patted her on the back.

"Well guys, thank you for that generous tip. I sincerely appreciate, but I need to get to my other tables if you'll excuse me. And I'll be seeing you Sunday morning at ten, promptly." Jill smiled and waved as she walked away.

Joe needed to get back to work as well. "It was a pleasure meeting all of you tonight. I look forward to seeing you Sunday morning." They all shook hands and Joe headed back to his office.

On the way back home, Jimmy made sure to tell everyone to be at his house a little before ten in the morning. Ken was going to buy Jimmy a car in the morning, and he was more than a little excited, and everyone already knew it. "I feel like a five year old going to the circus right now. I don't even know if I'm going to be able to sleep tonight."

Betty Joe ruffled his hair. "My cute little five year old. Suddenly I feel like I'm dating a little boy." Everyone laughed. "I am so proud of you Jimmy. That tip you left was more than generous. That was really nice of you."

Zane was beginning to feel that adult thing again. "I'm telling you buddy; it sure makes a person glad to be your friend. Jill's face lit up light a Christmas tree when you handed her that money. It actually warmed my heart as well." Zane reached his hand out to shake Jimmy' hand, which he did without hesitation.

Rebecca was just as proud of Jimmy. "Not only that, but I was also thinking of asking Betty Jo if she wanted to trade boyfriends for about five seconds. But I think my guy is as good a guy as you are Jimmy." Rebecca reached over and gave Zane a playful push on his shoulder.

Jimmy was shaking his head. "Alright you two. You're laying it on pretty thick. I actually think that all four of us would have done the exact same thing if the circumstances were different. We all qualify as pretty decent people. And it's me who thinks I'm the lucky one in the bunch to call all three of you, my friends. I think the same way about all of you. All three of you make me a better person just being in your presence and I love you all more than words can tell. I'm not kidding. Also, Rebecca, you're out of luck trying to get me to switch with you and Betty Jo. I'm in love with her and no one else. So there. Neener neener." Jimmy called for a group hug, and they all obliged and shared a good laugh.

Zane started the car. "Well then, I better get us all home at a decent hour so we can all make it over to Jimmy's for his big day in the morning. Betty Jo, I'll drop by and pick you up, okay?"

"Perfect! I'll be ready and waiting on you when you get there. But you better be prompt." Betty Jo said with a laugh, which caused the others to join in.

Saturday morning finally arrived after a restless night's sleep for Jimmy. He went downstairs when he heard someone in the kitchen. He saw his mom making breakfast and headed straight for the coffee pot.

This surprised Sally. "Since when did you start drinking coffee Jimmy?"

"Oh wow. Let me think." Jimmy stared at the floor for a moment. "I guess it was right after Zane got his car. He had been drinking it for a while already and wanted to stop and get a cup one day. So, I guess about three years or so. I don't drink it every day like he drinks it, but here and there. Since I didn't sleep well last night, I'll be drinking every drop I can get my hands on today. So don't lay your cup down if you want to drink that coffee, because I'll steal it from you?"

Sally held up her cup. "Cheers to my new coffee buddy." They bumped their cups lightly and giggled. Sally was just finishing breakfast when Ken came into the kitchen and gave her a kiss on top her head. "I thought I smelled coffee. But is that steak and lobster over there? I could eat two steaks and three lobster tails before taking a breath this morning."

"Well, it's something like that. You're getting a cheese omelet with sausage patties. So close, but no cigar for you buddy." She put his plate down in front of him.

"She's a cruel woman Lord. What did I do to deserve this kind of person in my life? She is kinda pretty though." Ken laughed and Sally slapped his shoulder. He reached his fist over and gave Jimmy some knuckles.

"You two get out of my house! I will not have strangers in my house, and I don't know who you guys are right now." Sally was trying hard not to smile but couldn't hide it.

Ken grabbed his plate coffee cup and headed toward the door. "I ain't leaving without my food or coffee." Jimmy was right behind him with his coffee cup. "Me either you mean ol' woman." He just started laughing as hard as could. He had never talked to his mom like that.

"Oh No Jimmy! I dropped your breakfast in the trash on purpose! How does that feel you little dirt bag?" Now Sally was laughing.

Ken turned his back on Jimmy and started eating his food really fast. "You ain't getting my food…. you little dirt bag!"

"Alright you. I'm tellin' my mommy on you." He was still laughing. "It probably wasn't fit to eat anyways."

Sally threw a sausage patty at him. Jimmy caught and ate it. Now they were all having a really good laugh. "Maybe I was wrong." Jimmy could barely talk he was laughing so hard.

Sally went around the table and had a group hug with these two. Sally kissed Ken's cheek while Jimmy kissed his forehead and giggled.

Sally said, "I think there's going to be a lot of laughter in this house from now on. Thank you for that Ken. Jimmy and I did have some minor doubts about your salvation, but we also noticed the change in your behavior. That's why they were minor doubts. Both of us know, for a fact, that the only one that change a person like this is God Himself."

At that point Jimmy's friends were knocking on the door. Jimmy opened the door and let them inside. Ken looked at Sally and gave her a nod.

"Well, let's not waste any time, Sally. Let's get this show on the road." Ken was walking towards the door. Jimmy echoed his thought.

Sally shut the front door behind her. As soon as it shut, she gasped. "Oh shoot! I just locked our keys in the house, Ken.

Jimmy's shoulders fell and he let out a lough sigh.

"Let me try the garage door and see if it might be unlocked." Ken opened the door and there sat that beautiful green car he and Sally got to drive home the night before.

Jimmy noticed the car, but it didn't mean anything to him. Sally came over and put some keys in his hand. "Why don't you take your friends for a ride in that pretty car?" Jimmy stood there with his mouth wide open.

Zane was really excited. "Whoa! An early fastback. Oh my! Wow!" He might have been the most surprised one of the bunch.

Betty Jo grabbed Jimmy's hand. "Why don't we go look at it Jimmy?"

"Oh yeah. I guess I should since it's mine." He looked at Ken. "Are you sure you want me to have such a beautiful car Ken? I was expecting to get a little four door sedan or something. And I would have been more than pleased with it. But this is too much Ken. I don't know if I can accept this, it's too much."

"Too late you little dirt bag. It's already registered in your name. I had the salesman do that when we bought it last night." Ken was wearing a huge smile. Jimmy's reaction was just what he hoping for.

Zane was already in front of the car and opened the hood. Jimmy got there about the time the hood was up and noticed a few chrome pieces. "Is this a show car Ken? This motor is kinda fancy." Jimmy was even more amazed than Ken was before.

"No, the lady's husband a just put that chrome on there for looks as far as I know. I don't think he did anything to the motor other than that. When I drove it last night it felt all stock to me. It didn't act like it had a super cam or anything on it. It runs great. Although there's a few dings on the interior and some scratches on the paint, this car will last you a while." Ken was really pleased with himself and that he found this car.

Jimmy was standing there shaking his head back and forth. "I don't know what to say Ken. I could say thank you a million times and it wouldn't come close to how thankful I am right now. I didn't even think of anything like this." He stepped over and gave Ken a huge hug and held on for a while. Ken hugged him back and enjoyed every second of it.

"Uh, hey buddy. That little blonde over there is starting to give me some stink eye. I think she's getting jealous." Ken was giggling.

Betty Jo began to point and give Ken stink eye with a big grin on her face. Jimmy let go of Ken and blushed every color of red and purple known to man. "I'll scratch your eyes out mister." Everyone was laughing at this point.

Ken walked to over Betty Jo. "I don't know your name. I'm Ken." He stuck his hand out.

Oh, uh, I'm Betty Jo. Jimmy and I are dating." Betty Jo was caught a little off guard there for a moment and blushed. She grabbed Ken and hugged him. Just not as long as Jimmy did.

Ken went over and greeted Zane with a hug, then met Rebecca and hugged her too.

"Is there anyone else to hug I haven't met yet this morning? I think I like hugging all you all." Ken was wearing that smile he had been wearing all week.

Sally walked over and grabbed him. "My turn husband of mine. Just in case either of these girls get any fancy ideas." Sally was laughing as she said it. "I'll scratch your eyes out!" She said while looking at the girls with a huge smile on her face. Now everyone was laughing.

Jimmy crawled into the front seat of his new shiny green car while he was still laughing. "Okay, let's hit the road. Maybe we'll get lucky, and I won't kill us before we get back."

Everyone else got in and they took off waving out the windows as they went. "How about some coffee? I only had about half a cup earlier and I would love some more."

They all agreed and headed to the coffee shop to partake of their favorite morning beverages.

Chapter 8

Sunday Service

Pastor Brown was up early almost too excited to sleep in anticipation of today's' service. He was enjoying a cup of cup coffee as Sister brown came into the kitchen. Sister Brown gave him a kiss on his cheek and started breakfast.

Across town Larry was in the kitchen visiting with Sister Wilson, telling funny stories of past church experiences. Bob was in the study going over his notes and making some last minute changes. He had a sense that God was ready to get back to work in Southwind.

Zane was in the bathroom primping when Laura came banging on the door telling him to get out, it was her turn to primp.

Rebecca was putting on her new dress she had bought when her and Carla had gone shopping this past week. She knew Zane was going to like it because it was his favorite color, green.

Betty Jo was in the living room at home trying to get her mom to go with her today like she had promised. But Louise was trying to back out of it.

"Mom, you told me you want to go and see if this was some weird hocus pocus thing. How are you going to be able to protect me if it is without checking it out yourself?" Betty Jo was standing her ground.

Louise shot back, "If it is some sort of weird thing, I'm going to call the papers and TV stations. Okay, I'll go. But I'm not promising to like it."

Betty Jo wasn't going to push her anymore; she was already annoyed at Betty Jo. "Jimmy said he would be here about nine thirty to pick us up in his new car. You should have seen his face mom; he was totally dumbstruck. He couldn't believe it was his. He finally walked over and took a look around it, then here came that smile of his. I'm sure he'll be wearing it again this morning."

"I know he'll be wearing that smile of his. He's always got that smile going. It almost makes a mom wonder what he's up to." Louise was teasing her.

"Good grief mom! Why would you ever say something like! You know he's not that kind of guy. And I'm not that kind of girl either. Shame on you!" Poor Betty Jo didn't like that statement at all.

Louise looked at Betty Jo with a big smile, "Gotcha."

Betty Jo's mouth fell wide open. "Why you evil old woman you!" And she started laughing,

"Listen sweety. I trust you and I trust Jimmy as much as a person can trust anyone. You have a good man there Betty Jo. I couldn't have hand picked a better man for my daughter. He has proven more than once in the past year or so how honest and honorable he is to me. In fact, if you two ever break up I still want to be his friend. What do you think about that, coming from an evil old woman?" Louise was still wearing that gotcha smile.

Betty Jo raised her eyebrows. "You know mom, one of these days I'm just going to push you out in front of traffic. That's what I think." Now they were both laughing.

Louise grabbed her and gave her a big hug. "I love you sweetheart."

"I love you too mom." Betty Jo was still smiling but shaking her head back and forth.

The Pastors and the two Evangelists arrived at the church parking lot about the same time. They all filed into the office and Sister Brown went in to start the coffee.

So, what's up with you two this morning?" Pastor Brown asked.

Larry pointed at Bob since he was preaching this morning.

"Well Parson, I've been with God all morning and let me tell you something interesting. Now God didn't tell me to say this to you, but something *interesting* is happening here. You and your lovely bride have hung on in this town far longer than most would have. And for that my friend, you are beginning to see the harvest of your sowing. Everyone knows you here in town. And they love you two for who you are. Last week we had such an awesome service and moving of the Holy Spirit and it's going to continue today as well. The Holy Spirit will show up again today and do what He sees fit to do. Lives are going to change for the better. Marriages are going to be healed. Friendships repaired. And lots of other fun stuff.

"As for my sermon today, I'm not going to say much of anything these people haven't heard before. I mean seriously, if they've been going to church as long as we have, they've heard it all. But here's the kicker, each time they hear it God does something different in them. Of course, the new people they're going to have their eyes opened and see things differently than they have. All of that is what I love about what we do, stand back watch God work. He uses our mouths to get them to listen, but He does what He wants to do and it's an all-out blast to watch Him do it. Counseling, therapy, psychotropic pills, elixirs, surgery, make up, illicit drugs, relationships, and everything else we can think of, can't match anything our God can do, or fill that void we all feel.

"Who else do you know that can make a tree? Or dirt? Or a blue eyeball? I mean, look at Larry! Nobody deserves to be that ugly, but there he is." Everyone started laughing including Larry. "Ain't no one can do what our God *has* done or *is* going to do. Other than that, it's been kind of boring around here." Bob was wearing a huge smile.

"Boring or not I'm ready to see how big this harvest is brother. There are so many people in this town that are just about ready to pray and get saved. I'm *always* inviting people when I see them around town, and they just put me off. But what they don't know is that I've been praying for years for this town and a lot of individuals. They can't outrun prayers for their souls, it just doesn't matter how fast or far they run. So, Bob, you get up there tell them what they've heard before and let God do His thing just like you said. And we'll stand on the side of the room and watch Him do it with smiles on our faces."

Larry spoke up. "Pastor, I think I'll sit in on the youth class this morning. I've kind of grown fond of a few of those kids and I'm wondering if any of them are ready to rise to the top, so to speak. Mike has done a great job with them, and I wonder who is going to be giving him a hand as that group gets bigger. It seems like it's already doubled in size, if not bigger than that."

Pastor Brown was all for that. Maybe Larry could help encourage some of the kids along in that area. "That sounds great Larry. In fact, Bob, would you mind taking over the adult class this morning and just basically telling them some stories about some of the things you and Larry have seen at some of the other churches you've been to?"

"That sounds like fun Pastor. I would love to do that." Bob said.

With that the four of them walked out into the sanctuary and knelt down on the steps leading up to the platform and began to pray for the morning service.

Soon people began arriving and visiting started before Sunday school got started. Lots of laughs and hugs and big smiles everywhere.

Soon everyone was in their proper rooms and Sunday School began. Bob started the adult class off in prayer and began talking about some of the experiences he and Larry had in times past. Most of all he talked about was how the churches grew and the successes they had on the local community after they had left town. He talked about how souls were saved and some of the miraculous salvation's that had occurred.

Pastor Brown was enjoying the stories when he was suddenly tapped on the shoulder by a man in a Fireman's uniform who wanted to speak to him outside. As they stepped out into the hot desert sun the man introduced himself and the local fire chief, Captain Don Roberts. "I'm here to inform you that you are exceeding the total amount of people that is allowed for your facility. You need to have everyone leave the building and I expect it to be done in the next five minutes." He did not smile or raise his voice. He spoke in matter-of-fact terms without regard for the time needed to carry out his orders.

Pastor Brown didn't hesitate. "And who exactly told you we were exceeding the capacity of this building sir?"

This took Captain Roberts by surprise. He didn't expect or appreciate being challenged on his orders whatsoever. He just expected everyone out of the building in five minutes as he had ordered. "That's none of your business! Just do what I told you to do, times ticking as we speak."

"Sir, if you'll wait just one minute, I'll be right back." The Pastor already knew how to handle this situation.

"You've got thirty seconds and not one second more. I'll be right here." He said.

As Pastor Brown walked away, he was thinking this man had no sense of humor at all. When he came back, he had the Chief of Police with him, Doug Lee. "Don! To what do I owe this unexpected visit today?"

"This church is exceeding the occupancy capacity for its size, and it must be emptied in five minutes Doug. I'll wait here while you folks get the people out of there." Again, he had the same matter-of-fact tone with Doug.

Doug rubbed his chin for a few seconds. "Don, you, and I both know that this church has been here for over one hundred years. It was here when the migration to California was going full speed. It was put here so the travelers would have a nice place to worship God and take a needed break for a few days. Since this church is so old, the city, nor it's fire department, haven't ever given it a seating capacity. So, your demands are simply void of any statute, or law, for that matter. So, your order for us to clear the building is not going to happen. I'm not being disrespectful to you personally or your position as Fire Chief. But since your here, why don't you come inside where it's cool and enjoy the service with us. Seriously, we'd be honored to have you here today. And by all means, please take off that heavy jacket you're wearing and just sit and relax with us. Please?"

Chief Roberts was looking at the ground. As he looked up, he said, "You're right of course Doug. I guess maybe we can work out an occupancy permit another time. But I do have a few men coming over here in a few minutes to board up the place. I don't have their phone number with me to call them and cancel the work order. I also think I'm going to pass on your invitation to attend with you today. I'll wait for the guys out here and tell them to go home when they get here though."

Pastor Brown spoke before Doug could open his mouth. "Chief Roberts, I've invited you over here I don't know how many times and you have always politely turned me down. But you're standing on my doorstep right now. With what we have going at this church right now, it be an all-out shame if you missed out on it.

"Chief, Jesus died for my sins just like He died for yours and Doug's. And you may find this hard believe but there are a lot of people praying for you. Doug and I have long talked about wanting to be a close friend of yours, but so far, you've kept us at an arms distance. So, consider this invitation from one friend to another. If fact, I can see you sweating your brains out. Why don't you let me get you a big glass of ice water while you take that heavy jacket off and relax with us this morning? Seriously, it would be my pleasure to have you here today." Pastor Brown reached out his arm like he was herding Don inside. "In fact, if you would rather have a nice cup of coffee this morning, we have some really good coffee in there for you too."

The chief started walking inside. "I'm not turning down that glass of ice water. My throat is beginning to think I ate sand for breakfast this morning. Doug, Pastor, thank you for being so pleasant and kind in speaking with me today. I honestly thought there was going to be a fist fight. I even had plans to call you Doug and have you and your guys come break it up. I think I like this outcome much better though. Which is totally out of character for me, but I think you both knew that already."

Doug escorted him into the sanctuary where he and his wife, Martha, were sitting. When Doug's wife saw Don standing there, she got a huge smile on her face and jumped up to give him a huge hug. This totally shocked Captain Roberts and he blushed every shade of red.

As he sat down with his new friends, he began to listen to Bob telling a story about a man named Albert.

Albert had lived alone for sixteen years since his wife Emma had passed away. Every day Albert would go to the cemetery and talk to Emma as if she were standing in front of him. He missed her so bad that some days he wondered how he could even make it another day without her.

One day while he was in the middle of his visit, he heard a Preacher speaking not very far away from where he was standing. He was telling the crowd about Heaven. In Heaven there was no more pain, no sickness, no arthritis, or diabetes. Nothing but happiness and joy and spending eternity with our Savior Jesus.

As the funeral service ended Albert walked over and talked to the preacher. He was really curious to see if Emma might be there waiting on him. The preacher, John Lockhart, was reluctant to tell Albert if Emma were in heaven since he had never met her. But from how Albert described Emma, he told him that there might be good a possibility Emma was waiting for him. Albert asked how he could make sure that he could see Emma again in heaven. Pastor Lockhart prayed with Albert for a moment and lead him to accept Christ as his Savior. With tears in his eyes Albert gave Pastor Lockhart the biggest hug he had even been given. A couple of months later Albert died and was buried next to his Emma.

Bob went on to tell what an impact "Father John," had on the two young preachers and the huge influence he had on their young professional lives. Even when things were going wrong, John still had a smile and a grace about him. He seemed to never get rattled about anything. He would say, "What does it matter boys? In the end I'm going to be in heaven with my Lord and nothing can change that. What does it matter if the devil gives me rough ride now and then? He can't take my reward away from me unless I let him. And guess what? I ain't gonna let him!" Which he followed with a big boisterous baritone laugh of his.

As they were saying their good-byes at the car the day the two preachers left town, Father John told them he would see them Glory and introduce them to Albert and Emma.

Captain Roberts got a tear in his eye and felt like he going to breakout crying. He hadn't done that in years, but he was tougher than that.

In the Teen class, Mike and Larry were having a wonderful time telling the kids more about Jesus. The newer kids were asking so many questions that the lesson was put aside in order to answer them and teach them the basics about God and Jesus, as well as Salvation. These kids seemed to be so excited about what had happened to them. They began telling where and how they accepted Christ as their Savior. Larry and Mike both noticed that a certain group of kids seemed to be involved with most of the stories.

Some of the kids were having a little difficulty understanding it all. Mike told them to keep coming to Sunday School and the Wednesday night youth meetings. He also told them to read their Bibles a lot and not take his word for it about all this stuff.

Some of the kids didn't have Bibles at home. Larry had those who didn't have a Bible to raise their hands. Mike went and got one for them on the spot. Larry announced that he and Bob had agreed to preach every night the coming week and invited all of them to come.

Sunday School was over way too soon and it was time to head toward to sanctuary. Larry noticed the truck with a load of plywood in it and asked Pastor Brown about it. Pastor Brown just told him the guys decided to take the day off and enjoy the service today. Larry made is way down to talk to Bob before things began.

As he caught up with Bob and bumped fists, Larry started encouraging his friend much like they often did with each other. "You know buddy, the healing of this church happened last week. So today is going to be a day of calling. We're going to see new preachers and missionaries, counselors, and the like. So don't hold back, let it all out. You're going to do great like you always do."

Bob smiled. "You know Larry, today is a little different. I always know what I'm going to do, how I'm going to do it and pretty much where it will lead. But today, all I know is how it's going to start. God has got a plan that I don't know about today. You know what that means don't you. This is going to be fun to watch brother" He gave Larry a big hug and made his way up the steps to join Pastor Brown with a huge smile face.

The song service began soon, and Tom was doing his best as he did every Sunday. He led the most anointed songs this week. Why they were more anointed today unlike other days was up to God. Even the musicians sounded better today which was hard to do. All of them were fantastic in their talents. A lot of hands were in the air and tears were flowing as the congregation was getting an extra big blessing. It was an excellent time to be praising our Lord and Savior.

As the song service ended, Pastor Brown made a few quick announcements. He told the congregation that they were beginning a weeklong revival starting Monday night and try to stay out of the bars those nights. He promised to do his best as well. Then he introduced Bob and let him go.

As Bob took his place behind the podium, he asked the musicians to stay in their places as he wouldn't be long this morning. He promised to get things started, then get out of God's way and let Him do what needed to be done. Whatever that meant.

He told everyone to open their Bibles to John 3:16 as he was going to continue with Larry's message from last week. As everyone was turning in their Bibles, Bob asked Pastor Brown if he would stand and read it for him. Pastor Brown obliged him and took his seat. Bob took a big breath and began, "If any of you have spent any time in church during your life, you more than likely memorized that verse years ago. One of the things that happens over the years of attending church is the fact that this verse loses its meaning to us almost entirely. That verse has become a cliche,' if you will, we almost don't even hear it when it's quoted or read aloud in our presence. It's just a bunch words spoken in a certain order that sound familiar but have no meaning any longer and that's an all-out shame.

"The fact that the maker of this universe and everything it, God Almighty, cloned Himself and came down here to sacrifice Himself on our behalf has no meaning. We go to church wearing our smiles every Sunday, sing songs and listen sometimes while we're not on our phones, then go home to our real lives. Monday morning, we go back to being ourselves, which may or may not be in line with God's word. We don't think we're hypocrites, but we don't have the warm fuzzies anymore that we once had in our lives. We don't share the compassion for our fellowman that Jesus has for them. We don't even have that smile that Jesus wears.

"Some of it's our fault that we don't look like Jesus does at the world. We watch the news on TV, listen to it on the radio in the car. We read even more on the internet, and we get caught up in that negative stuff. Before you know it, you're up to your neck in the muck screaming for help.

"This Bible is not a negative book. None of these books are negative in nature. They all point us towards God, to Jesus, towards the Holy Spirit. The three most powerful beings ever to exist.

"If we read that Bible and take it to heart, really pour our lives into it and live the way it instructs us to, then we can make it to Heaven when it's our time and enjoy the fruits of God.

"Listen, I know this has been harsh and I've hit you right between the eyes with my words. Some of you are ready to head for the back door to save yourselves. Give me just a few more minutes, I'm almost done then God's going to take it from there. Is that okay? Just a few more minutes?" He got a small response, but it was positive.

"How many of you want to go to Heaven, raise your hands." Almost everyone raised their hands. Some people just don't like to participate with rhetorical type questions. "So, how are you going to get there? Are you to keep that negative attitude you're walking around with now? Are you going to continue to live a life you know isn't worthy of heaven? Or are you going to look towards Jesus and His love to help you get there?

"Let's take a real look at what Jesus did for us. Better yet, let's do this. Everyone in this room has someone we truly love. Maybe even someone we would literally die for. It could be your spouse, your kids, your parents, the list goes on. Well, let's look at that person in a different way this morning. What if that person got a crown of thorns smacked down on their head. There's blood running down their bodies now. Now look at them without any clothes on and being beaten with a whip and punched in the face. Now their body is torn to shreds and they scream out in agony. Wouldn't you want to yell out for that to stop? That person that you love so much is falling beneath the weight of that heavy cross they've been made to carry. Wouldn't you want to step up and carry it for them?

"Now your loved one is being thrown down like a rag doll onto the cross. Some mean looking dude comes over and begins to drive stakes into their hands and feet as they scream in pain. Wouldn't you want to do something to make it stop?

"Okay, now instead of your loved one hanging up there, it's now Jesus. Can you see the love and compassion in his eyes? As much as you wanted for all that to stop, as much as you wanted to trade places with your loved one, Jesus was actually able to step in and take your place. He wore that crown for you. He took that beating for you. He took those spikes for you. Look at His face as He hangs there. Can you see the love and compassion that He has for you this morning?"

Bob stopped talking for a moment and looked over the crowd. He could see that many of the people had tears in their eyes. Some of them looked like a deer in the headlights. Some had their heads bowed and already praying. He turned and gave Tom a nod and the musicians began to play softly.

"All you that need to ask Jesus into your hearts, why don't you just come down to the front and meet me over here on the right side of the platform. Everyone else, these altars are open for you get closer to our God. Please don't leave here without spending some time with God. Please." Bob walked over to the right side of the platform and waited for the people to come forward. He began to get tears in his eyes as he realized almost the entire crowd was standing in front of him.

Chief Larson opened his eyes and was going to invite Captain Roberts to go down and pray, but he was already down there. The crew that was going to board the church up today was making their way down right behind him.

As the two teen couples made their way towards the front, Joe and Jill were following them. As they approached the front, Justin tapped Jimmy on the shoulder and smiled. Steve was there as were most of the kids from the frosty that night. Jimmy turned and saw his mom standing there with Ken and he began to sob out loud. He made his way over to them and hugged them both as tight as he could.

Larry made his way over to Bob and put his arm around his shoulders. At that point Bob began to cry out loud and was basically inconsolable. Larry stepped forward to lead the group in the sinner's prayer.

"Folks, I'll tell you that I've never heard a sermon like that before. In all my years of going to church I've never heard one so in your face and blunt. But look at us now. A crowd the size of Vegas standing here ready to go to heaven. Let's pray. Father, we stand here knowing we don't deserve what you have done for us. But we also stand here asking for one more favor. Forgiveness of our sins.

Repeat after me you, guys. Dear Lord...please forgive me of my sins...wash me clean with Your blood...help me to live a life.... that is pleasing in Your sight and Your ways...Amen."

Jimmy finally released the hug on Sally and Ken, and they stood and cried together. Jimmy looked over and saw Betty Jo with her mom standing close by with tears and make up running down their faces. He grabbed Betty Jo's elbow and lightly pulled her and Louise towards him and his parents.

Zane was standing in between Dustin and Steve and the crowd of kids from the frosty. Rebecca was right next to him with her hands on a couple of those kid's shoulders. They were going to have to learn a bunch of new names today when this altar call was over, which might take a while from the looks of it.

Nearby Joe and Jill stood hugging each other and crying as well. Today turned into an all-out cryfest for the entire church it seemed. Jill had reached over and hugged Joe just because she needed someone to hug, and it just happened to be him. Joe hugged her back without hesitation. He loved this girl like she was his own daughter.

Some other people had a little group hug going on. As Larry looked over at them, he realized it was Doctor Bob, Cindy, and Roxanne. He tapped Bob to get his attention and pointed them out. Bob got a surprised look on his face and waved at them. "We'll see you guys in the back in a few minutes. Please don't leave without saying hi." Doctor Bob gave him a thumbs up and turned back to the ladies.

Larry continued to stand with his arm around Bob's shoulder as they watched God do His work with the folks standing in the front of the church. It still amazed these two preachers to stand back and watch this happen. In times past they would go down and pray with people, but as time went on, they found that wasn't needed. God did everything He wanted to do without their help most of the time.

"Stay as long as you like or as long as it takes. Bob and I as well as the Pastor want to meet everyone before you leave. I'm quite sure some of you have some questions for us, so we'll stick around as long as we need to today. We'll talk to you in a few minutes, but seriously folks, spend some time on your knees." With that, he and Bob headed towards the back of the church and Pastor Brown met them there when he finished his time with God.

"Wow! What a response to an alter call. These people were hungry to get closer to God today. Just Wow! Thank you, Bob, for facilitating this. I know all that you did is tell us what God laid on your heart. Personally, I was wondering if people were going a be offended at your delivery, but apparently, it was exactly what they needed." Pastor Brown was smiling as he spoke.

Bob smiled, "Pastor, I'm not sure if I have ever been so in-your-face before. I do that a lot when I'm kidding and teasing people. But I don't remember ever doing it in the pulpit. Do you Larry?"

"No brother, I don't either. I know at times we've been chatting back and forth and still having difficulty understanding what the other one is trying to say. Then one of us with tell the other to talk like we're only five years old, then we can understand each other. It kinda looks like what happened here today. There was no misunderstanding what you were saying at all. I guess God has to do the same thing to people in order to get done what He wants to get done." Larry was looking in the direction of the alter while he spoke. "There's twenty or thirty people down there right now. They're all going to walk out of here happy people today, no doubt about it."

The three of them stood there for a few minutes just watching the crowd with smiles on their faces. They all knew this was going to continue all week. The Holy Spirit was only getting started at this point. This church and town were going to be a bit different in the coming days and months, all thanks to a group of people who gave themselves entirely to God.

Dr Bob and the nurses were the first ones to meet up with Bob and Larry. It looked like the ladies may have walked in wearing makeup, but it was all gone at this point, with a little bit of black on their chins. Roxanne almost ran Larry over as she rushed to hug him a little too fast. Cindy in turn grabbed and hugged Bob. They two ladies began sobbing as the held onto the preachers as tight as they could. Dr. Bob had tears in his eyes as well. They all stood there until the ladies regained their composure.

They exchanged hugs and remained silent for a moment. Dr. Bob was the only one of the three that could talk, barely. "Guys, I've never had an experience like this before. It was like being wrapped in a warm blanket from the very top of my head clear down to the end of my toes. The girls felt it too. We were just saying that as we were walking over here. It's the most awesome thing I have ever felt. What just happened here guys, cuz I have no idea, but I know I liked it a whole bunch." Cindy and Roxanne nodded in agreement while they wiped their eyes.

Pastor Brown answered the question for all three of them. "That was the Holy Spirit paying you guys a nice little visit. That's what it feels like. And you're right Bob, it's one of the greatest experiences ever when He does that. What makes it even more amazing is that it's not a one-time deal.

"When the climate is ripe for the Holy Spirit, He shows up wherever and whenever that is. I've had Him visit me in my office here at the church. And, of course in the services like this one. I've had visits in my study at home, while driving in my car, even while just sitting somewhere reading my Bible and praying. In fact, one night He woke me up in the middle of the night to calm my anxieties I had about some issue I was dealing with. So, the very fact that you had that experience, is an assurance that if you can follow Christ and keep yourselves close to Christ, you'll have more of those experiences. You're in for a treat guys, I assure you. You met God in a very real way this morning and its life changing to say the least."

Dr. Bob reached over and gave the Pastor a hug. "Why should the girls be the only ones to get a nice hug. I like them too." Everyone chuckled. "I have to tell this to you guys. Since you were in the E.R. the other day and prayed with us, we've been praying for some of the patients that come in and might be in real trouble for doing it. We've seen those people get up and walk out the door. In times past, those same people would have been admitted to the med/surg unit or even the ICU. All three of us know why that's happening too. We got our own personal view when that bullet that fell out of your back pocket that day Larry. When we pray for people, we have no doubt that Jesus is going to touch them in some way. To be honest, not all of them have gotten off the gurney. We still have some people pass away like we have on a regular basis. We know God doesn't heal everyone. Sometimes He heals them in heaven. But the healings are so amazing.

"For instance, just yesterday we had a man come in by ambulance who had a major heart attack. Before we began praying for people the other day, he may not have survived. He was really in bad shape. But yesterday the three of us stood there and said a really quick prayer, and almost immediately his heart rate and respirations began to come around towards normal. That's only one of the many that have happened in just a few days. He went upstairs, but he'll be home in a couple days and not the cemetery. You don't have to convince the three of us God is for real, we get to see it every day right now. I guess today's experience seems to be the icing on the cake perhaps."

Larry grabbed Dr. Bob's shoulder. "That's just a small sample of things to come. Getting a visit from the Holy spirit isn't a one-time experience. It'll happen from now on, sometimes when you're not expecting it even. That goes for all three of you. You're Christians now and you have plugged into God in a great way. You guys just wait and see, it'll happen."

As Larry was speaking a young couple was pushing their way through the crowd to get to the preachers carrying a young child in a car seat. They were breathless as they got to them. "Pastor, Pastor, you're not going to believe this.

I know we don't know each other because this is our first visit here. But God healed our little girl just now. Sarah had a pretty difficult pregnancy, and we had to decide whether or not to end it. But we knew God had given us this baby after years of trying. Anyway, she was born with a deformed skeleton, but other than that she was normal. We've had to carry her everywhere and pay attention to her while she moves around in her walker, so she doesn't tip herself over, which seems to happen for some reason. But while we were down there in the front praying to God, I looked down at the car seat and she wasn't in it. At first, I thought I was imagining something. But after a few seconds I noticed she was standing next to one of the chairs about three rows away wearing the most beautiful smile. I grabbed my wife's arm and pointed, and we both screamed at the same time. My wife started to walk towards her, and she took off running, wanting us to chase her, still wearing that smile. So, we chased her down, picked her up, and hugged her tighter than we ever have and just cried while she laughed." The man was talking so fast it was a little difficult to keep up with what he was saying. But now both of her parents were looking at their little girl shaking their heads. The little girl was giggling and seemed like she was never going to quit either.

Mom put her hands over her face and said she felt like she was going to pass out. Billy Warren was standing behind the couple, grabbed a chair, and got it behind her just as she began to wobble. Dad got on his knees and held mom's hand for a few minutes. The three preachers reached their hands over and began to pray. As they did the Holy Spirit began to fall again. Larry looked at Bob with wide eyes, "Here we go again buddy!" Bob stood up, raised his hands, and shouted, "HALLELUJAH!" He let it go for an entire breath. "PRAISE YOUR NAME FATHER! WE LOVE YOU JESUS!" Then he stood there clapping his hands.

The crowd of people around the preachers began to raise their hands and praise God with raucous voices. The two nurses fell to their knees and began to openly sob as the Lord began to bless everyone all over again.

The praising and worship continued for a little bit while the little girl danced and ran around everyone's legs, letting out cute little squeals. As things began to die down her parents were able to corral her and pick her up.

Pastor Brown reached over and tickled her cheek as she gave him a huge smile. "What are your names folks? I don't think I've seen you here before.

"We're Louis and Leona Campbell and this is our little girl Kimberlyn, or Kimmy, Kim, Little booger, whatever seems right at the time. Of course, I'm Louis and this our first time here Pastor. We just moved to town and are looking for a church. I'm pretty sure we found it today. Kimmy here is only fifteen months old. The Doctor told us she would never walk because the bones in her legs were not growing correctly, which was having an impact on the muscles not being able to grow correctly, so her balance and strength weren't enough for her to walk. They may have been right at the time, but not anymore, they ain't, Praise God." Louis and Leona were wearing the biggest smiles that Pastor had seen in a long time.

Kimmy was enjoying all of the attention. She was dancing around with a huge smile. The hugs seemed to edge her on even more. "Louis, we have to get home and make a lot of phone calls today to let everyone know what happened here. I hate breaking this up though. But I'm in a hurry to let our doubting family know what happened here today. Most of our family is agnostic and they haven't held back on what they think of a god that would allow this to happen. Now we can brag on our God and their god can take a hike. Who knows, maybe we can get them to come up here for at least one service this week."

"Ooh! That's a good one." Bob said. "Well, this crowd is really growing, and we have more people to meet, but I would love to talk to you tonight or tomorrow if that's possible. I want to hear this entire story."

Larry and Pastor Brown agreed and said as much. Kimmy gave everyone a big fat sloppy kiss and the family left with wet faces and big smiles.

Billy and Helen Warren were right behind the Campbell's and started hugging the three preachers. "Boys, I've never heard preaching like this before, but it hits the spot." Billy was looking down and shaking his head a little. "I feel like I just grew into a giant spiritually. I don't know how else to put it, but this is good stuff. Even the worship songs and music seemed totally different today, even though we sing those songs all the time. But that's neither here nor there. I know you three are really busy right now, so we're just going to get out of your way. Pastor, I'll be by this week for a visit. In fact, I might even bring some lunch for the four of us. Love you guys." Billy waved as he and Helen walked out the door.

As the ministers were greeting everyone as they filed by them in the foyer, Jimmy had a thought and wanted to share with Ken. It took him a few minutes to find him and his mom through the crowd, but when he did, he grabbed Betty Jo's hand and started their way.

"Hey Pops!" Jimmy started laughing when he said it.

Ken raised his eyebrows and gave Jimmy a quizzical look. "It's Pops now, is it? I guess it could be a lot worse." He reached over and messed up Jimmy's hair like a real dad would have done.

Sally, Ken, Betty Jo, and Jimmy, all gave each other hugs, but Jimmy was itching to ask Ken a question. "Ken, I just had a thought a moment ago and I like it a lot. But I need your permission to walk it through."

"Okay, what is it, Jim?" Ken was genuinely astonished but happy at the same time that Jimmy would approach him like this.

Jimmy was nervous, but he proceeded on. "I haven't had a chance to tell you all about our date the other night. But our waitress and her boss came this this morning at our invitation. Jill's boss, Joe had to drive Jill because her boyfriend left with her car and never came back. Ken, she has a small daughter and leaves her home with her roommate when she's at work. She has to ask people to take her to the grocery store and Doctors appointments for that little girl. I want to buy that car from you and give it to Jill if that's all right with you. At least we know that car will be going to a good place and really be a blessing to them. Ken, her life is really hard right now and according to Joe, she never complains and is always wearing a smile, regardless of her circumstances. My heart goes out to her, and I want to help her. That's all. What do you think?"

Ken grabbed Jimmy and pulled him really tight to him and hugged him like he was own son. He even got a little teary eyed while he was hugging him. "Jim, save that money and give her that car. That thought you're having right now is absolutely perfect. I don't need any money from that car, so let it bless someone who could really use a blessing. If it's really on its last legs, let's get it fixed for her too. Do you know where they're at right now?"

Jimmy looked around and found Jill and Joe talking with Zane and Rebecca just a couple feet away. He was able to reach over and grab Zane's arm to get his attention. "Hey, you guys, come over here for a minute I want to introduce you to my mom and dad." That got both Sally's and Ken's attention when Jimmy called Ken "dad."

Everyone shook hands and smiled at each other then Jimmy looked right at Jill. "Remember the other night Jill when you told us that you didn't have a car? Well, we have an answer for that. We have a car in front of our house that we want to give to you. A gift from my dad, Ken."

Jill immediate began to cry and covered her face with her hands. Rebecca reached over and gave Ken a huge hug and told him "Thank you." Joe had tears in his eyes when reached over and shook Ken's hand. Jill made her way over to Ken and hugged him as she continued to cry. Ken kissed her on top of her head. He was really uncomfortable with this, as he wasn't used to this type of affection from anyone. Hugging Sally was natural to him, but hugging anyone else was a foreign concept.

Finally, Ken couldn't take this any longer. "Okay, okay you guys. This was Jim's idea, and he should get all the hugs and stuff. Really, it's the truth. So go hug on him, lick him, kick his knee whatever it is you kids do these days and have fun doing it." He was smiling while he was talking.

Immediately, Jill, Rebecca, Betty Jo, and Zane grabbed Jimmy and gave him a big group hug. Zane, not to be outdone, licked his cheek, which made everyone laugh. Jimmy looked at him and told him, "Do it again Zane, do it again," so Zane made it long and wet. Now everyone was belly laughing. The three preachers were laughing right along with them. Poor Jimmy is now wiping his face on Kens jacket because he started this whole thing.

As they were all walking outside, Don and his crew, as well as Doug and Martha were walking up to say good-bye. Pastor Brown stuck his hand out to Captain Roberts. "How did you enjoy the service, Captain. It was a great pleasure having you here."

The captain shook Pastor Brown's hand as the tears began to run down his face again, to the point he wasn't able to talk. Doug reached his arms around his shoulders. After a couple of minutes, the captain was able to speak through his tears. "Pastor, I am not a well-spoken person. I don't have the right words to tell you how I feel right now. I know that I feel like I only weigh two pounds right now. The world has left my shoulders. Looking at you right now I actually feel love for you." He began to cry again. "I can't remember feeling love at any time in my life, even when I was married. I didn't really feel love for my wives. In fact, now that I'm standing here thinking about it, I can't believe how miserable of person I've been my entire life. I thought people who felt love were weak and no good for anything. And now I'm really feeling it. I mean I love everybody and everything right now and that's never happened to me before. I might even love anchovies for the first time too." Everyone chuckled. "I'm pretty sure I would have never said anything humorous to anyone before I walked in here today. I don't even know how to act."

Pastor Brown had as big smile on his face as he had ever worn before. "Don, you had a personal experience with God Almighty today and what you're feeling right now is the result of that. If everyone in the world could ever have the same experience you're having right now, there wouldn't be any more sinners anywhere. I'm fairly sure this might be the best thing that's ever happened to you in your entire life, isn't it?"

Don started shaking his head up and down. "Pastor you are so right about that. But even that seems like an understatement right now."

"You're absolutely right Don. I don't think the English language has words that can describe how awesome an experience this is. But it's always the bestest feeling in the world when a person gets saved. Ain't no doubt about it. As us Preachers like to say, it's better felt than telt. End of discussion.

Doug spoke up, "Pastor, I promised Don and his crew a steak lunch. I think we're going to be having a fun conversation in a few minutes. I promise to do my best to explain things and answer questions. But if I get stumped, which is likely to happen, we will be bringing it to your attention tomorrow night, okay?"

"I've got a better idea." Pastor Brown offered, "Let's just get together about six o'clock before service starts tomorrow. I want to hear about this conversation anyways and then we can answer any questions at that point. Can we do that?"

Everyone shook their heads in agreement, and it was settled, so off the gentlemen went to lunch and meet with the Pastor another day.

Chapter 9

Sunday's Afterglow

Sally and Ken had to stop by the store for a few groceries before going home today. As they pulled up in front of the store Ken looked at the entrance. He watched two of the employees on their break walk away when they noticed him. Ken lowered his head and let out a big sigh. "Well, Sally, let's go do this. I hope they're in a generous mood and accept my humble apologies. But we won't know until we walk in there."

Sally leaned over and kissed his cheek. "It's going to okay Ken. Do your apologizing and let's see what happens. These are really nice people here. It's going to be a pleasant experience I bet." With that they walked hand in hand into the store.

As they walked in, they noticed no one would make eye contact with them. One elderly woman walked out leaving an entire basket full of groceries behind. She must have been there quite a while with all those groceries in the basket.

Soon they were by the checkout counter. Ken looked at the girl standing there and saw an unfriendly face. "Miss, can I please talk to your manager?"

The girl paged the manager and let out a sarcastic sigh. While they waited, Ken stuck his hand out in her direction. "Miss, I owe you an apology the size of the Pacific Ocean. I am terribly sorry for the behavior I have exhibited in here. No one deserves to be treated the way I have treated all of you guys that work here. I would totally understand if you didn't accept my apology, but I assure you that it's very sincere."

The girl shook his hand with total bewilderment on her face. "Is this a joke? Are you okay Ken? This is very strange."

Ken was smiling as he answered her questions. "No ma'am this is not a joke. I'm feeling great and as for what is going in here, that's a bit of a story. But the short version is that I have given my life to Christ, and I don't even know how to tell you about the change it's made in me. As you know, I was just a miserable man who hated everyone and everything. That's no longer the case. Look at me, I'm smiling today, and I can't begin to tell you the level of remorse I feel for how I have treated all of you. I am so, so sorry."

"Well Ken," the girl began, "that smile tells me that you're telling the truth, so your apology is easy to accept. But if you are indeed a Christian, I want to hug your neck." With that she moved forward and pulled Ken toward her. Ken began to weep as soon as they embraced. The girl told him "Those tears aren't necessary Ken. We have been praying for you for years now. So, let's just make those happy tears."

The manager was standing behind Ken during his entire apology. After the hug was finished and Ken had regained his composure, he asked, "Ken, did I hear correctly when you said you're now a Christian?"

"Yes sir, that's what I said." Ken replied.

The manager had a huge smile on his face while he spoke. "Ken my name is David, and this is Kelly that you've been hugging. She's telling you the truth that we have been praying for you for a quite a while now. It's so good to see you walk in here with a smile and not acting like you used to. But now I know why that's the case. Welcome to the family Ken, you're going to really enjoy your new Christian life."

"I can assure you that I already am enjoying it a lot. What I've realized the most is how light I feel. I'm not bogged down with all that mess, or whatever you call it, anymore. Makes it easy for a guy to smile a lot." Ken chuckled.

Sally had already gone around the store and got what they needed. Now she was back at the checkout counter. After Ken finished his chuckle Sally said, "It's so nice to hear that little laugh again. I have the husband I married again. He really is a nice man and really easy to love."

Ken had a thought. "Hey, can you ring those groceries up that lady left over there. I want to pay for them. I just don't know how to get them to her house."

David smiled. "That was my mother, I'll take them to her later today. Just wait till I tell her about this. She's gonna jump and down I'm telling ya. She's the one who told us to start to praying for you."

"I don't even how to say thank you for that. But please pass my many thanks and kiss her all over her face for me." Ken let out a big laugh.

"Oh, she'll like that. Getting kisses from a good looking man after all the years since my dad's been gone. She might want to kiss you back." Now David was laughing and everyone joined him.

"I would welcome a kiss on my cheek, but she's getting more than one when I see her next. Thank you isn't a sufficient word for what she started. Thank you all of praying for me. I know there were more than just your group and I owe them a thousand thank you's as well. I didn't know people could be this happy. I'm not even kidding. I was a pretty happy guy before I went all sour on everyone, but this is over the top. I'll probably die with a smile at this point." Ken was smiling and shaking his head back and forth as he spoke.

With all the thank you's and you're welcomes completed, Ken and Sally headed home, with Sally snuggled up and against Ken in the car.

Over at Jimmy's house, he had given Jill the keys to the car, and she was still in tears. "This car is way too nice to be a gift. I can't accept it, Jimmy. Thank you, anyway, but it's just too much."

"Oh, no you don't. Take a look at that car I drove to church and back today. Ken bought that for me yesterday. Now *that*, is over the top. This is just a car. So just get yourself in there before Zane starts licking your face." Jimmy chuckled as Zane started walking in Jill's direction. Now everyone was laughing.

Jill yelled, "I give up, uncle, uncle, uncle!!" She gave everyone a huge hug and said thanks. The last hug was for Zane who licked her face anyway. "Oh, my good heavens, you guys are a lot of fun. I will definitely see you tomorrow night. I'll bring my baby with me so you guys can lick her all over and stuff like that too." Then she drove off waving out the window and smiling as big as she could.

Joe stood there shaking his head. "I don't even know what to say to you guys. What a gift! And you guys are so much fun to be around. I'm so glad you came in other night. I knew you guys were nice, but this over the top. Anyway, I've got to get the restaurant and check on things. I doubt I can make it tonight, but I'll be there every night this week that I can. Jill has the week off with pay, but she doesn't know that yet. That way she can come out every night she wants to. Man, I love you guys." He gave everyone a hug before he left.

The group was left standing outside Jimmy's house with big smiles on their face. Zane announced he wasn't done licking faces, and they all scattered as fast as they could go. The fun wasn't finished yet for these kids.

Over at the restaurant the Chief of Police and the Fire Chief were laughing and having a fun time with the team of guys that had brought the plywood to the church earlier in the day. The Police Chief was enjoying the laugh of the Fire Chief and said as much. "Dan, it's so good to hear you laugh man. I was beginning to think I might never hear that from you."

"To tell you the truth Doug, I never even thought about laughing, or smiling, or anything like that. I was just getting along in life doing what I did. That was my life. I didn't even know how miserable I was until a few nights ago. I went into a bar and struck up a conversation with a guy there. We talked for a while, when he suddenly walked away and call me a miserable so and so. I went home and thought about what he said, and he was obviously correct. Instead of trying to do something about it, I embraced it and got meaner. It's twisted, but I enjoyed making people angry enough to hate may guts. I know now that the devil was using me as his puppet to get you guys at church to hate me too.

"But what I found today was a couple of guys who were able to stand their ground politely. Neither of you pointed your finger in my face, or even yelled at me. But you stated your case and offered me a cool glass of water. Which is exactly what I was wanting at the time. In fact, I was sort of mad at myself for not thinking to bring a cool thermos with me. I'll tell you one thing right now, that's the best glass of water I've ever drank in my life. That glass of water came with Jesus in it." He laughed again and everyone joined him. That whole group was having the time of their lives.

Doug began to ask the group if they had any questions, but he had a thought first. "I know you guys have questions but let me tell you something first. The devil is the biggest liar in the universe, and he's really good at it. He is able to convince us of things that aren't true, he's that good. However, what happened to you all today was the real deal. Every last one of you asked Jesus for forgiveness and He forgave you. Your sins are forgiven, and you are on your way to heaven when your time is up on earth. The devil is going to tell you otherwise. Things like, you're too far gone for Jesus to forgive. He is going to remind you of things that you did in your past and tell you that it's unforgivable. None of that is true. The devil does this to every new Christian.

"So, here's how you stop him from doing that to you. Every time he tells you there's no way you can be a Christian, without delay, ask forgiveness of your sins. There's no limit to how many times you can have your sins forgiven or get saved for that matter. After you pray like that, he'll stop doing that to you. He did it to me when I was a brand new Christian, and they told me about this little trick. It worked for me. In fact, I still do it. I have a bad day sometimes and my attitude can use a little adjustment. The devil will tell me I can't be a Christian and act like that. I immediately ask for forgiveness and ask for an attitude adjustment. Before long I'm smiling again or feeling better and happier than I was before. So now you know how to fight with that stinker, and he fights hard. Keep in mind that this is an all-out war for your very soul and where you're going to spend eternity. The devil absolutely hates your guts and want to drag to hell right next to him. So, when he starts in on you about your past just remind him of his future burning in hell. Now, let me start answering questions for you guys."

Pastor Brown drove home with Sister Brown to get the gourmet lunch started for his new friends. Bob wanted to grab a shower before they came over for some reason. Sister Brown had asked that they bring Sister Wilson along so they could visit.

Larry had a good idea what they were having for lunch when the Pastor said the word "gourmet," but he was kind of hoping he was wrong. Sure enough, as soon as they walked into the Pastor's house he could smell the gourmet tube

144 ~ *Ed Wacaster*

steaks. Also known as hot dogs. What Larry didn't see coming was all the things Sister Brown had chopped up for the hot dogs. She had chopped up onions, tomatoes and put out different kinds of mustard and mayonnaise. Then she had some relish and chopped black olives to boot. How was all that stuff going to fit on a hot dog bun? The he saw the buns coming out of the oven that were the size of a cowboy hat. Lunch was going to be good today. No time to talk, just chow down baby. Pastor Brown prayed over the food, and they sat in silence for a while as they enjoyed today's gourmet lunch.

After enjoying such a great meal, they all retired to the living room to discuss the upcoming week. Larry already had Monday nights sermon ready to go. Bob said he had something he was working on, so after some study and prayer time it would be ready to go. That took care of Tuesday. Suddenly Larry and Bob were looking at each other with a thoughtful look on their faces. "Tag team," they blurted out at the same time. So that took care of Wednesday. After that they couldn't decide what to do, so they just decided to let God do as He saw fit. God seemed to keep these two flying by the seat of their britches most of the time anyway.

Later that afternoon after the teenage boys had taken their girls home, Jimmy, Betty Jo and Louise were sitting in the backyard eating bologna sandwiches. They were talking about the morning church service and Louise was discussing what happened to her.

Louise was shaking her head back and forth. She had never had an experience with God before. She definitely knew it was going to completely enhance her life. However, the happiness she was feeling right now was even greater than the day Betty Jo was born. She cried like a little girl with happiness when they laid that little baby on her chest. But today was so much more than that. It was all consuming down into her entire being.

"I know God made everything. He made this entire universe and everything in it. He is the creator of life itself and now I know Him personally. I know that if I hadn't said that prayer with that preacher this morning, I'd be on my way to hell in a hurry. I had no intention of going to the front of the church until Betty Jo grabbed my arm. At that point I was more than ready. When that guy talked about your heart beating fast, he was talking to me. My heart was beating so fast and hard that it was all I could hear for a couple of minutes. Now Betty Jo has an all new mommy. Maybe I won't be so paranoid around men anymore. Who knows, I may end up as a missionary in Africa and marry a cannibal or something like that." Now she was laughing historically. She was showing her sense of humor she had lost so many years ago. She was wearing a new smile, and she liked it a lot.

Betty Jo was so excited for her mom. "Mom, you have the biggest smile I have ever seen on you. I want a picture of it. Look at me and give it to me." She put her phone up and snapped a quick picture before her mom could even react.

"Well crud, now I'm going to have to buy more lipstick if you're going to be snapping pictures like that all of the time." Louise started laughing again. She was a giddy little girl all of a sudden. "Did I ever tell you guys about how pretty you are?" Both of the kids shook their heads no. "That's because it isn't true." Now everyone was laughing. Louise was going to be just fine.

Jimmy enjoyed Louise's banter. Betty Jo looked over at Jimmy and noticed his gaze was far away from the current laughter. "Hey there. I can see your mind is elsewhere. Which way did you go? If you're still wondering about Ken then your faith shouldn't be in Ken, your faith should be in God. Even Ken isn't too far away that Jesus can't save him. I'm pretty sure you already know that though. So let it go my honey and enjoy yourself. This has been one of the greatest days in my life and I was already a Christian." Jimmy leaned his head over and rested it on Betty Jo's head. "Thank you, sweet lady."

The phone rang and Louise jumped up excited to see who it was. "Jimmy, it's for you and you owe me a quarter young man." Louise still that huge smile on her face.

Jimmy was thinking this must be the last house in America with a land line as he walked in the house. Jimmy picked up the phone and to his surprise it was Ken. "Hey Jim, your mom and I just got home from the store, and we bought a lot of steaks. So why don't you and Betty Jo and Zane and his girlfriend come over here for a nice lunch, dinner, whatever it is at this point. Anyway, they're getting ready to go on the grill any minute now."

"Wow." Jimmy was actually shocked at this. Not in a million years would he have ever thought about a phone call like this from Ken. "That sounds great, but we would be leaving Louise here by herself."

"Who's Louise?" Ken asked.

"Oh, that's Betty Jo's mom. She was at church this morning and she got saved and she is making us laugh a lot over here." Jimmy was wearing a big smile again.

"Well bring her along with you then. I bet your mom would love to get to know her. In fact, is Zane's girlfriend's mom single too? If so bring her over as well, I'll bet the three of them would make for some good company." Ken was enjoying his new salvation and wanted to meet as many Christians as he could.

Jimmy hung up with a smile on his face. He was beginning to realize that Ken did in fact accept Christ as his savior. That being the case, life was going to be completely different now, whatever that meant. He called Zane and told him to grab Rebecca and meet him at his house. He told Zane that Ken was in fact a Christian, but there was a lot more to the story than they could talk about right now. Zane was happy to hear everything Jimmy had to say about Ken and told Jimmy the two of them would be over shortly.

Jimmy walked out on the porch, put his hands on his hips and started talking like a Drill Sergeant. "You two beautiful ladies have been invited to my house for a barbecue. We will be leaving this residence in oh five minutes, drive to my home and partake in said activities and you *will* like it!"

Louise didn't hesitate in her response. She jumped up out of her seat and pointed a finger at Jimmy. "Oh, blow it out your backside there Drill Sergeant! We may go over there and partake, but we refuse to like it! Okay?!" Then she began laughing. Betty Jo was on her knees laughing hysterically before Louise ever finished her sentence. Jimmy was bent over holding his midsection laughing just as hard.

Soon everyone was over at Jimmy's house and hanging out in the backyard. Ken was doing the cooking while the ladies were basically getting things in place. Ken insisted on everything paper and plastic, so Sally didn't have to work so hard in the kitchen. They had bought a few different salads but served them in their plastic containers and put a plastic spoon to serve. The four kids were sitting around the pool with a cool drink enjoying the shade of the big tree.

Ken yelled at everyone that the meat was finished, and they all gathered around the outdoor dining table under the veranda. Ken said the blessing over the food and the meal began. Soon Ken just spoke up, "let me tell you what God has done for me this week." He went on to tell exactly what happened in the car and then how God had done even more amazing things within his heart this morning. He apologized to everyone again for his previous behavior and even asked God to forgive him again. Then he pointed at Louise. "You've been cracking jokes since you got here. Let's hear about your experience today."

Louise smiled and covered her face with her hands for a moment. "Well, all I can tell you guys at this point is that I see the humor in everything. My leg could fall off right now and I would change my name to Ilene and get a job as a car hop at the frosty down the street." Ken spit his soda out his nose as he was laughing so hard, which in turn made everyone else laugh even harder.

It took a while for everyone to gain their composure so Louise could continue. "Well, I guess it kind of started when Betty Jo came home one day and was telling me what was going on with the youth group at the church. She told me there were two new preachers preaching over there and she was really excited about what was happening. I had gone to church when I was a kid because my parents made me go. They would drop me off for Sunday School then go get breakfast and pick me up when it was over. So, I had a decent idea of who God and Jesus are. But I was skeptical about it when she told me only because I'm a little skeptical about everything. I told her I was going to have to check it out and make sure everything was on the up and up. So, she forced me go this morning by telling me she was going to kick my dog. But I don't have a dog.

"So, we get into the sanctuary, and I could feel something almost immediately. I felt really warm, I was a little scared and calm all at the same time. That's the best way I can explain it and I don't know if I'm saying it right. But anyway, the songs were beautiful and really stirred my emotions. I teared up a couple times as I was listening. I didn't know any of the songs so I couldn't sing along. But as soon as the guy started preaching my heart was trying to jump out of my chest. I was at the point where I wanted him to shut up so I could go down to the front and pray. I was finally down in front, and I was saved, saved, saved I'm telling you. I was so happy I just wanted laugh out loud as loud as I could. I knew that would make me look a bit weird, so I sat down on the front bench and bowed my head while I laughed to myself. That's pretty much it in a nutshell. I'm just a happy person again and I'll be that way until I get to Heaven. I bet it'll be more fun when I get there." Louise looked as happy as Betty Jo had ever seen her.

"But as I'm sitting here and listening to you guys talk and noticing how all of you interact with each other, this is totally different. I can tell that all of you actually love each other. You have been saying kind things to each other. Of course, you've been teasing each other too, but it's in good fun. I have laughed more today since I've been here than I have in a long, long time. This is the kind of religion I could get involved with I think."

Jimmy was the first to speak. "Louise this is what Rebecca, and I have been talking about at your house. One of the things I've learned lately, I'm not sure if anyone else caught it, but God doesn't care about a religion. He wants to have a personal relationship with all of us, including you. I know a lot of people who think as long as you're a good person and do kind things, you're going to heaven. They're a pretty good person compared to others and things like that. But on judgment day we won't be compared to other people, we are going to be compared to God and how perfect He is. It tells us that in the New Testament I think, but I'm not sure. The Bible tells us that the only way to get that perfect is to allow Jesus to wash our sins away. That only happens when we ask Jesus to forgive us, like Ken did the other day in his car and Louise did this morning. It really is that simple."

Louise was beginning to get tears in her eyes, but she didn't know why. "Well Jimmy, had it not been for being here in this backyard right now, I would not have believed a thing you said. But I have just seen what you talked about in action, so it's really easy to believe it. But right now, my heart is so happy I think it might break through my chest and I feel like I need to do cartwheels.

The first thing out of Rebecca's mouth was, "I'm sure glad she didn't wear a dress today."

Louise looked over at Sally, "Hey lady, what did you put in that punch?"

Sally responded, "Cartwheel juice." Now everyone was laughing and having an enjoyable time.

Chapter 10

Revival Rages On

Monday morning came around and none too soon for Pastor Brown. He got up and made coffee for him and his bride, which woke her up when the smell of coffee hit the bedroom. She walked into the dining room where her proud hubby was reading his Bible. When she greeted him with, "hey" it startled him, and he jumped in his chair totally surprised.

"Can't a girl get a decent night's sleep around here anymore?" She actually sounded irritated which was very uncommon for her.

"Nope" was the Pastors answer.

Sister Brown started toward the coffee pot whispering to herself. "Why you dirty rotten, low down, good for nothin,' why I aughta` ..."

"Did you say something dear?" The Pastor was looking at his Bible again.

"Oh, yeah, I said what a beautiful morning and thank you for the coffee." She had a sarcastic tone to her voice.

The Pastor didn't hear her sarcasm. "Oh, sweetheart, anything for my lovely Bride. You know I love you."

"I love you too sweety, but it's a good thing I don't have a frying pan in my hand right now." They both laughed and pastor got up and gave her a big hug.

"Dennis I am so excited about the meetings this week. Is that what got you up so early this morning?"

"It sure is honey. I can't wait to see the crowd tonight. I talked to so many pastors this past week about it. A good amount promised to be here, as well as announce it to the people yesterday. But even more than that, with what God has done so far, I'm more anxious to see what He's going to go to this town and the surrounding areas also. I sure hope Captain Roberts hasn't backslid since yesterday." Dennis was choking up as he spoke. "He's one of meanest men I've met and now he's a Christian Rachel. And another thing that boggles my mind is how long we've been in this town with not much success. But now that things are hopping like they are God has shown me that we weren't here just wasting our rime like we thought we were. God does things in His own time and his own calendar, not ours. The encouragement I've gotten these past weeks is so much more than I ever thought about. I'm beginning to learn from these guys. I had no idea how ignorant I was. It's not like I have no idea what I'm doing or how to do it, but this is overwhelming. I guess I had become really comfortable where I was at, but this has been humbling and enlightening at the same time. There isn't an English word to describe what's happening here right now. Wow doesn't do it justice. Mega wow doesn't do it either. Anyway, I like it, and I like it a lot."

Rachel looked at her husband and his tears. "Quit being so hard on yourself Dennis. Maybe you're not as perfect as you thought you were, but you're not as unwise as you're making yourself out to be either. God has shown all of us some things lately and some of it is bigger than we were ready for. We've all learned things about ourselves and how big God really is. We've all been ignorant if you want to use that word. But God has shown Himself to us. Now we know for certain that God is real and all over the place at the same time. He's the Lord of Lords, the King of Kings, the beginning and the end, the author and finisher of our faith. God is all knowing and all supreme, everything to everybody. Have I made my point yet?"

"Yes, you have sweetheart, and I heard you loud and clear. Thank you for not letting me sit on my pity pot for any longer. I was really getting hard on myself there. Thank you. I'm amazed at how much we take God for granted when we start getting cold spiritually. We go through the motions by praying but not as sincerely as we once were. Things become hollow and stagnant for us as we just go through the motions. And it happens to every one of us as we go through life, for a plethora of reasons. It just happens. But once we realize where we are, we get back in touch with God again and our relationship with him becomes so much deeper again, more enjoyable even. Life becomes fun again for us because of those times we spend in the dessert.

"I was going through just such a time when I asked God to do something in this town. It was about two years ago. Do you remember that, Rachel." She shook her head yes. "Well, it took two years but here comes Larry and Bob and they had a huge hand in blowing the top off this circus. Those two have their time with God every day and is they get into the presence of God every morning. I've never seen even one man that focused on God, much less two of them on the same team. Those two are to be learned from and congratulated for their dedication. Without that time alone with God, none of this would be possible. God has really given them a special ministry and I'm kind of jealous of them actually. They both have the energy of a five year old on the playground I'm telling ya. Maybe even a dozen puppies playing in their box. I love those guys and we're going to be friends with them forever." Pastor Brown was getting excited all over again. As he looked over at his beautiful wife he saw her face.

Sister Brown had tears in her eyes again. She looked at him and spoke so sweetly. "This is absolutely awesome sweetheart. How can we be so lucky to have such a powerful force, the God who made everything we've looked at our entire lives, has come to this place out here in the middle of nowhere? I was just thinking of all the people that have been in the alters these past few services and all the healing that's happened. Little Nancy is probably the most noteworthy, but I mean the healing among the families. People hugging and crying and asking forgiveness of each other. Only God could do that on such a large scale like that. Every day now I wonder what miracle He's going to do today and not one day have I been disappointed.

"Remember that incident with the shotgun? That was a huge miracle! Larry's hip wasn't hurt that day, just a little pride maybe. And to beat everything that had just happened, you end up at the hospital where those three people had just been talking about God the very day before and they got saved right then and there on the spot. Then there's Ken and that fire Captain! Wow! I agree, there's no English word to describe what's been happening here Dennis. And here we are getting to watch it all happen right in front of us. We are so lucky! Oops, let me take that back. And this was all orchestrated by God right in our little town and we just happen to be pastoring one of those churches. Ken alone is going to be the talk of this town for years to come as well as the Fire Captain. Those two are going to be wearing smiles wherever they go now, instead of being so mean and cantankerous. They are going to be two of the biggest witnesses of God's grace this town now."

Pastor Brown was shaking his head back and forth while his wife was talking. "This town is already on notice my dear. They are going to be noticing the changes that have taken place recently. That alone is going to make them ask questions, especially when they see Ken. I've got a feeling Ken is going to tell them exactly what happened. I think we might need to teach him how to pray with people to do the same thing he did. Then we have Captain Roberts who has his office over in Wesley. Those people over there are going to have the same questions. We better teach him the same thing. Those two alone are going to be responsible for people getting saved." Now the Pastor was shaking his head again. This truly was the most amazing thing this Pastor had ever witnessed.

Sister Brown laid breakfast on the table and kissed her hubby on the head. They had a nice visit as they ate, they continued to talk about the church and people in the congregation. Once in a while they stop and pray for the individual they were talking about. For some reason, this breakfast seemed to be a bit better this morning. Now it was time to get to the church and get busy getting things put together for the week.

Bob and Larry walked into the office just as Pastor Brown was setting down in his chair with a hot cup of coffee. Larry was the first to notice the coffee smell. "That's really fresh isn't it."

"Yes sir, it is. Grab yourselves a cup and let's get to chattin,' I'll wait here."

The guy's got back to the office and noticed an unusual smile on the Pastors face. "So, what's up with the smile this morning Pastor? It looks really good on you, but it's a little bit bigger than normal." Bob was pretty sure of where it came from, but he was curious as to why.

This made the Pastors smile even bigger. "Rachel and I had a good time of fellowship for breakfast this morning. You know, we were talking about what's been happening around here since you two came into town."

"Stop right there Pastor." Larry looked more serious than the Pastor had seen him since he got into town. "We haven't done anything at all. All the credit goes to God and the moving of the Holy Spirit on this town. We deserve absolutely no credit whatsoever. None at all. You know that's the truth." Pastor Brown suddenly felt like he had been scolded and he said as much. "Oh, Pastor, I didn't mean it like that. I'm so sorry. We're both a little sensitive to being given credit for things that God does. I'm really sorry."

"Oh Larry, I didn't feel like you paddled my bottom, and I know that God deserves all the of the credit. But it is true that none of this happened until the two of you got here. That is the truth, which is what I meant. So, just to make things clear, we're all on the same page. You two have an unusual ministry though. Do things happen like this everywhere you guys go? I've been curious about that almost since day one. Especially when you got shot in that tooshy of yours Larry."

"Actually Pastor, I should be the one to apologize. I overreacted. I am truly sorry. But, to answer your question, no. This doesn't happen at every place we go. Southwind will rank up there in the top five or so. But in reality, not every town is ready for God to show up on such a large scale. But things do happen. People get saved and some even get healed. We like to think that we leave a church in better condition than we found it. So far that's been the case, we think. This town has been like a sponge since we got here. We've been talking about it too. We know that you were praying, but we're both convinced that you weren't the only Pastor or church that's responsible for the town being so accepting. There are others that have been praying for this town. Obviously, God has heard all of you guys. That's pretty obvious to us at this point in our ministry."

"Oh, you are so correct wise one. Every Pastor I've talked to here in town has almost hugged me through the phone when I called them to let them know what was going on over here. I invited one Pastor down the street, and he completely lost it. He dropped the phone and began praising God right then and there very loudly. I think he's more Pentecostal than he lets on. You'll be meeting him tonight, no doubt. In fact, most of the other Pastors I talked to mentioned they had been praying. The ones that didn't mention their prayers, probably were, they just didn't say so. This building is going to make Captain Roberts pay attention to how many people are here at some point." They all began to laugh.

Bob asked, "Was he the one who showed up here yesterday and was literally going to close us down and board the place up?"

"Yeah, that's him. But God showed up and saved him too. Guess who won that battle?" Pastor Brown started them all laughing again. "I think I'm going to have him form a committee to build us a larger church." They kept laughing for a little bit. "I apologize guys. I mean no disrespect towards Captain Roberts. God really showed us that he's bigger than any circumstance yesterday. That man getting saved just took a huge tool away from the devil, no doubt about it. I was telling Rachel this morning that he was the meanest person I have ever met. But now that we're talking about it, I think Ken could match him toe to toe in that category and God saved them both. I have to confess this here and now, I know there isn't anyone outside of Gods reach, but I had my doubts about Ken. My thought was if there is such a person, Ken would qualify. But then God would remind me to pray for him, so I would. I knew it was going to take more than my infrequent prayers to get to him though. Now look at him. That man is as saved as saved gets and he's loving this new life God has given him." Now the Pastor had tears in his eyes again.

The two newest townsfolk agreed with everything that Pastor was saying and enjoyed listening to him brag on God. "Well, why don't we pray about tonight and the rest of the week, so we get this week started right." Bob was a really anxious to see what God had in mind for the area churches this week. The three took turns praying specifically what their roles would be this week and for lots of new souls to be brought into the kingdom.

As they were praying the front door of the church opened and in walked Zane and Jimmy. They walked over and realized they had just interrupted their prayer time. Zane was embarrassed. "I'm so sorry guys, we had no idea you were in prayer. We can come back later if that's okay."

Pastor looked at them with that huge smile of his. "No Zane, we're glad to see you two. What's up with you two today?"

"We just wanted to come and help with the repairs you're doing around the church. We've seen you guys out there working as we drive by and just wanted to help where we could." Jimmy was really shy as he spoke.

Pastor Brown shook their hands and patted both their shoulders. "We could sure use your help of course. Zane, do you have something you want to ask me?"

Zane's mouth dropped open. How could this guy already know what he was thinking? "Uh, ya, I guess so." He looked at Jimmy whose eyes were as big as saucers. Well, I guess first of all, I should tell you that I've canceled my plans for the military. We both feel like God is pulling us to help out with the youth in the church, but we have no clue how to get started, much less if there is a need for that. Mike seems to have a pretty good thing going at this point. So, to form a question, is there a place for us to help here? We would really need a lot of help and some sort of guiding, training or whatever you call it."

Pastor Brown stood started clapping his hands. "Praise God in the highest! Oh, you two are going to get more help than you ever thought you would need. And yes, we could use some help with this suddenly huge youth group we have here. I'm sure you two had a lot to do with that. Am I right?"

Jimmy was a little dumbfounded by the Pastor's response. "So, *you*, need *us*? I don't understand. We both think that Mike has things under control. The group follows every direction he gives them, as well as being quiet and polite the entire time. What are we missing here?" Zane had the same questions and nodded his head as Jimmy spoke.

Zane wanted to answer the Pastor's question as to who had anything to do with the sudden growth in the youth group. "Pastor, I'm not sure who is responsible for all of the kids that have started coming here. The four of us mention the group all the time and everywhere. But that night we went to the frosty was a huge reason for it. In fact, our girlfriends are the ones who lead that entire group to become Christians. I can't remember who started witnessing to them, but she was spot on with everything she said. When it came to praying with them, she didn't know how, so, the other girl stepped in and prayed with them. Jimmy and I just stood there watching it all happen. Is it okay to be proud of the one you're dating so much you want to hug them as tight as a teddy bear?

"So, it's not just us, you guys. I'm pretty sure it's a package deal with the four of us. Of course, the girls are a little shy and will make us take the lead. But when they step up, they step way up; if that makes sense?" Jimmy was beginning to think maybe he and Zane had this all wrong and that they had no business getting involved.

Pastor Brown saw the look in Jimmy's eyes and realized what he might be thinking. "Listen you two. Mike is a great guy and is able to do everything I ask of him. But he was hesitant when I asked him to help out with the teens. He *needs* your help. Your two friends are a definite bonus, especially if you're mature enough to lead an entire of group of teens to the Lord. My goodness that's a remarkable story. I want to hug them myself right now.

"For now, I agree that the Lord laid this on your hearts, which means He's going to bless it as well and the four of you kids. So, here's what we're going to do. I'm going to give a Mike a call in a few minutes and tell him what you have told me. I'm pretty sure he's going to want a group hug at that point. If you guys can get here a little early, I'll have him meet with you and you can discuss the details. How's that sound?" Pastor was on his feet the entire time he was speaking. He was so excited about this. God was doing everything he had been praying for since he got to this town. Now that it was happening right in front of his eyes, his heart was about to jump out of his chest.

Bob gave Larry a nod. They both went over and gave the boys a group hug, Pastor Brown was a little tardy getting there. Larry began praying. "Father, we want to thank you for these two guys and their friends. We know that You put this together and we look forward to what You're going to do through them. Please put a hedge of protection around their health, their safety, as well as keeping their focus on You and don't allow them to be distracted with all the stuff that comes through a church Father." Larry asked who was next to pray.

Zane didn't hesitate. "God, I'm scared. I have no idea how to do what I feel You calling me to do. I need so much more wisdom than I have right now. I need You to hold my hand like I'm a little boy and tell me everything is going to be okay. I don't know what else to say but help!"

Bob was next. "Lord, we know that since You're the one that laid this on their hearts that it's ordained by You and that You will bless it. Please keep them encouraged and focused on You and Your leading."

Pastor Brown was next. "Lord, You have been so good at showing me more about how You can work and get things done these past couple of weeks. I was ready to quit and call it a career and be happy for the rest of my life. But No, You had to send these two boys into town and turn everything on its head. I want to thank You for the huge amount of growth I've experienced during this time. But right now, Lord, I'm asking you to pour out Your Spirit on these two boys and fill them up to the top with the Holy Spirit. Let them be sensitive to Your leading and direction. Help them to lives their lives as a model to the others their age. Thank You so much Father for all You've done thus far and what You're going to do in the days ahead. Amen"

Jimmy was a little hesitant to pray but finally chimed in. "God I thinks these guys have prayed for everything I wanted to pray for. But I agree with Zane, I'm a little boy who needs You to hold his hand and tell him everything is going to be okay. Remember that both of us are new to this, so please don't be too hard on us." The others laughed. "That's about all I can think of to pray for God. Just be with us and let us be a blessing to the group. Amen"

The huddle broke up with hugs and slaps on the back and big fat smiles all around. God still had a lot of work to do in this church, but it was already beginning to show signs of a huge growth spurt.

In the meantime, the paint for the inside of the building was still in the paint can and Larry was the first talk about it. "Boys, that paint ain't gonna put itself on these walls. Why don't we help it out a little. Sound like a plan?"

Everyone agreed and acknowledged as much as they headed for the kitchen for a cool glass of water that was waiting for them in the refrigerator.

Afterwords, the Pastor excused himself to his office to make some calls and invite other churches to the services. He was also thinking about calling a few people he wanted to take a leadership role he would need shortly, to see if they would be interested in helping out.

A Few minutes later the four guys were painting the walls in the fellowship hall and had it finished in no time flat. They began washing everything up and getting ready to start on one of the classrooms down the hall. As they were just about finished, Larry told Bob he was getting some ideas for tonight's sermon, so he was going to get going to finish praying and studying for it. Bob and the two new youth leaders gave him hugs and out the door he went.

Bob decided that was a great time for a cold glass of water and the others agreed. As they sat down in the room they just finished painting, Bob decided to encourage these two new guys in their roles as leaders. "Guys, I gotta tell you this; there is nothing more sobering than to stand in front of a congregation and watch God change lives right in front of you. You can tell by looking at the faces as to who God is talking to. Those people have a look something like getting caught with their hands in the cookie and they know they're in trouble. Once they have asked Jesus into their lives that face changes from worry to huge smiles. Now it's all smiles and tears of joy and big fat hugs. It's brought me to tears more times that I can count. The feeling you get from being such a small part of. That is bigger than the high you can get from any illicit drug. That's not a lie at all. That's one of the rewards Larry and I get to experience at times and it's the most awesome feeling in the world man, I ain't even kidding you."

Zane and Jimmy were looking at each other with big eyes right now. Both of them were really looking frightened at being in front of a large group of people. They hadn't thought about being in front of people and giving the sermon until just this moment.

Zane asked the questions for both of them, "So, how do we get into a position to pray with people like you just described?"

Bob was absolutely dumbstruck and his face as much. "Dude! You guys just did it the other night at the frosty from what I hear. I am so proud of you guys. People your age just don't do that. They invite them to church to do it. You guys lead an entire youth group to Christ right there in the parking lot. Your question has me confused. Am I missing something here?"

Jimmy and Zane smiled at each other. Jimmy kind of chuckled and said, "Yes sir you sure are missing something in that story. It was our girlfriends who did that entire thing. Rebecca kind of preached to them a bit and got them ready to pray. But she said she didn't know how to do that part, so Betty Jo led the prayer. We were both totally amazed and proud at the same time. We teased that maybe they should be the preachers, and we could preachers' husbands, or something like that. It was as amazing as you probably heard it was. It just wasn't us doing it."

Zane piped up, "I was standing there with mouth open in total surprise. I don't know about you Jimmy, but I was totally surprised. I was like, I didn't know she knew that stuff. Then Betty Jo came over and started a prayer. She sounded like she had been doing those things her entire life. I'm still amazed at those two. I'm serious."

Now it was Bob's turn to be amazed. "Are you kidding me. They are so quiet. They stand there with a smile looking all pretty and stuff. They don't even talk to us. Well, if that's the case, you two better keep these relationships going. If I ever hear of you guys going different ways, I'm going to hunt you down and beat you in the head with a twenty pound Bible and you're gonna like it!" They all shared a good laugh at that threat.

After they gained their composure, Bob told them that it was really exactly like it happened at the frosty. "One point you're talking to someone and the next you're praying them through to God. You just have to be ready at a second's notice. Remember in second Timothy, Paul tells us to be ready in season and out of season. I'd say your friends were ready that night, no doubt. In fact, I'm really looking forward to seeing them tonight. I gotta tell ya, I've never seen the likes of the four of you. At your age you are so far advanced than most others. At least as far as your willingness to get in the fight and mix It up with the devil when it comes to souls. Not only does this church and city need you guys, but the world could use thousands more just like you. You two flat out amaze me."

Zane and Jimmy just looked at each in total bewilderment. "I didn't know it was such a big thing, did you Zane?" Jimmy was starting to feel a little bit awkward about it all now.

"No, I had no idea what we were doing that night was really a big thing. I mean handing out burgers and drinks was so much fun that night. We met so many people that night that I still don't know all of their names. But I could feel something when we were all standing there listening to Rebecca. She knew what she was talking about that night. I was kind of surprised when she didn't know how to pray the kids through. But here comes Betty Jo, she walked right up there and said repeat these words and by golly they all did just that. I got a tear in my eye while she was praying because I knew that prayer was going to change lives that night. But Bob, really, we can't be the only young adults that do such things. That makes us sound something like...I don't know what it makes us. I don't know which word to use even." Zane was still bewildered.

"The word is unique," Bob said. "Don't misunderstand me. I'm not saying you guys are weird or some kind of spiritual super star. Well, you kind of are, but it just makes you different from most of your peers. That's all."

Jimmy spoke up, "I've known Zane I and were a little different from most of the other boys we've grown up with. We didn't stand around gossiping about our dates on Friday night and the things that happened. We didn't go around talking flashy to the girls while we walked the campus. We did talk to girls, but we never tried to pick up on them or tell them how great we thought we were. I noticed a change in us when we started coming to church these past few weeks though. I can feel the presence of God in the church at different times. You know during the worship, during the preaching and then a whole bunch during the alter calls, while people are down front praying. It gives me goosebumps and makes the hair on my arm stand up sometimes. In fact, that's what we felt while Rebecca and Betty Jo led those kids to Christ the other night. It was so cool I'm telling you right now. We weren't even in a church. Just a dirty parking lot. But Bob, we ain't no different from any other guys our age that's a Christian. That's what I think anyways."

Bob looked over at Zane, "Do you agree with that Zane?"

"Absolutely! In fact, Jimmy, you may have even given us too much credit. I don't feel like I'm any different from anyone. Certainly not any better than any other person alive, I don't even feel like Jimmy, or I are any better at sharing the gospel, or praying with people to receive Christ as their Savior. Doesn't everybody do that?"

Bob Chuckled, "Dudes! No one does that! Most Christians leave it to the preachers and Evangelists because that's their job. Everyone else just goes to church on Sunday and get blessed by God and go home. In fact, if you keep this up, Larry and I can retire already. So YES! You two are different than most

Christians. Don't get me wrong, those who come and go home are really good people and I meant no disrespect to them at all. The issue is that there are millions of Christians, but only thousands of preachers. You see, we can't do it all by ourselves. Its people like you and your girls that make a real difference. God needs you to be the ones that step up to the plate when the opportunity presents itself to do just what you have been doing. That's exactly what makes all four of you different. Do you get it now?"

Zane and Jimmy were looking at each other with wide eyes. "I do now, how 'bout you Jimmy." Zane was shaking his head back and forth.

"I'm right with ya brother. Wow. I was doing what came natural to me. In fact, the night Rebecca was telling that group of guys about Jesus and didn't know how to pray them trough, I was getting ready to step in and take charge of that. Then Betty Jo had to jump in ahead of me do it. I can't even tell you how surprised and proud I was of her. Is that natural for you Zane?"

"Ya, same here. I was getting ready to step into the crowd and do just what Betty Jo did. And I'm with you Jimmy, I was so proud to be Rebecca's boy that night. Maybe it's just natural to them too."

Bob was a tad bit surprised to hear them say that it came natural to both of them and probably the girls too. But he wasn't going to argue with it or mess it up. He decided to leave it alone and let them continue doing what they had been doing. He looked at his watch and decided it was time to get to Sister Wilson's house for a shower. "And with that, guys, I've got to get back to the house for a shower before church starts. I can only say to you guys to just keep doing what you have been doing. You'll learn how to know when it's time to pray with someone. Besides, it comes natural to the four of you."

With that, Bob stood up and began walking down the hall, with the two boys right behind him. They stopped at the Pastor's office just as he picked up his ringing phone. Pastor Brown put up a finger to take the call and he would be right with them.

As the Pastor answered the phone to see who he was going to be speaking with, he was a bit surprised to find out that he was live on the air with a local radio talk show host Leo. Leo wanted to get Pastor Brown to talk about what had been going on at his church, but he wasn't very polite. Leo began quite sarcastically in asking, "So tell me Pastor Brown, does this God of yours heal people and save them from hell?"

Pastor Brown could feel God's presence in his office immediately. He took a deep breath and decided to go slowly in speaking to Leo and his audience. He said a quick prayer while took his big breath. "Leo, this God that you're talking about is your God too, if you need healing or salvation. God will hear your request for healing and salvation. He will heal you and forgive you. But I can tell in your voice Leo, that this isn't a social call. But I will talk to you until you decide the conversation is over. Is that fair?"

Leo was almost drooling on himself and decided to go in for the kill. "That's just great Pastor! Well, isn't it true that this Jesus you believe in, actually died about two thousand years ago?" Leo's voice was even nastier at this point.

Again, Pastor Brown took a deep and prayed at the same time. "Leo, I can tell by your tone of voice that you're not much of a fan of the God that created this universe and everything in it. But Jesus did die two thousand years ago. However, He walked out of that tomb three days later just like He said He would. And because of that, we are healed, saved, and have an everlasting life waiting for us when our time here on earth has finished. So, Jesus ain't in that grave anymore Leo. He's sitting at the right of God Almighty. As far as god's go, I think you have Jesus mixed up with other pretend god's or other religions."

Leo didn't have a snappy come back so fast this time. "Okay Pastor, tell me and those listening to this program right now, just why we should serve a God we can't see or touch? Why should we believe in your God, instead of any other gods?"

Pastor took that deep breath again and said a prayer. "I have already mentioned that this God I serve made this entire universe. To believe that we evolved from pond scum, or a monkey is an insult to every ounce of intelligence that God gave to all of us. If you want to believe that you came from pond scum that's your choice, but God made man from a fist full of dust and breathed life into it and created man. You can find that in Genesis chapter two verse four."

"That's why you preachers use the phrase ashes to ashes and dust to dust at funerals. Now if this God made us like the Bible tells us He did, would it be appropriate to recognize him as a Supreme Being and worthy of some type of honor?"

"As to the fact that we can't touch God or see him, that takes faith Leo. Jesus told us, blessed is he who has not seen me but still believes in me. That a paraphrase but it's accurate. Thus, it does take bit of faith to believe Leo. Do have any faith like that Leo?"

This preacher was eating Leo's lunch right in front of his listeners and Leo felt powerless to stop it. So, he came up with a new question that was sure to paint this preacher into a corner. "Okay Pastor, you have a point there. But what about all of the bad in the world. Why does your God cause so much bad?"

Pastor Brown knew this answer and didn't hesitate. "Oh Leo, you are really misinformed. But you're not alone. This is a common misconception. I promise to make this very clear and easy to understand, but may I first ask you a personal question?"

"Yeah, sure."

"Do you believe in a battle of good and evil?"

Leo got a big smile on his face. "I sure do, and you guys are the evil empire!" Leo was almost giddy with that answer.

Pastor Brown chuckled at Leo's giddiness in his answer. "Okay, that's fine Leo, but here's where it gets simple. If there's a battle of good and evil, wouldn't it make sense for all the bad in the world to come from the evil side of the battle?"

Leo thought for a quick second. "Yeah, I guess so, that makes sense."

"Okay then, let me keep this simple again so you can understand. God created this universe and everything in it. But this world has rejected God as it's maker and Jesus as the Savior He truly is. In fact, there's a verse in the Bible that tells us that this world rejected God because it's deeds were evil and it loved the darkness, even though God brought the light. Or, if you will, they would rather live in their sins and face the consequences, than accept the free gift of salvation and eternal life, which is the only way to be genuinely happy. So, this bad that you see in the world Leo, actually comes about because of all of the sin in the world. God gave us a free will and He doesn't intrude on our decisions. It's our own personal decision as to whether we want to accept Christ as our Savior, or not.

"Now, to show you what I mean, if there's a battle of good and evil, would it not make sense to cloud the issue and blame the good side for all of the bad crud going on? To take it one step further, the Bible tells us in the book of Romans that the world will begin to call good stuff, bad stuff and the bad stuff, good stuff. Thus, confusing everyone who isn't paying attention to the facts. Does that make sense Leo? The good is bad and the bad is good. Which is exactly what is going in our society today."

Leo had to think for a moment which created some dead air and silence on the radio. "Okay, you made another good point Pastor. But I don't know whether I believe in your Bible though. So how should we conclude this discussion? How would you sum up what has been happening at your church these past few weeks?"

Pastor Brown took another deep breath, but without the prayer this time. "What we're seeing happen at church for the past few weeks is exactly what God has wanted to happen. I had been praying for two years that this town would begin to take God seriously. Three weeks ago, two guys showed up at the church. They've been all over the country and have been involved with these types of events before. They have truly been instrumental in what has been happening at our church these past few weeks. We've seen the altars filled at each service as well as the church packed wall to wall. People are humbling themselves before the Lord and having some great experiences with God moving on their lives and families. We saw a very sick little baby healed the other day. Also, we had two men in our town accept Christ as their Savior, that everyone thought were so bad, God could save them. They were wrong. That person does not exist as far as God is concerned."

Pastor Brown took another deep breath. "Leo, the issue here isn't who's right or wrong. The issue really is where are we going to spend eternity when we pass away. We can cloud the issue with all kinds of questions, and they seem to be good questions on the surface, but underneath they're hurtful. We're told in the Bible that if we confess with our hearts that God raised Jesus from the dead, then we can be saved. This God that gave us His Son is waiting for us to ask one question. And that question is for forgiveness. Three simple words, Jesus forgive me, spoken with a sincere heart is all it takes to receive forgiveness for your sins and make you a child of the most high God. Then Leo, we get to visit with each other in heaven for eternity. I for one Leo, would enjoy that very much. In fact, I would enjoy visiting with your listeners as well. What you think of that Leo?"

Leo didn't answer right away this time. After a few seconds of dead air, Pastor Brown was wondering if he had hung up. Finally, Leo spoke in a broken voice and sounded as if he might be crying though his words. "Pastor Brown, you have made your point quite clearly today. I sincerely apologize for my tone at the beginning of this conversation. I can't speak for my listeners, but I think I now understand what you have said on the air today. I see things totally differently now than when I called you. This is one radio host that's willing to put aside his professional pride, and even put his career in jeopardy and ask you to help me say that prayer sir. I don't know how to pray and I'm sure a lot of my listeners may be in the same boat. So, Pastor Brown, can you pray for us? I mean, say that prayer that will allow us to have those long visits?"

Pastor Brown's lower lip was beginning to quiver, but he could do this. "Yes, Leo, I can. I'm going to say that prayer, but can you repeat what I say? It's simple and your listeners who what to follow along can repeat it as well wherever they are, and it will have the same effect for them. So, let's get started. Just repeat what I say. Okay"

"Okay Pastor, go right ahead." Leo was ready and ever a little bit impatient.

"Dear God...I ask right now...that You would forgive me of my sins...help me live a life...according to Your word...I invite Your Holy Spirit...into my life...

Please help me through each day...to live for you... and to know you more each day...Thank you Father...Amen...

"That's all it takes Leo, you and whoever else repeated that prayer are now new Christians. Welcome to the family you guys. I really hope you don't lose your job Leo. I'm pretty sure you're going to be better at your job now that you have a new understanding about God and everything He does for us. As well as being in control of this entire world whether we think so or not."

Leo was still talking in a hushed voice. "Thank you, Pastor, for letting me interrupt your busy day and leading us in that prayer. If I'm right, aren't you having some kind of a weeklong meeting this week at your church?"

"Why yes, we are Leo. Please come and invite your audience. It doesn't matter if they prayed with us or nor. We won't turn anyone away." Pastor Brown was smiling that big smile of his.

"Why don't you give us you address so we show up at the correct church. I'm sure some of the audience prayed with us, but I for one will definitely be there tonight." Leo was now smiling and feeling better than he ever had felt before. He felt as if the weight of the world had just left his shoulders. He was wondering what was going to happen when he invited his girlfriend to come with him tonight.

Pastor Brown told them the address and Leo hung up. The Pastor hung up and looked over at Bob, Zane, and Jimmy with that grin of his.

Bob jumped right on him; he couldn't wait for the Pastor to tell the story. "What just happened here Parson?"

"Bob, I know you're not going to find this too far out with your history in the ministry you and Larry have. But I was live on the air with this guy named Leo who called to make us look bad to his audience. He was pretty ornery when the call started. Called us evil and such even. But as we went on, I was able to get him to see the battle of good and evil we all face every day. Then I was able to get him to pray the sinners live and on the air. *TAKE THAT DEVIL!*" Then Pastor Brown began to cry. That experience really touched his heart.

All three guys were standing with their mouths open. Bob turned the other two, "Now you see what I mean about being ready when the time comes. That man right there stood tall when it came time to face the devil and looked him right in the eye.

"Dennis, you did it brother. You led that man to the Lord when he had no idea that he needed to do it. And who knows how many in his audience did the same thing. *GOD YOU ARE SO AWESOME!* We don't deserve anything You have done for us, but it sure is fun to watch You work. Hallelujah!"

Pastor Brown went on to tell more. "The Holy Spirit was already in the room when Leo called. I had been sitting here praying about tonight when the phone rang. Man, Leo jumped on me like a hungry Lion right from the get-go. He was convinced that the church was part of an evil empire of some sort, and he was going to expose us or something like that. But he wasn't so far down the road that he wouldn't listen to a reasonable explanation of how things worked with God. After just a few minutes he caught on to what I was telling him. In fact, after I mentioned salvation and it being so simple, *he asked me to pray for him and his audience!* I have never been so nervous in my life saying that prayer, but we got it done and now we have a bunch more Christians in the area. Praise God Hallelujah!"

Bob was ecstatic. "Pastor, you have to tell that story tonight. I'm serious, people need to see how God works when we may not be ready for Him to."

"I'll do you one better. I think I'll introduce Leo while I tell it. He promised me was going to be here tonight." And with that, Pastor Brown began to cry all over again.

Bob went over and hugged him. "Pastor, you are one dynamite dude if I met one. Of all the Pastors I have met, you have got be one that stands out among all of them, and I mean it sincerely. I've told you about some of them, but you are truly a giant among men. I don't know how else to say it. Wait until Larry hears about this. He's going to go ballistic! You've been asking us for advice, but I'm pretty sure it's me and Larry that can learn a lot more from you before we leave here. This is so awesome!"

Zane spoke up, "I'm definitely going to be telling my family about this at dinner tonight for sure. Jimmy echoed it for Sally and Ken. This was already more than these two young men had ever thought they would encounter. What was next?

When Bob got to Sister Wilson's house, he was walking so fast that he almost knocked Sister Wilson over just inside the door. "Excuse me Sister Wilson, I'm so sorry, but I have the most awesome news to tell you and Larry." He was so excited he was almost shouting.

"It's so good you had knock around an old lady?" Sister Wilson was laughing as she said it.

"Well, I'm not sure about that, but good enough to rush through the door. You have got to hear this." By that time Larry was standing with them in the kitchen. Bob shared about the phone call and how rude Leo was at the beginning and then what happened at the end of the call.

Larry was so excited about this news that he started jumping up and down, clapping his hands and praising God that same time. "How is God going to beat this in the next town we end up in? Bob, that has to be one of the most exciting things I have ever heard of! This is even more exciting than a carnival ride." He gave Bob a high five and hugged Sister Wilson.

Sister Wilson was smiling and crying, and so happy for Leo. "I used to listen to his show not very long ago. Something happened to him, someone dear to him died, or something like that. Afterwards, he became ornerier in his show, and he hated God. It was clear to me that he believed in God and had some knowledge of the Bible for him to be that angry with our God. This phone call makes sense to me and even how it ended. WOW! God was truly watching out for him! Even through Leo's anger, God still loved him and was ready to welcome him home. You guys are right. This is going to be hard for you to forget. Did Leo say if he was going to be at church tonight? If so, I want to give him a big hug. I've been praying for him since I quit listening to him. He just got so mean I didn't like the show anymore. Praise God! Hallelujah! Man, I am so glad you guys stopped at our church that day." She gave both of them tight hugs.

"How is God going to top this one? What's going to happen the rest of this week? Even with all of the churches we have been to, this is the most memorable by far. This is the biggest movement of God we have seen so far Bob. Am I right?" Larry was so excited right now he was having a hard time standing still.

"You are correct ol' wise one. We haven't seen a movement even close to this! And yes, Sister Wilson, Leo is going to be there tonight, so hug on momma!" Bob was having the same issue Larry was having, he was pacing all over the room and clapping his hands.

"I told the Pastor before I left, that this was the most memorable place we had been to so far. But Larry, you know as well as I do that as soon as we think we've seen and heard it all, God's going to do something even bigger. So maybe we should just be ready for another amazing event before we leave Southwind. That's what I'm thinking anyways." Bob was now standing with his arms crossed and shaking his head.

"I was just thinking the exact same thing, Bob. I think we are seeing the just the tip of the iceberg here brother. It's going to be really exciting what our God is going to do the rest of the week. Just expect it bro." Larry was beginning to grasp the vastness of God's abilities and willingness to meet every need a person might have. God's awesomeness was a true understatement. Now the two were looking at each other and shaking their heads acknowledging just how dear God is.

Church time finally came around and the crowd was getting pretty big pretty early. The Pastor had already asked a couple guys to be ready to grab some chairs from the fellowship hall if need be. As he hung out at the front door, he was able to greet the Pastors of other local churches he had invited to come to the meetings. Billy Jones from Wilton brought some of his congregation as well as Pastor Ribeiro. Pastor Ribeiro had a church a little outside of the area and it was a bit of a drive to get here tonight. Pastor Brown had long wished for the time to spend more time with these two preachers. He had such love and respect for them both. It hurt his heart not to know them better.

Sister Brown was on the piano and Sister Wilson was at the organ. All of the other musicians began the music a few minutes before the service started and it sounded like heaven to Pastor Brown. He was wondering what was going to happen tonight as it was going to be hard to do more than God had already done.

Pastor Brown went to the podium to greet the crowd before the service began. He welcomed everyone to the first revival meeting at this church in three years. He was very liberal in his praise for Bob and Larry and talked about when they had shown up in front of his office three weeks ago.

The Pastor talked about the conversation with Leo earlier in the day. He wasn't able to greet Leo before the service began because of the size of the crowd, so he asked if Leo was in the crowd. Leo raised his hand, and the crowd busted out in applause. Pastor invited him to the platform to chat a bit in Pastor Brown's home turf. Leo said some very kind words towards Pastor Brown and God. Then he asked those who prayed with him on the air to stand up. Twenty people stood up. Again, the crowd applauded. After they sat down, Leo told his side of the conversation. He had heard what going on here and wanted to expose the cruelty and all out evil of today's church. But when he called, he found a Pastor that seemed to be ready for him. Even though he was mean to the Pastor, he answered with a very kind voice and was completely in control of his emotions. As the conversation went on, Leo realized that God had set this up. He had been running from God for a long time and he was feeling the prayers of those who had been praying for him and it made him mad. Mad enough to pounce on an unsuspecting Pastor on live radio. But that's not what happened. This Pastor lovingly and graciously led him and twenty others to Christ live on the air instead. Leo let the tears roll down his face as he spoke and then went over and gave Pastor Brown that big hug he wanted.

Now the only question was if he had a job tomorrow. He had gone looking for the General Manager of the station after the show was over but her couldn't find him.

As he said that, the General Manager stood up to Leo's utter surprise. "Dave, did you say that prayer with us today?"

Dave giggled a cute giggle and then began to tear up. He was able to talk through the tears and even smile a little. "Your job is secure Leo. If anyone is going to be fired, we're probably going to get fired at the same time. But tomorrow, it would be appropriate to talk about what happened today and what happens tonight. So, we can just add God to our subject matter for the show from now on. We talk about everything else, adding this subject in a positive light would do the audience some good and maybe grow the audience as well. Be in my office at nine in the morning and don't be late." Then he sat down. The crowd laughed as Leo saluted and said, "Yes sir."

Leo handed the microphone to the Pastor and went back to his seat. Pastor Brown looked over at Sister Brown and said, "Hit it maestro!" and the worship service began with a strong band in proper tune and an audience with a strong voice.

The worship service was better than it had been in a long time. God was already moving on the crowd tonight and it was awesome to watch as the three preachers were amazingly blessed watching it happen. As pastor Brown looked out over the crowd, he wondered how so many people could squeeze in there. He couldn't find an open seat anywhere. There were even people sitting behind the people on the platform. They were going to need to open the fellowship hall tomorrow night. It was definitely true, that where God moved, people would show up and here they are. God was definitely moving on this town.

After the worship was over Pastor Brown again greeted the crowd. He was noticing that there was no room for an alter call in front. It was just packed all over the room. Larry would figure it out, he's probably done this a few times before, was the Pastor's thinking. He announced the other meetings coming up this week and turned it right over to Larry.

Larry took his place behind the pulpit and realized there was no room for an alter call tonight. Oh well, it's God's job at this point. He began talking about the conversation he and Bob had earlier in the day. How this has been the greatest move of God they had ever seen. This hadn't happened at the other churches they had been to through the years. Again, the audience applauded God for His infinite mercy and grace. Larry went on to tell what happened with the shotgun blast, then had Dr. Bob, Roxanne and Cindy stand up. Even more applause, but now people were shaking their heads at the awesomeness of God. What the devil had meant for bad, God turned into a really good outcome.

Larry had them open their Bibles to Psalm ninety-one. He was going to point out the protection we have through our God who is all mighty. The person who dwells in the shelter of the most high will dwell in the shadow of the Almighty. And in verse seven, a thousand may fall beside you and ten thousand on your right, but it won't come near us. "So, looking at the event of that shotgun blast, not only do I have buns of steel, but that bullet didn't have the effect it usually would because it was between me and the bullet" The crowd was really clapping now. "Take that devil. Eat that bullet your own self and leave us Saints alone. You can't hurt God's anointed or those of us who walk in His shadow."

He then asked how many would do anything without consulting God first and waited for people to raise their hands. After a minute he asked, "Then can you explain to me why you drive your car without praying first?" Now the audience let out a big groan. "You guys don't pray because you take it for granted that nothing is going to happen to you on the trip you're taking. Be it to the grocery store or three states over. We already know that God is with us. Especially if we're in that shadow of the Almighty. God rides on top of our car singing the entire trip. I'm sure God changes up the songs He sings while He rides along with us. Singing one song over and over is really boring. Basically, my point here, is that God never leaves us. He tells us that in First Kings. He loves us so much that He will fight our fights if we get out of the way and let Him. He heals our body's, He heals our minds, He heals our marriages. Yes, our marriages. In fact, that happened for one couple on, or soon after the day we got to town. People, that's a huge miracle. How many divorces are you aware of? I heard a preacher say once that divorce creates more problems than it solves. Although I have never been married, I can say I've seen exactly that happen because of the position I'm in. I get to watch people live their lives right in front of me. And not that I'm watching anyone, but I see them in their darkest hours at times. Conversely, I get to see their high points too. That's the part I like the most. That's the part Bob and I talk about when we get back to the hotel, or wherever we might be staying.

"One of the things I like to point out at each place we go, is this, God sent Jesus down here to live among us. He walked like we walk, one step at a time. He was tempted with the same temptations we go through yet was without sin. In short, our God knows exactly what we go through. He's been there, done that, bled on the shirt. When we hurt, He hurts. When we cry, He cries with us. God has first-hand knowledge of our sorrows and our joys. He has firsthand knowledge of what goes on down here. He's not one of those ogre's who sits high up on his throne that's so far away he has no idea what our life is like.

"He knows how it feels to get in a splinter in our foot and step on a big sticker. He knows what it's like to stub your toe. He has laughed when someone fell down because it was funny. Okay, I might have made that part up. But my point is that He has been in our shoes.

"He has every reason to banish us to hell, yet He forgives us every time we ask. His love for us is like the way we love newborn kittens and puppies. He picks us up with a huge smile on His face and snuggles our noses and holds us close to Him. He gives us loving hugs and smells our puppy breath. Ya, it really is like that. We could never love someone like that, especially if they treated us the way we treat Him at times.

"He knows exactly how it feels to be stabbed in the back by one of His closest friends. He knows what it feels like to be abandoned by all of His friends when He needed them most. His father even turned His back on Him at the lowest point in His life.

"Let me put it this way, He has walked in our shoes. He knows all about it and maybe even more than that. He even heard you say that bad word when you stubbed your toe or smashed your finger. No, He didn't do that part. But yet after everything He went through on your behalf, he still loves you enough to want to smell your puppy breath. He wants that intimacy with you. He wants to hug you and kiss you on top of your head because He loves you that much. He can see your pain. He can see your happiness too. He can also see your future and that's where the concern comes in.

"Are you ready to look Him in the eyes? Are you ready to see His smile? Are you ready for that hug? Well, are you? Are ready to get told you did a good job? Did you do well? Have you asked Jesus to forgive you of your sins? Because that's all it takes to get that hug and smile and that kiss on your head.

"Bow your heads and let's all say this prayer together. Man after preaching like that I feel like I need to get saved all over again.

"Father forgive me of my sins… I admit that I'm a sinner… Please guide me and direct me through my life… from here on out… Help me to live according to Your ways, not mine… Thank you for taking that beating for me and shedding Your blood…Thank You for Your love. Amen.

"Now that we're all Christians, let's all go get a piece of pie." Larry waved at the crowd as he turned it back over to Pastor Brown. As he walked away the crowd began to clap for him. Larry wasn't going to allow that. "That's right, clap for the Risen King of glory. Praise His Holy Name!" The musicians started to play, and the worship leader started singing. And right on cue came the Holy Spirit began blessing the entire room. Hands were raised everywhere with shouts of praise as they all sang praises to God and wept as they did. There was something cathartic about singing praises to God from the bottom of your heart. It gets clear down into your soul and makes you feel so clean from the inside out, one can't help but naturally shed tears.

As the worship and praise continued, the three preachers made their way towards the back door. Periodically they would stop and pray with someone as they felt led to. It took them a while to get there but the breeze coming through door felt so good right now.

Bob grabbed Larry and hugged like never before. "Puppy breathe? Are you kidding me? That really touched my heart! Where did that come from?"

"The Lord told me to say it. I would have never thought of that in a trillion years brother. And it touched my heart too. I teared up, didn't you hear it?" Larry was beginning to tear up again as he spoke.

"No, I didn't, but I did the same thing." Bob said. "That's got to be the most precious way of expressing God's love for us I have ever heard. Just WOW! I'm going to remember that the rest of my days."

Pastor Brown was shaking his head back and forth. "You two still blow my mind. I have never heard anyone preach like you two. You stand there and tell an all-out blatant truth while having a good time doing it. Even the crowd enjoys being hit between the eyes when you guys do it. It's like you punch 'em in the face and make 'em smile at the same time. But I absolutely love the way you present the entire gospel and God's love. I hear people say all the time that they hate the fire and brimstone preaching. But it's not *ALL* hell fire and brimstone. It's the love that Jesus freely bestows on all of us. Yeah, there is a bad part to the story for those that don't accept Christ as their Savior, but that's their decision to make alone by themselves. God wouldn't choose an eternity in hell for them. He did everything within His power to help them make the right choice," He took a big breath. "Here I am preaching to preachers. But I love you guys more than you deserve. You need to know that."

Bob and Larry gave him a big hug with big smiles and held it for a while.

After a lot of people had their made their way passed the preachers, Leo finally got there. He grabbed Pastor Brown's hand and gave it a good firm handshake with both hands. "Pastor Brown, it's my all out pleasure to be here tonight. I know that you know I called you look bad live on the air. I am so glad my little plan didn't work. I knew as soon as I heard your voice that I was totally over-matched. You were so soft spoken and wise with everything I threw at you. This is one of those few times in my life I am so overjoyed to show who I really am in public. I have always been a softhearted kind of guy, but I present myself as someone totally different on the air. But because of our encounter today,

Pastor Brown, I'm a Christian again and I can feel it ALL THE WAY DOWN TO MY TOES!" Leo shouted it out and started crying at the same time." I don't care who knows it and I don't care how they found out about it either." Now he was laughing. "God made sure to show us all that He's so much bigger than a radio hosts ego!" He reached over gave Pastor Brown another big hug like he just had from Bob and Larry.

"Leo, you were so forthright and honest on the radio today. I have a feeling that's why you had twenty of your listeners show up tonight. Had you been completely abstinent and argumentative it would have been totally different. So, being softhearted worked in everyone's favor today. Have you run into your boss yet?" Pastor Brown was still hugging Leo as he spoke.

"Not yet. But I'm going to wait outside for him so we can go get that piece of pie." He winked at Larry and giggled.

Right behind Leo came the Fire Chief, Don Roberts. He grabbed Pastor Brown and gave him another great big hug. If this kept up tonight Sister Brown was going to get jealous. "Pastor, I have got to tell you what a great day this was. I have never in my life, walked into work so happy and flat out relaxed. When I walked into the office the guys started to leave the room like they always do when I walk in. But today I pulled rank on them and told to sit down and like it. I told what had happened yesterday, the entire story. When it came to the part where I went down and prayed their eyes were as big as dinner plates. I apologized for who I was before and told them I would do my best to be a better boss and better person. I even told them if I needed redirection in my behavior I wanted to hear it. I told them that I was ashamed of myself and who I was and the nastiness that I brought to work every day. I apologized about nine hundred times until one of the guys finally raised his hands and told me to stop. I had been talking so much that I was repeating myself. I gotta tell ya Pastor, I was so impressed with every last one of those men. Every one of them stood in line to shake my hand and tell me to my face they forgave me. I was in tears after the second one, but they just kept coming. I am truly a blessed man. And here's the kicker Pastor. The last man in line had tears in his eyes too. He told me that God had been dealing with him for a long time, but he just kept pushing Him away. His wife is a Christian and had been praying for him for years. She asked him to go to church with her for years. She even asked him to pray with her at times to accept Christ as his Savior, but he wouldn't do it. He told her when I get saved then he would think about it. He told me yesterday that he almost went to church and got saved, but for some reason he didn't. Then I walk in this morning and make this big announcement. It pushed him over the edge and now here he was standing in front of me crying wanting me to pray for him to get saved, but I had no idea what to say or much less how to pray. So, I looked straight up and said out loud God help me. Then I grabbed the guy's hand and told him to repeat what I said. So, I repeated what the guy said yesterday because it worked for me. Now there are two Christians at work that I know about. There might be more, but I haven't spoken to everyone yet. So, in closing," Don giggled, "it was the best day of my life so far."

Bob heard the entire story and butted in. "And that's our God in action Don. You don't have to be a preacher and go through a twelve point sermon to lead someone to the Lord. All you have to do is be ready to do it. It sounds like you didn't think you were ready yet, but you were, and you did. Now you'll be even more ready for the next time. Do not ever hesitate to tell your story; what God did for that miserable person that you were and also for that guy you prayed with today. That's a great testimony of God's love for both you and his family. Did he come tonight."

"I don't think so. I kept looking for him before the service started and didn't see him. He was such a basket case after we prayed that I gave him the day off with pay. That felt good to do even. I've never done that before. But you have a huge crowd that wants to talk to you right now, so I'm going to stand outside for a while to see if he did come tonight. I'll see you all tomorrow night." He shook hands with everyone and stepped outside to stalk his prey. He ended up in the yard chatting with Leo while they both waited.

Chapter 11

Tuesday

Rachel and Dennis woke up early today. They were lying on their backs staring at the ceiling when Rachel began to hum one of the songs they sang last night. Dennis decided if they were awake enough to hum a song, they were awake enough for coffee. "I'll let you make some coffee while I go grab the paper off the porch."

Rachel was feeling a little giddy already today. "Let me tell you something Mister Preacher man!" She laughed as she was getting out of bed.

"Hey! Just cuz you're married to a preacher man doesn't mean you can call him names! You short, sawed off at the knees, stubby woman you. Who is very beautiful I might add." Now he was laughing. He added the last part because he knew who was cooking his breakfast. And besides, she *was* kind of short.

"Why you old fat knuckle head. I'm gonna have to give you a big fat kiss for that one. You mean, mean bushy eyebrowed old man!" Then she tackled him onto the bed and started giving him sloppy wet kisses all over his face. It was pretty easy to see that these two really liked each other. "Stop screaming little boy, you're going to wake the neighbors!"

"I'm telling my mommy on you!" Dennis was getting his own sloppy kisses on Rachel's face too. He pushed her off of him and started running down the hallway. "You can't catch me! Nanny nanny boo boo!"

Dennis went and grabbed the paper while Rachel got the coffee started and then started getting breakfast put together. As they both got seated and relaxed, Rachel began to smile and shake her head. "Sweety, can you remember where we were at mentally just before Bob and Larry showed up? We were both ready to quit. I mean, usually it was only one of us that was ready to call it quits and the other would be the encourager. But this time it was both of us. God's timing is impeccable. He's never late. I sure wish He would show up early once in a while, but He never does. I think I may need to address that issue with Him when I get to heaven. What do you think Dennis?"

"I'll tell you what I think. All of you people who want to give God a piece of your mind when you get to heaven, don't have a piece to give to him, because your brain ain't there. You don't even have a little piece of it to give to him. That's what I think." He chuckled a little. "Besides God's clock and sense of timing is nothing like ours is. His is exact and precise, but it just doesn't look like it to us. And at times it ticks me off too. Just like everyone else who wants

God to do something at a specific time. Problem is, His timing ain't our timing and we're asking for something to happen at a time that isn't convenient to Him. And His is the timeframe in which he works. Not ours. And besides, you need that piece of your mind while down here, cuz you ain't none of that smart anyways. So there, neener neener." He looked at her with a big smile on his face.

Rachel looked across the table at her wise husband. "Well Dennis since you made it so simple to understand, I think I can agree with you. I love our time like this every morning. It's so quiet and just you and me chatting like we love each other. It's these times when I fall deeper in love with you. I hope you feel the same way.

"I do absolutely Rachel. I love our morning visits. We let each other talk about anything and everything and I love it. I look forward to this part of the day. I love it even better than the dinner table. I love you so much and I really love visiting with you every time we get the chance. But this is the bestest time of the day with you. You always make a nice breakfast regardless of what you cook. Your coffee is always better than mine. I know for a fact that God gave me the best woman on the planet when He put you in my life. You can't even argue with that, it's a fact."

Now they were both just sitting and smiling at each other with sweet smiles on their faces. God had done a great thing when He allowed these two to grace each other's lives. Right now, they were more than thankful for that, and they never wanted it to end. To say they both loved each other was a huge understatement.

Over at Sister Wilson's house, Bob and Larry were gulping down the last of the coffee. They were just finishing the best breakfast ever. Sister Wilson was really making it difficult for these two to figure out who was going to marry her first. This breakfast of eggs and bacon, as well as biscuits as fluffy as clouds. That gravy she put with them was to die for. Whatever she put in there they wanted it every day for the rest of their lives. It was going to be a sad day when they had to say good-bye to this food they had been eating these past few weeks.

Zane and Jimmy had just left Jimmy's house and headed for the church. Jimmy was shaking his head with a smile on his face. He finally answered Zane's question about the smile. "I'm telling you Zane, that Ken really is a Christian at this point. I have no questions as to that fact anymore. When I came down for breakfast this morning, he and mom were chatting and chuckling and having a great chat. I actually stopped about halfway down the stairs and just watched for a couple minutes because it was fun just to watch. They were talking about the church, his work, her daily chores, and stuff. But as they did, they threw in some little funny items which made them laugh. Every time they would laugh, they would reach over and grab each other's hand, and it was so sweet. The smiles they had were so big, I mean huge man. There is no question in my mind that those two are in love with each other. I didn't want to interrupt them. But my mom finally saw me standing there and called me down to the table.

Zane reached over and patted his leg. "I am so happy for you man. I heard every word you ever said about how bad of a man he was before this. And I'm hearing every loving word you're saying about him now. I have to admit though, I thought he was way too far gone for God to ever get to. I am so glad I was wrong. I'm also amazed at how huge a difference God has made in Ken's life. I mean for realsies, that man is the polar opposite of what he was before. He has become as sweet a person as he was a mean old booger snot person. But now, you can't help yourself but to love that guy. I mean, what a different person he is now. I can see why your mother fell in love with him if he was like this when they met. Shoot, what woman wouldn't marry the other Ken, and neither would anyone else. If he was our age and acting like this, we might have competition with our girls even."

They were pulling into the church parking lot at this point just as the Pastor and Bob and Larry were getting out of their cars. Everyone greeted each other with smiles and handshakes. Bob suggested they all go in and introduce these two youngens to the best beverage in the world, also known as coffee. "Best invention since the coffee bean." Bob said. But those two boys had already discovered it for themselves long ago, and the joke was on the elders of the group.

When they got to the kitchen, they found out that coffee was depleted, which made the entire group very sad. Larry grabbed Zane and said, "Come on, let's go to the store before we have to mop up the tears of fully grown men. That would just be sad."

Once at the store Larry found his favorite brand of coffee and was at the checkout stand before anyone knew they were even in the store. Larry turned to Zane, "A man can't survive even one day without coffee in his guts. That just a fact of life. Can't even argue with it."

The girl at the counter looked as if she hadn't had any coffee in at least thirteen weeks. She looked over at the two men at the counter a little surprised as she didn't hear them walk up. "Oh, I didn't know you were there, you startled me."

"I'm sorry about that. But I have men back at the church waiting for us to get back with this coffee or that church just may have to close for good, because they're going to rip it apart and leave it in a heap of dust." Then he flashed her a big smile.

"No, I should be the one to apologize. I haven't been able to sleep very well this week. I keep thinking about the church down the street and what's been going on there. People come in after the services and just beam their happiness. I just want to punch 'em in the face. I'm only kidding about that actually, but I envy them so much. I'm not sure I've ever had a smile that big. And it's so sincere, that's what's got me out of sorts. The happiness that they wear in here is obvious to anyone paying attention. I'm not the only here that has noticed it either." She brushed her hair off of her face so she could see who she was talking to.

Zane jumped right in without hesitation. "I actually go to that church. In fact, my friend's stepfather came in here the other day and apologized to everyone. That man got saved somehow and it changed his life completely and totally around. He's just as sweet as he was mean, is how I put it this morning. So, what have you been thinking that's keeping you awake at night?"

She was shaking her head back and forth as she spoke. "I can't sleep because I don't know if I would make it heaven when I die. I think my hubby might be doing the same thing. He checks on me at night to see if I'm asleep and I act like I am, so he doesn't worry. But he said something about hell the other day that got me to thinking about it. So do you have something to say that might answer my question?"

Zane looked at Larry. Larry just nodded at him encouraging to keep going with the conversation. Zane looked at her asked her for her name.

"I'm Wendy."

"And what's your husband's name?"

"Jake."

"Well Wendy, it just so happens that this guy right here," he pointed at Larry" and his friend are the ones kind of responsible for what's going on down there at the church. But Wendy, you don't have to wait until you go check it out to answer your question about where you spend eternity. We can do something about it right here, right now, right where we stand."

Wendy interrupted him right there. "Tell me right now and let's get this over with. I can't continue living like this. I'm dying over here and I'm not kidding. So just do it already!" She genuinely looked scared.

Zane looked at Larry again and got the nod. "All we have to do is say a short prayer, but you have to be sincere, okay?"

"You have no idea how sincere I am. I am so scared I'm going to hell. So PLEASE, let's pray." Wendy had tears in her eyes and her voice at this point.

Zane reached over and grabbed her hand. "Repeat what I say okay?" "Okay."

"Father forgive me of my sins...I confess my sins, and I repent...help me to live life according to your will...Amen." Zane looked at Wendy and noticed a smile begin when they finished praying.

Wendy came around the counter and gave Zane a hug like he had never had before. She was crying and hugging him so tight, and he was enjoying every moment of it. Zane caught a glimpse of Larry who had his eyes closed and both hands in the air.

At this point, the manger had come over to see what wrong with Wendy. Once he figured out what had just happened, he raised his hands like someone had just scored a touchdown! "Praise Your Holy Name oh God!" He was a Christian and had been praying for all of the store employees. He just didn't think it was going to happen at work. Now he was shaking Larry's hand and still wondering exactly how this happened.

Wendy came over and grabbed them both and gave them a group hug as she jumped and down with joy. Now all three of them were jumping up and down. It only took half a second for Zane to grab the bunch of them and join in the gymnastics. The manager suggested that they come back later when the store is full and repeat that prayer for the other employees. Now they were jumping and laughing.

It took a few minutes for them to gather their composure and be able to talk normally. Wendy went behind the counter and gathered some tissues to wipe her face. The makeup she was able to get on her face before coming to work this morning was all over the place now, including her shirt. She looked Zane right in the face, "You look like you're twelve years old. But after all this I'm guessing you're older than that. What's your name?"

"My name is Zane and I'm nineteen years old. This is my good friend Larry who happens to be the reason for most of what is happening at the church down the street." Wendy gave him another quick hug.

Larry couldn't let what Zane had said about him go too far. "No Wendy, I'm just one of the traveling Evangelists visiting for a short time. God is responsible for everything that's happening down there. Honest."

Wendy grabbed Larry and gave him another huge hug. "I don't care who's responsible for what, I'm just glad you made it in here just now. I was literally afraid to drive here this morning in case I got killed in a car wreck. I'm not kidding. I was miserable."

Larry being Larry said, "Well, it's okay for you to die now." He started laughing which got everyone else laughing. "Well listen Wendy, I know you have to get back to work and we need to go get our friends caffeinated before they turn that church into a national news story. But bring Jake tonight okay. And if he hasn't said a prayer like you did just now, we can take it from there at the end of the service. Sound like a plan?"

Wendy was shaking her head "yes" before Larry finished talking. "You guys had people standing all over the place last night, didn't you? Maybe we should bring our own camp chair or something tonight. People talk while their standing in line here, so I hear things. That's how we know everything that going on in this here town." Now she was laughing again.

David heard the comment about the camp chair and came over with an offer. "If that's true, let me talk to my Pastor and see about bringing some chairs from our fellowship hall for you guys tonight?"

Zane told him that was a great idea, but they hadn't broken out the chairs in their own fellowship hall yet. But they might need more chairs tomorrow night if tomorrow night's crowd is too big again.

Zane began shaking his head back and forth as he and Larry got back to the car. "Before you guys showed up in town here, I never knew it was possible to become a Christian unless you were at a church. But that's the second time in just a short time now. It's nice to know it's not required to be inside a church because these people who asked Christ into their heart are as saved as anyone I know right now. It amazes me what's been happening here since you guys showed up."

As they walked into the church Bob knew something happened at the store. He had seen that look on Larry's face a lot through these past two plus years. "What happened at the store?"

Larry smiled and pointed at Zane. "Tell 'em." Zane blushed as he looked at the group of guys, "The cashier got saved while we were there. It was really cool."

Bob was instantly excited. "You can't stop there, tell us what happened!" Larry just gave that nod again and Zane took it from there. "Wendy was looking so tired when we got to the counter, and I said as much. I should have kept my mouth shut, but I always enjoy teasing her, because she gives it right back to me. But today she tells us that she hasn't been sleeping very well since she's been hearing what's going on here at our church. She was afraid she was going to die and go to hell. Her husband was going through the same thing. So, I looked at Larry thinking he would take it from there, but he just nodded at me and basically told me to keep going. Ya big chicken! Anyways I looked at Wendy and she was beginning to get tears in her eyes. At that point I knew she was ready to pray, so I offered to pray with her, and she accepted Christ as we prayed and she started crying a little out loud, but not too much. Dude! I'm telling you even I could see the relief that came over her at once. Her shoulders literally dropped, and she let out a big sigh.

"At that point Dave was standing there and had pretty much figured out what had happened. After seeing Wendy's condition, he told her to go home and get her husband ready for church tonight, or something like that. I'm pretty sure he's going to show up and get saved too.

Zane was getting a bit giddy at this point. "Well guys, I'm whooped. Carrying the load has just worn me out. You rookies are going to have to take over from here. I need a nap." Zane started to giggle as he couldn't say that with a straight face.

Bob, Larry, and the Pastor looked at each other with big smiles. Bob was the first to speak. "Let's kill him!" He rushed over and got Zane in a fake headlock and acted like he was punching him in the face, then gave him a big hug. "I'm proud of you Zane. That's exactly what we were talking about yesterday, or whatever day it was. Just being ready and so full of Christ that you can do just that when it's called for. You did it bro."

Zane was looking at the floor. "I kind of feel like I passed a test."

Larry smiled at him. "That was no test Zane, that was the real deal. Wendy needed someone to pray her through to Christ and God made sure you were there to do it. Again, that wasn't a test. Someone got saved and the angels in heaven are having a party for it. Cake and ice cream for everybody up there right now." Both Bob and Pastor Brown raised their hands and shouted "Hallelujah" at the same time.

Jimmy pointed his finger at both of them. "We ain't got time for choir practice you guys. We've got work to do." They all laughed and slapped each other's palms.

"Well praise our good Lord for bringing Wendy into the kingdom, but yeah, we gotta get to work." Pastor Brown stood up and looked around the fellowship hall they were sitting in. "There's got to be a way get a decent crowd in this room and involve them int the service. Any ideas guys."

"Pastor we've had this happen before. We can use a camera in the sanctuary and a projector in here, but we'll also need some speakers. We have the camera and projector in our trunk, but we still need speakers. Where can we get those?" Larry looked at the Pastor and the two other guys.

"I've got some speakers I'm not using for my stereo anymore. Jimmy and I can go get those right now." Zane reached in his pocket and grabbed his keys.

"Why don't we go down to the electronics store and grab some wire and connectors while they're doing that Larry. Then we can come back here and figure out to get everything attached and working." Bob reached into his pocket and grabbed his keys. "You ain't the only one with keys in his pocket young mister." They all laughed and got in their respective cars as the Pastor went into the kitchen and made the much awaited coffee.

As Zane and Jimmy began to drive away, Jimmy called Betty Jo to see if her and Rebecca would come over to the church and give the kitchen a good scrubbing. With a crowd in there tonight that kitchen just wasn't up for company. Besides, it would give the four of them some time to see each other before the service started tonight. Betty Jo said she knew Rebecca would like that idea, so she would have her mom bring them over in a little while.

The two Evangelists walked into the little electronics store and found a rather angry looking man reading the paper behind the counter. "How can I help you guys today?"

"Well," Bod said, "We need to a good amount of stereo wire for some speakers and the right connecting jacks for the sound system. Can you help us with that teeny tiny list?"

"Yeah, I can." The guy didn't even look at them as he passed by and walked down an aisle. "I'm pretty sure I still have some that wire around. Since everything is going to Bluetooth, I don't have very many people beating feet to grab it anymore. You two aren't from around here, are you? Where you from?"

"We're actually just passing through sir, but we've been in town a couple of weeks helping out at the church down the street." Bob didn't want to tell the entire story.

"Well, if this is for Pastor Brown's church it's on the house. I love that Man. He did my mom's funeral a while back and he was so nice. He just made me feel like we had been friends for years, but I had never met the guy. He is one of nicest people I have ever met." Ralph was kind of smiling as he spoke.

Larry and Bob looked at each other and smiled. Larry told him it was indeed Pastor Brown's church they needed the supplies for. "In fact, sir, there's been quite an event going on down there for the time we've been there. It's really fun to see God work like He has. People are getting healed and even more getting saved. Do you go to a church here in town sir?"

The guy turned around with a really angry look and "NO!"

The two preachers looked at each other rather shocked at this intense response. "Did we miss something Ralph? I thought you liked Pastor Brown?"

"I do, I love that man. But God took momma before she was ready to go. I can't forgive that." He still had an angry tone to his voice.

They found the stereo wire and Ralph put it in a big bag for them and wished them well. But as they got to the car, Bob turned around and went back inside. Larry went ahead got the air conditioner going as it was a pretty warm day.

Larry watched Bob chat with Ralph through the big window. He watched Ralph shaking his head back and forth. Suddenly Ralph's head came up and he looked astonished. After a few minutes Bob and Ralph shook hands and Bob made his way to the car.

Larry was a little dumbfounded at what he just saw. "So, what just happened?"

Bob had a big smile on his face, "He'll be at church tonight."

"How did that Happen? He was mad when he walked out of there?" Larry was still confused.

"He knew about what's been happening at the church, he just didn't want anything to do with it because of how he feels about his mom. But when I told him about Ken and the Fire Chief, he almost broke his neck. He said if that was the truth he had to see them there for himself." Bob was still smiling. Larry pounded knuckles with him, and they drove back to the church.

Zane and Jimmy were inside wiping the dust off of the speakers when they walked into the building. The girls were in the kitchen working hard and the morning just seemed to be getting busier now. Pastor Brown was a little curious what took so long to get some wire.

Bob told him about Ralph and that he would be at church tonight. Pastor shared how hard Ralph took his mother's passing and that he seemed to get angry about it, but Pastor didn't know the big reason. But now it all made sense. "That makes my heart happy for him. He's a bit quirky but has one of the biggest hearts I've ever seen. He's easy to love that's for sure. I can't wait to tell Rachel. She's going to be so excited! God has done so much around this town it's getting the attention of a lot of people not only here, but in other towns in the area. All I can say is WOW God! God's getting bigger by the day around here! I might have said that already."

"Pastor, there's not a person in this town that would argue with that right now. This revival has almost gotten out of hand and it's opening the eyes of people that have been spiritually blind for a long time. It seems that those who haven't seen what's going on for themselves have at least heard about it. The Holy Spirit is having more conversations than we can count right now with just about everyone around this city. At least it seems that way to me." Larry was still smiling all over the place about what had happened this morning already.

"You keep wondering what's next, but you don't have to wait very long to find out. You know God will have more in store for this town, so let's just keep praying and smiling about it." Bob was smiling just as much as Larry was.

Zane and Jimmy were in awe of what these two guys were talking about. They knew they hadn't seen the things these guys had seen God do in other towns before. The stories they told were amazing, but Ken getting saved was just about the biggest thing these two had seen so far and that was going to be hard to beat anywhere.

As the five guys were standing around chatting about everything, the two girls came out and enjoyed the conversation with them. Both of them had grown so much and became closer to God since this revival began. They had never been a part of a conversation like this before and they both found themselves smiling along with the rest of the group. Neither one of them had even imagined that God could be this big or do so much in such a short time. To see all the miracles that had happened in this town in just a few days was absolutely mind boggling. And it appeared that they were only just getting started.

To end the chatter and get everyone back on task, the Pastor announced that the extra chairs would here in about ten minutes. He also told them that sister Wilson, sister Brown and Jimmy's mom were bringing a lunch big enough to bloat an elephant's tummy. So, it might be a good idea to get everything finished before they got too full to work afterwards.

Without saying a word Bob, Larry, Zane, and Jimmy moved faster than they had ever moved before getting things done. The girls worked just as hard finishing the kitchen, then started in on the fellowship hall working just as fast before the chairs got there.

Bob was moving so fast that he kept falling down. Finally, he fell pretty hard on his head which brought a huge round of laughter from the rest of the group. "Lord, knock 'em all in the head for laughing at my pain. What kind of friends do I have anyways?" At that point, the lunch arrived, and everyone's eyeballs got huge. To say it was a big lunch was an understatement. There was no way those seven people, plus the ladies could eat all of that today.

All of the guys filled their plates to the brim but could only eat about half of what they had taken. Rebecca and Betty Jo got more salad than anything and one piece of chicken. They had a figure to watch out for, of course. Sally, sister Brown and sister Wilson helped themselves to a little bit more than the girls and finished their lunch in no time flat.

Bob and Larry were the most vocal in letting everyone know they had eaten way too much and were probably going to have their innards splat all over the freshly painted walls. They will never get out of town if this keeps up. How many coats of paint does it takes to cover up innards anyways? They were hoping not to find out.

Finally, the three cooks started putting the food away and got it all in the refrigerator. Jimmy apparently had been hanging out with the preachers too long already, announced he was just ready to go for a second helping. Everyone got a good laugh at that. Betty told him to be careful with that, cuz she wasn't gonna be dating no fatty! Now everyone was really laughing.

Jimmy got his plate and sat down with the other guys at the table. The rest of them did a quick huddle and made a game plan for the rest of the day, then began painting in earnest. The girls cleaned up the kitchen after lunch, then got the bathrooms cleaned for the service tonight. All in all, it turned out to be a really productive day at the church itself. Then you have to consider the people who got saved before the day even started. By the time everyone had left, the place was as clean as a whistle and the speakers were hung properly and had finally quit hissing after quite a few tweaks. Now it was time to go home and get ready for church.

Zane and Jimmy didn't want to take the girls home, so they went over for an appetizer at the steak house in town. They talked about how much they had grown spiritually since this revival had begun. how much closer they were to God and how much all of them had really found it great fun to read their Bibles every morning and spend some time in prayer to start their day.

Sister Wilson had made some snacks for the boys as she knew they weren't going to be very hungry for a few months after that lunch today. The three of them were having pretty much the same conversation the four teenagers were having at the steak place. But they both could tell something was going to happen at tonight's service. They didn't know what, but they knew something would happen.

"Larry, have I told you that this has been the best revival we've been part of by far?" Bob was shaking his head back and forth in mild disbelief.

"You say that at every place we've been to Bob, but you might be right this time. I find myself wondering if it's really true, or have all the others been just as good, but this is the latest one, so it just feels like the greatest to us maybe." Larry really wondered sometimes if that were the case.

Sister Wilson's eyes got really big when she heard what Larry was pondering. "You mean to tell me that these things have happened in others places too?"

The two boys looked at each other with a smile. Larry spoke up. "Oh yeah Sister Wilson, every place we have had the privilege to stop. God does this every place He is welcome to do so. It doesn't happen just because we show up, but the people there are ready and hungry. That's when God can move and save and heal and do all kinds of things. He even healed a guy's car once, because he didn't have the money to fix it.

"God uses those people to keep His people ready to go to heaven when the time comes too. Pastors are great at doing their job and loving the flock. At times, they have to preach some things that can be hard to hear. Maybe someone has been blowing it in a certain part of their life. The Lord tells the preacher to preach about it and the consequences involved. Now it's up to that person to accept the correction or not.

"We have it easy, in that, we don't know the people at all. So, when the Lord puts it on our heart to preach about something, we just do it. We have no idea who we're preaching to, or the back story to what's going on. But so far in our little "road trip", God has been so faithful to not only bring a large crowd of new believers into the family, but He has also helped a lot of Christians set their feet more firmly onto the foundation of God, giving them a better experience with the Holy Spirit and basically help them grow in the faith. It's been fun for us to watch. I'm pretty sure I can speak for you on that one Bob. Am I right?"

"I was getting goose bumps just listening to you Larry. This "road trip" has really been a trip for both of us. No doubt." Bob was still shaking his head at the magnitude of the events that had taken place thus far at this church. This stop on their road trip had seemed to be more eventful than the other stops they had made. There were always people saved and maybe a significant healing or two, but this place had been like all of the previous places combined.

Chapter 12

Wednesday Night Service

When Bob and Larry entered the church, they found Pastor Brown and Rachel in the alters already praying for the service. They both went down and joined them as a few people had already straggled in.

There was already a sweet spirit in the building. Soon the four teenagers joined them for prayer as Louise knelt at her seat.

People began to fill the pews and knelt for prayer themselves. As they prayed, the Pastoral group went to the door and greeted people as they arrived. Ken and Sally came in and greeted them with smiles and saying hello. But Ken seemed a bit off tonight. Perhaps he was just a bit tired. Pastor Brown was hoping he was doing his morning devotions he had advised him to do. That morning time with God is a life changer for everyone who does it. There's nothing better than putting on your Spiritual armor every morning. Maybe Ken was having difficulty getting his armor in place.

The Youngs' came early so they could get a good seat. Others were coming for the same reason. Half an hour before the service started, the crowd was already crowded in. The fellowship hall was already full and now the people were finding a place to stand. Some began standing on the sides of the platform so they would be able to hear everything that was said tonight.

As the worship service started, the crowd was still growing. Now it was to the point that people were standing outside the front door. They sang along with worship as best they could hear. The neighbors came outside to see what was happening. Some of them came and joined in singing along with the others.

As cars passed by some of them would stop just to see what was going on. Most of them stood in the crowd and joined in. Others got back in their cars and drove away. By the time the worship was over, the parking lot was full of people standing and singing. One of the Police officers drove up to the opening of the parking lot and noticed people standing there. He put his lights on and parked there so no one would accidentally drive into them. He locked his car doors and went inside looking for Chief Doug just to let him know what was going on outside.

Doug went outside just to see for himself what the officer had told him. As soon as he saw the crowd he raised his hands and starting crying out loud. When he looked at the crowd, he found them with their hands raised and some faces full of tears. It touched his heart to see so many people singing out

186

loud and surrendering themselves to God at the same time. He had never seen anything like this before and he couldn't hold his composure, nor did he really try. It appeared that this crowd outside was pretty close in number to the crowd inside.

Doug looked at the officer and asked him if he knew what was going on and if he was a Christian. The officer said that he was a Christian and he could feel the presence of God before he made it to the church, but he didn't know why. He found out why he was feeling it when he got closer to the church. He even told Doug this crowd had to be bigger than the crowds that showed up at the carnivals in town. Doug easily agreed with him.

Doug told the officer to stay by his cruiser and run the motor from time to time to keep the battery from dying as he went inside. Doug went and talked to Mike to see about opening all the windows on that side of the building so more people could hear the service. Mike was on his feet before Doug finished asking. They both went and opened the few windows they had on that side of the church. As they opened each window the crowd outside pressed forward toward the sound.

The worship was so anointed, and God's presence was so strong, the worship went an hour long at least. People were praying for salvation without being prompted to do so. Prayers were being answered tonight that had lingered in times past. The same thing was happening outside. If there was someone not raising their hands, you couldn't tell. It appeared that everyone was being blessed tonight before the message even started.

Bob realized what was going on a few minutes after Mike and Doug opened the windows. Now he was shaking his head again and nudged Larry. Larry saw him shaking his head again and gave him a high five. Bob said, "I'm pretty sure this is the biggest crowd we have ever preached to brother?"

Larry had begun to shake his head along with Bob. "Bob you are right again oh wise one. But can you see that crowd outside? They're just as blessed as those inside. AND they've been standing for about an hour already."

"I can't wait to hear all the stories tonight. So don't be long winded this time, okay?" Bob said with a smile.

"It just so happens that I have a short one tonight. God gave me a short one tonight and now I know why. The thing I love most about these types of services is that so many things happen to the people in the crowd that we don't see happen. Plus!, we don't have anything to do with it. God does it all and we are only spectators. It's my favorite part of our ministry, we get to stand and watch." Now Larry had a huge smile, and he was ready to go snatch the microphone away from the worship leader. The two preachers looked at each other laughed for a bit and enjoyed the worship.

Soon the worship was over, but the instruments kept going for a little while as the crowd continued to worship God and be blessed. Pastor Brown made a few short announcements and handed it over to Larry.

"Wow! That's all I can say right now. So, we'll see you again tomorrow night. Be careful going home." He acted like he was setting the microphone down. The crowd laughed as he stood behind the podium. "Again, WOW! That was an amazing time of worship, wasn't it? Let's give a huge appreciation hand to the worship team." The crowd erupted in applause for a good while.

While they applauded, Larry worked his way over and opened a window and took a look outside and began to let the tears flow down his cheeks. He was able to see the crowd with wet cheeks and he noticed the Holy hunger in their eyes. He and Bob had seen this everywhere they had been so far on this road trip. It took him a few moments to get himself together, then he turned and looked at Bob.

"Bob, find yourself a microphone as I ask a couple of questions here." He looked over the crowd outside and asked, "How many of you asked Christ to be your Savior during the worship?" Dozens of hands went up, both inside and outside the building. "Okay, please make your way to the platform after the service, okay? We want to talk to you and get you a Bible and some other stuff. We'll wait as long as it takes, so take your time and don't run anyone over. We'll be there when you get there. Okay, next question. Was anyone healed during the worship?" About a Dozen hands went up. "Okay, same thing for you. Please make your way to the platform after we're finished here tonight. We'll be there waiting for you."

Then he turned to Bob with a microphone in his hand. "Heya Bob, how you doing about now?"

"I think I'm doing about the same as you are my friend." As Bob put his hand on his chest and appeared to be weeping.

Larry gave him a moment to get it together as he addressed the crowd from the windowsill. "One of the issues Bob and I face everywhere we go is that there's a good amount of the people who are new to Christ and all this church stuff, if you will, is this. Bob and I get the credit for what God has done for people. Such as those of you who asked Christ to be your Savior tonight and those that have been healed. Bob, did you do that?"

Bob had a good idea where Larry was going before he asked the question. "No Larry I didn't. Did you do it?"

"I'm so glad you asked that question Bob. So, if you didn't do it and I didn't do it, did you do it, Pastor Brown?"

Larry caught him off guard. He looked at Larry with a blank stare. Bob walked over to him and put the mic in front of his mouth. "I had nothing to do with nothing that has happened so far here tonight, Larry. So, if we didn't do it, then who did?"

"That's another great question Pastor. I think I shall answer it now. God did it. Did you hear me?" Now he raised his voice. "GOD DID IT ALL! Pastor didn't do it; Bob didn't do it, and I didn't do it either. I'm doing this to make a point so hear me and listen to my words as best you can. Bob and I get the praise sometimes when God does things like He has tonight. But we don't deserve one bit of that praise. That praise goes to the very source from where it came from, God and God only. The only thing Bob and I do is preach. We talk and say things and we teach at times. But when a person asks Christ into their heart it's because the Holy Spirit showed up and invited them to do so. And moving on from there, when someone is healed, God did it. Only God did it. At the time it happens, Me and Bob don't know a thing about it, until someone tells us what happened.

"In fact, if you noticed the two of us laughing earlier, it's because we were talking about this very thing. I was telling him, or he was telling me, I can't remember who said it now. Anyways, one of us told the other that we knew people were saved and healed and we had the privilege of being able to stand there and watch it happen. So, when you get happy about being saved or healed or whatever else may have happened, the praise and glory and honor belongs to God and Him alone. Lift your voice your hands to Him and say think you." The crowd began to praise and worship God for a moment. "Does everyone understand what I've said? I don't want anyone to be confused. The creator of the universe showed up here tonight and forgave some of you and healed others. So, I think I made my point on that and times getting on and I have a message for you tonight. I'll only be a just a few minutes though.

"Hey Pastor, Bob we can't have people hanging through the windows like this tomorrow. Can you two and whoever else you need involved, come up with a plan to make a place for everyone tomorrow? Maybe we can announce that tonight before we dismiss later. Can you guys do that for these nice folks?" Larry was still amazed at the size of the crowd tonight.

"So, while they work on their assignment, let me get into tonight's message. Open you Bibles or whatever digital device you have to Matthew chapter seven. I'm going to stand here by this window and preach tonight so that maybe everyone can hear a little better outside." Larry noticed a guy sitting right in front of him with his Bible open. He put his hand on his shoulder. "Sir, would you mind reading verses thirteen and fourteen for us?"

The guy turned about fifty shades of red but agreed to read it for the people. Larry thanked him and had everyone give him a hand. Again, he turned a bunch of colors of red. He was a really shy and bashful person, but he served God with his entire being tonight. Larry held the microphone in front of him as he read. "Enter by the narrow gate for the gate is wide and broad that leads to destruction and a lot of people enter it. But the gate is narrow and small that leads to heaven and small is the number that find it."

"Let me start by asking a silly question. Why would the majority of humanity decide to walk through the wide gate and into eternal damnation, when it is so easy to walk through the narrow gate and into eternal bliss? They've been deceived. Others, knowing who God really is, don't mind making their way through the narrow gate. They just refuse to bow their knees to the devil. Satan has this thing about a person thinking that if they live a good life and are better than the other person, they'll make it to heaven. The problem with that point of view is that God doesn't grade on a curve. Jesus tells us earlier in Matthew chapter five and verse forty-eight that we are to be perfect just as our Father in Heaven is perfect. That doesn't sound so hard now does it?" Most of the crowd had wide eyes as they realized exactly how difficult that would be. "So basically, it's a pass or fail grade.

"Let me talk about that a little bit at a time. Becoming a Christian is simple isn't it. That's a statement not a question. Praying and asking Jesus to forgive us of our sins is a simple thing to do. The hard part is getting your heart into position to do such a thing. That's where the Holy Spirit comes in and makes your heart feel like it's going to pop out of your chest. Then He prompts you to pray and ask forgiveness. Now we're Christians and we're so glad for that.

"So, here's the most fantastic thing about asking forgiveness of your sins. Second Corinthians chapter five and verse seventeen tells us that once we say that prayer that all things become new in Christ. Old things have passed away and all things are now new. In other words, you're a completely new, or different person at that point. That means that it's no coincidence when you feel like the weight of world has just left your shoulders and you feel lighter than air. How many times have we heard that since we've been in this town Bob?" Bob stood up and held his hands apart as far as he could. "That's still an understatement brother.

"Okay, let's get into that perfection thing. When I was growing up, I used to hear this analogy once in a while and it made sense to me. Maybe it'll make sense to you as well. When Christ bled all over that cross for our sins, our sins were covered by that blood. So, when God looks at our condition of being a sinner, it kind of goes like this. If he can look at our life and sees sins popping up out of that blood, it means we have sins that aren't covered by the blood of Christ. That's not good, and out future will be quite hot. But if He looks at our life and doesn't see any sins at all, but only the blood of Christ, the next thing we're going to hear is God welcoming us into heaven.

"I've also heard people talk about a courtroom scenario where Christ is our attorney. As God is getting ready to slam the gavel down on us and give us the bad news, Christ speaks up and tells God not so fast Dad. This person has accepted Me as their Savior and is as perfect as you are. It's okay in this case, they should be allowed into Your paradise. God hears His Son, and that all is forgiven, and we are allowed to enter into heaven at that point.

"And just take this one step further in Hebrews chapter ten and verse fourteen we are told that Christ has perfected us. That's a loose quote of that Scripture so I suggest you find it and read it for yourself. Again, that was Hebrews ten, fourteen.

"So don't be afraid of that issue about being perfect. The fact of the matter is that none of us are perfect within ourselves. But if we are in Christ, we are perfected through him. We can never get there on our own. But Christ makes us perfect. You have to admit that bar is set so high we can't achieve that on our own. But again, Christ is so gracious and forgiving. As soon as we ask to be forgiven, we get the full package. We get saved and our new future is in heaven singing with the Saints. We are going to see Jesus face to face some day. I like to think of that day often.

"I have a few different scenarios in my mind. I think of running into His arms like a two year old girl and wrapping my arms around Him and hugging him so tight he has to tell me to ease up. Another scenario, which might be more realistic, is that I see him and fall on my knees in worship to Him. Another is that we walk and chat while we have our arms over each other's shoulders.

"Those are just my ideas; you may have your own. But here's the plain truth friend. We only have two choices about our future when this life is over. One is so fantastic we can't even imagine how great it is. The other is so horrible that we don't even want to think about it. The fact that we will be on fire for eternity is a scary thought. But the devil keeps telling you that I'm a liar and it's not that bad. But the Bible tells us that it is that bad and the Bible doesn't lie, so I'm going with what the Bible says.

"Folks this sermon tonight has been as simply put as I know how to put it, I prayed over this sermon for quite a while before I was comfortable with it. I don't like to point my finger at people and tell them they're going to hell and that's what this has felt like to me tonight and I'm sorry. But forget the words that I spoke tonight. But pay attention to the words that you heard in your heart. Does your heart tell you that you need to ask for forgiveness. Is your heart telling you it's time to quit fooling yourself and get real with God? Is your heart telling you it's time to quit running from God? Is your heart beating so fast and hard that it feels like it's coming out of your chest? Well then, let's get this over with. Let's bow our heads. Even you guys out here in the parking lot, bow your heads and let's say a prayer. If you need to ask for forgiveness, let's do it. Just say these words out loud. Father, please forgive me of my sins... Please guide me and direct my life... Draw me towards You... Thank you Jesus for dying for my sins... Amen.

"There you have it. Now you're perfect and walking in through that narrow gate. It was really easy wasn't it. Just say a few words with a sincere heart and that changed your life forever. Now that you have prayed and become a Christian, the devil is going to be coming at you from every direction at the same time. He's going to tell you that I lied you. That there's no way that God could save someone as awful as you are and all sorts of other things. So, here's what we're going to do now. Bow your heads again because we are going to pray for protection for those of you that accepted Christ as your savior tonight."

"Father, we know how the devil works and what happens when people first get saved. We know how he comes in and tells these people big fat lies and tries to discourage them from believing that they really are saved. So, we ask right now that You will guard their hearts and minds and let them know without a doubt that they are indeed and new creature and perfected in You. Thank You once again for what You did on that cross for us Jesus. Amen.

"Now, here's something for every one of us to do before we go to sleep tonight. Read John the first chapter before you close your eyes. Those of you that have gotten saved since this revival started and even tonight will learn a few things about Jesus. The rest of us will just be encouraged in what we read. There will be a test tomorrow night, so take a lot of notes.

"Don't forget to make your way to the platform you guys. Whoever accepted Christ tonight and were healed. We want to see you before you leave, okay."

Suddenly Larry looked lost. He looked at the platform to find Pastor Brown. There were so many people up on the platform that it took him a few minutes to find him. "Pastor Brown, if it's okay with you I'll just go ahead and dismiss this crowd of four million people and invite them all back tomorrow night."

Pastor Brown told him he an announcement About tomorrows seating. He found a microphone and told everyone to come and there would be plenty of seating in the parking lot under tents, so they didn't have to get burned by the sun.

Larry prayed for safe travels for everyone and a safe return tomorrow night and wished everyone well. The crowd was slow moving as it was so crowded. A lot of people took advantage of the slow pace and met the people around them and began visiting right where they were.

Pastor Brown was trying to get to the platform so he could shake hands and meet the new people, but it was tough going. He ran into Leo, who had some fun news for him. "I still have a job but get this!"

Pastor Brown could tell it was really good news just by seeing the look on Leo's face. "What?" he said,

"I'm playing Christian music now as my bumper music! Can you believe that! It was my managers' suggestion too! He was listening to our conversation the other day and said that prayer with all of us. I had to call some larger stations to see if they could loan us some music or sell it to us until we could get our own supply. Most of them were sending us all they had. Others were more of a corporate station, so they had to get permission from the corporation. I can't even put into words how happy I am since we talked the other day. But what's even more fun is to watch God work like this. This is more than amazing man. I really don't know the words to use to describe it because this all so new to me."

They stood and chatted for a few minutes with huge smiles acknowledging how big and great some of the things were that had been happening just since their conversation on the air. They concluded that God was getting bigger every day and the more they learned the bigger He got.

As the conversation with Leo ended Pastor Brown walked towards the platform shaking his head back forth. He began to talk to himself out loud, "Father, this entire area has done a one-eighty since You started this *thing* a few weeks ago. All I know to say is that You are so awesome! It's the only word that comes close to this and even that is an understatement." It took a while, but he finally made his way to the platform.

Mike Lewellen took it upon himself to grab a box of Bibles and brought them to the platform. Billy Warren was right behind him another supply to make sure they had enough.

They met and spoke with as many people as they could before it was time to let everyone go get some sleep so they could function tomorrow.

After the last couple left the foyer Pastor Brown looked at his watch and it was midnight. He told the gang what time it was, and they all seemed to gasp. "Wow! Once again, that's the only word I can think of to describe the moment. Have any of you come up with a different word yet? Bob was the first to answer. "Wowzers Dude! That one is working for me right now until I come up with something better.

Larry smiled as he looked at his best friend. "You know, for once I agree with your weirdness. I like that one." About that time Larry noticed to two young couples standing there with them. "What are you guys doing here? Isn't waaaaay past your bedtime?" Then he chuckled.

Jimmy decided to join the fun. "Awesomer than awesome! Works for me. I think."

Zane nudged him with his elbow and smiled. "What are we doing and who are we talking about?"

Pastor Brown answered him. "With what God has done since this has begun, I can't come up with a good word that describes how good this has been. Every word I can come up with seems so shallow and an unworthy description of how large and awesome God has been to us. So, I'm open to suggestions. So far 'Wow'! and 'Wowzers' are as close as we've come."

Betty Jo nudged Rebecca with a quizzical look. Rebecca just shook her head as she said, "I'm not sure there's an English word that even comes close to describing this."

"That seems to be the answer we've come up with so far." Larry said.

Rebecca decided to make herself and Betty Jo seem special. "Well, since Betty Jo and I are the smartest ones in the group, we'll start to put some serious thought into the matter and get back you all at a later date." The group got a good laugh out of that one.

Pastor Brown suddenly remembered about his conversation with Leo. "Hey, Leo stopped me on the way to the platform tonight. He told that' he's playing Christian music on his show. It was his boss's idea. Apparently, his boss was listening in that day I was on his show and prayed the Sinners Prayer with us." Pastor Brown began to cry. "This just gets better by the minute you guys. His boss will be here tomorrow night with his wife. I'm guessing she might have gotten saved when the boss made it home that day. If not, I like her chances while she's here tomorrow."

He raised his hands began praise God again. "God, my faith has never been at this level. You have done so much more than I could have ever imagined in all of my days at this point. I'm going to be bold here and ask for more. I don't know that means but keep doing what You have been doing and give us more.

Thank You, God, thank You Jesus, thank you Holy Spirit. Hallelujah, hallelujah, hallelujah."

The rest of group joined in with praise as the Pastor was praising God. The room filled with the presence of the Holy Spirit, and this little session of praise lasted for a little while. Jimmy looked over at Zane and the girls. All of them had their hands in the air and tears on their cheeks as did Jimmy. He closed his eyes and raised his arms in praise as he rejoined the group.

After quite a while it was quiet, and they could hear noises in the kitchen. A few minutes later, Rachel and Sister Wilson brought out the leftovers from earlier in the day. Rachel walked over and kissed the pastor on his cheek. "Sister Wilson kind of figured all of you would be hungry at this hour. It's one-thirty in the morning. Why don't you guys eat a big fat early breakfast and come in here a little late this morning. You guys have been working so hard on everything, including this building, you deserve at least a couple hours of sleep. I think." Dennis grabbed her and kissed her forehead and gave her a big hug.

Sister Wilson looked over at the two preachers. "I'm not going to wake you two up for breakfast like I have been, at least not today. You two are starting to look tired. Rachel and I aren't making a demand here, but we're concerned about how tired you all might be getting. Just give yourself a few hours of extra rest. Can you do that so she and I can relax a little bit for you guys and girls?" As she was talking, she and Rachel were dishing up the food for the group.

Larry spoke first. "Okay ladies, we're going to need you to make a couple of important calls for us in the morning. We need you to call Mike and tell him we need a few things. Tell him that we need a couple of those big tents for the parking lot. In fact, we're going to need enough of them to cover the entire parking lot. We're also going to need at least two port a-potty's and one for disabled people. I'm sure there's a rule about that somewhere. Did I miss anything Pastor?"

"Well, now that you brought it up, why don't you call Doug and Chief Larson for direction on those tents. Maybe we should also get some guidance on the seating arrangements if we need it. Also ask Doug what we can do about parking. We may need to close a street or two. Can you guys think of anything else?" The Pastor looked like he could really use a good night's sleep.

Zane piped up. "Call my dad first. I swear that guy knows everybody in the United States. I'm pretty sure he can get you everything you're asking about. In fact, I'm sure my dad will be over here giving directions and ordering people around, nicely of course. I swear he was a drill sergeant at some point in his life."

At that point it all seemed settled, and it got quiet as they all sat and enjoyed some really good leftovers.

Pastor Brown woke with jolt. "What time is it? The sun is high I can tell. What's going on?" As he rubbed to eyes to gain some focus, he noticed Rachel sitting in her chair looking over her book with that beautiful face of hers.

"Dennis it's okay. Remember you were going to sleep in a little bit today and take a short break. We knew you guys were getting tired and needed a little more rest than you've getting these past couple of weeks. Everything is fine. I made all the phone calls we needed to make. The two chiefs were going to go over to the church and take a look at our parking lot to see how to get the maximum seating out there tonight. So just lay back down and relax for a few more minutes. God has it all under control and He doesn't need your help at this very moment." She was still smiling as she spoke.

"Man, I tell you what, those two young preachers are going to leave me with a mountain range of work when they leave town. I'm actually looking forward to it too. I'm going to need a bigger staff; I know that much already. I'm going to need a janitor and an associate. I'm going to have to figure out time for my wife, whoever that is. At this point I haven't seen her in like four years. Does she still have those cute dimples in her cheeks and those beautiful eyes? The most beautiful eyes in the world. Do you have any idea where this woman might be? You look familiar, but you're not as pretty as my wife." Rachel punched him in his guts and hugged him at the same time.

Pastor Brown laid there looking at her and wanting to grab her face and kiss it. "That smile of yours is making this room a lot brighter. It ticks me off!" Then they both laughed. "I remember everything now that I'm awake. Man, waking up like that can kill a guy. That was instant fear, but I'm okay now. No wonder most of the heart attacks are in the early morning hours." He looked around the room for the clock but couldn't find it. "Rachel, where the clock?"

'I took it out last night when we got home. I didn't want you waking too early and getting right back at it. That's why I'm sitting here with my book. I was prepared to bonk you on the head with it if you woke up earlier than you should? Old guys like you tend to get a little cranky if they don't get enough sleep. You guys have been getting to the church early and leaving late every night. We suggested just a couple hours of extra today, but only today." You look well rested at this point you ol' coot. Now get your clothes on and get out of here. You've got leftovers to eat in about thirty minutes. And you need to shower because you stink. Other than that, you're perfect." With that, she got up and walked toward the living room.

Dennis intercepted her as she walked by the bed, pulled her down with him and acted like he was giving her a noogy. "How did I ever marry such a heartless woman? She's so mean dogs run from her and wet themselves. She's so mean tomatoes refuse to grow in her garden. She's so mean the paint melts off of her car. She's so mean all twelve of her husband's went bald. A couple went cross eyed, and one never came home from fishing because the fish were treating him better than she did. Should I continue my dear?"

"Yeah, you should because it's the last time anyone's going to hear your voice. I'm going to poison your drink today."

Dennis laughed. "Oh, you think you're so smart. Well guess what? I'm going to drink it too. So there, neener neener." Then he started kissing her all over her head.

Bob and Larry were awakened by the smell of coffee and biscuits in the oven. Sister Wilson let them sleep in today, but that biscuit smell would wake the dead with a smile on their dead face. They began to talk about the weight Sister Wilson had put on them since arriving in town. Their clothes were getting a little tight at this point. Sister Wilson reminded them that there was something wrong with a skinny pastor. As they thought about it, almost all of the pastors they had met while on this road trip had a few extra pounds around the middle. They were still arguing about who was going to marry this precious woman first when they headed out the door.

Zane didn't sleep very well and ended up getting up with his parents this morning. While enjoying their great breakfast, compliments of his mom, Helen, they had an enjoyable conversation about the revival. Billy noted that the people bringing their cars in for repair weren't as angry about it. The church came up more often with his customers and some of them wanted to hear stories about it. He was really good about inviting them to come find out for themselves.

Zane told them how much he had learned by being around Larry and Bob as well as how much he had grown in his walk with the Lord. They had been a huge influence on him since he decided he wanted to hang out with them. According to Zane, those two were perfect in how they lived their lives and treated people. He just wished he could have that character as he went forward in life. They had definitely made a huge impact on him already. But he was careful to let Billy know that he was his only hero and always would be.

Billy had no trouble believing anything Zane had to say about the two preacher's character. He pointed out to Zane that at about ten or eleven years old, kids begin to make their own decisions about things and not pay so much to their parents. So, what Zane had said just now was actually great news. Considering the people he was talking about; he knew his son was in good company while he was making decisions about what kind of man he was going to be.

Jimmy was eating breakfast with his mom and Ken this morning and enjoying a good visit with them. Jimmy found himself looking at Ken this morning, while he ate and realized how much he had grown to love him since he got saved and said as much to Ken. Ken smiled and reached over to grab Jimmy's shoulder and told him that it was a mutual relationship at this point. So, they sat there and tried to out complement each other and laughed about it.

Sally told them they were funny and was enjoying the show. Then she began to talk about the churches in the area that had been coming on their nights off from their own churches. She was hoping that this revival would empower those churches to expand on the momentum and keep it going when the revival ended. She looked at Jimmy. "Gods called you into the ministry hasn't He."

"As a matter of fact, He has. In fact, me and Zane went into the church one day and announced that the Lord had put it on our heart to begin helping with the youth. When I told Zane I wanted to do the same thing he did, his face looked totally confused. We never even talked about it before that day. It would be kind of cool if we ended up in the same type of ministry in a few years.

Over at the church there was a group of people preparing the parking lot for tonight. Billy Warren called every person he could think of that might have something to offer.

Billy had the tent guy out there measuring to see how many tents it would take to cover the entire parking lot. He even had an audio and TV guy out there figuring out how to display the biggest TV's he had. He and Billy figured two in the parking lot and one in the fellowship hall. They were even talking about putting the church service online. A couple of the churches had gotten together and sent over every chair they could spare for tonight.

Chief Roberts came up with an idea he thought might be important but wanted to run it by Chief Lee. He started walking over to where he thought he had seen him last. As he got there, he was a little confused as to how fast he and Officer Mark had vacated the area. He looked down the street and saw them talking with a couple on the sidewalk. As he walked in their direction the conversation ended.

"Doug, how's it going for you today my friend?"

The two shook hands "Well Don, I'm at a loss for words for what's been going on here in town since this revival began. I've never been involved with anything like this. And I started going to church nine months before I was born. This is more than amazing. What about you Mark? You've been a Christian for a long time too?" He nudged Mark with his elbow.

Mark started shaking his head back and forth. "Doug, I have never seen anything come close to this. I know how big God is. Or at least I thought I did. I don't have words for this Chief. As I'm thinking about it, awesome, magnificent, overwhelming even far out man don't do this justice." Then he shrugged his shoulders.

Chief Roberts looked at Chief Lee and shrugged his shoulders. "This is my first rodeo through this stuff. Are you telling me it's all downhill from here? They all chuckled. "Doug, I have an idea but I'm not sure I like it."

"Okay, what is it, Don? It can't be that bad." Now Doug had a concerned look on his face.

"Oh, it's not a bad idea, I just don't like it. I'm thinking we probably should put one or two portable toilets out here. If I was the same old man I was, I would insist on them but that's not the case anymore thank the good Lord. But if someone from the county shows up, we're going to get a good tongue lashing. What do you think about it?" Don had a hurt look on his face.

"I think you're dead on right to have them brought in. It's our job to oversee things like that Don. If we don't do our jobs on a professional basis, the professional Doug and Don will get in trouble. But the bottom line is that we really need them here. It's only common sense. But I don't know anyone who owns one of those companies. Do you?" Doug had his hand on Don't shoulder.

"I sure do. I've had to call him in times past. As far as I can tell, he's honest and his customer service is pretty good. He's not my greatest fan, but that's never kept him from being polite to me. I trust him anyways." Don said.

Doug gave him a thumbs up. "Give him a call and we can mark that off the list. Mark and I have a good plan for parking tonight. It'll give some our guys some overtime that they can use. So how 'bout your stuff Don?"

"I've got it worked out with the tents and chairs at this point. I only need to call for the toilets, so I'll do that now." Don turned and walked back toward the church while making the call.

Inside the church the group of preachers and soon to be preachers were all enjoying the last of the leftovers from yesterday. It was unusually quiet today inside the church. On the outside it was like a beehive. People were all over the place getting everything in place for tonight and beyond.

Zane was the first to speak. "I've got to say this while I'm thinking about it. Larry and Bob, I have learned so much and grown as a Christian more than I ever knew was possible while you guys have been here. I feel like a totally different person too. My thoughts are different and the way I feel about things is completely different. Things that use to frustrate me or aggravate me don't anymore or do it less than before. You two are so calm all the time and it's amazing to watch. If I can be half the person, you two are, that would make me a really good man." Then he looked at Jimmy and shrugged his shoulders.

Jimmy didn't hesitate. "I'm the same way as Zane. Everything he said I say ditto for myself. I've noticed a change in Zane since you guys have been here. I'm not sure I've changed that much though."

Zane told him, "You have changed as much as anyone has Jimmy. I'm pretty sure we're on the same path."

"I hope that's true Zane. I know my thoughts and attitudes have changed a bit. I don't know what else to say, but I sure have enjoyed hanging out with you two. Well, Pastor Brown also, but he's old so I don't know if that counts."

Bob and Larry had been siting there with mouths open as they listened to these two kids that were so mature well passed their years. When Jimmy made the comment about the pastor Larry couldn't let it go without getting into it as well. "Well, ya, he is kinda old and a little ugly, but I think he preached pretty good some weekends. What do you think Bob?"

"I ain't getting in trouble with God just because you silly boys ain't smart. But he really is ugly. Rachel only married him because she felt sorry for him." Bob chuckled a little as did the others. Then Bob looked at Pastor Brown and said, "Brother, I love you more than I deserve. You have proven yourself to be rock solid with all of the crud the devil has thrown at us these few weeks. I mean it. You have proven yourself to be a strong leader and an even stronger warrior, I'm not kidding you. And Rachel married you because she fell in love with you and it's easy to see why." Then he smiled at the pastor.

Dennis waited for a few seconds expecting a punchline, but it didn't arrive. "Oh, you're being serious all of a sudden. You can't sneak up on a guy my age like that, it scares us into an early grave. I'm lucky I only to have to change my britches this time." Now everyone was laughing.

"It's kind of nice to be serious at times, I guess. Thank you for those kind words, Bob. To be totally honest this experience has brought that out of me. I've never had a fight like this. What boggles my mind right now is the fact that you two have been through this stuff before. So, you can stand there not fazed by being shot in the rump with double-ot buck shot and come out almost laughing about it. I almost passed out when I saw that hole in my chair that day. That would have hit me square in the middle of my chest. I'm mean seriously, how does this kind of thing NOT scare you guys?" He shook head. "I'm not kidding about that passing out thing. It flat out scared me to think that the devil tried to kill me that day. Then to find out that little zing I heard was a bullet whizzing by me in the hall. He tried two different ways that day and yet I'm standing here talking to two of the most amazing people have ever met.

"I've had other Evangelists come through here from time to time to get a revival going here, but after the meetings are over it only takes about two minutes before the effect is finished. To say it's discouraging is a monumental understatement. But with you two, I've got job security for a long time now. There's no way this church and town are never going to be the same when these meetings end. And to be honest with you, I don't want them to end. I have grown to love you two like my own sons at this point. Then I look at Zane and Jimmy over here and they're just a younger version of you two in some ways. They're amazing you men with a similar character. If they start preaching or evangelizing like you two, this country ain't ready for that." Now the pastor was laughing and shaking his head.

Zane's head almost popped off of his head when the pastor compared him and Jimmy to Bob and Larry. "I can assure you Pastor Brown that I'm not ready to preach or be an evangelist yet. And if God calls me to something like that, I'm going to lock myself in my bedroom and never come out. I have no desire to be shot at or anything like that right now. I just want to go to church and college and maybe get married in a couple years or something. Don't scare a young guy like that. It just ain't the right thing to do. You silly old man you. You're just lucky I only have to go home and change my pants this time" Now Zane was pointing his finger and frowning at the pastor in jest.

As Zane was talking, Rebecca and Betty walked in the back door. Rebecca saw Zane pointing and frowning. "Ya! You silly old man you!"

The group of guys started laughing and holding their abdomens. These friends had learned to have a fun time together. Pastor Brown just laughed and told them that he loved them all and kept laughing.

Outside Doug and Officer Mark finally had a minute to take a break for a quick minute. "Hey Doug, I was talking to a friend of mine last night. Apparently, he had been thinking about that murder last year. He told me he used to see that old limousine around town when he and his wife would do date night. He says he doesn't think he's seen it since then though. I'm wondering if maybe the guy was living here in town at the time and if so, maybe he still has that car in his garage somewhere here in town."

"I guess maybe we should start paying attention to open garage doors as we patrol now. My thinking has been that one of those guys involved would get caught for something, then rat out the others for some kind of deal. That is interesting that no one has done just that. Maybe the guy that killed her decided that was enough and quit. Like he has a conscience or something. Hmm, date night. That's a good idea man, I'm going to tell the wife about that one. That sounds like fun." The chief had a habit of talking about several things in one sentence like this.

"You know Doug every time I drive by this place, I feel something. Especially since whatever has been going here, I guess. Actually, I can feel it now. It's like just all over the place. Stuck in the cement and the street. I'm looking forward to tonight. My wife and I talk about this revival every day now. It's been a really big part of our spiritual growth since it began."

About that time one of the guys the video equipment arrived. He knew about the TV's coming over to be used outside tonight, but he wondered how that was going to work because no one said anything about a camera in the sanctuary.

He met Billy as soon as he got out of his truck. "Where should I set up this camera?" He asked.

Billy introduced himself to the guy. "Hi Billy, I'm Walt Smith. No one contacted me about this. I found out about it talking with the other guys at the store. I thought maybe someone should bring a camera over here since they said no one had thought of it yet. I have a nice camera in my van, but someone needs to operate it. It's not a set it up and forget it type."

"Well, let's go inside and figure it all out. I'll let you figure it out since you're the expert on this sort of thing." Billy was getting excited about how big this operation was beginning to get. A few short weeks ago they only had a few dozen people attending this church. Now it seemed like thousands and there just wasn't enough room for all of them. They went into the sanctuary and found a great spot immediately. There was a place in the back corner that wouldn't be in the way of the congregation, but it also offered a clear view to the platform and the windows if it needed to. It would need to be elevated a little, but it was a perfect spot.

Walt told Billy he needed a few more things and went out to the van and got a control table he could operate from the corner to make sure the camera views made it out to all the TVs. "I think we've got it all set now Billy. Any idea how many people are going to be here tonight?"

Billy began to tear up a little bit. "Walt...I don't know... Hundreds is all I can come up with right now...It could even be a thousand for all I know." He began to cry. It took him a few minutes to gain his composure. "I'm sorry Walt, this is getting overwhelming to me at this point. We've had so many coming the past week or so. Now we can't contain it in our building anymore. People seem to be coming to Christ by the dozens every night. We've had marriages restored and people have been healed. We even had a little baby with disabilities get up out of her seat and start walking around the other day. I've been in the presence of God quit a few times Walt, but not at this level. It always feels like being surrounded by a comfortable warmth. Now it's so thick, it feels like it's going to carry you away. Are you a Christian Walt?"

"No sir I'm not. But as we were working in there just now, I could feel something. It was almost coming out at the walls at me. I was talking to my grandma yesterday and she asked me when I was going to quit running from God. I think right now would be a good time. How do I become a Christian? Can you help with that Billy?" Now they were both crying.

Doug and Mark heard them crying and came over to find out what was going on. As they got closer Officer Mark began to tear up and put his hand on Doug's shoulder. Now the group was standing together, and Doug had no clue what was going on yet. "Okay, what's going on here. What am I missing here Billy?"

Billy couldn't talk yet, but he reached over and hugged Doug tightly. So, Doug just stood there hugging him.

It took a few minutes, but Billy was able to tell Doug that he was getting ready to lead Walt in the Sinners Prayer.

At this point, the preachers came out with the four teenagers to get busy but were met with people crying. So, they walked over to see what was going on.

Billy was finally able to tell them what was about to happen. "Pastor, do you want to lead this prayer?"

"No Billy you got this, go right ahead." Pastor Brown had never had a smile this big as far he knew.

"OK Walt just repeat after me, ok? Walt nodded because he couldn't speak very well at the moment. "Father forgive me of my sins...thank you for dying on the cross for my sins Jesus...please come into my heart... help me to live my life...according to Your ways...Amen."

Bob lost it. He raised his arms and started yelling, "Hallelujah, Hallelujah, Hallelujah!"

Larry started to laugh as he raised his arms in praise to God. The rest of the crowd around them began to do the same thing. The others that had been working outside walked over and began praising God right there on the sidewalk. Church started early today.

After a little while the crowd began to disperse and get back to what they were doing even though they were pretty much finished. It was starting to get pretty hot outside as well, so they all finished the final details and called it a day.

Jimmy just remembered that he had a sizable number of folding chairs in his garage and decided to go get them. He told Zane what he was going to do, and Zane told him he would bring his car over to help. Besides, Jimmy's car only had a small trunk and Zane's was much bigger, plus he had four doors making the back seat available for the large haul.

As they got to Jimmy's house, he was thankful his garage was in the shade. As he looked around for the chairs, he found them in a corner behind the car that Ken left covered. He had never seen that car, but it was big one. He wiggled his way back into the corner and handed Zane a couple chairs over the trunk lid of the covered car. As he did, he brushed something with his leg, and it fell of the car onto the floor.

As Jimmy knelt down, he thought it looked like teeth. He had Zane go over and turn on the lights so he could see better. It was indeed teeth, and they were broken. Whoever these teeth belonged to still had the roots to these teeth in his mouth. Then he looked at the car cover and noticed a pretty large spot of blood that these teeth had probably been stuck to.

Zane got curious and asked what he was looking at, so Jimmy walked around the car and showed him. Zane was no good at being around blood and got a queasy. As Zane took some deep breaths to keep from throwing up Jimmy looked at the car.

Jimmy lifted up the corner of the cover enough to where he could get a look at the car underneath. He noticed a tire with wide whitewalls. His heart fell and Zane's eyes got really wide. They uncovered the car and looked inside. It seemed that every place they looked there was a spot of blood. Zane had to walk outside and take some deep breaths. That was too much blood for him.

Jimmy got the keys out of the dashboard and opened the trunk to see what might be in there. He found a bag containing a fake beard and mustache, fake eyebrows and a small plastic case that had colored contact lenses in it. Then Jimmy saw something that made him as nauseous as Zane was. He found a black head band. "Zane, was Linda wearing a black hair band that night?"

"Ya I think so why?"

"Look at this. I think it's hers."

"I think you're right Jimmy. Now that I'm thinking about it, it wasn't there when I found her that night. It just might hers for sure." Zane ran outside and heaved.

Jimmy got tears in eyes. This can't be real. Can it? There's no way Ken or anyone he knew could have done this. Jimmy was scared now and had no idea what to do or how to handle this.

Not only was Zane scared out of his wits, but he was also afraid Ken would come home and catch them. "What time does Ken get home from work?"

Jimmy looked at his watch. "In about ten minutes. Let's closed this up before he gets here."

Just as they got the door closed Ken pulled up. Jimmy and Zane walked around the garage in the opposite direction like they were doing something. "Zane, I don't know what to do. I don't have a clue what to do. I want to call the police, but then I don't want Ken to go to jail. He just got saved and turned into the nicest guy on the planet and now I love the guy. Now what?"

"I'm with you, bud, I don't know what to do, but we can't just stand here and let it go away. It doesn't work like that." Zane and Jimmy were crying because of what they had just figured out.

Jimmy realized he had the head band in his hand. "Well, let's get this over with then." He grabbed Zane's hand and headed for the front door.

Ken and Sally were sitting at the dining room table to get ready for dinner as Jimmy and Zane walked in. Jimmy held up the head band. "You killed Linda didn't you Ken." Jimmy was very calm, but his voice was shaking.

Both Ken and Sally were shocked at this announcement. "What did you say Jim?" Ken wasn't sure he heard him right.

"I said you killed Linda last year. That's what I said. How could you do that Ken. She was such a sweet person, and you killed her." Jimmy was crying as he spoke.

Sally grabbed her stomach. "What's he talking about Ken? Who died? You didn't kill anyone. Jimmy! Stop saying things like that! You know they're not true!"

"Mom, he killed Linda last year. That girl that we took to the movies with us last year. Remember? He killed her. We just found all the evidence in that car you keep covered up in the garage. You killed her!" Now Jimmy was screaming at him at the top of his lungs.

Now Ken was standing and looking guilty. He was looking at the floor with sagging shoulders. He didn't know what to do. As Jimmy kept screaming at him, Ken got more and more confused. He finally walked over to the bureau, reached in, and grabbed a pistol as he went upstairs and locked the door.

Sally began to scream in terror. "Ken! Ken! Put the gun down Ken!"

Now Jimmy was angry and started screaming at Ken. "What are going to do Ken shoot yourself. Do it! Do it!"

Zane called nine one one as he watched this unfold. He grabbed Jimmy and tried to get him to go outside with him, but he wouldn't let Zane pull on him.

Sally ran to the top of the stairs screaming historically. Jimmy ran after her afraid she was going to try to get into the bedroom with Ken and the gun.

Over at the church the song service had just started when Chief Larson and Officer Mark got the nine one one call being told a gun was involved. People watched as they hurried out and left with their lights and siren going.

Rebecca and Betty Jo looked at each other and shrugged their shoulders. They both knew their boyfriends were AWOL at the moment, but didn't think the sirens would be for their guys.

As the two police cars pulled into the front the house, Zane was outside waving at them frantically. Both officers came out of their cars and drew their weapons. Zane told them where Ken was and no one was in danger, except Ken, but they entered the house with their weapons drawn just in case. They found Jimmy and Sally at the top the stairs hugging each other.

Officer Mark asked Jimmy what was going on. As Jimmy talked, Officer Mark pulled them both to the back porch, out of sight of the bedroom door. Jimmy was able to tell Officer Mark what he found in the garage, through his tears.

In the meantime, Doug was upstairs trying to talk Ken into giving up the gun and coming out of the room. "But you don't know what I've done Chief!"

"Come out here and tell me then Ken. No one has to get hurt and you don't have to kill yourself or anyone else tonight. Come on Ken, you just got saved and you're one of the nicest people I know right now. We can figure this out. Come on out and tell me friend to friend. Please man, this is all really unnecessary." Doug was completely taken aback at this. Ken was doing so well since he accepted Christ into his life.

"Let me think for a few minutes Chief. I'm not going to hurt anyone but myself. I'm not even sure if I'm going to hurt myself but I have the gun pointed at my head.

Mark listened to what Jimmy had to say, but he needed to get upstairs with his partner. So, he got Jimmy and Sally, as well as Zane seated on the patio furniture outside and took his place on the opposite side of the door.

They kept trying to get Ken to put the gun down and come out of the room but the more they talked, the more Ken got worked up. Now Ken was shouting at them to leave him alone or he was going to shoot himself. As Ken kept screaming Sally made her way to the top pf the stairs but remained quiet. Jimmy was trying to pull her back downstairs. Suddenly Ken tried to shoot himself, but he pulled the gun away at the last second. At the gun blast Chief Lee kicked the door, and it fell to the floor. Ken had lost his grip on the pistol, and it fell somewhere. Officer Mark got him rolled over on his stomach and got his hands behind him and cuffed. Meanwhile the Chief was looking for some type of wound to Kens head or shoulders. Mark rolled him over on his back and noticed a burned on the crown of his head as well as a good amount of singed hair, but he was okay.

Zane began crying like a baby and was unable to control the tears. The blast scared him that bad.

Now Sally was screaming completely out of control and Jimmy couldn't calm her down. She rushed for the door, but Jimmy tackled her and held her to the floor. Doug and Mark kept asking Ken where the gun was, but he couldn't hear a thing other than the ringing in his ears.

Finally, Jimmy picked his mother up and carried her outside again and held her on his lap until she quit screaming. Zane had been at the top of the stairs and saw what was going on inside the bedroom and explained it to Sally. It helped only slightly for her to know that Ken was okay. Physically, Ken was okay, but he was still hysterical. Crying and sobbing as hard as anyone these two cops had ever seen.

Mark was afraid to let him go, so he just held him on his back and let him cry. Mark and Doug kept wondering what was going on, because all they knew at this point was that Ken had a gun to his head when they got here. They would look at each other once in a while with questions on their faces, but no answers. Doug finally found the gun under the bed after he took the door out of the room.

Sally was still in the same condition, absolutely inconsolable. She kept trying to get out of Jimmy's grasp, but he wasn't about to let her go. He looked over at Zane. "Are you sure he's all right Zane. He didn't shoot himself."

Zane was crying too but only because he was so scared. "I promise Jimmy. Mark has him on the bed and he's crying about like Sally is here. I couldn't see any blood at all. But I don't know what he shot at." He sat down in one of the chairs on the patio feeling like he had just finished the most difficult workout of his life, completely exhausted.

Now that Sally was able to hear that Ken was still alive, she was starting to calm down. "Zane! You better not be lying me right now. You better be telling me the truth!"

"He's alive Sally I promise. He's up there crying as bad as you are right now. There is no possibility of a head injury with him acting like that. I promise he's okay." He was beginning to calm down a little bit himself.

Jimmy spoke into his mother's ear. "Mom, if I had any idea that it was going to go like this, I would have never said a word. I am so sorry."

"This isn't the time for that Jimmy. It's out in the open, so let's just deal with it. But I still don't know what's going on. Something about some girl getting killed and Ken did it. I think that's what I know, but I'm not certain of anything yet." At this point she had turned around and was sitting on Jimmy's lap letting him hold her. She needed that right now.

She saw Ken coming down the stairs and wrestled out of Jimmy's lap like a bolt of lightning. She grabbed Ken around his waist and started crying again. Ken's hands were cuffed behind him, but Officer Mark took them off. This guy was no threat to anyone at this point. The two cops just stood there and let them cry it out.

Zane went into the kitchen and looked for the coffee pot made a fresh pot. This was going to take a while, and he could use the strongest cup of coffee he's ever had right now. Then he walked outside and tried to call his dad, but he didn't answer. Church must be pretty loud right now. Then he noticed dinner on the table, and it looked good, but he started to take the dishes into the kitchen. He needed to be doing anything but sitting in a chair.

He finally had the table cleared off and the coffee was done so he suggested everyone gather around there and figure out the situation.

Doug set the rules as they sat down. No hitting, no yelling, no losing control and crying out of control. No kicking the dog, or tipping over the fish tank. He had learned to use humor in situations like this from one of his partners when he was a young patrolman. Sometimes it worked and other times it didn't. It seemed to fall flat here tonight.

"So, what I need to hear right now, with only one person talking at a time, is what happened. Start from the very beginning. If we can go in order has to how things happened tonight, it's easier for us. So, what happened?" The Chief looked from Ken to Sally and Jimmy waiting for an answer.

Jimmy started with coming over to get chairs and knocking the teeth off the car cover. Then he went into how they uncovered the car and found the head band. At the point where he confronted Ken and accused him of murder, Doug stopped him and advised Ken of his rights before he incriminated himself, if that's what was about to happen.

Ken did in fact do just that. He blurted out that he had killed her, but he needed to tell the entire story. He started at the beginning of the evening when he had his driver show up at the house and pull the car out of the garage and went on the from there. He told how Linda had put a fantastic fight and had hurt all of them. A couple of them needed surgery on their knees, others needed dental surgery and other things. Then he told them what he did to Linda and the fact that he had to drive out of the park because everyone else was too injured.

"Can anyone tell me what happens to me after I accepted Christ as my savior. That's the part that scares me the most. I've been reading my Bible and spending time in prayer, but I have no idea what I'm doing yet. I can handle jail, but am I going to hell because of this?" Ken was crying a little, but nothing like he was earlier.

Everyone looked at Doug for the answer to Ken's question. He raised his hands and said, "I'm the wrong one to answer that question. I think I might know the answer, but I'm not even close to being sure of it myself. That's a preacher question. I'm just a cop."

Zane's phone rang at the moment, it was his dad. Apparently, church had ended. "Dad, I can't go into detail right now, but could you get the pastor and Larry and Bob to come over to Jimmy's house right now?"

Billy was a little puzzled, but he didn't like the tone in Zane's voice. "Zane, is everything okay?"

"I can't really talk right now dad, but I'm okay. Tell the girls that Jimmy and I are fine, and we'll let them know more tomorrow, okay? Can you come now? I really need one of your hugs." Zane was crying as he spoke.

"No Zane, you tell me what's going on right now son. You don't cry so that tells me everything isn't okay. Tell me now son. It'll be okay." Hearing Zane cry really rattled Billy. Zane was so mentally strong nothing made him cry. Ever.

Doug reached for Zane's phone, and he handed it to him. "Billy, it's Doug. Everything is fine. We had an incident earlier, but everything is calm and settled. No one is hurt and Zane's telling you the truth. So, don't go rushing over at two thousand miles an hour like you want to right now. I don't need any more calls tonight okay. In fact, put Dennis on the phone. I'll wait while you go get him."

"Doug, you know I'm a take charge kind of guy. If everything isn't like you're telling me when I get there, I' going to punch your face." Billy was more emotional than Doug had ever heard him.

"Billy, I promise everything is okay. Let me talk to Dennis." Doug already knew that punch would hurt. So, he needed Dennis to get him calmed down before they got over here.

Finally, Doug heard Dennis's voice on the other end of the phone. "Dennis, do you know where Ken and Sally live? I thought so. I need you to bring Larry and Bob over here right now. Get here as soon as you can without killing yourself or anyone else. In fact, it would be smart for you obey the speed limits. And lock Billy in the trunk." Doug winked at Zane who smiled back at him.

Dennis had to hunt down Mike Lewallen and ask him to lock up when everyone was gone and get the TV's put away. Then he and the two other preachers got to Ken and Sally's in no time flat. What speed limit, he didn't know anything about a speed limit.

As the three preachers and a scared daddy walked into the house, Doug gave Dennis the evil eye, knowing he got there way too fast. "Did you stop at the stop signs pastor?"

"I didn't see any of those Doug. Why?" Doug shook his head and smiled while the pastor looked around trying to figure out what was going on.

Billy grabbed Zane and hugged him then put him at arm's length. "You promise me you're alright son and you do it right now." Billy had never been scared like this. He could handle a big situation that he himself was involved. But when it's his son, there was no way he can handle that. Billy had tears running down his face and the look of total panic.

"Dad I'm fine. I promise, I'm fine. No one got hurt, no one died, but this is not a good thing right now and you're getting ready to hear all about it. But everyone here is ok. Calm down okay. Take a breath. We're all good here." Now Zane was concerned for his dad. He had never seen him rattled like this. It was kind of scary.

Doug got everyone gathered around the dining room table and filled them in what had happened. But Ken had a question that stopped The Chief from taking him into the jail tonight. Is murder a forgivable sin?

The preachers looked at each other trying to figure out who was going to answer the question. Larry pointed at the pastor. "Pastor, since this is your flock I think it would be appropriate for you to answer this one."

Pastor Brown leaned forward in his chair. "The simple answer to your question Ken is that yes, it is forgivable. But I have to explain that answer, so pay attention, okay? The ten commandments tell us not to kill. We're also told that whoever does murder someone, they themselves are to be killed. But in today's society we don't do that anymore. We have a death penalty that just isn't enforced any longer. In Mark chapter 12 Jesus Himself tells us that the only unforgivable sin is blaspheming the Holy Spirit. To teach you what that actually is would take at least one sermon, if not an entire series of messages. But the bottom line is that you do it on purpose, and you know you have done it.

So, when the devil tells you that you have done this, he's lying to you. The devil is pretty good at using that one on new Christians that haven't grown in their faith yet. So, Ken, if you have already asked forgiveness of this murder, then you have already been forgiven and God doesn't know what you're talking about the second time you asked. Did I make that as clear as mud for you?"

"That's what I need to know pastor. Thank you. So, since I've asked forgiveness, I can go to heaven when my time is up. That's what I needed to know. It doesn't seem right to me though, but I'm not going to argue with it. Thank you, Pastor Brown." Then he stood up ready to go.

Doug told everyone if they wanted to get a hug or a handshake this was the time. Sally was the first with a lot of crying and tears all over Kens shirt. After everyone was finished with their good-byes Doug reluctantly put the cuffs on Ken and took him away.

Larry, Bob, and Pastor Brown sat in the fellowship hall praying for Sally, Jimmy and especially Ken. He was in for the biggest challenge of his life, and they didn't want him to begin to question God. Being such a new Christian and going through such a huge experience can not only set a person back on their heels, but sometimes they get to a point where they question God, themselves, their salvation, and everything in between. And the devil will take it as far as he can. Sometimes life just isn't fair.

"I was flat out impressed with the amount of money Ken mentioned to Sally last night. That guy has done very well in his businesses. I had no problem believing him when he told her that it was all honest money. Of course, I never met him until he was already a Christian, so it's easy for me to believe." Bob found himself proud of Ken even though he didn't know him other than casually. It's a shame that he let himself get into the condition he did last year, and that poor girl died because of it.

Pastor Brown was a little upset that he had a murderer in his congregation. It just so happened that guy turned out to be a murderer, then turned out to be one of the nicest people he had ever met. After he got saved, Ken was the epitome of the change God can make in a person when they commit their life to Him. The pastor was just concerned that the town would see this church in a different way now and things would get ugly. He finally told that part to Bob and Larry.

Bob walked right over and put his hand on his shoulder and began to pray. "Father, this is one of the finest people I have ever met in my life. As far as pastor's go, he has been one of the biggest blessings to me and Larry. Comfort his heart Father and continue to bless his heart and his life. Keep Your loving arms wrapped around him and Rachel. Give him wisdom as he questions himself here and let him remember that he's not the one in control, but You are. Thank you so much for being such a loving God. Amen"

Pastor Brown looked up at Bob. "Thank you, Bob. I literally felt that prayer. Thank you. Going forward please pray that the town will begin to heal and trust each other again. They started locking their doors for the first time ever when that girl was killed. Maybe they won't feel to that anymore. For the most part, this town is full of really good people. We have our element like any other town. But here in Southwind it seems to be a smaller percentage of the population than in other towns I've pastored in.

"While you were praying Bob, I got a thought about the church going forward and we're going to accommodate a much larger crowd. Until now, it's just been me doing everything. Well, that's not entirely true. I call Mike Lewellen from time to time to help. That man never tells me no and he has the energy of thirty two twelve years olds I'm telling you. I can't ever remember him saying no when I've asked him to help out. Well, you guys saw that when all those kids started coming. But I think we've got that department handled with Jimmy and Zane helping him out. It's just a matter of time before Mike hands it off to them. Those two kids are so much more mature than their age. Zane has got some leadership skills that I'm envious of. That kid knows how to take charge in an instant.

"It's the other departments that I'm going to need help with and need it right now. The mothers have been helping themselves to the nursery. We probably should have someone in there to point them in the right direction when they need something. At least let them go to the restroom without worrying about the baby. We're going to need more teachers. We've had all the kids together in the same classroom up to eleven years old. Mike takes the twelve and over crowd. But we can't do that anymore. We have the rooms; they just need to be cleaned up, I think. Unless Rebecca and Betty Jo have already done it, they're going to need some attention. I think I'm going to ask Billy Warren to be our Sunday School Superintendent. Zane got his leadership skills from his dad. Billy has some great leadership, he'll be great at that spot, if he'll do it. Sometimes he's reluctant because he thinks someone else would be better at a position he would be, but he's wrong on this one. He's the best fit." Then he sat back and began to finally take a drink of coffee and stare at the cup.

"Pastor, we've seen this more than once. One of the Pastors called a meeting for those who want to be volunteers early one morning and they got things put together for the coming Sunday morning. But we have all day tomorrow, so we can use it to do the same thing. If we can get people here around ten tomorrow morrow morning, we should be able to get the materials and the copies of everything finished before classes start. I can even get it organized for you if you want me to. Been there done that and it was successful." Now Larry had a big smile as he looked at this worn out pastor.

Bob spoke up kind of quietly. "We have an announcement too pastor. Sunday night will be our last meeting. Apparently, God needs us at another place. We never know where it is until we get there, so we'll be heading out early in the week."

Pastor Brown smiled at him. "I kind of knew that was the case when I woke up this morning. I can't even come close to communicating to you how much I have grown as a Christian since you guys got here. You guys don't seem to waste your words when you're delivering a message. I just might do the same thing from now on. But then I'd probably be driving my car right behind yours if I do. But besides that, I have fallen in love with both of you. In fact, I'm quite sure this entire town has done the same thing.

"Hey, why don't we call for a workday tomorrow and a volunteer meeting. That way we can get the rooms cleaned, the rest of the painting finished and be ready for Sunday School on Sunday. I'll call Billy in a little while. Besides, I need to check on him. I never heard him threaten to hit anyone before. He was more than upset before we left here last night. I'm glad everyone was okay. Physically anyways. What do you think?" Now the worn out pastor looked like he got a new burst of energy. But if the workday panned out, these guys could go home and enjoy some rare down time before service tonight.

Bob and Larry smiled at him. This church was in good hands going forward with this guy at the helm. "That sounds like a beautiful idea pastor. I think I'm going to read my Bible and take a nap before tonight. I could use it, what about you Larry?"

"I'm going to do the same thing you are, but in reverse order, I think. I'm ready for a nap right now, not later." Larry was smiling and ready to go to Sister Wilson's house to get the napping going on right now.

Suddenly, Sally Foster was standing in the doorway of the fellowship hall. She was smiling because she had been standing there for a few minutes now and heard the banter going on between these guys. They were funny and she enjoyed being invisible for a little while.

Pastor Brown jumped to his feet when he saw her there. She startled Larry and Bob who both jumped when they realized she was there.

"Pastor Brown, can I steal a few moments of your time?" Sally was looking at the ground as she spoke. She was tremendously embarrassed to be seen in public right now.

Pastor Brown went over and gave her a huge hug. "Sally, don't you ever lower your head when you talk to me. You have every reason to raise your head high around here. With what you've gone through these past few years and now with Ken being in jail, most people would have folded up and quit with a not so gracious exit. You are very well loved here and in town, trust me, I've heard them talk about you at the store. This town feels so sorry for you, and they love you at the same time. You'll be finding out that I'm telling you the truth in the coming days and weeks. But besides all that, yes, you make steal a few minutes of my time and I'll just give you a lot more than that if we need to. Let's go into my office." He looked and Bob and Larry and asked them to hang around until this conversation was over.

Sally wanted to know if the pastor would go with her see Ken today if they would let her. "He had talked about a lot of money last night, but I couldn't understand anything he was talking about because I was so emotional at the time. But at this point, it's time to go get groceries and I need to figure out where to get the money. I don't even care about the money, but we need to eat for the rest of our lives and that won't be very long if we starve to death." She smiled sheepishly as she wasn't sure it was appropriate to be joking right now.

"Hey, that was a good Sally! Bob and Larry would be so proud of you for that. Yes, I would be happy to go with you to see Ken today. I'll bring Rachel along with us, so we don't give the wrong impression to the town." Pastor Brown said it all with a smile. Sally buried her head in her hands, she was so embarrassed.

Zane was still lying in bed today. He wasn't asleep, but just lying there praying for Jimmy and his mom. He found himself being thankful that Ken had received Christ as his Savior before being found out. Becoming a Christian for Ken might not have happened after he was in jail.

Suddenly, Rebecca was beating on his door yelling at him to get out of bed, he was being too lazy on a day like today. Who did he think he was anyway?

He went over and was greeted with the biggest hug he had ever had in his entire life. "What's going on Rebecca? Why such a big hug?"

Rebecca didn't let go but talked to him while choking the life out of him. "I'm only glad you're ok. We saw them take Ken away last night, but we couldn't see into the house. We waited for a while and when no one came out and we couldn't see what was going on, we left."

"Wait. You were there at Jimmy's last night? With whom?" Zane was totally shocked. He never dreamed that she would even know where they were.

"Yeah, we were there. After the crowd got smaller at the church last night, Sister Brown came and got me and Betty Jo, and we went over there to see what was going. Sister Brown was as scared as we were, so she took us with her just in case the pastor was hurt or anyone else. We stood out in the street so we wouldn't be noticed. We didn't want to get arrested for being in the wrong spot. We were so scared we stood there crying and holding onto each other. When the Chief brought Ken out, we still had no idea what was happening. I think we noticed that there weren't any ambulances around at that point, so we quit crying so much. And when the Chief opened the door, we could see people standing inside even though we couldn't make out who they were. After a while of no one coming out or moving around we just figured everything was okay, so Sister Brown took us home.

"When I started to tell my mom what I thought was going on last night, she started to cry thinking maybe you got hurt. She made me skip all the details and tell her that you were okay. She was crying really hard there for a little bit Zane. My mom loves you maybe more than I do, I think. But she finally calmed down so I could finish telling her everything. And here's the kicker though. I ain't got one clue as to what happened last night. So, it's time for you to spill the beans mister!" She had only slightly released the strangle hold she had on Zane, but now he really couldn't breathe.

"Tell you what Rebecca. Let me call Jimmy and see if he has told Betty Jo yet. If not, let's all get together, so we only have to do it once. Sound good?" Zane was not looking forward to this at all. He knew he was going to lose it and cry like a baby while he told the story. He was also thinking that Jimmy wouldn't even want to tell it, so he could do his bestest friend in the whole wide world a favor by telling everything.

He called Jimmy and found him lying on the couch just thinking about everything. Zane found out that he hadn't talked to Betty Jo yet. So, he volunteered to go get her and meet him at his house in a little while. Jimmy easily agreed because he didn't think he could move right now. He felt paralyzed by what had happened yesterday and seeing his girlfriend would be great. He just didn't have the energy to go over there. Besides, he had a bit of a depression going on. One second, he was fine, then suddenly he was crying again.

Pastor Brown called Rachel to let her know what was going on and gave her a few minutes to get herself ready to go to the jail, which she genuinely appreciated. But now that they were on the way to the jail, Sally was wishing she had thought to bring Ken some decent food. When she said as much to Dennis he began to laugh. "Sally, they don't allow outside food in jails for safety reasons. You could put a gun or a file or an aircraft carrier in there."

Sally started to laugh at herself. She wasn't thinking about that part of it. "At least I meant well.

Rachel suddenly was feeling a little hungry. "I'll eat his part. He don't deserve it anyways." Now they were all laughing.

It took a little while, but they finally were able to get into see Ken. Rachel waited out on the lobby, or whatever it was called and read a book, while the pastor and Sally did business inside.

Sally took one look at Ken in his orange jumpsuit and began to cry out loud.

She was afraid of this, but she was powerless to keep her feelings hidden. Ken sat down on the other side of the partition and began to cry as well.

"Sally I am so, so sorry. I can't even put it into words how awful I feel about what I've done to you. Last night while I was trying to go to sleep, I kept remembering what a sweet, sweet woman you are. And treating you like this is off the chart the meanest thing to do to you." Ken kept wiping the tears out of his eyes.

It took Sally a moment to get herself together, but she was finally able to smile. "Well, I never dreamed of a day like this one. You have definitely put a crimp in my lifestyle here Ken, no doubt about it. The reason I'm here today is because I need to figure out how to pay for groceries. You said a lot of things about money last night, but I couldn't understand a thing you said about it. I was so messed up in the head, nothing was making sense to me. So, I have no expectations as to how much money you have, but I need to get some food in the house today or tomorrow so we can eat and not die of starvation." Then she gave him a meek smile.

He smiled back at her glad that she had a little bit of humor in this terrible situation. "Once I found out you were coming today, I made arrangement for you to get my wallet and phone. I didn't realize I had my phone in my pocket until I got here. Anyways, it has my ATM card in it, and I wrote my PIN on the back but memorize it as soon as you can and get rid of it. Also, on my phone is a lengthy list of names and their titles. So go down the list until you find my friend listed as financial planner. Call him, he knows what to do. Then find my friend listed as Attorney and tell him what's going on. He might want to come down and see me for a minute, even though he's an estate attorney. Find the Manager at work and let him know what's going on. He already has instructions as to what to do if I'm ever incapacitated. We were thinking medically at the time, but yet here we are.

"Sally, every penny I have ever made in an honest penny. All of the money I have earned is from honest transactions without cheating even one person. My work ethics are higher than anyone else I know of. And Sally, you are filthy rich. You don't have to even think about getting a job. Ever. I had put together a trust fund for Jim for him when he hit eighteen years old. I knew he wanted to go to college, and I didn't want him using that money for school. So, I didn't tell him about it. I was going to pay for college and anything else that came up until he had graduated at whatever level he wanted to. Even a doctorate if he wants to go that far. And now he can still do that, and you can pay for it.

"All of these professionals I've told you about are the most honest people I have ever met. That's why they're on my team. So, if you're comfortable with them going forward, let them continue to represent you on anything you need. The financial guys are the best I've ever seen. I hired them away from other companies to work in my businesses. The Attorneys are the best in their fields also. Keep them in your pocket. If you can trust them like I do, you'll be fine the rest of your life. Crud even your grand kids will be fine and never have to work if they don't want to.

"Now that I'm thinking about it Sally. You could take yourself and Jim and Zane and the entire group on a long vacation to anywhere in the world if you want to. Oh! I just had a thought. Pastor Brown, what kind of car did those two guys drive into town?" Ken was going to get rid of everything today. He didn't need money or things anymore.

Pastor Brown had to think for a minute. "It ain't pretty and it's on its last legs Ken. It's ready for the junk yard and that's not a joke. I was going to look for one for them when I get back to the office. Why?"

"Sally, give them my car. I just had the engine maintenance done on it and put new tires on it a couple of weeks ago. I had the air conditioning looked at; it's started to get too cold in there at times. I'm not kidding. And keep in touch with them so you can pay for the yearly registration on it." Ken was fairly sure everything was taken care of with the car. It was going to last forever.

"You don't need to do that Sally. One of them is a trust fund baby and the other has a rich uncle that gets mad when the other one uses his trust money. I don't why they were driving such a terrible car when they got to town. But they've got the registration taken care of as they can afford it. You can take care of mine if you need to though." Then he chuckled.

Ken slapped his hand on the counter. "Done!"

Now they were all chuckling.

Sally was still worried. She knew she would never be able to enjoy Ken's company again, lay in bed and just talk or watch TV. She was going to miss that, even though it had just begun for them. "So, Ken, what's going to happen with you now? Are you going away for the rest of your life? Can I come visit you once in a while. What? I have no idea what to do or what to think right now."

"Well Sally, I'm told that I will have a hearing on Monday at some point. I'll need to enter plea. I'm going to plead guilty. I did this and there's no reason to drag this out any longer than we have to. I know how much this rocked the town. Now they can begin to heal and unlock their doors again. Oh yeah! Send that girls parents a million dollars. If they want more than that, give it to them. Within reason anyways. I've been wanting to do that since it happened last year, but I knew I would get caught."

Sally's mouth fell wide open. "A million dollars?! Just how much money do you have Ken? My Word Ken!"

Ken smiled. He just realized that this hadn't made it into Sally's consciousness yet. "Sally, you're filthy rich. I'm not kidding you or joking with you sweetheart. You probably have more money than you ever dreamed of. It's a lot of money. I'm not going to say how much out loud in this place, so call the financial guy on the list in my phone. In fact, you should do that as soon as you get home."

"I still don't get it. You were tight fisted when it came to money. So, it's hard for me to believe that you have all this money. So, what happened, or maybe, how did you get all that money? She was completely dumbfounded about where all of this money came from.

"Sally I've done well with almost all of my businesses since I was a young adult. I would make a bunch of money in one of businesses and go buy another business. When that business made money, I would go buy another one. I continued to do that until a few years ago. I had too many businesses and some of them were beginning to fail because of the lack of attention they were getting. So, I sold a few of them and made a huge profit. If I had been a politician, I would be under investigation for all that profit. But Sally, it's all yours now. In fact, if you want to go into my office, look on that list for the office manager and make an appointment. I'm pretty sure that if you want to keep everything going like it is right now, that team of professionals that I have around me would figure out how to make it happen. So go talk to all of them, they're all really good people and you'll fall in love with some of the on your first meeting. But for right now, getting groceries, use my ATM. That account has a decent amount of money in it. You'll be able to keep yourself and Jim going just on that account alone.

"I'm so sorry to do this to you Sally. This is the meanest thing I've ever done. I had no intentions of killing anyone that night, but I did. Pastor, tell me again about how I can be forgiven for this. It just doesn't seem fair to me I guess." Ken had his head in hands again shaking his head back and forth. Sally wanted to hug him so bad, but there was a huge screen between them.

Pastor Brown said a quick prayer, asking for wisdom and the right words that would help Ken know he was forgiven and let him sleep at night. "Ken do know anything about the Ten Commandments?"

"Not really pastor. I know that they say not to steal, not to kill, don't lie about others and something like that. But I know nothing about the Bible, Jesus, or God really. I was just getting started with this new life and I was enjoying it. Church was one of my favorite things now too. I was learning so much just listening to you guys. I was even learning things when you guys would talk about silly things in your personal lives. You guys seemed to be so happy and have the right motivation, or whatever you call it. I was just hoping to get to be a small piece of that kind of person. I'm sorry pastor, I'm so nervous right now, but I need to know about being forgiven here." Ken was just trying to find out if he could still go to heaven. But if so, it still didn't seem fair to him.

"There was a guy that used to go around persecuting Christians and killing them. He thought he was doing the right thing because of the way he was taught and then because of his studies as a young adult. He was what was called a Pharisee in Christ's day. One day on his way to another city to kill more Christians, he was knocked off his horse by a bright light. Jesus himself asked the guy what he thought he was doing killing all these people. So, he ended up being blinded and led away to a Christians house. When the Christian man prayed for this guy, scales fell from his eyeballs and the guy was saved. Now he was a Christian his own self and became just as zealous for God and Jesus as he was when he was killing everybody. Ken, that man's name was Paul, and he wrote most of the New Testament in the Bible. We preach from his teachings. If God can forgive such a wicked, vile person like Paul, He can forgive you.

"As you read through your Bible, you'll find that God used a murderer to lead the Jews out of Egypt. King David was an adulterer and a murderer. Not everyone that God uses has a squeaky clean life. I know I'm not squeaky clean. But I think I know where your problem is coming from. Are you afraid that the girl went to hell, or something like that?" That thought just hit him as he was speaking. God knows how orchestrate things and He proved it just now.

"That's exactly it! I couldn't put it into words, but you nailed it right there." Ken had a puzzled look on his face, but he was also excited to hear what this preacher had to say about that.

"It's okay Ken. I'm told that she was a Christian. She only accepted Christ as her savior just a day or so before all this happened. So, you will see her again, but it'll all be smiles and hugs between you both when that happens." Pastor Brown watched as Ken's shoulders relaxed. "Apparently that helped out a little bit, didn't it."

"Oh man pastor! That's why I thought it was so unfair. It never crossed my mind that she might be a Christian. I just figured I had sent her to hell. That's why it was so unfair! I send her to hell, and I get to go to heaven. It's just not fair to me. But I can relax a whole bunch about that now. Thank you, thank, you, thank you. I want to kiss your face so bad now." He looked at the guard and told him to open the door so he could kiss the preachers face. They all got a good laugh for a quick moment until the guard acted like he was going to open the door and faked them all out. Now they were really laughing.

It was getting on into the afternoon and Pastor Brown needed to get going in order make it to church on time tonight, Sally told Ken that she would see him tomorrow with a new set of questions. She was sure she would have a list of questions after talking to his staff after she got home.

The staff at the counter made sure that Sally got everything Ken told her about. But Sally really didn't appreciate the way they looked at her she walked out.

Chapter 15

Friday Church

Pastor Brown was still in a little bit of a funk as he walked around his backyard in a big circle. Rachel stood watching him with tears in her eyes. This situation with Ken was ripping his guts out. For some reason Dennis decided it was his fault Ken killed that girl last year. How in the world could he be taking that on his shoulders, he had enough already to worry about. Now that she was watching him torture himself about it, she found herself wanting to slap some sense into him. He wouldn't have been able to stop it when it happened. But now he just walked and prayed. Maybe that was the best way to handle it after all.

Suddenly Dennis lifted head, took a deep breath, and said out loud, "I praise Your wonderful name Jesus. Thank you for everything." Then he turned to walk into the house and noticed Rachel. "Hey pretty girl. Are you stalking me again?"

Rachel grabbed him and held him tight. She loved this man so much, it hurt her heart to watch him go through things like this. Even though it wasn't very often, it still hurt. She shed a few tears while she was choking the air out of him. Dennis finally pulled her off so he could breathe again. 'Sweety, it's over. I gave it to God, and I won't be taking it back. I'm practicing what I preach. Give it to God and don't ask for it back. It's God's worry now, not mine. And I'm sure He ain't gonna worry about it much."

"You are a silly man, Dennis Brown. And I love you with all of my heart. It hurts me so bad when this happens. The weight of the world is too heavy for one man, yet there you stand holding onto it like a god. Your posture says, I got this, leave me alone. But you're not that strong Dennis." She grabbed him again even tighter this time. He began to laugh as he tried to get her off of him, but she held on even tighter.

"Rachel, I have to get to the church. I love you too sweetheart. More than I deserve, to tell you the truth. I just gave it all to God. I'm not carrying that weight anymore. Besides, it looks good on me, you can't deny it." Now they were laughing and enjoying the hug.

Over at the church Larry and Bob were going around thanking all the people that were helping with the TV's and chairs. They wanted to thank that little mouse for running away as fast he could, they couldn't catch up to it. This place was looking good which required a hot cup of coffee to truly enjoy the view.

As Larry turned around, he saw Zane and Jimmy standing there with their own cups of hot coffee. Larry nonchalantly walked over to Jimmy and took his cup away from him and drank it all down, then handed him the cup and told him "Thanks."

As Bob noticed what Larry did to Jimmy, he decided he would do the same thing to Zane. But Zane figured out what was about to happen and gulped down his coffee. As Bob got closer, Zane handed him the empty cup.

"Did you see what he did to me Larry? That's a friend right there, buddy. Pull a trick on his buddy and then rub it in like that. It takes a true friend to do that to a guy." They all chuckled and walked into the kitchen where the coffee pot was and got themselves a fresh cup.

As the group stood around the kitchen leaning on the counters, Larry had a big thought. "Pastor Brown tonight belongs to you. With what went down last night, it would be more appropriate for you to deliver the sermon. You're the one who needs to break the news to the congregation about Ken. I have no advice on the matter though. We haven't had a situation like this before."

"I was already thinking the same thing, Larry. I'm not sure how well this revival message will be received, but you're right. It's my flock and my responsibility to be their Pastor tonight. That being said, I think I'm going to bow out of here and go to my office and pray and study for it. This has been a fantastic time with you guys here, but it's about time for you two to be moving on soon."

Bob smiled. "You are right ol' wise one. This is the part I hate about this ministry. We make really good friends at every church we've been to, then we leave with the possibility of never seeing them again. But I'm going to ask this without asking Larry first. Would you invite us back at some point in the future?" Larry looked like he going to cry.

"Oh, you better come back buddy boy. Maybe we can pick a date before you leave this week. Or is that how this works?" Pastor Brown was already sad to see them go.

"Yeah, let's do that. But right now, you got to get into that office. We'll get to that when we get a spare minute." Bob was looking at Larry. Bob couldn't remember a time when he and Larry were so sad about leaving a town.

As the pastor went around giving out hugs, Larry held him a little tighter this time "I love you, Pastor Brown. I'm already missing you and Rachel."

That made the pastor tear up. "I love you too Larry." He reached over and pulled Bob into the hug. "I already miss you both too." Now all three of them were teary eyed.

The teenagers had no tears, but they didn't want these guys to leave. These two had been here when they began to really get their feet planted spiritually, and they had such a fun time with them and learned so much just hanging out and listening to them talk. What was life going to be like with them not in it?

Pastor Brown finally let go of the two best Evangelists he had ever heard preach and headed for the office. As he passed Zane and Jimmy, he shook their hands gave them a teary smile. The pastor was definitely going to be leaning on these guys going forward. It was going to be fun watching these two grow in the Lord. Pastor Brown should have just stayed home today. He hadn't done a thing here today but feel sorry for himself. However, at this point, he was beginning to relax and get himself ready for the service tonight. He knew God would be there and help him to pull this town back together and get back to being the loving community it had been for so many years.

Zane and Jimmy decided to go see their girls and try to just relax for a little bit before church tonight. Last night had taken a lot out of them both. Zane knew that he was only collateral damage from last night, but Jimmy was full on damage.

Before they left the church, Zane called Betty Jo to sneak an indication of how Rebecca was doing. They chatted for a few minutes and decided for the four of them to meet at one of the parks in town. Betty Jo was going to go pick Rebecca up on her way. In the meantime, Zane was going to bring Jimmy so he could take a big breath on the way over there. Maybe the smell of the pizza they would pick on the way would help.

Jimmy was doing much better than Zane had thought he would be doing. He showed his humor was intact with that coffee incident just a few minutes ago, but he had a good poker face sometimes. It was one of the few things Zane found annoying about the guy.

Zane and Jimmy pulled into the parking lot at the same time as the girls. As they looked around the park, they noticed that huge group of kids they led to the Lord at the frosty that night. That group seemed to be bigger though. This should be fun to hear how this happened.

Betty Jo was out of the car before she even got it into park. She couldn't get to Jimmy fast enough and almost knocked him over backwards when she jumped into his arms. "Jimmy Drummond, I love you more than you'll ever deserve, trust me, but you need to remember that God is on the throne and whatever happens with Ken is none of your concern. God has it under control, so just relax, okay. Can you do that for me?"

Jimmy was taken aback at this but enjoyed that big hug. "Betty Jo, yes, I do deserve it, and God has been really good to me today. I woke up this morning after almost no sleep last night. But my sleepless night was because of my concern for my mom, not myself. Trust me, I'm not perfect right now, but I'm doing much better than I expected to be doing today. I even gave those two preachers a bad time a little earlier. I promise my dear sweet lovable, cracked in the head, girlfriend, I'm doing fine."

At this point that large group and their new friends was standing there with big smiles and warm greetings for these leaders. Justin was the first to greet them. "Hey you guys! We were just talking about that night at the frosty when we all got saved and how much we have changed since then. We've been inviting our friends and their friends to church every night since that night, and everyone is getting saved man. High school is going to be totally different this year, I can promise you that. We haven't been able to get to you guys after church because the place is just too crowded. I told these guys we would run into you soon enough. Man, you have got to hear some of these stories. Some of these guys got saved while they were high before church one night. Some of our parents are coming to church now and getting saved. Not everyone that's showed up had got saved, but man this is just blowing my mind how God has just taken over the entire town. Even some of the kids from other towns have been coming around too man. We skate a little bit, but we mostly just sit around here and talk about God man.

Zane's tummy was beginning to growl out loud. Dustin finally heard it and took the crowd away so the four of them could eat. They pretty much ate in silence while they enjoyed the beautiful day and the company. Finally, Jimmy broke the ice by announcing, "guys, I'm okay. I go from being so angry at Ken I want to punch his face one minute. Then the next minute I'm so, so glad that he became a Christian before he got caught. I know that'll help him while he's inside a prison. Then I have other thoughts coming from all over the place. But I'm okay. Nothing better than okay, but at least I'm okay."

The other three chuckled a little at that. Betty Jo, being the closest to him, reached over and hugged him. "Jimmy, you know how we all feel about you. There is no way on earth that we are going to leave you alone right now. If you need a hug, I'm your girl. If you need a kiss, talk to Zane." Now they were all laughing.

"Hey! That ain't funny!!! Well, maybe a little bit." Zane was laughing. "I might lick your face though."

Rebecca didn't appreciate the competition all of a sudden. "I was all set to lose it when I found out about Ken being found out last night. But I haven't and I'm a bit surprised about it. I guess God is really helping me out, because I remember how I was when Linda died. I thought the pain of her death was kill me. Don't get me wrong, I'm feeling a lot of things, but nothing like it was that night.

Zane shook his head. "All I know is that it was a memorable first date. It took everything Jimmy and I had in us to call you two beauties and ask you out. And then Linda is murdered. I'm not trying to be funny or make light of what happened. But who else has a story like that? What if we end up being preachers and telling that story from the pulpit. I mean, it's funny, but not funny. How many people would laugh at that? Saying things like our first date was a killer! That might bring a laugh or two, maybe. But do we really want to go there?"

Rebecca reached over and put her hand on Zane's arm as he was talking. "I'm not proud of this, but I had some similar thoughts last night before I went to sleep. Does that make us bad people? I was as close to Linda as I could possibly be, being that she lived so far away. But we were instant friends when we met as little girls. I didn't get to see her very often, but I have missed her every day. I am glad we can laugh about it, but not that glad. You know what I mean?"

"Don't be hard on us yet, we're all still working through all of this. We didn't know her like you did, but we all made instant friends with her. She was just flat out good people." Zane leaned over and kissed Rebekah on the head.

Suddenly Jimmy noticed the time. "Zane, I need to get home and check on my mom before church starts. It's getting pretty close to church getting started already. It looks like I'm going to be late tonight, but I'll be there. We need to get going."

The group didn't hesitate, they were on their feet and cleaning their table off. They all said good-bye and headed in the proper directions. As the boys took off Zane was beginning to feel really bad for his best friend. "Jimmy, don't you dare bear this burden alone. I know how close you are to Betty Jo, but if you need to talk and let your emotions fly, do it in front of me, not her. I would hate for this to ruin you two, because you suddenly had a moment that anyone would understand. You hear me? Shoot, I want to lose it sometimes, but I just don't let myself go there. There's no way I would be able to hold it back if the roles were reversed right now. You understand? I want to be there when you lose it okay. I might even lose it with you, who knows?"

"Thanks Zane. I am having a bit of a tough time keeping it together, but I'm good right now. I just wonder how my mom is doing after her visit with Ken in jail today. I mean, looking at the pastor a little bit ago I was wondering why he was feeling the way he was. It wasn't his stepdad who killed anyone. What's his deal anyway? Someone in his church did a bad thing? Really? Who cares you little wimp!" Jimmy shut up because he was on the verge of losing it and talking about the pastor like that didn't taste good. He liked that guy a lot, so he just shut up.

"Wow, I didn't think of that. But it's not my family involved. Your mom is one of the sweetest people I have ever met. My problem is Ken going out and raping a girl, forget the murder part. Why would a guy with a wife like your mom even have that idea. I don't care what his reasons are, he deserves to be where he is right now, and I can't feel sorry for him at all. I'm sorry if I made you madder than you already are." Zane was shaking his head as he drove into Jimmy's driveway.

"Not at all my best buddy in the entire world. I don't feel sorry him either right now. In fact, I'm not sure feeling sorry for him is even appropriate. I'll see you in a little bit. Thanks for the ride." Jimmy reached over and shook hands with his bud and went in the house.

As Jimmy walked into the house he found his mom with her head in her hands. "Mom, what's going on. Are you okay?"

Sally looked up startled. She didn't hear him come in the house. "Oh! Yeah, Jimmy I'm okay. Just overwhelmed with everything Ken told me today. Holy cow! I just got off the phone with some of Ken's business associates. Sit down a minute, I have news. I think we might have more money than God right now." She let out a shaky chuckle. "We won't have to worry money at all for the rest of our lives. That guy is loaded! Well, we're loaded! Ken made money and a lot of it. He told me this morning every dime he made was honest money. Now that I've talked to his team, they assured me that Ken was telling the truth. Those people are the nicest, smartest guys. Anyways, if you want to go to an ivy league university, we can afford it. In fact, we can pay for Betty Jo to go with you and buy you a mansion to live in if you want to. I'm not kidding. Then after you graduate, if you don't want to work for your entire life, it's all good. We even have enough money for your grandkids to be deadbeats, maybe a few more generations too."

Jimmy looked at his mom and smiled. "What are we doing sitting this little dump then? Let's go buy a mansion!" He reached over and ruffled her hair.

Sally slapped at his hand. "I guess we could, but you're going to be moving on to college here pretty soon and a big house is going to be too much for me. I was beginning to have those thoughts before all this happened, but this is a big house. Ken bought it after we were married thinking we could grow old here. Plus, it had plenty of room for grandkids when they came along. But I'll have to think about that another day. I have enough to wrap my head around right now.

"You buy whatever house you want mom. If you want to get a new home before I'm out of college, I'll live in it with you. That might be a nice transition for both of us. This house has a few rotten memories in it at this point."

Sally started thinking about different things she might want to do with all this newfound money, so they began to go through a bunch of scenarios they might want to see play themselves out in the near future. Before long Jimmy noticed that church had already started, and he promised he would be there.

Sally was way too embarrassed to go. She didn't want to see people giving her those sideways looks and stuff like that. Maybe tomorrow she would feel different, but tonight she was staying home. Jimmy texted Zane to let him know he was on his way but would end up out in the parking lot. So, they could just connect after the services.

When Jimmy did get there, Tom was just finishing the worship service, and everyone was greeting each other. The first one to grab Jimmy's hand was Dustin. He had a huge group of teenagers all sitting together. This kid had been busy recruiting new believers his own age. Jimmy was impressed. Anyone would be.

It took a little while, but everyone finally found their seats again and got set for whatever God had planned to tonight. Jimmy caught his breath when Pastor Brown stepped behind the pulpit. He had forgotten about this part for tonight's service.

Pastor Brown bowed his head and immediately began with prayer. He didn't pray very long and got right down to business. "Friends, tonight is going to be a bit different, as I have something I need to talk about. Let's start with a question though. Did Moses kill someone and run away?" A lot of people inside said, "yes."

"Did King David have someone murdered after he slept with his wife?" Again, the people answered with a "yes."

"Did God forgive them?" Again, a huge "yes" from the crowd.

"Well folks, we have someone *we* need to forgive. It was revealed last night that Ken Walker was the one responsible for that girl's death at the park last year." There was an audible noise from the crowd. Pastor Brown could even hear the people outside this time.

"Guys, let me point out a few things. We live our lives, and we commit these little sins all day, that will never make the news or headlines in any news publication. But let me ask this question. Is stealing from the store a worse sin than murder?" Again, there was murmuring in the congregation.

"We know that sin will separate us from God. If you read the laws in the Old Testament, there are differing punishments for all of the sins mentioned.

But stealing from the grocery store and murder have the same consequence when it comes to being separated from God. They both separate us from God. Can God forgive you if you sin? Regardless of which one? Didn't God forgive Moses and David? Of course He did. So, there's no reason to sit here and pass judgment when we, ourselves have sinned.

"As crimes are committed in our society, we also have a tier system of punishment for breaking the law. Murder of course, has the most severe punishment attached to it and we would all agree it should be that way. And please, please, don't think for second that I'm making any excuses for Ken. I promise I'm not. Ken will be punished for this, and we will not see him on the streets for a long time because of that.

"BUT! Who are you to judge him and hate his guts?" At this point Pastor Brown folded his arms and stood back from the pulpit for a couple of minutes while he let that statement settle in amongst crowd.

"Larry, stand and quote John three sixteen to the crowd." Larry stood and quoted the Scripture. "Now, Larry, quote us John three seventeen."

"For God didn't send Jesus to condemn us but to forgive us. Or something like, but I'm pretty close on it. I guess it depends on which translation you're reading. That was the Owens translation." The congregation laughed.

"So, if Jesus doesn't condemn us at this point, who are to condemn anyone? Bob! It's your turn.

"Go easy on me preacher I ain't that smart." Bob said as he stood up.

Pastor Brown had to take a moment to quit laughing "And he's telling the truth!" Again, everyone laughed. Quote me Matthews seventh chapter and the first couple of verses.

Bob put his finger on his bottom lip. "Uh, I dunno." And everyone laughed again. "Actually Pastor, that's where Jesus told the people on the Mount of Olives not to judge others because the very way you judge them, will be the way you are judged when your turn comes in the hereafter. That's the Watson translation." Now everyone was howling in laughter.

"Give them both a hand of applause for being such great translators for us all tonight." Pastor Brown applauded along with the crowd.

"Folks this is one of those times when we can learn a huge lesson on human interaction and how to be a better friend, perhaps. But most of all, my goal tonight is to help you become a better Christian. Can you react to what you heard tonight with the proper Christian attitude? How many of you wanted to kill Ken when I told you the news a few minutes ago? Or punch his face, or kick his dog and drown his cat, or whatever?

"We all know that Ken was mean. In fact, he was a cruddy snot ball to the highest degree. But he became a Christian, just like you guys, a couple of weeks ago. And the change in that man was complete. If you had a chance to interact with his after he accepted Christ, you know what I'm talking about. He is the epitome of the drastic change Jesus makes in people's hearts, souls, and character when they accept Him. One of the first things Ken did was go the grocery store and pay for a lot of booze that the store bought, knowing Ken would purchase it at a later date. Well, Ken wasn't going to drink it anymore. So, he went and paid for it so the store wouldn't be out all the money and stuck with that much booze. I have no idea where it went, but the store wasn't out all that money. He is always wearing a smile now. He greeted everyone with a warm friendly handshake and a huge smile. He was a little awkward at it, but he was getting there. His friendly smile and warm handshake were genuine though. Every one of you would like this man if you had given yourself a chance to truly know him. Again folks, I'm not making excuses for him; only pointing the difference that Christ had made in Ken's life. It's the most remarkable change I have ever seen after these many years in ministry. There's no question about it, it's true.

"I feel that I need to point out that some of us need to ask for forgiveness because of our reaction to this news. Sometimes Christians can be the worst people around when these events occur. We judge, we point fingers of condemnation and can be really nasty in times like this. But I'm pretty sure I was effective in showing that's what we need to avoid here. I love every last one of you, but I also know that we're all human. Sometimes our knee jerk reaction can be brutal. So, let's repent of that behavior, if that's what happened within you tonight. You're still good people, just human. So don't let the devil beat you up about it either.

"I'm going to close with this, so Tom, can you guys find your way back up here and start playing again? Sally Walker needs more prayers than you can imagine right now. Again, she didn't come tonight because she was so embarrassed and tremendously devastated by what happened last night. It got a little hairy there for a little bit. The Chief and Officer Mark had everything under control by the time the three of us got there, but when I heard all that had happened, I actually got scared just listening to them talk about it.

"So, seriously pray for Sally. We also need to pray for Ken. He's in a place where nice people aren't in great supply. He going to need prayer cover if he's going to be able to keep that smile if it's not already gone. I know the Chaplain over there, so I'll pull as many strings as I can on his behalf, but it won't amount to much.

"With all that I've talked about tonight, it really hasn't been much of a salvation message. But now you know how God judges us. What I didn't really talk about is how much He loves you and died for you on a cross so that you can spend eternity in heaven with Him. These meetings have been going on for so long, I'm sure those of you who haven't accepted Christ as your savior yet, you have heard about those whose have. And with a crowd this size, there has to be some people here tonight ready to accept Christ. If I'm talking about you, we have some people standing around outside to help you. Guys, wave your hand up high, so they see you out there. You people in here, just raise your hands. We're getting ready to pray."

Jimmy was standing in the back of the parking lot because there were no seats available when he got there. Suddenly, Dustin lunged at him with a huge crowd of kids behind him. Most of them had been to the church before and had prayed through already. But along with them were about a dozen or more kids ready to pray the Sinners Prayer. "Hey man, we brought some of our friends from the skate park and those we've talked to at the park. They want to get saved, we don't know how to help them do that, so they all waited until now. I know you can help us. Or if we need to, we can wait on that other girl to come out and help us."

Jimmy's heart was so touched by the size of this crowd of kids that he teared up and began to cry. "I got you Dustin." He said with a shaky voice. "Let's get all the people who want to pray over here in a circle, and we'll help them pray and get saved." Dustin's eyes got big when he realized Jimmy was crying.

It took a minute for the kids to get to the front of the group. Jimmy had them all hold hands with him as he prayed and had them repeat the Sinners Prayer after him. Once he was finished, a girl grabbed him and hugged him really tight. She was absolutely sobbing and repeating "Thank you Jesus! Thank you, Jesus! Thank you, Jesus!" He could only hold her and let her cry until she was finished. The makeup she was wearing was now all over her face and Jimmy's shirt.

After the girl settled down, she slowly let him go but didn't quit sobbing. Dustin was still standing there with wide eyes as Jimmy was still crying. "Man, are you all right? Why are you crying man?"

Jimmy put his arm around Dustin's shoulder. "Dustin, this crowd you have here is huge man! It moved me to tears, I'm not kidding. You'll have to believe me when I tell you this is really touching to a person's heart. This is amazing Dustin! You need to learn how to pray with people like this if you're going to keep doing this, I'm serious. My goodness Dustin! Look at this group you have here. You could almost start your own church." They laughed. "Keep it up

Dustin. Don't ever quit whatever you're doing. Let's get together in the next few days, because I want to hear how you're getting all these guys to come to church with you and we can teach you how to lead them in that prayer, so they don't have to wait like this. I'm going to be busy with my mom for the better part of this week, so maybe late in the week. I want Zane and the girls to hear this too. Okay? So, hang out here until they get here in a few minutes. Cool?

"Yeah man, whatever you want. It's really not hard you know. I just talk to everybody and tell them what a huge difference Jesus has made in my life. They want to know moré, but I don't know anything about it really. That's when I invite them to come here. They can hear more and pray here. I don't know how to do it man. I get these guys here and you guys go take care of business.

Inside the church at least as many people that attended this church were quickened in their spirit and needed to repent for their poor behavior and thoughts about Ken and the entire situation. About a dozen or so people also accepted Christ as their Savior. There were tears everywhere as well as people mingling and talking quietly,

Zane, Rebecca, and Betty Jo were looking at each other rather quizzically wondering where Jimmy was. Betty Jo finally told them that if he really was late, he was probably out in the parking lot, so they headed in that direction.

Larry, Bob, and Pastor Brown were on the platform looking at the crowd after everyone finished praying and getting saved. "I have no idea how that sermon is going to be chewed on after everyone gets home tonight. Hopefully, they'll be able to go forward with a Christian heart and spirit. I'm really concerned about how many people are going to quit attending here and it's going to break my heart. I love these people. A lot of them are like my own kin even. Oh well, it's in God's hands now and I need to quit thinking like that."

"Pastor that was probably one of the best sermons I have heard when the chips were down like they are tonight. I can think of one church we were in when something happened that wasn't even close to this, and the Pastor basically scolded everyone and told them they were all going to hell." Bob had his hand on the pastor's shoulder as he spoke to him.

"The meetings that followed that sermon were a skeleton of what they had been before that. It's probably the only time I ever wanted to grab a pastor by his collar and shake his teeth out. I never, ever even thought a pastor was capable of doing something like that. Pastor Brown, you preached from your heart, and we were all able to feel the love you have for Ken as well for every one of us. That alter call should have been encouraging to you. A good amount of people accepted Christ as their Savior. Then of course, you had a good amount of people that seemed to be asking forgiveness for exactly what you preaching against tonight. Those people that prayed that prayer are going to be much better in their Spiritual lives going forward now. Their attitude will be much better about things now." Larry had really grown to love this Pastor. He really loved this church and everyone in it.

Zane, and the two girls finally found their way to Jimmy. After Jimmy told them about what Dustin had been doing, he pointed to the large crowd of teenagers gathered around laughing and having a good time in the parking lot. Betty Jo was the first to blurt out, "There's got to be ten thousand kids here Dustin!" She was exaggerating of course, but it was a large group.

Zane shook his hand and congratulated him on such a fantastic job, sharing his testimony around town and in the parks. Jimmy looked at Zane, "Perhaps we're the wrong ones to be leading the new youth group."

Jimmy laughed. "He's definitely going to be our right hand man, there ain't no doubt about that."

"Great idea Jimmy. I'm pretty sure we can all learn from him. At least on how to attract a crowd of kids this huge. Man, this is impressive Dustin. I don't think you know what you've started here." Zane was smiling from ear to ear while he spoke.

"No Zane, I can't do that. I have no idea what to do here. I only know how to tell them how Jesus changed my life, then bring them over here where you guys can tell them more and pray with them. I don't know how to do any of that." Dustin was getting a little nervous about getting involved in anything right now.

Rebecca laughed a little as she grabbed Betty Jo's arm. "Dustin, we didn't know much just a few months ago either. Remember when we prayed with you guys that night? We stumbled through the entire thing; Betty Jo and I did. One of us preached to you, sort of, then the other one helped with the prayer. I don't even remember which one of us did what. We barely know anything now even. Jimmy and Zane are the experts here." The two boys looked at each other with huge eyes.

Chapter 16

Sunday Morning

Sunday morning was a beautiful day. As the sun came up Pastor Brown was on the porch watching as the colors changed while the sun came up. He couldn't sleep for a lot of reasons, but he was enjoying this sunrise. It had been a while since he had gotten up before the sun. The big issue this morning was how many people would be left in his church after breaking the news about Ken. He was much less concerned about it this morning than he was Friday night though.

He found himself getting anxious to get to the church and letting Tom get the worship service started. How many were going to get saved this morning? How many would get saved tonight? Would they board up the church when they found out that meetings were ending tonight?

He found himself smiling as he sipped his coffee. Overall, this had been more than he ever thought possible. He had no idea how many people had received Christ into their lives thus far into the revival, but it was definitely in the hundreds and that was no exaggeration. He was also so thankful that the other churches in the area and been coming and some of those that got saved would be attending some of those churches. Pastor Brown realized that he had no idea how many people had been healed, or marriages restored, other family relationships restored, and the list just keeps getting bigger. God had showed up in a huge fashion these past few weeks and it was sad it had to end.

Sister Brown had been leaning on the wall watching her hubby smile to himself. She had no idea what he was thinking, but it must be good stuff. She startled him when she spoke. "I sure do love that smile. You must be thinking something ornery."

"Not this time sweety. I'm just enjoying the morning and the coffee at the same time. I was definitely enjoying the fact that your fanny wasn't blocking my view this time." Then he smiled really big and took a drink of his coffee. "You should put a sign on that thing to warn people." Now they were both laughing but Rachel was punching him in the guts. The coffee ended up on both of them, but they didn't care. Once the wrestling settled, they enjoyed a nice hug and just sat for a few minutes.

"You spilled my coffee you mean ol' woman. Go get me some more and make it quick, chop chop!" Dennis was awake now and feeling his oats. Perhaps too many oats.

Rachel grabbed his cup and ruffled his hair as she went inside. When she came back out, she had her own cup which was full of coffee and Dennis's cup only had a little coffee in it. She didn't make eye contact with him as she handed him his cup and acted like she was going to spill it on him.

"Did you drink all of my coffee already? Why you dirty rotten woman. I'm going to throw you out into the street." He acted like he was going to pick her up, but instead let his coffee spill on her.

She gasped as it ran down her clothes, then started laughing. She hadn't seen this side of her husband in a long time. He had been so burdened and sad before this revival broke out. It was good to have him back. This wasn't the first cup of coffee she had worn, but she loved it every time it happened. She had her husband back, that was worth wearing dozens of full coffee pots on her clothes and watching him laugh. She loved that man, and it was hard during the struggle and getting no help from anywhere it seemed. Then God showed up and blew the roof off the town. This was going to be fun to watch now as the town settles into itself.

Rachel grabbed Dennis's coffee cup and kissed his head. "I love you Dennis Brown, more than you deserve." As she walked away to go fill their cups again, he slapped her leg as she walked away. "I don't deserve it at all darlin'." That made her smile. At least both of them agreed on that issue.

As Rachel sat down next Dennis with a full cup of coffee for both of them, Dennis put his arm over Rachel shoulder and pulled her close. "This is the last day of a hugely successful revival my sweety. In fact, it may just be the most successful revival this area has ever known. We've had about four million people get saved, five hundred thousand get healed of everything from cancer to hangnails and even had seventeen thousand marriages restored. I'm kidding about the numbers, but man this place has been like walking in heaven itself. I'm not kidding Rachel, I didn't think that God could impress me any more than he had, but with all of this happening right in our church, I don't have the words to describe it, much less how to describe how thankful I am." He noticed Rachel smiling as he spoke. "What?"

"It's so good to see you back. Smack dab in the middle of a church that's on fire for God again. It was really hard to be here when things were so bleak. No one was coming to church anymore it seemed. The people had gotten pretty apathetic, and we were basically just spinning our wheels. At least that's what it felt like. But there you were Dennis, working as hard as ever. Doing things for people that you knew would never thank you or even appreciate your efforts. But there you were being a Christian right in front of them. I loved watching you do all of that, but it was hard to watch the effect it had on you. You're an all-out hero to this town Dennis Brown. Don't even argue with me." Rachel felt like she was falling in love with this man all over again.

"Come on Rachel! Don't start with that hero stuff again. I did what every pastor would do who is worth anything. I did my job. And the reason the church was getting apathetic about everything was because I was losing my drive. I wasn't feeling it during my morning devotions. I'm pretty sure it's because I was feeling sorry for myself and couldn't get off my pity pot. I had pretty much decided to quit the ministry all together, but I loved these people so much I couldn't leave them without a pastor. Even with that, I was getting really close to walking away." Dennis remembered how dejected he felt as no one seemed to care about the church, or even he and Rachel back then.

Rachel knew how hard it was on him during that time. She cried at times seeing her best friend so hurt. "Dennis, you did for this town, exactly what you did for me when my husband died. Your wife had died about the same time, but you were there for a lot of us. You let us know that you loved all of us and that God was still in control of everything when our world had crashed and was buried at the funerals. Dennis! You're the most loving and giving person I have ever met. There's not a person in this town that would disagree with that. You have single handedly touched every single life in this town! For the better! You're walking hero Dennis Brown! Not every hero is a soldier in the military and carries a gun. Some of them carry a Bible and live it daily."

"All right, all right Rachel. Maybe I have risen to the top a few times now and then. But it doesn't matter at all if people aren't going to heaven. If that's the case, then I have failed as their pastor. I did what every other pastor would do and no less than that. So just drop it okay sweety. You know I don't like you talking like this." His tone of voice carried some irritation with it.

"Let me tell you something you worthless man you. When my husband died, you single handedly kept me from staying in bed all day every day. You are the best person I have ever met Dennis. I was so lost when my husband died, and I would lay on my couch and just cry. When the phone rang, I knew it was you on the other end wanting to cheer me up and comfort me. I even knew that you had bad days too, but you cared so much for others. You are one of a kind Dennis. As time went on after we were all alone, I began to fall in love with you. I even questioned if it was because I was so lonely. But one day one of the guys in our grief group was talking about you during a break. He said if he was a woman he would have nailed you down and married you already. That you had helped him so much and he needed you just as much as we all did. Dennis, what you have dome for this town is exactly what you did for our entire grief group. You carried the heavy burden and did the heavy lifting for all of us. And God showed up right when you need Him, and you deserve everything He has done for you, and for this town." Rachel had tears running down her cheeks as she spoke about this brilliant man that she was so lucky to have married.

Dennis began to shake his head side to side. "I tell you what Rachel. I was at a point of desperation when Larry and Bob walked up on the sidewalk that day. They're the ones that have done all the heavy lifting here. Things started working in this town before breakfast the next day I swear. It was so fast! And God came into this town and got stuck, I think. He sure has lingered here, and I have enjoyed every single minute of it. Thank you for those awesome words, Rachel. I know you're thinking I'm a hero and maybe I am to you. But in the large picture of everything, I'm only one dot on that picture just like everyone else. Let's get ready for church." Dennis kissed Rachel's forehead, and they walked inside holding hands.

Bob was laying on his bed awake wondering where God was sending them to next. This part of the job was both exciting and frustrating, but the results were always awesome once things got going in the church. He told Larry to meet him in the study.

Larry moaned. "Why can't we ever meet in the coffee shop or the ice cream parlor. We always go to the study and work. I'm going to tell my mommy on you Bobby. I want ice cream for breakfast today."

Zane was awake on his bed wide awake. He had slept like a baby last night, but he was praying for Jimmy and Rebecca. He knew Rebecca blamed herself for what happened to Linda. That was so much nonsense from the get-go it almost made him mad. He was praying for Jimmy because Jimmy needed a good friend and also needed some help to keep his emotions in check sometimes. Apparently exposing Ken set Jimmy off and He even told Ken to kill himself. That was not the Jimmy Zane grew up with.

Sally was in her room still thinking of how to go forward now that Ken was going to be in jail for the rest of his life. She already knew money was not going to be a problem, but what now? What was she going to do? She had a growing boy that she needed to care for, that was becoming such a better man than she had ever thought possible. She was married to one like that once. Jimmy was turning into his dad and that was a most awesome thing.

Billy and Helen were in their room discussing everything. Billy was feeling really bad about being part of the group that had threatened Ken that night. Helen told him that God had already forgiven him and had forgotten about it. Maybe he should too.

Louise and Betty Jo were eating breakfast and taking turns praying for everybody they could think of. One would pray while the other ate and then they would switch. It was a new tradition the two of them were enjoying. They had prayed for everyone in the church that they knew and even some of them that they didn't know their names yet.

Sally was the first one to the church this morning as she had some questions for the pastor. She found him and Sister Brown sitting in the back row enjoying some coffee. They both went right to Sally before she could even get into the sanctuary. Sally was looking at the floor as she asked if she could have a private word with Pastor Brown. Rachel lifted Sally's head. "Sally, don't you ever look down when you talk to us. You have nothing to be ashamed about. You're as welcome here as anybody. And yes, you may have a private moment with my hubby. I'll go make some more coffee since tubba guts here drank it all."

As Sister Brown walked into the kitchen the Pastor motioned Sally to the chairs on the back row. What can I help with Sally? Do you need anything?"

Sally chuckled at that last question. She didn't need anything right now really. "Pastor Brown, would you go with me to Ken's hearing tomorrow. I don't know if I can do that by myself. I still love that man even though I know what he's done. It just won't go away. I'm so mad at him though. I want to beat him senseless."

"Of course, Sally. Anything to help. Anything at all. Why don't you meet me here and we'll take Sister Brown with us in my little putt putt car. Will that work for you?" Pastor Brown was going to go with her to that hearing anyways. Apparently, Sally didn't know it yet.

"Your little putt putt? I don't understand," Sally said.

"That's just what I call my car. It's getting so old it makes old car noises. But it still gets me around town. It's my little buddy I guess." The Pastor smiled as he spoke about his car.

"Pastor Brown, Can I take you and Sister Brown to lunch today after the service? I could really use the company, and I have a ton of questions. Sally had a plan about that little putt putt car.

At that very moment Sister Brown walked in and handed them both a cup of coffee. "Sister Brown, Sally here wants to take us to lunch today. Do you think we should allow her into our most esteemed company?" Pastor Brown was still feeling it from earlier this morning. That ornery stuff was going to get him into trouble, but first it was going to get him lunch in town somewhere.

"I don't know about taking you along with us, but Sally and I could sure have a nice visit. What do you think Sally? Should we leave him out along the road some place?" They all laughed but agreed the pastor would be allowed to eat with them. But only French fries.

At that point, others were making their way into the church, so Pastor Brown needed to get busy. He helped the guys put the TV's outside and rearrange the chairs all over the place. The Pastor realized while he was moving chairs that this building was just too small for this crowd and the ones to follow. They were going to need a new facility or something. This church was ridiculously too small now.

As the Pastor was standing enjoying his thoughts, a man came up to him and shook his hand. "Pastor Brown, my name is Mr. Williams. I'm the Principal of the high school. I have been coming to the meetings this entire past week and I noticed that this church is too small for you now. I have been authorized to offer you our gymnasium until you can find another facility or build one. The only stipulation is that you have to clean up after yourself. There are two of our janitors that attend this church, so I'll bet they'll help you out. Besides, I already asked them and offered to pay them overtime for it. It's a done deal if you want it. I know you need to talk to your board, so just let me know after that meeting, okay?"

Pastor Brown began to weep. "Mr. Williams. I was just standing here thinking this building was too small for us now. And immediately you were standing here offering me more space before I could even say a prayer about it. God answered my prayer before I had even formed a real thought." Mr. Williams got goose bumps that made him shiver.

"I'm not finished yet pastor. I've also been authorized t off you as many classrooms as you need for Sunday School and youth groups." Mr. Williams was just full grand offerings this morning.

Now Pastor Brown wanted to dance he was so happy. He hadn't even had that thought yet. Much less prayed about it. God was smiling on this church today before things could even get started. "Mr. Williams, you have made this Pastor's day already and church ain't even started yet." He reached over and hugged Mr. Williams as tight as he could and said a prayer of thanks before he let him go.

As Pastor Brown walked into the kitchen, he found Bob and Larry enjoying a cup of coffee. "What are you mumbling about over there Parson. Do we need to call the guys in the white coats over here?" Bob liked that smile the pastor was wearing this morning.

"I just had an amazing conversation with Mr. Williams, the principal over at the high school. He offered to house this entire church for our weekly services since it appears we have outgrown this place. To include all the Sunday School rooms that we need! I hadn't even thought that far ahead, and God was ahead of us on it. Isn't God a little more amazing than He was yesterday. He just seems to get bigger every day right now."

Bob and Larry looked at each, then back at the pastor, "We agree," they said at the same time.

"Wow!" Larry said. "Can you believe that? God did that miracle without us even asking for it first. God wants this town bad brother and He's going to get it regardless of what the devil put in the way. The devil already has a black eye over this town, and he might be getting a bloody nose pretty soon. That school may not be big enough with the size of the crowds that have been here lately though. How long would it take for you get the funds to build a new facility on this property?"

Pastor Brown puffed out his chest. "I have the money in my pocket already believe it or not." Now he was smiling the biggest smile these two guys had seen since they got here. "Sister Brown and I were going over the books the other day and realized that since these meetings began the giving has been a lot bigger than we anticipated. With what we already had in the future building fund, we're pretty comfortable with what I just told you. If he had a set of plans already, we could probably pull plans this week. But there are no plans, so we have to wait, dog gone it." He was smiling the entire he spoke.

The boy's eyes got huge in amazement. "Are you serious pastor? That's astonishing!" Bob didn't even think that was possible. He was expecting the pastor to lower his shoulders and cry like a baby when Larry asked that question. "Okay, that might be more amazing than the high school thing. Thank you, Jesus, for the start of another terrific day! Take that devil!"

Larry looked at his watch and realized they were missing the service. As he began to listen, he could hear Tom and the worship team already going at it. "We better get in there guys, or someone is going to start preaching and it might be better than anything we could do. And we can have that. Taking money right out of our pockets and stealing our blessings." They all laughed and headed to the sanctuary.

Bob slapped Larry on the shoulder. "The way we're set up, they could take out money and we wouldn't even know about it." Larry slapped him back and let out a huge laugh. Bob was right. They didn't need to worry about money at this point in their lives, with a rich uncle and trust fund in hand, they were going to be just fine.

As they got to the platform it was obvious that God had been moving before they got there. They settled into their places and joined in the worship. Suddenly there was a blood curdling screaming from the crowd which got everyone's attention. A mother just realized that her blind baby was looking at her and smiling. She started moving toward the platform as Tom kept the worship going until she got there and told them what had just happened.

As she told the preachers what happened they began to praise God and His presence fell all over the property. The parking lot erupted into a loud sound of praise. There were even people across the street praising God because the parking lot was full.

Bob walked over to use Tom's microphone and Tom just backed away. "Folks, let me tell you what just happened." He told them that the baby was born blind, but her mommy just saw her looking at her and smiling. "If you need healing today, this is the time to ask because it's going on around you right now. The place is too crowded for any of us to get to you and lay hands on you, but you don't need us, you only need Jesus." With that he motioned Tom back to the podium and worship music filled the place again.

One of the people that arrived in a wheelchair, stood up and walked away from it. Huge men were crying like babies. Even in the parking lot it was hard to hear the music over all of the people crying in praise to God. The huge group of teenagers were in the parking lot crying almost out of control, but everything was right in their world.

People began to make their way to where the TVs were set up on the sidewalk. As they passed by the TV's, they began to drop things. Piercings, cigarettes, pipes, drugs, bottles of alcohol. One guy had written the word "porno" on a piece of paper and told one of guys standing by the TV's he was going to throw it all away when he got home. Others dropped chains, knives, guns, a satanic bible, and other things that apparently were keeping them from serving God.

Word made it to the platform what was going on outside. Bob made his way down to the wall where the windows going into the parking lot were. As he looked around and saw what was happening, he knew God didn't need him to say a word today. People were jumping up and down in worship. There were people kneeled at their seats, couples in full embrace letting God do whatever they needed Him to do. He then turned around to see the crowd inside and saw the same thing going on in here. He worked his way back to his place next to Larry and told him what was happening. Larry shrugged his shoulders and smiled.

At the scheduled time Tom looked over at Pastor Brown, who looked at Bob and Larry. Bob just motioned for Tom to keep going. God was doing His work right now and Bob had no intentions of getting in His way. Once in a while Tom would look over at them and they would encourage him to keep going.

After quite a while the Spirit of God began to withdraw, and things began to settle. People were sitting in their seats watching what was going on around them or praying quietly. Bob took his place at the podium and just stood there not wanting to interrupt anything else still going on. When he was satisfied God was finished, he addressed the crowd. "Well folks, I can't say one thing that will add anything to what's already happened. God Himself came down here and did all the preaching that needed to be done this morning. I am convinced of that. We've already seen people healed, I'm sure there were others we didn't see. I also know that a lot of you have accepted Christ as your Savior during this worship time. If you did not do that while all that was going on, please raise your hand." Hands went up all over the property. He then asked if there were any others that wanted to accept Christ as their Savior and hands went up all over the property again.

"Okay, listen to me and hear what I'm going to tell you. All of you that asked Christ into your heart, you are as saved as all of the rest of us and are a Christian just like we are. Don't let the devil tell you that because we didn't pray with you that it didn't work, or anything like that. God answers that prayer every time and you are no exception. Now, those of you who raised your hand, let's pray. Wrap your heart around these words as we pray. Father forgive me of my sins... Take my life and direct it according to Your ways... Take my bad habits and everything that has kept me away from you, away from me... Thank you for dying on the cross for my sins... I claim you now as my Savior and my friend... Thank you, Jesus, Amen." The crowd clapped for those who said that prayer. Some even reached over and gave the new Christians a hug.

Bob looked over the crowd again and couldn't think of anything to say that would make any sense. God had really worked hard this morning, and this crowd received it all. Every last drop of it. "Okay guys, we'll see you tonight at six. Don't forget your sunscreen."

Some of the people sat down while everyone else was in a hurry to get stuck in the parking lot and surface streets. You could still feel the presence of God in the building, just not as intense as it was earlier. Those sitting and waiting were visiting quietly, while others were praying. Some of them just didn't want to leave at all.

The entire crowd of teenagers was looking for Zane and Jimmy and their lady friends. They all wanted to go to a restaurant for lunch, but where was a place in town that could manage a crowd that large? Jimmy still had quite a wad of that money Ken had given him, so he told them all to meet them at the skate park. He looked at Zane, "We're buying a whole bunch of pizza today brother and it's going to be more fun than we deserve, I think." Zane and the girls chuckled and got into Zane's car and headed to the pizza parlor as Jimmy called the order in before they got there.

Sally went and found the Pastors and told them it was time for high tea, and she was hungry. She knew that Pastor Brown was driving so she told him which restaurant they were eating at before he started the car. He turned around to the backseat and mildly declined to go there. It was too expensive. "Pastor, after I got off the phone yesterday with Ken's team of money guys, I know right now that I can buy that restaurant if I want to. But all I want is a nice meal and good company today. At this point, only one of those items is missing." She gave the Pastor a big smile, "Let's go Jeeves!" And off they went.

Bob and Larry had to hurry to catch Sister Wilson before she took off to get lunch ready for them. They each grabbed an elbow and got into their automobile that sounded like it was going to die and took her to lunch. She tried to protest at first, but they literally picked her up off the ground and carried her to the car by her elbows. She began to smile as she kicked her feet in the air while being carried.

She sang their praises all the way to the restaurant and wouldn't quit, even though they told her she was laying it on way too think. As they pulled into the parking lot, they saw the Pastors and Sally. They all greeted each other and traded jokes at each other's expense. The boys however asked if it would be okay to eat at separate tables because they wanted to have a nice visit with Sister Wilson. The Pastors understood completely.

Jimmy and Zane and Rebecca and Betty Jo walked into the pizza joint which didn't seem very busy for a Sunday. Jimmy ordered two of every pizza on the menu to be delivered to the skate park. The manager looked at him and asked him if he knew what he was doing. The four of them laughed and Jimmy assured him that he was perfectly sane. That manager wasn't worried about his sanity, he was concerned about the coordination of such an order.

Zane got the staff out at the counter, and they all came up with a plan to take care of the order. The pizzas would be arriving at the park at different times because the delivery cars were too small to carry that many pizzas. When the manager visibly relaxed after Zane did his thing, he rang up the order and announced it was a record order for his establishment. Jimmy took out the wad of money in his pocket and counted out the amount of the order and added a bunch more to it. He was feeling pretty generous with Ken's money. From what his mom told him, there was a lot more to come. Maybe he would buy an island or something. They left with the first two pizza's and headed for the park.

Sister Wilson was fit to be tied because of the restaurant they were at. She had never been here before because it was so expensive. Bob and Larry didn't eat at places like this very often either, but today they had a special friend that deserved this and so much more. As soon as they had ordered, they began to heap praises on their little friend. How much they appreciated her kindness. How much they really appreciated her study and all of the Biblical reference books. They were able to add so much more to their sermons because of those books. They were able to open up the Bible to the congregation because of reading those references. They loved her cooking and may never be as skinny again as they were when they got to town. They really enjoyed her motherly charm during the time at her home. She was truly one of the sweetest people they had ever encountered in their lives. She was going to leave an impact on their lives after they had been gone for a long time. No one was going to be able to match her generosity and warmth they had felt every day since they arrived at her home. Sister Wilson was holding her face in her hands because she was so embarrassed while the boys spoke about her.

As Pastor Brown and Rachel enjoyed their meals, Sally announced she needed to stop by the car lot on the way back to the church. There was something she needed to do there. When the Pastor asked her what she needed there, he was wondering if it was something he could manage for her without spending so much money there. She didn't want to tell him what she needed to do there, but he just kept pressing her. Finally, she told them they were getting a new car today. Ain't no Pastor of Sally Walker going to be driving around in a putt putt car as long she has anything to do with it. Pastor Brown came unglued and absolutely refused to take her to the lot. She told him she didn't need his permission and would just have a car of her choice, delivered to the church this week. Or they could go pick out the one they wanted. It didn't matter to her, but they were getting a new car regardless of their pride.

The kids at the park had literally destroyed about nine thousand pounds of pizza and enjoyed every ounce of it, but they couldn't eat it all. Some of the other kids that weren't in the group would look over every now and then to watch the party going on over there but didn't bother them at all. Once the group realized how much food they had left, they started telling all of the others to come over and help eat it.

Of course, all of them were appreciative until one of the kids asked what was going on. One of Dustin's friends told them that they had just come from church and that Jesus was really stirring things up with the group of kids at the skate park. One of the other kids became sarcastic and asked how Jesus was able to supply so much pizza on a Sunday. It didn't sound very "religious" to him.

Dustin walked over to the guy and wrapped his arm around his shoulder. "Well, my sarcastic friend. There ain't nothing religious about pizza, I don't care how Italian you are. Jesus isn't even religious. He came down here to save us all from hell and allow us to be happy about everything. I used to be so angry that I wanted to punch everybody in the face. I hated everyone at the same time. I didn't hit anyone, but I just hated so hard on people. But one night these guys were having a free hamburger night at the frosty and told me about Jesus. How he made the earth and everything in it. How man turned his back on Him and God. So, Jesus came down here and became a man, just like us. But He gave His life for us and paid the price for our sins to keep all of us out of hell. Once I asked Him to come into my heart, I started smiling all the time. I want everyone to have the joy I have now. I don't hate anybody anymore; I almost love them all. C'mon dude, even you asked me why I'm smiling all the time. Now you know. It's Jesus dude, I ain't lyin' or nothin' man. I tell you what, if you want to be this happy, I just told you why I smile. So, let's get Jesus living you, then I can ask you what you're smiling at, and we can tell each other about it. Did any of that make sense, because that's the best way I know how to tell you about it?"

"Enough to know that I want to be happy like you are man. That smile you have lights up the world and I want one just like it. So how do we make it happen man?" The kid looked a little frightened, like he didn't know what was really going to happen.

Zane stepped in at that point. "What your name friend?"

"Marty. And you're Zane from school, right? I remember you and Jimmy all over campus smiling a lot just like Dustin here. I guess there really is something behind those smiles. I remember a bunch of what he was saying. I went to Sunday school when I was a kid. But my parents got a divorce, and my mom quit going to church after that. So do we say a prayer or something to get this happiness inside, I don't know exactly what to do." Marty still had a look of trepidation on his face.

Zane just grabbed Marty and hugged him. "Marty don't be scared. It's Jesus that we're going to pray to, and He loves you more than you ever thought anybody could. But He will be your Savior and be closer to you than you can imagine. Here, take my hand and we'll pray, okay?"

Marty yelled over to the other kids in the crowd that were standing around eating pizza and listening to what was going on. "Hey you guys! Come over here with me and Zane, we're getting ready to say a prayer to Jesus. If you want to have a big fat smile like Dustin has, join in here." The gang meandered over to where they were standing. Even after listening to the entire conversation with Dustin, most of them had a quizzical look on their faces like they had no idea what was going on.

Zane told the other kids in the crowd what was going on and encouraged to join in the prayer. "So what Marty is asking you guys to do, but only if you want to, is to pray with us and accept Christ as your Savior. You see, Jesus came down here to Earth and became a man just every other man. He had skin and hair and blood just like us. But He came here to be a sacrifice for our sins. I don't have the time to go into everything right now. It would take weeks and you guys have skating to do." They all chuckled. "So, in order for your sins to be forgiven you just have to ask Jesus to forgive you. He always says yes to that prayer. Then after your sins are forgiven, you can have that smile like the one Dustin has all the time. What's really neat about that smile he has, is that he really is that happy and that's why he smiles so big. So, let's all hold hands and say this prayer. What do you think?" Everyone either nodded in approval or voiced it. It took a few minutes for everyone to get each other's hand. "Okay everyone, just repeat my words, but be sincere in your heart when you say them okay? Here we go. Dear Jesus...please forgive me of my sins...give that happiness that Dustin has...and that smile too...stay with me the rest of my life...and help me live...according to Your plan for my life...thank You for dying for my sins Jesus...Amen."

Zane opened his mouth in astonishment. He could literally feel the presence of Jesus during that prayer. He had never had an experience like this before. He looked out over the huge crowd of teenagers and saw some of them crying softly, while other were smiling that huge smile they had all talked about. He looked at Jimmy and Jimmy just gave him a thumbs up for helping these kids get saved.

Zane walked over to where Jimmy, Rebecca and Betty Jo were standing. "How many kids are here right now. It looks like about six or seven thousand. Jimmy, we have our work cut out for us if this group gets any bigger before Wednesday night. We might even need another person or two to help us out." He looked over at the girls and winked at them. They both winked back at him and made him and blushed a little. Zane told them about feeling the Holy Spirit as he prayed and asked if any of them felt it as well. All three of them agreed that they did, and this was going to be one awesome youth group. In reality, the group was only about twenty or twenty five kids in total. Bu the experience of praying with so many at one time was a trip for these four kids that were new to this.

Over at the car lot the Pastors were finishing up the paperwork on their new luxury car. Pastor Brown was wondering how he was going to explain his new car to the other Pastors at their monthly breakfast next time. The truth seemed to be the correct answer to that question and that's exactly what he would tell them. Plus, the fact that Rachel looked good in it. That car was his and hers and they were going to wear it out, just like they did that putt putt they drove over here.

Sister Wilson knocked on the door frame of the room that Bob and Larry were taking their naps in. "One last motherly thing boys. It's time to get up for church tonight. Or you can take the night off. It's up to you." She giggled at herself and walked back into the kitchen.

"Larry, I just figured out why neither of us are married." Bob started laughing.

Larry even found that funny and laughed right along with him. "Please remind me of this very event when I mention getting married, even when I'm kidding around." They laughed some more before they got up and readied themselves for their last service in Southwind Nevada.

As the two preachers were driving over to the church Larry looked at Bob and said, "This heathen town doesn't deserve people like us, Bob." Then he laughed.

Bob responded, "Yeah brother, they deserve much, much better than anything we can offer."

"Quit getting so serious on me all of a sudden. You know I'm joking. This town is full of wonderful people that deserve everything they already have and so much more, you Debbie downer dude." Now both of them were laughing. This was the part of this job they hated the most. They always made such good friends and then it was time to go make newer friends and leave them too. Sometimes it pulled their guts out. This town was going to be the worst one yet.

They had never been in a series of meetings where so many had accepted Christ as their Savior. This place was so much different than the other towns they had preached in. The entire town and all of the churches had been so supportive and attended every service they could. It appeared that all of those churches were going to grow just like this little church already had. God didn't just have a revival in this church, He had one in the entire town, maybe even further out than just the town.

It was so late when the pastors finished signing all the papers that they had to drive straight to the church. This car was so nice the two of them found themselves just wanting to go for a drive in it during church time. But tonight was a special night for the church and all of the surrounding churches. It seemed that most of the churches canceled their own services and had their congregation coming over here tonight. It was going to be an awesome ending to an already more than awesome Revival meeting. Pastor Brown was thinking that he had no idea he was going to have to wait this long for God to show up, but it was definitely a work of God Himself. There's no way Dennis, or any of the other Pastor would have been able to pull something like this together and have the results they have had. Yap, tonight was going to be a good night.

Chapter 17

Sunday Night

As Pastor Brown and Rachel got close to the church, they found it was not possible to get to their normal parking place. The parking lot was already at least half full of people trying to get a decent seat. Dennis parked his new car as close as he could and walked over to the church with a huge smile, while holding Rachel's hand.

Tom had just arrived in the church. He had to park a little way away from the church as well. He looked around and found the musicians already getting their instruments in tune for tonight.

Jimmy, Zane, Rebecca, and Betty Jo arrived a few minutes later and had quite a walk in order to get there. If Dustin and his crew didn't get here soon, they were going to be watching from the neighboring county. They walked inside to see if there were any seats available and found some. They all looked at each other and ran towards them so they could all sit together. Betty Jo was laughing the loudest. "This is like a general admission rock concert."

Bob and Larry had lingered a little too long in front of the mirror and had parked forty-two miles away and hoofed it to the church. That's what they told Pastor Brown when they got there right as the music was starting anyway. They were stuck in traffic and watching the cars in front of them look for a parking place for tonight's service. They found themselves enjoying the show and laughing at some of the things people were doing in order get a parking place almost anywhere. They found their place on the platform and enjoyed the worship service as Tom led the biggest crowd that had attended these meetings so far.

Dustin and his friends ended up just across the street, but they could see the TV's and hear everything that was happening. Marty and all of his new friends were there tonight as well. Some of the kids had called their parents and told them where they were going and asked them to come along. There was no way they could see them if they did come, but they would find out when they got home tonight.

The worship went a little longer than normal as the Lord was moving all over the place tonight. People were getting blessed both inside and outside of the building. People were crying out loud and letting themselves feel the full impact of the blessing they were getting.

As the worship began to settle Zane nudged Jimmy and motioned towards the back of the church. Someone was making his way into the church wearing a grim reapers robe that covered his face. Zane nodded for Jimmy to follow him. About the same time Larry noticed the person and got Bob's attention. Pastor noticed the person as they made it to the isle and began walking down the middle of the church.

As the music stopped things seemed to happen like it had been choreographed in Hollywood. The person raised his arm and pointed toward the platform. Bob and Larry pointed back and yelled quite loudly "In the name of Jesus!" At which time the guy seemed to fly through the air until they hit the back wall. The clock on the wall fell off and conked them on the head. At that precise second Zane Jimmy were on top of him holding him down.

Larry and Bob ran back there and held onto the person too. The guy was motionless for a few seconds, then began to shake his head back and forth trying to get oriented again. Finally, he raised his head and looked around with total surprise on his face. It was a young man, maybe in his twenties or thirties. "Where am I?" he asked.

Larry put his hand out towards Zane and Jimmy to let them know he had control of the situation. "You're in a church. Where did you think you were?"

He then began to contort his face, and his eyes began to roll around. Jimmy and Zane got scared and moved away from the guy. Again, as if it were a Hollywood script Both Bob and Larry stood and pointed at him. At the same time, they yelled "Be gone Satan!" And the guy went totally limp on the floor. Bob and Larry held their stance for a while ready to re-engage the person if they needed to.

It seemed to take an eternity, but the guy finally leaned over on his elbow and asked, "Is it gone?"

"If you mean that demon, it does appear to be gone, yes. Who are you and why did you come here tonight?" Larry was in total control of this situation and had certain command to his voice.

"Please, please, don't hurt me. I've been trying to get of that demon for so long now I thought he was going to kill me. I have been trying to get to one of these services for days now, just hoping that would help. Please tell that I'm really inside of a church. Please."

Again, Larry with his command voice asked him what his name was. "Lonnie, my name is Lonnie. Am I going to be okay now?"

"There's really only one way to find out Lonnie. Will you pray to Jesus with me?" Larry was going to find out if this guy was genuine or acting cool to deceive him.

"Yeah, I'll pray with you. That's what I came here for. To pray and get rid of that demon." Lonnie looked sincere, but there was only to find out.

Larry stuck out his hand for Lonnie. "Take my hand Lonnie and repeat this prayer after me, okay?"

Lonnie took his hand and agreed to repeat the prayer.

"Jesus, please forgive me of my sins." Larry waited until Lonnie said those words and then waited a few more seconds as he looked at Lonnie who had his eyes closed. Larry had purposely used the name of Jesus as the first word. If Lonnie was still possessed by that demon, there would have been a huge reaction from Lonnie. But at this point, Larry continued with the Sinners Prayer" and led Lonnie to Christ right there on the floor in the back of the sanctuary.

It was so hot tonight in the building, Bob asked Lonnie if he was wearing anything else under the robe. Lonnie pulled the robe away from his body and smiled. He looked up and told Bob he was wearing a shirt and jeans, but he wasn't wearing shoes. "Don't worry about the shoes, let's get that heavy robe off of you."

Zane and Jimmy looked at Larry to see if everything was really okay. Larry nodded his head, "Everything is okay now guys. Lonnie is going to be one of the newest members of this church." Then he took Lonnie's hand and walked him down to the front of the church where he could keep an eye on him while he preached tonight.

Larry found a place for Lonnie to sit on the steps to the platform and then took his place at the podium. "That is not the way I am used to starting any of my messages. But that needed my immediate and full attention. Bob has yet again proven to have my back when things hit the fan like that. He was there the day I got shot right out here while we were scraping paint. In fact, he was there the day I got hit by a car in the parking lot of one of the churches we were at last year. Bob! You are bad luck dude!" Everyone began to laugh, even Lonnie. Larry was looking right at Lonnie to make sure of it.

"None of you are here by accident tonight, especially Lonnie here. We'll let Lonnie tell his story another night because tonight belongs to Jesus and our Mighty God who has already proven himself here tonight. Man, you guys," Larry lowered his head and began to shake it back and forth. He was just beginning to realize what happened with Lonnie and now he was getting scared. He called Bob and Pastor Brown over to him and told him what was happening and told them to pray for him.

Larry cried like a baby while his two friends prayed until he was able to regain his composure. Bob took the podium for just a minute while Larry grabbed some tissue. "Do we serve an awesome God or what?" He waited while the congregation gave praise to that very God." He didn't have to do anything tonight, but He has been all over this place tonight. First, He blessed you guys' big time. It is so much fun to watch a congregation get blessed like you did tonight. Seriously, it warms out hearts to see that. We get to see people's faces when something real happens. Like this morning when that blind baby was looking at her mommy for the first time. Those are my favorite times as a minister. We get to watch God work like that quite often."

Now Larry was standing next to Bob with that smile of his, which let Bob know he was okay. They gave each other a huge hug. Larry told Bob, "I love you brother." Bob told Larry, "I love you right back brother." and Bob took his seat.

Larry pointed at Bob as he went to his seat, "That is a friend right their ladies and gentlemen. A true friend. I hope there comes a day that people will talk about me even a little bit like they talk about him. That man is a true Christian, I tell you. He doesn't just preach it, he lives it. He knows more about the Bible than most universities. Well, at least the one we went to together. I could go on and on about my friend Bob, but tonight belongs to God and what He has already done here in Southwind.

"Bob, would you mind going over to the window for a moment?" Larry waited for him to get there. "Okay, raise your hand if you have received Christ as your Savior since this Revival began." The number of hands that went up was huge. It completely surprised Pastor Brown, Larry, and Bob and probably every Pastor in attendance tonight. It was almost half of the crowd there, both inside and outside tonight.

Larry, Bob, and Pastor shook their heads in amazement. "Again, you are not here by accident. I'm going to do this service a little different tonight and you'll notice in just a few minutes. With a crowd this size, there is bound to be some people who have not accepted Christ as their Savior yet. I want to talk to you specifically that are in that category. Don't be scared or angry at me yet. There will be time for that later." The crowd chuckled.

"Regardless of where you are in your life right now and how happy or miserable you might be, Christ died for your sins, just like He did mine and everyone else's. Ask yourself this question, seriously. Did you deserve for the Maker of this universe to die in your place on that cross for you sins? An honest person will say no to that question. But let me ask you another question, because I don't think the first question is really the right question to ask. Are you *worth* that Maker of this universe and everything in it dying in your place for your sins?" Larry took a step back from the podium and he saw quizzical looks on almost everyone's face. "Jesus and His Father God obviously thought you were. So let me tell you something my dear sinner friend, you *are* worth it. Not deserving of it, but worth it. There's not a person sitting here tonight that's deserving of what Christ has already done for us. There's not a person on this entire planet that's deserving of what Christ has done for us, not one. But He offers Salvation to us as a free gift. The only catch is that we have to ask for our salvation. God isn't going to mess with your will or desires. He won't beat you into subjection in order for you to become a Christian. But He will stand there with His hand out offering it to you free of charge if you will simply just ask forgiveness of your sins. Do you want to go to heaven when this life is over? Ask for forgiveness. It really is that simple.

"I have no idea how many times, over the years, that I have heard people say something to the effect of, 'I won't believe in any god that sends people to hell.' Well, neither do I. But I do serve a God that will allow people to make the decision as to where they will spend eternity. God doesn't send people to hell. We get to choose to go to hell by ourselves. We make our choice and God honors it. That's how that works. And still, there's God or Jesus, one of them anyways, standing with their hands out offering you a free gift of eternity in heaven with His angels and His golden streets and the best banana cream pie you ever did eat. Or you can choose to pass on that for the other destination.

"Here's the difference though. I just described heaven to you. But let me tell you what hell is. Hell is so much different and so much simpler than heaven. It's fire. That's it, one word describes it, fire. It was made for the devil and *his* angels, and you can join them if *you* choose to. There will no beer parties or any other kind of party there, just, fire.

"That was not God's intention when He made man. That came about when Lucifer got too big for his britches, so God had to remove him from heaven. And what sill puzzles a whole bunch of intellects and Bible scholars is why and how did he take one third of the angels in heaven with him? Down here we call that staff splitting. Where one person will go around and get people on their side of an issue. That's how you get on the wrong side of God and lose your place in heaven. That means that the devil and one third of the angels ain't smart.

"My friend, I don't care how unintelligent you think you are, you ain't that unintelligent. Of course, you are not an angel in heaven either. But you do have a decision to make. Are you going to live in heaven or hell for eternity? Do you want to visit with Jesus and God Himself? What about some of your relatives that you know are there? You can even have your own banana cream pie. Or you burn on fire for eternity. It's your decision alone and no can make it for you. I can stand up here and make a sales pitch, if you will, for heaven. But you still have to decide." Larry stood silent for a couple of minutes just looking around.

"Okay, enough of that. If you want to make the decision to go to heaven tonight, stand up. Simply just stand in front of your seat. Normally we try to get people to come down here in front, but we don't have the room tonight." Larry noticed people standing as he was speaking so he quit talking and began to weep silently. So many times, he had stood and watched people make the decision for Christ and it touched his heart, just like it was right now. "Come on you guys, just stand up, I know there's more of you. Don't let your pride or whatever it is get in the way. Just stand up. Yap, people are going to see you there, but this is called a public declaration of faith, and the Bible says it's a good thing. Are there anymore that need to be standing? I'll wait for just a moment more. It's the most crucial decision you will ever make in your entire life; that's why we're waiting." Larry quit talking and looked around. A few more people had stood, but he couldn't see outside to see if there were any standing outside. But as big as this crowd was tonight it made sense that there were.

"Okay, those of you that are standing, I'm going to say a quick prayer, then I'll ask you to repeat a prayer that I pray with you. Here we go, Father, I thank You once again for this time of repentance and this group of your people. Okay guys, repeat these words after me and wrap your sincere heart around them. Pray these words with a sincere heart and you will the newest Christians in town. "Father, please forgive me...please take away my sins...change my heart and make it like yours...help me live my life...according to Your ways, not mine... please open Your Bible to me...help me to understand what I read...thank you Jesus for dying on that cross for my sins...Amen.

"Come on guys, let's give them a hand. Make sure you come toward the front of the church after the service is over so we can give you a Bible if you don't have one." Pastor Brown tugged on Larry's pants leg and told him they didn't have any more Bibles. "Scratch that, we have given all of our Bibles away. Well, stay tuned and I'll make an announcement after we're done here tonight, but don't leave, okay?"

"Okay, let's get on with part two of tonight's message." Larry went on with his message at this point.

Bob leaned over to Pastor Brown. "Pastor, do you have a computer in your office that's hooked up to the internet?"

"Why yes Bob. Even in Southwind Nevada, we are hooked up to the twenty first century?" He smiled when he said it.

"Oh, Pastor I didn't mean that, a lot of the churches we visit only let the secretary, if they have one, have access to the internet. Let's go order some Bibles right now. Then we can announce when they'll be here after Larry's finished." Pastor Brown led the way.

Bob knew exactly what he was doing when he got to the computer. He had ordered more Bibles than he could count. As he got to the number of Bibles to order he stopped and looked puzzled. "Pastor, how many other churches are attending these services?"

Pastor Brown didn't know. "I honestly don't know Bob. I have talked to at least eight, maybe more. I honestly can't answer your question."

Bob suddenly nodded, "I'm ordering twenty-five cases of Bibles. I want to see if we can get every one of the churches a case for their own church. If there aren't twenty-five churches, then you just keep the extra cases and check with other churches once in a while. But! If you even get to the point, you're getting low on Bibles and you don't have much money, you better call me. I'll take care of it. Promise me you'll do that. I'm serious, don't ever run out of Bibles again. You got me?"

Pastor Brown smiled. "I got you Bob. But with all the money we have right now, I'm not sure that will be an issue. But I promise to call if we get to that point."

Bob reached over and slapped the pastor's knee. "Good man." Then he finished ordering the Bibles and headed back into the service.

Larry was talking about being a new Christian. "One of the things that I need to really stress is daily devotions. Please, please, please read your Bible and pray every day. Most people like to do it as soon they wake up in the morning. They enjoy starting their day off with some time spent with God. It seems to help them have a good day as that day progresses. Other do it before they go to bed. They say it puts their mind in a place where God can give them a good night's sleep and they wake up refreshed and ready to go. Still others say they do it during their lunch period, however long that is. All I know is this, if you don't spend a few minutes with God every day, you're opening yourself for failure as a Christian. I'm not saying that you won't be a Christian anymore, please understand me here. If you go without reading your Bible and spending a few minutes in prayer, it can lead to a bad day.

"Spending time in prayer and Bible reading is the best thing you can do for yourself. Especially as a new Christian. It's all new to you, so everything you read is the awesomest thing you've ever read in your life. And the more you read and pray the more wisdom you gain as a human.

"Some people believe it's okay if you never go to church. They say that you don't have to go to church to be a Christian. Well, they're right, you don't need to go to church every week to be a Christian. So, don't beat yourself silly when you have to skip a week or two. Hopefully, someone in the church will call and check in on you to see if there's something they can pray about.

"But let me address those who refuse to go to church at all. They miss the relationships they could have with other Christians on a regular basis. Those are the people that can prop us up when things get tough. Those are the good friends that will stick with you. Friends you can invite over for dinner and enjoy the time you spend together. You can go golfing with that guy and not hear him say vulgar words when he misses that six inch putt. That guy does exist, I promise.

"Those of you that have received Christ as your savior since these meetings began, I have just given you a playbook for success, if you will. You're still going to have bad days, that's just life. But now that you're a Christian, you have a helper in your heart. He's even closer than your hip pocket or your purse. Don't forget God is there when you need Him. Even if you blow it big time, just ask him to forgive you. Here is a very likely scenario that plays out in a lot of our lives, that something makes us angry, and we say every bad word known to man in every language possible. Then the Holy Spirit gently reminds us that we shouldn't do that. All that's needed right then, is for you to ask forgiveness. And the Lord hears that prayer. He sticks closer than a brother. Inside your heart is almost closer than your blood and definitely closer than a brother. You've got this because God has you. The Holy Spirit is right there too, so don't get too frazzled when you get frazzled. Let's pray."

Larry prayed for everyone, and every church represented tonight.

"That's about what I felt like the Lord wanted me to cover tonight. Please don't get in hurry to leave yet. We have some things we need to cover before you leave, so just hang tight. Bob, do you have info on those Bibles?

Bob came over to the podium and stood next to Larry. He told them what he had done earlier ordering the Bibles. He asked if the churches could get together on Tuesday night for another meeting and hand out the cases of Bibles. It seemed all of the pastors that were there shook their heads in agreement.

Now here came the boom. Bob told them that tonight was the last night of the Revival. "If you guys show up here tomorrow night there won't be any lights on." They could hear people already beginning to cry. "Hey, hey, there's no reason to cry because we're leaving town. There's so much more to be happy about. Millions of people have been saved since this Revival started. People have been healed and set free from all kinds of things. By the looks of the things, we collected after the service this morning, people have been set free from everything from weed to porn to whatever else you can think of. So, there are so many reasons to be happy. One of them is that we are leaving town and now you can stay home and watch a baseball game for Pete's sake." The crowd laughed at that, so the boys took that as an opportunity to leave the platform.

As they began to leave applause broke out. Larry went back over to the podium. "Guys, let me set the record straight here. All of the miracles, all of the blessings that have happened, you need to know that Bob, nor myself, had anything to do with anything. God healed those people. God blessed those people. God saved all of those people. We did nothing but stand here and show you that God was in control. We only moved our lips. In a way we're just facilitators for God. We show up and open the door. That's not a perfect analogy, but it's something like that. The only thing we've done is make some wonderful memories for ourselves. We hope we made some good memories for you too, but our participation in what has happened has been absolutely nothing. God gets all the glory and Him alone."

Bob had come back with Larry to the podium. "Guys, this is what we do. It's what our calling is. We travel the country and hold Revivals all over the place. Then we leave and go to the next town. God does a bunch of God things there too. Then it's time to move on. I think I can speak for Larry about this, Southwind has been the most successful Revival that we have been blessed to see. More people were healed, saved and everything in between."

Larry stepped over to the microphone. "We've already told Pastor Brown that we want to come back for another meeting. This is the first time we've even felt like we wanted to go back to a place. Not that the other ones were bad or anything, it just didn't work like this town did. And those were all really nice towns. Of course, if they were to call and ask us back, we would go. But the way we end up at a church is that we just drive up and announce ourselves. We drove into this parking lot and the pastor could hear our car coming from three hundred miles away. He was waiting for us on the sidewalk with a big glass of ice water. We were here for week before we started meeting every night. Larry got shot in the rump, but the bullet didn't even break the skin because God was watching over him. In that same instant, the devil tried to take out Pastor Brown twice. He had a bullet whiz by him in the hallway and another lodge in his chair right where his heart would have been if he had been sitting there. So don't ever think this a little thing we do. It has eternal consequences, but we have nothing to do with the outcome. God does all of the work. In fact, in a lot of ways, Tom over here had more to do with it than we did. He did an awesome job with the worship services. All of those who played instruments did such a fantastic job too. They had at least as much to do with it as we did. Seriously, when you think about this in the future, all of your praise belongs to God and Him only. I think we've made our case here brother." Larry nodded his head in agreement and they both walked off the platform, again.

On their way out of the church tonight, the two preachers had never been hugged this many times in their lives. Some of the hugs were so tight, they actually hurt. These guys were going to really miss Southwind. As they made it to their car Sally Walker approached them.

"Hey you guys. Can I talk you into coming to Ken's hearing tomorrow morning? I could really use you there. I am so sorry to ask, but I'm still so...so... lost I guess."

"We'll be there Sally; it would be our pleasure. But we're going to need to get directions to the courthouse." Larry was almost excited about it. He had never been in a courtroom before.

"You know what, I'll meet you at Sister Wilson's house and you can follow me over there. How's that sound?" She was so sweet as spoke.

"We'll make sure Sister Wilson sets another place at the table. Don't you even begin to think about protesting. If you don't eat breakfast, she's going to give you stink eye for the rest of your life. Just go with it and enjoy the food. We know what we're talking about when we tell you it'll be one of the best meals you have ever eaten." Larry knew what he was talking about. Sally reluctantly agreed because she knew Larry was right.

Just as she walked away from the car, Pastor Brown and Rachel arrived at their window. "Follow us to dinner boys, our treat. Don't argue just do it. Sister Wilson is riding with us. Come on, it'll be neat."

The boys laughed, "Lead the way old man. Does your car need a walker to help you get there?" Pastor Brown just waved his hand as he walked away.

Chapter 18
Kens Day in Court

Sally woke up early today. She just couldn't sleep with what was going on with Ken today. She had no idea what was going to happen. Was he going to be given the death penalty or something maybe worse? Will he have to spend the rest of his life in prison with the likes of all those criminals. Ken had been a really bad man, but he wasn't a criminal. Well, until he killed that girl anyways. She decided to go on over to Sister Wilson's house. Maybe she could help with breakfast. If not, maybe she could learn a thing or two for her next husband. Now she was laughing at herself. She needed that, even if it was a little early to be thinking like about a new husband.

Jimmy was upstairs looking at the ceiling hating today as much as he ever hated a day. He had been so proud of Ken in the days before he was arrested that he even called him dad. He was kind of mad at himself for calling him that, because he didn't deserve to even be in the same room with him or his mother. Now Ken's life was in the hands of the court and even God had no idea what they would do. Jimmy had no faith in the justice system anymore. They were letting everyone go that had committed some of the worst crimes. Then they were sentencing people to life in prison for jay walking. Maybe today would be a little different than he thought it would,

Pastor Brown had got up a little earlier than normal and went down to the donut shop. He got his and Rachel's favorite donuts and waited for her to wake up. Fortunately, he had got a couple extra of his favorite just in case she slept for a year like she would do once in a while.

Zane was a little worried about Jimmy this morning as he went downstairs and got himself a cup of coffee. Helen and Billy were sitting and chatting and enjoying their first cup of the morning ritual. A few minutes later Laura came down and got her a cup and joined in the silence.

Finally, Laura couldn't take it any longer. "Would someone at lease moan a little? It too stinking quiet in here." The rest of the family laughed at her as she tried not to smile back at them.

Zane asked his dad what he had going today, and Billy just told him it was basically the same as yesterday. Only it was today this time. Then Billy remembered that today was Ken's hearing. "Are you going to go with Jimmy today over to the courthouse?"

"You know dad, as soon as I think I have that guy figured out, he changes on me. The other day when he found that hair band in the trunk of that car. You were dead on about that car dad, good job on that. When Jimmy pulled that out and showed it to me, I knew immediately what it was. I think he did too, but he asked me about it. I saw a rage on his face that kind of scared me at first, but as I followed him into the house, he seemed to calm down a lot. When he walked in and confronted Ken, he was so calm as he spoke. When I first saw that look on his face, I thought he going to try to kill Ken. I followed him as fast as I could to keep him away from the guy, but I didn't need to. After Jimmy told Ken that he knew what he had done, Ken just walked to that bureau they have at the bottom of the stairs, grabbed that gun, and went upstairs and locked the door.

"Poor Sally just started screaming as loud as she could scream. She was so scared. I wanted to go over and make sure she was okay, but I was afraid Jimmy was going to go after Ken. I called nine one one and told the operator what was going on and she had the called going to the cops before I even got off the phone with her. Jimmy had to tackle Sally at the top of the stairs to keep her from getting to the room Ken was in. Jimmy told him to go ahead and shoot himself a couple of times. I know Jimmy was more than angry, but I have a hard time believing Jimmy wanted Ken to kill himself. Once the Chief and Mark got there, things seemed to be calming down, but then Ken shot the gun, and everything went haywire. I just started crying I was so scared." Zane was beginning to tear up as he spoke. "A couple of minutes later they had Ken cuffed and brought him downstairs. After they were sure Ken wasn't going to hurt anyone, they took the cuffs off and just started talking to him. I got them all a cup of coffee and they seemed to be just having a regular friendly conversation like it was Saturday morning or something like that.

"I was so glad when you got here dad. I was so scared. I don't think I was ever that scared of anything in my entire life, even as a little boy. That level of scared was not a fun thing to go through. I'm still kind of feeling it just talking about it." Zane wiped the tears away from his eyes as Laura came over to hug him. This was the first she had heard about what happened that night.

"Shoot Zane, you could have been killed too that night. What were you thinking even being there?" Now Laura was crying.

Billy reached over and hugged her. "Laura, Zane was okay while he was over there. We just didn't know anything was going on or me and some of my friends would have been there before Ken even got the gun out of the cabinet."

Helen needed to vent too. "Zane, you are such a take charge kind of guy, just like your dad. But, son, you have to take a look around you before you run into that burning building. As soon as Ken grabbed that gun, you should have run out of there. Sometimes our instincts can lead us in the wrong direction." Now she was holding onto Zane and crying like she never had before. She had the feeling that she almost lost her son the other night and it scared her death.

"Mom, I was never in danger. I didn't need instincts to tell me that. Ken was the only one in danger of dying. Seriously, I was never in danger, neither were Sally or Jimmy. Neither of them even acted like there was any danger to themselves. It was just a scary thing to be involved in. Even the Chief and Mark said that this was the best scenario that could have happened that night. No one got hurt or injured or killed. Of course, Ken singed his hair and may never hear out of that ear again, but he's okay." Zane kind of chuckled at the singed hair.

Billy shook his head a little. I realized just how much I loved you when I was holding you that night Zane. If anything had happened to you, I don't know what I would have done. I would do the same with your mom. I love that woman right there. And Laura, don't get into a situation like that just to make realize that I love you just as much as your mother and brother. That night took four hundred years off my life I ain't even kidding. So, what time does his hearing start? I might go with you and let Ken know that some of us will support him, even through this.

"I'm not sure, but I'll call Jimmy here in a minute to find out. I'm pretty sure Rebecca and her family will be there. Betty Jo will be there for Jimmy no doubt. They might have to hold that hearing down at the church if too many go. That room ain't that big." They all laughed.

Bob and Larry made their way into the kitchen to the smell of bacon and coffee. Apparently, there were biscuits in the oven, so Sally and Sister Wilson were having a little girl time.

Sally seemed to be holding up better than the preachers thought she might be when she asked them to go with her today. "So, are you boys leaving today?" Sally asked.

Bob answered, "Not today, Sis, we have been invited to hang around a few days for some relaxation and recovery. Honestly, we could use it. Not only has this visit been physically involved, for some reason it's been emotionally draining. I swear that emotional stuff takes more out of you than the physical stuff does. So, what time do we need to be to court?"

"They start things off around nine I'm told but they don't know when Ken's case will be held." Sally was anxious but holding it together.

Ken was in his cell when they brought his tray of breakfast to him. He was quite sure that it was going to take a long time to get used to the low quality of food. He had been praying and asking for God's help while being here in jail, but so far nothing had happened to him. Maybe that was because he was praying. He knew others were praying for him too. If they asked him for a plea today, he made up his mind he was going to plead guilty. There was no sense in dragging this thing out with a long trial. He had killed that poor girl and that was the truth. So just get it over with and let her family can get along with their lives.

Suddenly he was overcome with emotions, but he could feel something in them. As he wept silently, he began to pray and ask God for wisdom. He prayed for the judge and his attorney that would be appointed to him. He knew without a doubt that he was a Christian, even though he was in jail on his way to prison. He asked for guidance and to be able to share his story with other inmates. Maybe some of them would be able to relate to him and give their hearts to Christ just like he had done. He laid on his bed and just allowed himself to weep silently so he wouldn't wake anyone.

Sally and Sister Wilson were having fun teasing the preachers this morning. These two guys had been staying in this house for a few weeks now and had never seen this side of Sister Wilson. She was just as ornery as the two of them put together, maybe even more than that. Sally was in a league all by herself and she was funny too. The preachers had decided that Sally was going to be just fine.

"And to think that I was sitting at my dining room table trying not to feel sorry for myself just about an hour or so ago. I really needed this today. With the hearing and everything, I was getting overwhelmed, so I came over here. I'm so glad I did." Sally had a huge smile as she was talking, and it looked good on her.

Of course, the two preachers were thinking this ornery humor was going to be attractive to the future Mr. Sally. It looked like Sally was going to be fine.

Zane went over to Jimmy's house to check on his best friend. He could have just called him, but he wanted to see him this morning and be his buddy. The girls could tag along later, but Jimmy was his priority right now. As Jimmy answered the door he gave Zane a nice smile, which kind of surprised him. Zane was expecting his friend to be a basket case, or something like it. "How you doing this morning Jimmy?"

"Surprisingly well, believe it or not. I'm okay with everything at this point. Mom went over to Sister Wilson's to help make breakfast for Bob and Larry a little while ago. I just laid on my bed and thought about it all and I'm fine with everything. I'm not really happy about everything, but I know in my guts, this is going to turn out about as well as it can. We'll see if I'm right in a couple of hours. How are you doing my bestest friend in the entire world?" Jimmy was really doing well, and it completely amazed Zane.

"I'm doing okay now, but I had a moment with my parents and Laura a little while ago. My dad had never heard what exactly had happened the other night. So, as I was telling him about it, I got scared all over again and cried like a little schoolgirl. That's why I just came over here without calling first. I have the best family in world Jimmy. We love each other so much and I can feel it to the middle of my bones. But at this point, I guess I'm about where you are, okay with everything. What happens today is going to be just fine and we will go on with our lives and put it all behind us." Zane put his arm around Jimmy's shoulders and Jimmy did the same thing to Zane. Then they sat down and had a good visit until it was time to head over to the courthouse.

Sally had something she was going to do for Bob and Larry, and it required the participation of both Zane and Jimmy. So, Jimmy filled Zane in on the details and they discussed how it should all go down. This was going to be fun to see.

Larry drove to the courthouse in their little putt putt while Sally took Sister Wilson with her. Sally wasn't sure why sister Wilson wanted to go, but she was sure welcome to do so. She could use all the friends she had to lean on today. This may not go the way Sally wanted it to go. If that happens, Sally knew she was going to be a basket case all over again.

Pastor Brown walked into the courtroom just as they brought Ken into the room. Ken didn't look at anyone and faced forward during the entire hearing.

The District Attorney stated what had happened last year, mostly relying on information Ken had provided to the two policemen that night at the house. Chief Lee and Officer Mark confirmed the information that the D.A. had already presented and took their seats.

The judge sat and read some documents in front of him before looking at Ken. Mr. Walker, do you wish to add or deny anything that has been said in this hearing so far?"

Ken's appointed attorney stated that he did not. Ken put his hand on the Attorney's arm and whispered to him that he would do the talking from here on out.

"How do wish to plead Mr. Walker?"

"Guilty You Honor. I killed that girl and there is no reason to drag this out and waste everyone's time. I'm ready to be sentenced today if you're so inclined sir?" With that Ken lowered his head again.

The judge looked at Ken for quite a while before he spoke. "Mr. Walker, you have no way of knowing that you and I have interacted out in the community for years. It was just passing you at the store and or seeing each other as we walked down the sidewalk in town. I know what kind of person you have been for years. However, we go to the same church, and I have seen the difference that Christ has made in your life. I have no issue saying that you are without a doubt the most significantly changed person I have ever seen get saved. I can't sentence you today Mr. Drummond because I don't know how to do that right now. You're going to prison, that's already decided for me. But for how long, is parole even an option here? Personally, if you remain the person, you have been for the past couple of weeks, I think parole is a possibility. But I have to look at the statutes and see what I'm compelled to do and what my options are. So, let's keep you here in the county jail for two weeks, then I'll let you know what your future is. And Mr. Walker, thank you for doing to right thing today. I know that you need to speak with your wife so we will make a room available to you that is secure immediately following this hearing."

At this point, the judge looked at the D.A. and asked if there was anything he needed to add to the hearing. "No, Your Honor, and I would like to second everything you have said about Mr. Walker today. I am not going to make any demands on you when it comes to his sentencing. It's been a joy to see the smile on his face and his wife's face as they have been in town. And yes, we go to the same church."

Ken had raised his head while the judge was speaking to him and now the District Attorney. With what they both had said, Ken didn't feel as scared.

Sally let out a huge audible sigh after the District Attorney made his announcement. Maybe Ken wasn't going to be in prison for the rest of his life. Maybe she could still get a few years with him when got out of prison. Then again, she might just move on without him she had no idea what to do, how to feel, or anything right now. She was just glad that Ken might have a chance at life again.

As she left the courtroom, Sally went into the side room to talk with Ken, and the rest of the crowd headed outdoors. As Bob and Larry got to the bottom of the steps, Jimmy came and asked for their car keys. He said he needed to put something in their car. So, Bob handed them over.

The group was chatting as they walked out into the parking lot when Larry noticed their car being towed away. "Hay! Hay, what are you doing with my car. We didn't do anything!" Then he looked at Jimmy. "You said you had something to put in our car, what's going on?"

"That's not your car anymore, this is your car," and he tossed Larry the keys. "It used to belong to some guy we know that's going to prison for a long time. He doesn't need it anymore. Besides, this was all his idea. It's got new tires and it's been serviced from head to toe." Jimmy stopped talking and enjoyed what he saw on the two preachers faces. Both of their mouths were wide open in total astonishment. "Don't worry guys, we got everything out of the old car before we let them haul it to the dump."

Everyone was now standing and looking at the guy's new car. Apparently, Ken had expensive taste because this car had everything a car could have. Finally, the preachers walked over and opened the door. Larry dangled the keys at Bob. "I'm driving it first." They both got in and took off leaving everyone in the parking lot laughing.

Jimmy didn't think they were going to leave so abruptly, but the look on their faces was worth the price of admission. It was going to take a long time for him to forget that look. Zane came over to him and bumped knuckles with him. This was a lot of fun. Maybe they could do that for someone in the future. Right now, they couldn't scrape together two nickels between themselves that they had earned.

Once Sally came outside, Jimmy told her what happened, and she laughed and laughed even though she didn't see it herself. That story made her entire day. Apparently, the conversation with Ken went well and the earth was turning on its axis again. Everyone was going to be okay now. Life was going to be good, no, it was going to be great. This town had just had a huge successful revival, and the effects were going to last for a long time.

Sister Wilson approached Jimmy. "Did you think to get my house key off that key ring before that guy drove off the with the car." Jimmy's face told her that he had not." Well, I hope that guy likes smoked brisket for dinner when he shows up to steal my China." Then she laughed. "Those two boys have brought me so much pleasure, there's no way that I can ever repay what they have done for me. Those two are real Christians. I've seen how they live, and they are real. All of us can learn more than one lesson from them."

Pastor Brown was standing nearby and heard every word that sister Wilson had said. "Sister Wilson, I don't think there are words that can describe the impact those guys have on people's lives. Just think of all the people they've met before they got to this town. Those are two amazing people. In fact, I'm not sure amazing is the correct word to describe them. They live what they preach and don't deviate from it. God definitely knew what He was doing when He called them into the ministry. I know I won't be the same and my preaching is going to be so much better because of this Revival.

THE END

Printed in the United States
by Baker & Taylor Publisher Services